CELIA'S GIFTS

A WHISPERING PINES NOVEL

ALSO BY KIMBERLY DIEDE

CELIA'S GIFTS SERIES

WHISPERING PINES (BOOK 1)

TANGLED BEGINNINGS (BOOK 2)

REBUILDING HOME (BOOK 3)

CHOOSING AGAIN (BOOK 4)

CELIA'S GIFTS (BOOK 5)

CELIA'S LEGACY (BOOK 6)

WHISPERING PINES CHRISTMAS NOVEL

CAPTURING WISHES (BOOK 3.5)

FIRST SUMMERS NOVELLA

FIRST SUMMERS AT WHISPERING PINES 1980

CELIA'S GIFTS

A WHISPERING PINES NOVEL

Kimberly Diede

Celia's Gifts Book 5

This is a work of fiction. Names, characters, organizations, places, events, and incidents are either products of the author's imagination or are used fictitiously and any resemblance to actual persons, living or dead, business establishments, events or locales is entirely coincidental.

Ebook ISBN: 978-1-7351343-1-4

Print ISBN: 978-1-7351343-2-1

This one goes out to my besties;
my sisters by choice:
Deneen, Darlene, Jodi, & Lynn

*Forever friends
are one of the
greatest gifts of all.*

WHISPERING PINES
SUMMER 2019

*V*icious pain shot through her foot. Renee bit her lip to curtail the stream of four-letter words.

She could hear Jess snickering from behind the closed office door to her left. "Did you stub your toe *again*, Renee? How many times have I told you to wear something sturdier than those four-dollar flip-flops you like? Maybe we need to put in one of those little nightlights. Your eyes aren't what they used to be."

"Shut up, Jess," Renee hissed through clenched teeth as she clutched her bare right foot, fumbling for the light switch with her free hand. She should have installed a window alongside the front door when she remodeled the lodge. The entryway was always too dark. Her eyes fought to adjust to the shadowed interior after the bright sunlight outside.

She couldn't see what she'd sliced her foot on, but Renee could feel wetness streaming toward her heel. No doubt blood was dripping off onto the scarred wooden floorboards. She found the light switch, then sank down onto the cool planks to sit and inspect the damage, her spine supported by a doorjamb.

She cringed at the jagged piece of glass protruding out of an inch-long gash in the meatier part of her foot, the pad under her big toe. Squeezing right below the wound helped squelch the sharp pain, but the sight of the glass brought on a wave of queasiness.

"Jess, grab some paper towels!"

Her brain barely registered her sister's sigh or the creak of the ancient office chair. A broken picture frame lay face down in front of her, clearly the culprit behind the shard of glass now embedded in her foot. Her eyes traveled up the wall. Sure enough, she spied an empty rectangle of dark paneling near the center of the collage of old framed photographs.

The office door creaked open.

"Oh man, Renee, that's going to take more than paper towels," Jess moaned, crouching down next to her. "Gross . . ."

Renee glanced up as her sister's voice trailed off. Ever since they'd been kids, the sight of blood had made Jess woozy. You'd think raising two—make that three—kids would have toughened her up. "Don't you dare pass out on me, Jess."

"For God's sake, I will not *pass out on you*," Jess said, thrusting a crumpled mass of paper towels at Renee. "But don't ask me to pull that out of your foot."

Renee grimaced. "Don't worry, I know your Florence Nightingale tendencies are limited."

"How did that even fall down?" Jess asked, diverting her eyes from the bloody mess.

Renee bent over her foot, better able to see the glass now that she'd used the paper towels to swab away some blood. "Not sure. But those frames are always crooked. I think the rush of air when we come in and out the front door does it."

She inhaled sharply at a fresh surge of pain and blood as she eased the glass out.

Jess stood, hands on her hips, and examined the wall of old photos, keeping her eyes off of Renee's injury. "Maybe we need to move these. We don't want guests getting hurt."

Grunting, Renee again eyed the fallen frame, one of its wooden arms jutting off at an odd angle. "Right now I'd vote to throw the damn things away."

"We can't do that," Jess countered, shaking her head. "These are an amazing visual history of Whispering Pines! I remember the first time Seth came out here. It shocked him that I hadn't spent much time studying these pictures."

"Yeah, well, your history-buff husband is a sucker for that kind of thing."

Nodding, Jess reluctantly turned back toward Renee and extended a helping hand. "He is. But I know you appreciate the history out here, too. You're just cranky because you hurt your foot." Jess took notice of

Renee's bare feet. "I see you've ditched your cheap shoes—going full Flintstones now?"

Grasping Jess's hand, Renee hoisted herself up, still holding her injured foot and keeping her back against the doorjamb for balance. "My Crocs were muddy, so I didn't want to wear them inside. I was coming in for a bucket to wash them off."

"All right then, my fashionista sister, give me a second to sweep this up so no one else gets cut today, and I'll run you in to the ER. That foot needs stitches."

* * *

"Here's the last of them," Robbie said, stepping carefully around the small ottoman where his mother was elevating her bandaged foot. He set a short stack of framed photos down in the only remaining open spot near the edge of the large folding table they'd set up in the kitchen. "What are you guys going to do with these?"

"Thanks, bud. Actually, I'm wondering the same thing," Renee admitted. She half stood as best she could, despite her injury, to scan the hodgepodge of pictures laid out on the table, her attention torn between her son and the old photographs.

"Careful," he warned as she wobbled.

"Jess and I want to reorganize these—she suggested maybe getting them all into matching frames. I was thinking we could hang them back up on a different wall where they won't get jostled around. They're an important part of the story of Whispering Pines."

Jess slammed a cupboard door. "Do you guys want coffee?"

"None for me, Aunt Jess. Nathan will be here in a sec. We're going fishing."

"Did I hear something about stories?" a deeper voice asked from behind Jess, followed by the smack of a screen door.

"Oh—hey, honey." Jess turned to greet her eldest. "Robbie said you're going fishing? You didn't have to work today?"

Nathan helped himself to one of the two cups of coffee his mother held in her hand, winked at her, and made his way over to his aunt and cousin. As Renee watched, she saw a flash of Nathan's father in her nephew's actions. Not that she'd ever mention the similarities. Nathan still struggled to forgive his father for the awful things he'd done.

"Not today," he was saying. "Frank kicked me out of the store. Said I needed less time with books and more time in a boat. What happened to your foot, Renee?"

Renee readjusted her bandaged foot on the ottoman. "Cut it on some glass a couple days ago. One of these picture frames did it, actually."

Nathan winced.

Jess opened her mouth to say something, but Renee cut her off. "But it's getting better. It only took a few stitches to fix me up."

"Now Mom and Jess are messing with *all* the pictures, instead of just fixing the broken one," Robbie added, his lack of enthusiasm over their project clear.

Nathan surveyed the haphazard arrangement of frames in front of Renee. "Aren't these the ones that usually hang by the front door? I've always felt like they had stories to tell."

"You sound like an author," Renee said.

"You also sound like Seth," Jess pointed out, taking the empty chair next to her sister. "He thinks we should try to document the history of Whispering Pines using these. You know, make it part of our advertising for the resort and our retreats."

Nodding, Nathan picked up one of the older photographs, studying first the front and then the back of it. "Look. This one's dated 'July 1943.' That's an impressive stringer of fish that guy is holding," he said, handing the frame to Robbie. "What do you think, cuz? Should we head out so we can catch something like that today?"

Robbie grinned, taking the picture from Nathan. "We've *never* caught that many nice walleyes in one day out here. These fancy dudes must have had a secret fishing hole. Who fishes in button-down shirts? Hey, Mom, if we come back with a stringer-full like that, can we get up on the Wall of Fame, too?"

"Absolutely," Renee agreed, laughing as Robbie angled the picture in her direction so she could see it. "I think it's about time we added some new pictures to the wall, regardless. We're part of the history of this place, too."

"I'm going to hold you to that, Mom," Robbie said, handing her the picture he'd love to replicate. "Come on, Nathan, Grandpa and Matt said the fish turn off by two. If we don't hurry, we won't get out there in time and we'll miss our chance at the Wall of Fame."

Nathan took a final slug of his mother's coffee, grimaced, and set the still half-full cup into the sink. "I can't believe you like it black. Besides, it's already hot outside. Beer would be better."

"If you recall, I didn't *offer* you my coffee—you helped yourself to it. Besides, it's too early for beer, young man."

"It's five o'clock somewhere," Robbie chimed in, his tone suspiciously casual. "Bring some beer in the boat."

"Nice try," Renee interjected. "Only one of you is legal drinking age, and it isn't you."

Robbie held up his hands in playful defense. "Not for me, Mom, for Nate. Jeez. Maybe it'll give him some luck. Last time we took the boat out, I'm the only one who caught anything."

"In your dreams," Nathan countered, slugging his younger cousin on the shoulder on his way out the back door. "Grab the boat keys off the hook. Let's go."

In the quiet that descended in the wake of their boys, Renee and Jess studied the photos, flipping them over occasionally to check the backs.

"I like your idea of transferring some of these into matching frames," Renee commented. "Whatever we don't hang back up can go into an album. And we should add more current photos, too. Maybe some from the Fourth of July . . . one from our big Halloween party after our first summer back out here . . . maybe even some from our retreats."

Jess nodded, her fingers tugging at the backing on a frame. "With everyone snapping photos with their phones these days, that should be easy enough."

"What are you doing?" Renee asked, nodding toward Jess's busy fingers. "We probably want to leave these as-is until we can buy all the new frames. We have to figure out how many we need."

Jess ignored her.

Renee's eyebrows shot up at the telltale sound of ripping paper.

A guilty look settled on Jess's face. "It was curling up in this corner," she said, holding the now torn piece up for her sister to see.

"And you couldn't just glue it back in place?"

Jess shrugged, letting the brittle brown paper fall to the floor. "Something about this picture has always intrigued me, but there wasn't a date or anything on the paper backing. I'm curious."

Renee tilted her head so she could catch a glimpse of the front side of the frame Jess was intent on dismantling. She recognized it immediately.

I've always been curious about that one, too, she thought, understanding why Jess might be impatient to inspect this particular picture more closely. Maybe there were names or dates on the back of the photo itself.

With the paper removed, Jess turned the frame over, her left hand supporting the photograph while her right tapped on the glass. "It's kind of stuck."

It didn't take much pressure for the protective covering to loosen. Jess set the frame and then the piece of glass to the side.

With a sigh, Renee struggled to bend over to retrieve the paper backing Jess had let fall to the floor, her elevated foot making the effort tricky.

"What the hell?"

Something in Jess's tone pulled Renee's eyes back to her sister as she straightened in her chair.

The thunderous crack of an explosion outside made both women jump. Jess dropped what Renee had thought was one photo but turned out to be a stack of them. They fanned out in disarray on top of the other frames directly in front of Jess. Dishes and pans rattled in the kitchen cupboards.

Both women shot to their feet, Jess's discovery already forgotten.

"That sounded bad," Jess declared, rushing for the back door their sons had exited through ten minutes earlier.

Renee's blood pounded as fear coursed through her. She followed as close behind Jess as she could manage, hobbling on her wounded foot, her cell phone already clutched tightly in her hand in case she had to call 911.

SUMMER 1942

CHAPTER ONE
GIFT OF A FAMILY DESTINATION

*C*elia breathed deep, savoring the tickle of the cool breeze on her face after hours inside a stifling car. The air smelled faintly of Christmas—a refreshing contrast to the cloying scent of leather. Helen's brother's 1941 Buick sedan might be all the rage, but it was beastly hot to ride in on a summer day.

"I hear the new Cadillacs offer this thing called 'air conditioning' in limited models." Helen slammed the heavy car door. "Couldn't you have talked Daddy into one of *those*, Leo, instead of this monster?"

Celia glanced back over her shoulder and grinned at her friend's flushed cheeks, then caught the driver's eye. "Thank you for the ride, Leo. Your new car is every bit as beautiful as you'd promised it would be. Ignore your sister. You know how cranky she gets when her stockings sag."

"I do," the tall man agreed, slamming his own door. He headed for the rear of the Buick and lifted the rounded hatch of the trunk. Pulling a white hankie from the back pocket of his trousers, he made a futile attempt at polishing off the dust clinging to the chrome bumper. "A month at the lake—minus her hose—should do her some good."

Celia turned back to the stretch of beach along the shoreline, biting the inside of her cheek to cut off the bubble of laughter threatening to spill out. Helen would only take so much ribbing before they'd all suffer her foul mood for the rest of the day.

A back passenger door opened. Footsteps shuffled to Celia's side. "I can't believe I let you talk me into this, Celia."

Celia turned and linked her arm through that of her friend's, making a sweeping gesture toward the two-story building in front of them and the grass lawns beyond. Log-sided cabins nestled on the green expanse and vacationers enjoyed the sultry, early July weather.

"Ruby, would you look at this place? You, my dear, are my oldest and dearest friend. I wouldn't dream of coming here on a month-long holiday without you. I still have to pinch myself that Eleanor even invited us. You know you would have been bored to tears at your grandmother's house in Duluth again this summer, learning the fine art of bridge playing. Maybe if we're lucky, Leo and his friends will let us play poker with them instead."

"All right, I admit I was dreading spending another July at Grandmother's with that insufferable cat of hers. I guess anything would be better than that."

Laughing, Celia gave Ruby's arm a playful squeeze, ignoring the dampness of her friend's skin. Color was returning to the girl's complexion, the greenish hue subsiding in the late-morning sunshine.

It had been a relief when Celia spotted the large wooden sign, sporting bright red letters announcing their arrival:

WHISPERING PINES
A Family Destination
Serving Minnesota Since 1926

The sign stood tall along the edge of the dense woods. The loud click-clacking of Leo's blinker as he'd pulled off the blacktop onto a shaded gravel lane had roused Ruby from a fitful slumber. Majestic pines high above served as a graceful canopy, filtering the merciless sun. Sitting in the backseat never boded well for Ruby's sensitive stomach, but Celia doubted Helen had even considered giving up her seat in the front, next to her big brother Leo. Celia was sure any more time in the hot car and Ruby would have been sick.

Helen joined her two friends at the edge of the gravel parking lot, busily scanning the lawns. "Where's Eleanor? I can't believe she's not here to greet us."

Celia looked around too, also surprised Eleanor hadn't appeared yet.

An outside observer of the three young women might find it odd that Helen didn't also link arms with Celia, mirroring the connection between Celia and Ruby, but it spoke to the dynamics of their friend-ship. They were an unusual trio with vastly different personalities, but they'd known each other even before their first day in Mrs. Green's first grade class. They'd recently completed their freshman year at a private, all-women's university, fondly referred to as St. Kate's. Their unlikely friendship had weathered the test of time.

Eleanor, their missing hostess, was a newer addition to their friend group.

While Ruby and Celia had been quietly brainstorming how to break the news to Helen that they were planning to room together at college, Helen was off making plans of her own to live with the daughter of family friends. Celia should have expected that Helen would maximize her opportunity to increase her social standing during her college years by latching on to someone a rung or two higher on the wealth ladder.

Unlike Helen and Eleanor, neither Ruby nor Celia would even be at the university without the scholarships they'd worked so hard to land. The past decade had been a difficult one financially for both Celia's and Ruby's families, much as it had been for the rest of the country. Those privileged few, like Helen's and Eleanor's families, weathered the economic storms of the 1930s with little apparent trouble, although Celia's mother often reminded her to never assume you know what goes on behind closed doors.

A shout pulled Celia's attention toward the lodge, and she and

Ruby spun in unison to see Eleanor rushing toward them, arms outstretched in greeting.

"I thought I heard a car pull up!" the young woman cried as she bounded in their direction, dirty white tennis shoes kicking up dust in her haste.

She caught them both in a rambunctious hug, squealing the entire time. Eleanor's raven black hair, usually meticulously caught up in a neat up-do, stood out from her head in a mess of shoulder-length curls, held back loosely from her face with a red band. Celia laughed and then spluttered as her friend's hair danced over her cheeks and into her mouth.

Releasing them, Eleanor turned to Helen. The girl stood uncomfortably to the side. "Hey, roomie," Eleanor cried, subjecting her to a similar embrace. Helen's arms remained at her side, her face reflecting her surprise and discomfort over the physical contact.

Unfazed by her friend's lack of enthusiasm, Eleanor stepped back, hands on her hips. Celia took notice of the casual outfit their hostess wore. She'd been right to pack plenty of play clothes for the month ahead.

"I've missed you three so much! Daddy has kept me busy working, but he's promised me I can set those duties aside now and focus on providing all of you with a delightful stay."

If Helen would have made such a claim about working while waiting for them to arrive, Celia would have doubted her, but Eleanor was different. Celia appreciated their newest friend's commitment to hard work, despite her family being extremely well-to-do, be it in her studies or the charitable endeavors she spent so much time on—an unusual commitment for a lowly freshman.

"Where is that brother of yours, Eleanor?" Leo strolled up behind the wild-haired girl and caught her around the waist, lifting her off her feet and spinning her around.

Eleanor roared with laughter as she clung to the arms wrapped around her middle, her rubber-soled shoes lightly kicking at the shins of her captor. "Leo Nielle, you set me down this instant!"

Leo did as he was told, but the second his arms released Eleanor, he gave one of her wild ringlets a playful tug. "How've you been, little Elly? Turning heads of all the boys who venture onto campus over there at St. Kates?"

"But of course," Eleanor assured him, clasping her hands demurely behind her back and batting her dark eyelashes. "Since you've always ignored me, I have to find myself some other rich, handsome young man to take me dancing."

Celia watched Leo and Eleanor spar back and forth as if they'd been doing so their entire lives. She could never act that freely around Leo, even though she'd known him for years. He'd always seemed rather unapproachable to Celia—Helen's older and more sophisticated brother.

"I'd have to bring a pretty big stick to beat off all your other suitors, were I ever to ask you to dance, little one. Where is that brother of yours?" Leo asked again.

Eleanor grimaced. "Not here yet. Daddy thought Tripp would get here either later this afternoon or tomorrow. He sent him on some business errand. But not to worry. You can hang out with us until he gets here."

Turning on her heel, Eleanor grabbed for Ruby's hand and headed off across the expanse of grass on the west side of the large, two-story building she'd just exited. Giggling, Ruby hurried along after her, pulling Celia along behind them.

"Wait!" Leo yelled. "What about all of this luggage?"

Celia spared a glance over her shoulder and hesitated, feeling a wave of guilt at the piles of luggage now heaped on the gravel behind Leo's Buick. Nineteen-year-old girls didn't pack light when leaving home for a month-long vacation. But the momentum Eleanor created made Celia's resistance futile. Ruby might just pull her arm out of its socket if she didn't follow.

"Thanks, Leo. We'll come back for it in a minute!" she offered, although his expression told her he didn't believe her.

* * *

"Where in heaven's name are you taking us, Eleanor?" Helen cried, following behind Ruby and Celia. "I was hoping we'd be staying in one of those quaint white cottages by the beach."

"Not this year, Helen. Sorry! Those cabins aren't big enough for all of you. They have two bedrooms, but they are rather small."

Celia hadn't considered what their sleeping arrangements would look like once they reached the resort. The glance Ruby gave her implied her friend hadn't thought about it either.

"Almost there," Eleanor said, holding her free hand up and pointing straight ahead.

Celia peered around Ruby. Two log-sided cabins nestled up against a row of tall pines. Theirs was most likely the one on the left, the larger of the pair. The cabin bore little resemblance to the white, clapboard-covered structures she'd noticed on the far end of the sandy beach, the ones Helen would have preferred to stay in. Bright red trim rimmed windows and the front door. Sturdy cement steps led up to a small, screened-in porch.

"This one is nice. Daddy just had it all redone this spring. I think you'll like it." Eleanor released Ruby's hand as she walked up the steps. "The only thing you might not like is the deer mount on the fireplace. When I cleaned in here earlier today, I felt those beady black eyes watching me."

Celia and Ruby followed Eleanor up the stairs. Celia stopped at the top, holding the door for Helen, but the girl still stood on the lawn, staring off into the woods.

"Come on, Helen. What are you waiting for?"

Celia's question pulled Helen's eyes away from the dense row of trees. Helen visibly shrugged, as if dispelling unpleasant thoughts, and plastered a smile onto her face as she stepped up the stairs. "Nothing. Let's check on the accommodations Eleanor and her father set aside for us. I hope it's nice enough for Mother."

It was Celia's turn to shrug. In her experience, little was "nice enough" for Mrs. Nielle.

They entered the small porch, only wide enough for a small card table with hardwood chairs flanking each side. But the screen would likely offer a pleasant reprieve when the infamous Minnesota bugs got to be too much in the evening.

Another screen door separated the small porch from a bigger room, dominated by an impressive stone fireplace on the right. Sure enough, beady black eyes on the mounted trophy head followed Celia as she walked through the front part of the cabin and into a bright kitchen, sunlight streaming in through windows on two walls. Following Ruby's and Eleanor's voices, she found them standing in a decent-size bedroom, connected to a second by a small bathroom.

"You ladies will be in this room," Eleanor was saying as she pushed up the sash on one window. "My, it's gotten stuffy in here since this morning. Don't worry, Daddy had Mr. Bell make sure all the screens were in perfect shape. *Mrs. Nielle* made it perfectly clear she'd only come for a visit if he could promise her a bug-free stay."

Celia snorted. "Hasn't your family known the Nielles for a long time? Is this the first time Helen's family has visited?"

Helen pushed past Celia, answering before Eleanor could reply. "No, we've been here before. I'll take this bed by the window. I don't sleep well if I get too warm," she claimed, plopping down onto the bed likely to get the best air flow.

Like mother, like daughter, Celia thought. The older they got, the more Helen acted like her mother—which wasn't a compliment.

"No problem," Ruby replied. "I'll take whichever one you don't want, Celia."

Celia turned toward Ruby, surprised at the overly compliant tone in her friend's voice. But the sparkle in her eye reminded Celia of the pact they'd made: they would try extra hard to keep things civil between the four of them. Their lofty goal was an entire month free from any Helen drama, although that was probably too optimistic. She shot Ruby a subtle thumbs-up as she reached up to smooth a fictitious strand of hair on her head.

The screen door into the front room banged against the wall. Celia hurried back out to hold the door for Leo. The poor man grunted and strained under the weight of four undoubtedly heavy suitcases.

"I really was going to come back out to help," Celia claimed, reaching for the suitcase on top of the pile.

* * *

Celia dug her heels into the damp sand and leaned against a blanket-covered mound she'd created following Eleanor's instructions. Sparks snapped, floating upward, as if pulled toward the twinkling stars above. She'd welcomed her friend's suggestion of a small bonfire down along the shore instead of sharing space with adults and strangers around a larger firepit near the cabins.

She half listened to her friends discuss the merits of the latest selection of bright red lipsticks in Revlon's summer collection. Celia cared little about makeup. If the conversation swayed to hair products, now *that* would interest her, but not cosmetics. She tilted her head back, eyes studying the velvet black of the night sky and the smattering of stars far above. She picked out the Big Dipper, something her stepfather had taught her to do while camping in the backyard at home with her two little brothers.

She wondered what her family was doing at this moment, and if they missed her. Spending time with them in June, after being away at college for the first time, had replenished her. A part of her wished she hadn't agreed to spend the entire month of July here, at this lake resort, with her girlfriends.

The only drama at home these days continued to revolve around Beverly's health concerns. For as long as she could remember, Celia had helped her sister and mother deal with one physical ailment of Beverly's after another. When Celia returned home after months away at college, Beverly appeared to have even less energy. She hoped it was her imagination. She didn't want to consider that Beverly was getting worse.

Promising herself she'd spend all of August with her younger sister before heading back for her second year of college at St. Catherine's, she attempted to turn her attention back to her friends' fireside conversation.

"Can we go dancing every weekend while we're here?" Helen was asking, her tone excited.

Eleanor shrugged. "If you want to. The dances are quite fun."

"I'd go every *day* if we could," Helen laughed, and Celia knew it was true. Helen loved to dance. She'd loved it ever since they were little girls and she'd taken ballet lessons. Celia still remembered how her friend had wept when the dance studio closed up shop, along with so many other businesses, in those early days of the Depression.

Helen cried easily and often, but usually it was a cry for attention or one of her tantrums. But when the studio closed, she wept genuine tears.

"They hold the dances at a resort called Grand View Lodge. It's down the road not far from here. And they hold one most every Saturday night during the summer," Eleanor explained. "The bands are usually good, too."

"I vote we go to every dance we can while we're here," Celia said, earning a thankful smile from Helen. She wasn't much of a dancer, but it sounded like a fun way to pass the time.

Ruby poked at the fire with a long stick, sending a shower of sparks up into the gentle evening breeze. "How long have you been coming here, Eleanor?"

"To the resort? I guess this is my fourth summer at Whispering Pines."

"Is that how long your parents have owned it?" Celia asked. Eleanor came from money, but Celia knew little else about the girl's family or where their wealth originated.

Eleanor didn't immediately respond. Wondering if her friend had heard her, Celia tried to read the girl's expression through the flicker of flames. Eleanor was tracking the path of a leaf as it floated out toward the inky black water, a flicker of flame slowly consuming it. Celia started to repeat her question, but Eleanor interrupted her.

"Yes, Daddy bought the resort four years ago. I think it was his way of coping."

"Coping?" Ruby asked, her tone soft, as though sensing the need to tread carefully.

Celia worried she'd accidently stumbled on something. "I'm sorry, Eleanor. We can talk about something else if you'd like."

Eleanor shook her head. "No. I figured this would come up at some point, so let's just get it out of the way. My mother left us. She was unhappy, and nothing Daddy tried helped. Finally, she said she either had to go home to England, or she'd die. I heard her say that to my father one night when she thought we were sleeping. When I went down in the morning, she'd gone. And she took my younger sister, Iris. Daddy said it would just be temporary, that they'd be back once Mother felt better. That was five years ago."

Helen sat up straighter, wrapping her arms around her knees. "I'm such a terrible friend. I complain about my mother to you all the time. I sometimes forget that your mom left like that. She was never around much, even when we were growing up. I should be more sensitive. But, honestly, it's almost like she's dead. No one ever talks about her."

Celia gasped. Even Helen should recognize how rude *that* sounded.

But Eleanor held up a hand. "No, she's right, Celia. It is like my mother is dead to me. And so is my sister. We've had no communication from them in over two years. Mother used to write once a week. Then the letters slowed and eventually stopped. It's not something we talk about. But I wanted you to know, so no one would say something awkward around Daddy. I know how badly he still hurts from her betrayal. Tripp, too. He pretends he doesn't miss them, but I know he does. He always used to say how he was Mother's favorite."

"I don't see how Tripp could be anyone's favorite," Helen said.

Eleanor's head whipped in Helen's direction.

"Don't talk about my brother like that, Helen. I tolerate your bad manners because I know your momma raised you like that. You are starting to be just as rude as she is. You need to learn not to say such hurtful things." Eleanor's voice broke, and a tear slid down her cheek.

"Me?!" Helen bit out, getting up onto her knees and glaring at Eleanor from across the fire, its flames now low as no one had thought to throw more logs on. "You just insulted my mother!"

Celia sighed. Helen's short fuse often spurred arguments. She considered stepping between the feuding roommates, but Ruby intervened, holding up both her hands and motioning for them to quiet down.

A cheerful whistle caught their attention, followed by the soft swish of sand. Four heads swiveled in the whistle's direction.

"Ladies, ladies, ladies," Leo admonished, shaking his head as he stepped into the meager light cast by the dying flames. "Is this any way to start a vacation? It's a beautiful evening, you spent the afternoon lounging on the beach in sparkling sunshine while I drowned a few worms, and you have full bellies compliments of a stellar fishing expedition by yours truly. Why don't we talk about something less controversial than the quality of our upbringings?"

"But Leo, are you just going to let her insult our mother like that?" Helen whined, her expression pouty.

"Dear sister, you know that our mother can be a bit . . . shall we say . . . *difficult*. And trust me when I remind you that sound carries clearly out here. Helen, I heard your little jab regarding Tripp. I'd call it a draw, so why don't you put the claws back in, and put those *polite* manners back on display that I know are deeply ingrained in you."

Helen looked between her roommate and her brother, debating whether to take the wise advice. Exhaling, she plopped back down onto her sand-strewn blanket. "Fine. You're right. Where are my manners? I'm sorry, Eleanor."

Eleanor stood and removed two logs from the small pile the girls had brought down to the beach. "I suppose our mothers have left us both a little scarred, Helen. Apology accepted. I guess we can't all have perfect parents like Celia."

Surprised and unsure how to take the comment, Celia watched Eleanor lay the wood onto their fire, flames quickly catching on the dried bark. Leo had dropped onto the sand nearby, half lying on his side, facing the fire, without the benefit of a blanket.

Eleanor and Celia hadn't been friends for long enough to know each other's history. She'd met Celia's parents and siblings on move-in weekend at the college. Celia rarely spoke of her earliest days.

Now she wondered if any of them would have any deep, dark family secrets remaining after this evening around the fire.

"My family hasn't always been so perfect, Eleanor." Celia kept a close eye on her hostess's expression and noticed a softening in the hard set of her jawline.

"I'm sorry, Celia. Ignore what I said. That was my bumbling attempt to deflect attention. No one's family is perfect."

Helen burrowed under Celia's skin often enough that she understood how infuriating she could be. She couldn't even imagine how it hurt Eleanor when her mother abandoned their family. Celia decided to attempt to lighten the atmosphere around the fire.

"You were right, though, Eleanor. My family is in a good place now. My mother is finally happy, and my brothers keep Beverly and me entertained. It's been so much better since Clarence came into our lives."

Celia read the confusion on Eleanor's face. She shrugged. "Things were harder before. When I was little. My father died when I was five years old. Bev was three. Mom was still really young. She wasn't even twenty-five yet."

Eleanor's face registered surprise. Ruby, Helen, and Leo listened quietly, already knowing Celia's history.

"It isn't something I like to talk about. It was a long time ago, and I barely remember my father. He was older than Mother. A *lot* older. Something happened at work, an accident. It had to have been pretty awful because Mother never would talk about it. There were some tough years between then and when she met Clarence. I like to say he saved us all."

Hoots of laughter filled the air, spilling across the dark lawns from the bigger group gathered around the bonfire by the cabins.

Celia glanced toward Leo when she heard him sigh. He fell onto his back, staring up at the same stars she'd enjoyed earlier, before their conversation had detoured from lipstick colors to family drama.

"Maybe I should have pulled up a chair around the other fire," he said. "Their conversation topics must be a little more light-hearted."

"Aren't you getting all sandy?" she asked him, thankful she had a comfy blanket to relax on. "I can spread this out if you want somewhere to sit."

"Nope, thank you, Cee, you are kind. But I'm good. I suppose you should keep talking. It would do Eleanor good to hear that sometimes broken-hearted parents can find love again."

Celia grinned. While she might never feel comfortable enough around Leo to joke and tease like Eleanor did, she felt she had an ally in him. She considered how best to share her story with their newest friend without boring everyone else around the fire.

Skip most of the depressing talk about empty cupboards and having to take in boarders in order to keep our home after Daddy's accident. Go straight to that fateful day when Clarence came to fix a broken window.

She opened her mouth to do just that when another man walked into the circle of light cast by their fire, a man she didn't recognize. She watched him kick one of Leo's outstretched feet and then sidle over to Eleanor and drop onto her blanket, jostling for room.

Leo sat up. "You're a sight for sore eyes, Tripp. All this henpecking was boring me."

Eleanor pushed against the intruder's shoulder. "Why didn't you bring your own blanket? I won't let you steal mine."

"Hello to you, too, little sister," the man said, slapping Eleanor's hand away. "Are you going to introduce me to your friends?"

Eleanor sighed, put out by her brother's sudden appearance. "Ladies, this is my big brother, Tripp. He's at the same level in college at St. Thomas with Leo here. Tripp, this is Celia and Ruby. Friends of mine from school. And you already know Helen."

Eleanor's brother gave Ruby a brief nod and then looked in Celia's direction. Their eyes met, and she felt a jolt, as though she'd somehow connected with him for the briefest of seconds on some deeper level than just a glance across a bonfire. It wasn't a pleasant feeling. His eyes were dark, nearly black in the flickering light, and his stare made her uneasy, although she couldn't have said why. She gave him a shy grin, immediately breaking eye contact and looking across at Helen instead. It was then she saw another wave of unease cross the girl's face, similar to the one Celia had noticed while she waited for Helen to enter their cabin earlier that day.

Did Helen have a crush on this brother of Eleanor's? Was that what

21

her rude comment earlier was really all about? A self-defense mecha-nism? She'd have to watch the signs.

Celia never did get to tell the story of how Clarence had saved them. Not that night. That night, around the fire, there was no more talk about romance or parents. Tripp had arrived, and he dominated the rest of the discussion until the firewood ran out and the mosqui-toes chased them inside.

The evening left Celia feeling unsettled.

CHAPTER TWO
GIFT OF BIG DREAMS

The bright red nose of the canoe slid silently through the water while the hum of insects competed with the small splashing sounds their paddles made as they dipped below the surface. Ruby sat in the front, Celia in the back, as they floated along behind a second canoe that held Eleanor and Helen. For once, the foursome's nearly incessant chatter had quieted, giving reign to the peaceful morning.

Humid, clinging air had driven them from their beds early. Celia welcomed the flow of cool air on the open water after the stuffiness of the cabin.

She grinned as she remembered how they'd tiptoed past the other bedroom, stifling giggles at the comical sound of competing snores emanating through the closed door.

"I'm not sure whether that loud snore is Dad or Leo," Helen had whispered as she turned the doorknob and fresh air rushed in through the outside door. "But the softer, purring snore is Mother."

Celia had brushed past Helen, her bare feet sensing the warmth still held deep within the cement step despite the early hour. "Does she know she snores?"

Helen made a harrumphing sound. "She's not one to admit to something so unladylike."

Now, as the surrounding air heated with the climbing sun, Celia pondered the mother–daughter relationship between Helen and Mrs. Nielle. She worried her friend received too little love from the one woman who should love her the most in the entire world. Mrs. Nielle saw to Helen's physical needs, spoiled her with material goods, but she was a hard woman. Celia couldn't remember ever hearing Mrs. Nielle laugh, and she seldom smiled.

Would Helen grow up to be a hard woman, too?

Indeed, she'd drilled those feelings of superiority into Helen's head from an early age. Mrs. Nielle was so different from Celia's own mother. She reminded herself of this when Helen's snotty attitude became unbearable.

When Helen spent time away from the overbearing woman, her better qualities would shine through again. It was why their friendship had survived this long.

Escaping to college had been good for Helen. She'd been much less catty—fun, even—as they'd traversed their freshman year together. But since Helen had spent the month of June at home, her negative attitude was back. A few days spent in the sun, before her parents arrived, had helped Helen relax again.

Celia knew her friend's fun mood might not last, now that Mrs. Nielle had arrived the previous evening. She'd try to ignore Helen's attitude in the coming weeks—just as she'd been doing most of her life. Her own mother had taught her that most everyone has a goodness, deep in their core, but sometimes that goodness gets buried under other people's influences.

"How are you ladies doing back there?" Eleanor asked, grinning back at them.

A crashing sound at the water's edge revealed a large-bodied doe, bounding up through the tall grass and quickly disappearing into the trees.

"Did you see that?" Ruby asked, pointing in the deer's direction. "She must have been getting a drink."

"I did. So pretty," Celia responded, then looked ahead to Eleanor and Helen. "Doing great! It's peaceful out here. Thanks for suggesting it, Eleanor."

Her friend nodded. "What do you girls want to do today? Daddy thinks it might be too hot for us to spend all day on the beach. He doesn't want us to burn. He suggested maybe a hike in the woods. Would that interest you?"

Celia glanced down at her bare arms, already a shade or two darker since spending the last four afternoons lounging on the beach. A change of pace sounded fun. "I think I'd like that, if you don't think we'll get lost."

Eleanor laughed, the sound echoing across the water. "We *probably* won't get lost. And if we do, Daddy will send someone out to find us. It's not like these woods are that vast."

* * *

"It feels at least ten degrees cooler in here," Celia said as they strolled deeper into the trees. After an hour on the water and a light breakfast of fruit in the lodge that was still so new Celia could smell the cut lumber and tang of paint, they'd donned long pants and headed off on their hiking adventure.

There was no clear path for them to follow, but the trees and underbrush weren't as thick as it appeared from the outside looking in. When they'd driven down the lane leading to Whispering Pines days earlier, the forest had looked dense—ominous, even. Now that Celia was walking through those trees with her friends, she could see she'd misjudged. The grass was sparse in places, much of the ground blanketed with pine needles. Plenty of sunlight kept the shadows at bay.

It didn't take long before the trees all looked the same and Celia lost her bearings. There was the occasional toppled pine, its nearly horizontal trunk offering a potential point of reference if they'd need help to find their way back. Hopefully Eleanor knew the way.

Celia switched the heavy wool blanket she carried from her left

arm to her right. The material caused her skin to itch. Eleanor and
Ruby each held one of the twin handles on a picnic basket as they led
the way. Helen was empty-handed. Celia would have to make sure the
girl carried something after they finished their picnic.

"Are there any cabins back here, Eleanor?" Celia asked, though it
seemed unlikely.

Her friend shook her head. "No, not back here. All the resorts hug
the shoreline. People vacation in Minnesota for the lakes. At least
that's what Daddy said when he told us he was buying Whispering
Pines."

"Why do you suppose he wanted to buy a resort?" Ruby inquired.
"Doesn't he work with metal or steel or something?"

Eleanor laughed. "Yes—steel and lumber for buildings. But he said
he wanted to *diversify*. I'm not sure what that means, exactly. Personally, I think he's always worked too hard. He was feeling guilty, never
having time to spend with me or Tripp, especially after Mother went
back to England. Buying the resort meant he could be here with us
during the summer months, but still be doing some kind of work.
Daddy isn't the type to lounge around."

"Is he worried that after last winter people will stop going on vacation?" Celia asked. She stared at the shadows as if expecting them to
encroach. "This war could really change things."

"You mean after what happened at Pearl Harbor? I suppose that's
possible. The need for steel is increasing, though, and Daddy seems to
have more demands on his time than ever. That's why he's been trying
to get Tripp more involved in his business dealings. I'm sure it's
possible that we could see fewer guests at the resort—at least until our
country can find its way out of the war—but I'm still glad he bought
it. He needs a place where he can unwind. Daddy always says this is
where he comes to rejuvenate. Did you know, the Indians that used to
live in this area, before it became Whispering Pines, believed this was
sacred ground? A special healing ground?"

"What nonsense," Helen piped up. She'd been unusually quiet up to
that point, slogging along empty-handed.

Eleanor stopped as they entered a small clearing in the trees, motioning to Ruby to set the picnic basket down.

"*I* don't think it's nonsense," she said.

Sunlight spilled through an opening in the canopy above. Two monarch butterflies danced around the picnic basket. Celia could hear the gurgling of water—there must be a stream or brook nearby. The rumbling in her stomach reminded her they'd been walking for a long time. She suddenly realized she could no longer hear sounds from the lake.

"This is where I thought we could enjoy our picnic. Celia, do you want to lay the blanket out?"

Celia held tight to one side of the dense wool blanket, fluffing the folds out as if making a bed. She kneeled, spreading the white blanket out on the grass; she admired the jewel-colored stripes adorning the edges as she smoothed it down. "This seems like an awfully nice blanket to use on a picnic. Won't it get dirty?"

Eleanor shrugged. "We have stacks of those things in the linen closet in the lodge. They won't miss one."

The four friends settled on the blanket, and Ruby folded back the cover on the picnic basket. Eleanor pulled out a stack of red gingham napkins and handed one to each girl. Next came various containers of food, all covered with pieces of cheesecloth.

"Who prepared all of this?" Ruby asked, grinning as she peeked into a tin container and pulled out a fried chicken leg.

"Mrs. Bell. She prepares all the food for the resort. Poor woman. She works so hard. She's the most talented woman in the kitchen I've ever known."

Celia could only imagine how nice it would be to have someone cook for her, instead of having to help her mother get nearly every meal on the table at home. She and Eleanor came from such different worlds.

They passed the various dishes around, each loading up their napkins. They'd forgotten plates, but no one cared about manners in the woods. They were hungry after an early morning in the canoes followed by plenty of walking.

"And let's not forget the perfect addition to any summer picnic," Eleanor declared, pulling a dark bottle of red wine out of the basket to squeals of delight.

"Wherever did you find that?" Helen asked, reaching for the yet unopened bottle.

Eleanor shrugged. "It didn't get opened at dinner last night. No one will miss it."

Celia watched as her friends expertly pulled the cork out of the bottle, Helen holding the bottom while Eleanor used the bottle opener, then cringed when droplets of the deep red liquid splattered on the white blanket.

"Oh darn, Mrs. Bell *will* notice that!" Eleanor sighed, brushing ineffectively at the stains with a spare napkin. "We may need to pick her a bouquet of wildflowers on our way home. That might convince her not to tell Daddy about our midday libations. I wasn't able to bring glasses. We'll pass the bottle."

Helen shrugged and then tipped the bottle up to her lips, drinking and passing it on to Ruby.

They enjoyed a few minutes of quiet, the twittering of birds and the sigh of the wind in the trees high above adding a musical note to their picnic luncheon.

After finishing her lunch, Celia wiped her mouth with the gingham napkin. "Thank you again for bringing us here, Eleanor. I've never had a full month off in the summer to just relax. Frankly, I feel like I should help with something."

Eleanor leaned back on her elbows and stretched out on their blanket, allowing her feet to rest in the grass. "I appreciate that, Cee. Daddy would, too. I'll mention your offer to him, but I'm sure he wants all of you to relax while you're here. He knows we work hard at school."

Nodding, Celia gathered up the remains of the meal and stowed them back in the basket. "You know, Eleanor, a successful man like your father . . . Maybe he could help me figure out what I want to study in school. Being undecided as a freshman wasn't much of an issue, but I need to decide where I want to focus."

"If Preston—Eleanor's father, I mean—is anything like *my* parents, he'll encourage you to study for your MRS degree," Helen said, a note of bitterness creeping in. She took another pull from the wine bottle. "You know, do what you can to leave college a Missus So-and-So, wed to a wealthy husband with lots of business prospects. Your life . . . neatly mapped out."

Ruby laughed. "My dad asked me something along those lines when I got home from school in June. But I think he realizes I'm there to get my teaching degree, not tie myself down with a husband and babies just yet. I can't travel the world to study art history—at least until this blasted war is over—but at least I can teach about it."

Celia set the picnic basket on the grass and lay back on the blanket alongside Eleanor. She gazed upward, taking in the fluffy clouds as they skated across the brilliant blue circle of an opening in the trees above. "Is that all we have to look forward to, my friends? To marry, become homemakers, then mothers? I don't think that will ever be enough for me."

"Mother says it isn't always about what *we* want," Helen replied, her tone a mixture of uncertainty and dread, without a hint of the normal haughtiness Celia knew her friend used as a front to hide behind.

"Helen, try not to take everything she says to heart. Just because your mother doesn't seem particularly happy in life doesn't mean you have to end up the same way," Celia said, wishing she could help Helen feel more optimistic. "If you could be anything, do anything, with no limitations, what would it be?"

Helen paused, considering Celia's question. Knees bent, she swirled the dark liquid that remained in the green glass bottle. Celia reached for it, surprised to find it nearly empty.

"Promise not to tell? And not to laugh?" Helen asked, handing over the bottle and glancing between her three friends as an earnest look stole across her face.

"Cross our hearts," Ruby declared, and the other two copied her action.

Helen reached up and fiddled with her hair, eyes focusing on something just beyond the trees lining their little picnic area. Or maybe she was focusing instead on something she'd built up in her own imagination.

"If I could do anything, I'd travel to Paris and become a fashion designer."

Of all the things Celia might have guessed Helen would dream of doing, designing clothes wouldn't have even made the list. She nearly laughed out loud, but at the last second remembered her promise and managed an encouraging smile. "You have an incredible sense of style, Helen. But I've never known you to enjoy drawing or the arts."

Helen dropped her gaze. With one finger she traced the thick yellow and red stripes at the edge of the blanket, sighing when her finger skimmed over the wine stain. "I have plenty of sketchbooks in my room, but I have to keep them hidden from Mother. She feels the arts are frivolous entertainment. Things performed and created by other people. People with heads full of butterflies and empty pockets."

Ruby, a lover of the great masters, shook her head. "That isn't true, Helen. Some of the greatest artists of all time were wealthy."

"Yes, well, I'm sure Mother would never think I could be anything great."

Helen's words threatened to dampen their lovely afternoon.

Refusing to let that happen, Celia broke in. "Helen, you will just have to make it your mission to prove your mother wrong. I ordain the four of us will do great things! We might not know what those things are yet, but we will figure it out. I have faith in us!"

Eleanor laughed and wiggled her fingers at Celia, taking the nearly empty bottle of wine and draining it. She set it in the grass and gave it a little push. The bottle rolled away. "Speaking of doing great things, I'm considering switching out of the nursing program."

Her declaration elicited surprised gasps.

"But Eleanor, nursing is an admirable profession!" Ruby countered. "Especially now, with the war hitting closer to home. Why would you switch?"

Eleanor shrugged. "I've spent time with Daddy in the factory. I want to help make bombers."

"Bombers?" Celia cried, stunned. A crow let out a loud squawk above them. "Really?"

Nodding, Eleanor sat up and began unlacing her tennis shoes. "Yes, bombers. Daddy says they are going to shift away from making steel beams and start supplying airplane parts for the war effort. But he's worried he'll have trouble finding men to work. He seems to think many will go off to fight the war. I suggested he hire *women* for the factory floor. You should have seen his face. It was hilarious! He looked like he'd bit into a lemon."

"Did you tell him you would like to *be* one of those women?" Ruby asked, intrigued by Eleanor's idea.

Their friend shook her head. "Not yet. He always calls me his 'little nurse.' I'm still letting him get accustomed to the idea of women working in his factory and not just in secretarial-type roles. If I've learned anything about men, it's that we ladies have to choose our timing for important discussions carefully. Sometimes we even have to let them think something is their idea."

Thinking back through her limited interactions with men, Celia had to agree. She'd even witnessed her mother doing the same thing with her stepfather, Clarence. The man was kind but stubborn. He had strong opinions on topics like religion and America's involvement in the war. Her mother didn't always agree with Clarence, but Celia had watched the woman pick her battles carefully. There'd been times when Celia argued with the man, his stubbornness butting up against her own, but her mother would stop her with a calming hand on her arm and a whispered "Not now."

Maybe that was what Eleanor was getting at, too.

Celia sighed. "Perhaps I'll just stay single all my life. It sounds like bowing down to the opinions and beliefs of men would be too exhausting. And limiting."

Eleanor, now barefoot, began rolling up her pant legs. "I don't think of it as bowing—I think of it as skillful manipulation, a way for us to still get our own way. And they don't even realize what's happening."

"What are you doing?" Helen asked, nodding at Eleanor's feet.

"Come on, can't you hear the stream back over there? Let's go cool off!"

Celia felt a trickle of sweat meander down her spine. Wading in a cool stream sounded like a brilliant idea. Standing, they gathered up the basket and shook off the blanket. She folded it as best she could and handed it to Helen. "Your turn to carry something."

With a sigh, Helen took the heavy, scratchy blanket, and they turned toward the sound of water gently splashing over rocks, their empty wine bottle forgotten.

CHAPTER THREE
GIFT OF RELAXING INHIBITION

*T*he sound of gurgling water grew louder as Eleanor led the way, shoes in one hand and the handles of the wicker picnic basket looped over her other arm. Celia marveled over her friend's ability to walk barefoot over the prickly forest floor.

Eleanor bent over and set the picnic basket on the ground. The handles left an indentation on her forearm. She dropped her white tennis shoes on the lid and instructed Helen to set the blanket on top of it all. "You'll love this place," she assured the girls, striding purposefully to the water's edge.

Celia kicked off her shoes, coaxed the stiff denim fabric of her pant legs above her knees, then stepped into the cool, dark water. Its caress soothed away the heat, and she curled her toes into the soft mud of the streambed. "This feels heavenly, Eleanor. I only wish I could sink my entire body into this water."

Ruby stepped in alongside them and bent down to scoop the cool liquid into her hands, splashing it onto her face and neck.

Helen struggled to untie her tennis shoe, finally giving up and pulling it off still laced. "Does that feel as good as it looks?" she asked Ruby, motioning to her white blouse, which had become nearly see-through as the water soaked her front.

"It does, but I hope it doesn't dry funny," Ruby said, plucking the wet fabric away from her chest.

Helen swiveled her head around in all directions, a mischievous glint entering her eyes. "Is there ever anyone else out here, Eleanor?"

Following suit, Eleanor scanned the area, a knowing smile stealing over her expression. "Only the lost boys. Otherwise, I'd venture to say we are very much alone out here."

Helen pulled off her other shoe, stood, and undid the fastening of her indigo blue jeans, the button giving her a little trouble. None of them wore pants very often.

"What are you doing?" Celia asked in alarm, worried she knew *exactly* what Helen was up to.

"I'm going swimming," Helen answered, her tone matter-of-fact.

"Swimming? But we don't have our bathing suits with us."

Shrugging, Helen pushed her jeans down her thighs. "Don't be a prude, Celia. Come on. We are all adults here. If my getting naked makes you uncomfortable, close your eyes and turn around until I get in."

Eleanor squealed in delight, much as she'd done when she'd greeted them upon their arrival. "I've never gone swimming without my clothes. You're brilliant, Helen," she said, untying the knotted tails of her red blouse and unbuttoning the top, her alabaster skin glowing in sharp contrast to her black hair and deep-red top.

Celia spun away, sure her cheeks were the color of her friend's blouse, now tossed in a heap on the knee-high grass that met up with the water's edge. "I'm not a prude."

Helen giggled. "You look like a prude to me."

Helen's voice sounded muffled, and Celia suspected that was because she was pulling her shirt off over her head. "Are you sure it's all right, Eleanor? No one will see us?"

"No one will see us, Celia. Don't worry."

She could tell by the splashing sounds and the trajectory of their voices that both Eleanor and Helen had ventured into deeper water, probably stark naked. She glanced at Ruby.

"If you'll go in, I'll go in," Celia said, trying to sound brave despite her own trepidations.

"Why not?!" Ruby declared, peeling off her wet blouse and the practical white bra underneath. The sight of Ruby undressing didn't bother Celia in the least—they were roommates, after all.

Caving to the peer pressure, Celia followed suit. She kept her gaze averted from her three friends, instead pretending to search the trees high above for the culprit responsible for some unusually loud squawking. It was as if the birds were scolding them.

But she wasn't a prude, and she'd prove it.

She'd been right about one thing: the water felt delicious, like cool silk flowing over her calves and then bathing her thighs. Her breath caught when the water tickled her waist and sides. It didn't get any deeper as she advanced, so she sunk down onto her knees, the water now covering her to the neck. Her knees sank a little farther into the muck, the slickness of it oddly soothing.

Celia willed herself to relax, to enjoy the soft lapping of the cool water and the play of filtered sunlight, glittering like diamonds on the surface. Her friends seemed much more comfortable with their own nakedness. Helen didn't even stay ducked down into the water, instead dipping low just long enough to cool off and then standing back up, the water sluicing off her bare breasts.

Celia wished she felt half as confident in her body as Helen appeared to be. Why were they so different? Eleanor was floating on her back, kicking her feet and raising her arms in a slow stroke. Ruby crouched low in the water, mirroring Celia. She tuned back into what they were giggling about, careful to keep her eyes on Helen's face.

"How formal is this dance tonight?" Helen was asking.

"Formal enough that we have to wear dresses, but no one will notice if you skip stockings. It's much too hot for that."

Celia was looking forward to the dance. When she'd imagined her summer at Whispering Pines, she'd looked forward to days spent on a sunny beach with friends, cute boys to flirt with, and kissing. She was the only one of their group that had yet to kiss a boy.

She thought back to the night of her high school prom—her only dating experience. She'd had fun with her date, a handsome football player, but only the two of them knew the truth of how their evening together evolved. He'd been nursing a broken heart, and she'd taken pity on him, allowing him to share the tale of his doomed romance. She'd hugged him and bid him farewell at the end of the evening, without so much as a goodnight kiss. He'd never reached out to her again, probably embarrassed by his actions, and she knew he'd joined the military shortly after graduation. She wondered if his heart had healed yet.

Would tonight be the night she'd meet someone special? Would this be the beginning of the summer romance she'd dreamed of?

She gasped as cold water splashed across her face. Ruby laughed, her raised hand marking her as the guilty party. "Where did you go, Celia?"

Celia splashed her back, then dipped her head below the surface of the water to slick the tendrils of red hair back from her face. She stayed there a second, enjoying the hushed quiet below the surface, her friends' voices a muffled drone above.

It was then that she remembered something Eleanor had said.

Breaking the surface of the water, Celia flicked the water from her eyes and turned her attention to their hostess. "What did you say about 'lost boys'?"

Eleanor let her feet drop, her body floating to a vertical position. Her long hair offered a modicum of modesty when she stood, and Celia didn't feel the need to look away. "Haven't I told you that story yet? About our ghosts?"

"Ghosts?" Ruby questioned, and Celia bit her lip to keep from smiling at the alarm in her friend's voice. Ruby was notoriously afraid of ghosts.

Eleanor nodded, her hands trailing over the water's surface, creating ripples that traveled out in circles away from her body. "Legend has it that two young ghost boys haunt these woods."

"So that's what you meant. No one would see us out here, except maybe two *ghosts*?" Celia shot back, relieved to hear *living* people wouldn't discover them, and amused at the nervous expression on Ruby's face.

Eleanor shrugged. "I didn't want to believe the story about the ghosts either, but Mrs. Bell swears it's true. She claims to have seen them with her own eyes. More than once. One time, she was taking sheets down from the line and one corner stuck. She had trouble getting the clothespin off, and when she finally snapped it down, she swears she heard a young boy's laughter and saw a flash of a blue jacket and white-blond hair. According to her, they cause all kinds of mischief around the resort."

Celia squinted at Eleanor, skeptical. "Have *you* ever seen these 'lost boys'? And why would there be little boy ghosts around here, anyhow?"

"No, I've never seen them with my own eyes. But Mrs. Bell seems awfully serious about them. Ask her. She'll tell you the same thing. When I asked Daddy about it, he said he's heard the rumors about ghosts but couldn't be sure about them. He said that shortly after this place opened, two young boys died in a cave out in these woods. So it *is* possible."

Celia suspected the legend was baseless, started up following an obvious tragedy and kept alive by a superstitious few. The way her friend's eyes scanned the surrounding trees, as if searching for a white, floating apparition or some such nonsense, reminded her Ruby would be the type to help keep a rumor like that alive.

Helen, quiet during their talk of ghosts and dead little boys, sunk onto her side, executing a graceful sidestroke toward the far bank. "I think I'll wear my blue dress tonight. It's rather patriotic. Appropriate, don't you think? So close to Independence Day."

Helen's strokes had separated her from the group. She stopped swimming and stood, facing the shore, the water not quite reaching her waist.

Celia whipped her head at a sudden rustling in the high grass on the far side of their swimming hole, off to Helen's right.

"Blue is *my* favorite color." The male voice skipped across the water and a dark head popped up out of the reeds, right in front of

Helen. It was Tripp, and he had an unobstructed line of sight to Helen's nakedness.

Chaos reigned. Screams and splashes drowned out anything more Tripp might have said. Helen fell back into the water, sinking below the surface, her body now hidden from view by the sparkling water. Eleanor screamed at her brother, her face contorted with rage. Both Celia and Ruby stayed low, using their feet to shuffle back toward their clothes; their hands roiled the water's surface to keep their own bodies hidden from their intruder's view.

"Tripp, where are you? Is that the girls I hear?"

Celia quaked under the water at the sound of Leo's voice. At least *he* didn't sound close to the pond. Yet.

Eleanor's screaming must have finally registered with Tripp. He sighed and turned his back on the swimming hole and the four younger women. The grasses rustled as he retreated toward the sound of Leo's voice. Celia noticed that Tripp had been *much* quieter during his approach compared to the noise he was making now.

Did he sneak up on us, knowing we were skinny dipping?

"Don't come any closer, Leo," Tripp yelled, his voice fading. "My little sister and her friends are cooling off in my favorite swimming hole. They need some privacy."

Celia had sensed Helen didn't like Tripp, and that was before he caught her naked in the middle of the woods. She could only imagine the gut-wrenching embarrassment Helen felt now.

She hoped Leo wouldn't kill Tripp when he found out he'd snuck up on Helen in her birthday suit. Eleanor's father might send them all home in disgrace if there was trouble.

"Your dress is pretty, Helen," Celia complimented her friend, trying to draw out a response. Helen had been quiet ever since Tripp had surprised them all in the woods.

"Thank you," she responded, her tone distracted.

Celia sighed. They'd arrived at the dance thirty minutes earlier, but they still hadn't made their way inside. Leo had been kind enough to give them all a ride, and Tripp was notably—and thankfully—absent. If the man had mentioned their nakedness to Leo, Helen's brother was enough of a gentleman to keep it to himself. When asked, Eleanor reported that her brother left again on some job-related task for their father.

Thank God, Celia thought.

Something about Tripp set her on edge. She barely knew him, but she didn't trust him. The episode in the woods only reinforced her feelings. Eleanor was a wonderful friend, and their father, Preston, a decent man. She hoped she was wrong to doubt Tripp's character. Maybe she wasn't being fair. It wasn't Tripp's fault they'd been foolish enough to strip down and swim naked in broad daylight.

Leo dropped them at the front door of the lodge at the nearby resort, famous for its weekend dances, telling them to have fun but to behave. He'd find them when it was time to go home. Celia avoided any eye contact with Helen's brother in case he knew more than he let on. She was embarrassed by their actions.

Instead of going inside, Eleanor suggested they walk along the beach to see the resort's famous summer sunset. The four girls followed a wooden walkway around to a sandy beach, removing their low-heeled sandals and carrying them as they made their way to the water's edge. This resort was considerably larger than Whispering Pines, the beach longer and deeper.

Eleanor told them a bit about the place as they walked. "I'm glad Whispering Pines isn't nearly this big. It would be so much more work. Do you know, at the peak of summer tourism, they can have upward of two hundred guests here? Mrs. Bell's son, Danny, works here. Maybe we'll see him tonight. If so, I'll introduce you."

Nodding, Celia scanned the large, three-story lodge behind them, enjoying the view of the façade from the beachside. The building sported dark brown siding, broken up by row upon row of multi-paned windows that popped with a white trim. Bright flowers in an array of jeweled tones lined an impressive stone staircase, leading from heavily carved wooden doors above down to an expanse of green lawns she imagined would feel like velvet under her bare feet. Threads of melody drifted down the massive staircase, mixing with shouts of laughter to give the summer night a festive atmosphere.

Celia felt a twinge at the opulence of it all. Maybe if her father hadn't died when she'd been very young, she would have spent childhood summers at a place like this with her own family. Her father, some twenty years older than her mother, had come from a wealthy family.

But everything changed when he died. It was shortly before the country fell into a time of economic hardship like few had ever experienced. Celia's mother, only twenty-four when widowed, struggled for years to maintain the family home that passed to her when her husband died—the only thing she had left from her husband, aside from their two daughters. He'd had no brothers or sisters, and his own father died ten years before he'd married; they hadn't been close to Celia's paternal grandmother. Even now, with her mother happily remarried, their family could never afford to spend time at a place like this.

She'd better enjoy these stolen evenings of dancing and mingling with the well-to-do.

"I know I keep saying it, but I'm really sorry about what happened out in the woods today," Eleanor repeated, looking between her three friends.

Celia could see the sincerity there. "It wasn't your fault, Eleanor. You couldn't have known Tripp and Leo would be out in the woods."

"Besides," Helen finally joined in, her perky nose slightly elevated, "it wasn't *your* idea to strip naked and go swimming. You'd never have suggested such a thing."

Eleanor crossed her arms over her chest, eyes narrowed at Helen. "Are you implying *I'm* the prude now?"

Celia felt a sting at the girl's words. *I'm not a prude,* she thought for the dozenth time that day. *I got in that water just like the rest of you.* But the two weren't paying her any attention.

"Of course not," Helen said, bringing her nose down a notch. "If anyone is to blame, it's me. Why don't we just agree to forget it ever happened? Let's never talk about it again. Can we all agree to that?"

Celia met Helen's pointed gaze and nodded. She was more than happy to do her best to put the whole incident out of her mind. No one disagreed.

"Well, that's settled then," Eleanor announced. "Anyway, I ran into Tripp as he was leaving and swore him to secrecy. We don't need him talking to Daddy about any of this."

A rush of relief coursed through Celia. Maybe they *could* stay for their full vacation.

"I don't know about the rest of you, but I'm ready for some dancing," Helen said, turning toward the main lodge.

"I'll second that," Ruby agreed, falling into step behind Eleanor and Helen.

Celia brought up the rear of their small group, again scanning the immaculate grounds and small knots of laughing people. The girls slipped back into their dancing shoes and clicked along the wooden boardwalk.

To her right a massive flower garden broke up the expanse of green; a man stood in the middle of it all, trimming errant leaves and twigs from a carefully manicured flowering tree. His sandy brown hair, longer than the current style, waved in the evening breeze. The gardening tool looked heavy, but the worker wielded it with little effort. Even from a distance, Celia could see the strength in his arms. The man reminded her of her stepfather.

"Come on, I love this song!" Eleanor cried over her shoulder, breaking into a slow jog, despite the kitten-heeled slippers she wore.

Celia laughed; Eleanor's enthusiasm was infectious. Hurrying, she kept a steadying hand on the railing leading up the stone stairs, the music drawing her in, the gardener forgotten.

* * *

While not technically old enough to drink alcohol in public, the girls helped themselves to punch cups full of ice-cold spiked lemonade anytime they stepped off the dance floor. Huge mechanical fans rotated slowly above their heads, the blades doing little more than stirring the heavy air. As the evening progressed, the mingling scents of perfume, cigar smoke, and perspiration permeated the heated air. The girls fanned both hands in front of their faces in a fruitless effort to cool down. When the band put down their instruments to take a break before their last set of the evening, Eleanor insisted they step outside for some fresh air.

Outside, the evening air felt heavenly, smelling faintly of fresh flowers instead of the man-made scent of perfume. Celia couldn't help but compare the way the fresh air felt to her earlier excursion into the cool water in the woods: like silk. She was sorry their evening was coming to a close. Bolts of lightning streaked across the horizon. She wished they could dance until the sun rose.

"Eleanor," a voice said from behind them, although only Celia responded. She turned, but couldn't see who'd been speaking. "Eleanor?"

This time she saw the speaker, a man, step out of the shadows and into a pool of light cast by the fixtures flanking the carved doors at the top of the field-stone stairway. Was it the gardener she'd noticed earlier? But no, this man was smartly dressed, wearing high-waisted trousers and a button-down shirt.

Celia smiled, blushing when the man noticed her and smiled back. Her heart did a funny little flutter in her chest. She nearly looked over her shoulder to see if the handsome young man was smiling at someone else, but there was no one directly behind her. He *had* smiled at her, although he was trying to get Eleanor's attention.

"Elly," she said, loud enough to snag Eleanor's attention away from Helen's animated retelling of her dance with a man she called the "most eligible bachelor at the dance."

"What?"

"I think someone wants to say hello," Celia said, nodding toward the young man.

Eleanor let out what was becoming her signature shriek, something Celia had never noticed her do at school before. She pushed past

Celia with arms outstretched. The man clasped her hands in greeting, then pulled her into a friendly hug. The other girls watched with curiosity.

"Oh my gosh, Danny, I was hoping we'd see you tonight! You didn't have to work? When did you get here? Your mom said you'd be in sometime soon, but she wasn't sure exactly when."

The friendly man shrugged, a sheepish grin lighting up his eyes. "It might be best if you don't tell Mother you saw me tonight. I'll be in trouble for not stopping over at Whispering Pines yet to see her. I wanted to, but they put me to work the minute I arrived. Honestly, when I got off work at nine, I barely had time to clean up. I wanted to rush over here, hoped I might run into you. How have you been? How is your family?" Following his litany of questions, the man paused, as if realizing he was being rude by ignoring Eleanor's friends. "And who might these lovely ladies be?"

Eleanor tilted her head, first at the young man, then toward her three friends. "Oh! I'm so sorry. Helen, Celia, Ruby—this is Danny. He's Mrs. Bell's son. We worked together at our resort last summer, but Whispering Pines couldn't compete with his love for landscaping, so he's working here now."

Celia held out a hand to Danny. He must be the man she'd noticed earlier after all. When his hand encircled her own, she could feel a strength there, a roughness to his palm that spoke to his passion.

He greeted each of them individually, then motioned back toward the heavy doors when the sounds of the band warming up again met their ears. "The evening is nearly over, ladies. Shall we?"

"Only if you promise to dance with me," Eleanor said, pinching his cheek as she passed him, an action Celia found odd—condescending, even. But he looked unfazed as he continued to hold the door for Helen and Ruby.

When Celia didn't follow, he looked at her expectantly. "Coming in?"

His question spurred her on. She held his gaze as she walked by him. Standing under the light, she could see those eyes were a warm

KIMBERLY DIEDE

brown. They twinkled at her, and she felt a wave of disappointment that he'd be dancing with Eleanor and not her.

But then, she told herself, they had all summer. There would be more dances.

* * *

Eleanor pulled Danny onto the dance floor as soon as they got back inside.

The "most eligible bachelor" whom Helen had been swooning over while on the patio approached them, and Celia stepped back out of the way, assuming he'd ask Helen to dance again. Her friend looked striking in her blue dress, with its cinched waist and the way the color set off her platinum-blond hair. Helen stepped forward, clearly thinking the same. The man smiled pleasantly at Helen but held his hand out to Ruby, leading her out to the dance floor instead.

Celia knew if the music wasn't so loud, she'd be able to hear Ruby's heart nearly beating out of her chest. Her oldest friend deemed herself to be a terrible dancer, although Celia didn't agree. Ruby just had a way of letting her nerves get the best of her.

Helen kept a polite smile plastered on her face until the dancing couple swirled out of view, after which she promptly pivoted on one heel, crossing her arms over her chest and thrusting out her chin like a spoiled child.

"Careful, Helen, your pouting will scare off any future dance partners if you aren't careful."

She rolled her eyes at Celia, took a deep breath, and dropped her arms. "You're right, as always, Celia. And we can't have that, can we?"

Celia watched as Helen scanned the room, zeroing in on Leo and a man he was visiting with near the entrance. Neither looked all that interested in dancing. Helen grabbed Celia's hand and dragged her in their direction. Celia resisted, sensing what Helen was up to.

"Hello, dear brother. Do me a favor, would you? Dear Celia hasn't danced enough tonight. Take her for a spin around the dance floor?"

Leo pinned his sister with a look. He didn't appreciate being inter-

44

rupted. However, years of breeding wouldn't allow him to be rude, so he excused himself to the man he'd been visiting with and extended a hand to Celia. Feeling manipulated, she grudgingly took it and allowed Leo to lead her toward the dance floor, shooting one last glare at Helen over her shoulder.

"I'm sorry your sister can be such a brat," Celia said, talking into his ear to be heard. "I never said I wanted to dance with you."

Leo pulled up short and dropped her hand, covering his heart instead. "You wound me, Celia."

She laughed, knowing full well he wasn't serious.

"I know you didn't say you wanted to dance. This is Helen we're talking about here. And that was Warren Arbuckle I was visiting with. He's someone Helen has had her eye on for the past few years. She isn't as sneaky as she thinks she is."

Celia looked back toward where she'd left Helen and this man named Warren. She couldn't recall Helen ever mentioning him before.

Leo must have read the skepticism on her face. "Trust me. I know my sister. And I love her. But I'm still often surprised that you can tolerate her. I have to. You don't."

The lead singer announced their last song of the evening.

Leo held his hand out to her again. "Shall we?"

Taking his hand, she allowed the brother of one of her oldest friends to lead her onto the floor. Leo was a skilled dancer, and Celia let herself get lost in the music.

As the final chords of the song faded, she glanced around, trying to catch one last glimpse of Danny, but she couldn't spot him. Someone else was spinning Eleanor around the dance floor now. She wasn't sure why the pang of disappointment cut so deeply. Many women in the room would have been tickled to wrap up the evening on Leo Nielle's arm.

CHAPTER FOUR
GIFT OF A WARNING

"I've had about enough of your sass tonight, Helen," Leo said, his voice tight. "I haven't run into Warren for over a year, and we were discussing something important when you so rudely interrupted. Now get in the backseat. Celia, why don't you get up front here."

Celia hesitated. "Ruby, will you be all right in the back?"

"That's sweet of you to ask, Celia, but yes. I didn't have trouble on the way over. It's usually the longer car rides, when it's too hot, that start to bother my stomach. You go ahead."

Leo, two steps ahead of the rest of their group, pulled open the back door of his Buick and motioned for his sister, Ruby, and Eleanor to crawl in. Celia gladly took the front passenger seat. She'd had enough of Helen, too.

Helen wasn't pleased to be stuck in the backseat, but it didn't take long before she joined in the animated chatter between Eleanor and Ruby as they dissected the prospects of their various dance partners. Celia wanted to remind them one or two spins around a dance floor wasn't enough time to determine anything important about a man.

Tuning them out, Celia faced forward, running an appreciative hand over the Buick's polished dashboard. The hands on the clock in the middle of the dash glowed half past one, and the rhythmic swoosh of windshield wipers quickly mesmerized her as Leo drove into the darkness, a summer rain shower quickly enveloping them. The car's headlights could only provide so much illumination, and Leo stayed quiet, intent on keeping a close eye on the road. They were about ten miles from Whispering Pines, but even during clear weather the road was tricky, full of sharp corners and switchbacks, trees crowding the shoulder as if someone had cut the lanes right through the heart of a deep forest.

Celia tried to help Leo watch the road, but the full day, the hypnotic motion of the windshield wipers, and the patter of rain made staying awake difficult. Her head bobbed.

She jumped awake just in time to see someone in the car's head-lights. She screamed, causing poor Leo to jerk the steering wheel. The tires lost their tenacious grip on the mud-slick road and the Buick fishtailed. Celia bumped her head against the side window and slid forward, hitting her shoulder on the dash. Tree trunks loomed ominously in the glare of the headlights. She squeezed her eyes tight and prepared for impact.

But the impact never came. The Buick stopped, its front wheels off the road. The rear wheels remained on the roadway. The nose of the automobile angled downward, but gently, so they could push back into their seats.

"What happened?" came Ruby's trembling voice from the backseat.

Celia spared a glance at Leo, noting the white of his knuckles where he still gripped the steering wheel. He turned toward her, wide-eyed. "What did you see? Did we hit something?"

"I . . . I thought I saw something—someone—standing in the road," Celia stammered, reaching up to touch the side of her head. She winced when her fingers found a tender lump no bigger than a marble.

Truthfully, it had looked like a child—a small boy—standing in the road, surrounded by a white light. But that couldn't possibly be. A child wouldn't be out here in the woods, in the middle of a rainy night. Then she remembered the tale of the lost boys. Had her mind played tricks on her, caught somewhere between sleep and awareness? Had her imagination gotten the best of her, only to lead to Leo nearly losing control of his brand-new car because of her ridiculous screaming?

Leo spun to check the backseat. "Is everyone all right?"

"Yes, we're fine," Helen replied, her voice calm and controlled.

Celia appreciated her friend's demeanor. This was the answer to Leo's earlier question, when they were alone on the dance floor. This was the part of Helen's personality that Celia appreciated, the one that kept their friendship intact. When things got rough, she could count on Helen.

Leo dropped a hand on her shoulder, giving it a light squeeze. "Are you all right, Celia? How hard did you hit your head on the window?"

She bit back a grimace. She'd hit first her head and then the shoulder Leo was gripping, but she already felt responsible for causing him to lose control of the car. "I'm fine."

He nodded, then opened his door. Celia grabbed for his hand, irrational fear sluicing over her. "Wait! Where are you going?"

He squeezed her fingers, then quickly released her hand and got out. "I have to make sure we didn't hit anyone."

Her breath caught. What if it hadn't been her imagination? Unable to resist the urge, Celia opened her door.

"Celia, stop, you'll get soaked!"

She ignored Ruby, stepping onto the rain-sodden grass. She slammed her door, squinting through the steady rain, searching for Leo. She spun, peering down into the woods, illuminated by the Buick's headlights, but the only movement was the dancing of leaves beneath the pelting raindrops. She swore she'd heard laughter behind her.

"Leo? Where are you?"

"Good God, Celia, get back in the car! What in heaven's name are you doing out here?" Leo scolded, coming up behind Celia and putting a steady hand at her waist. He opened her door again, practically pushing her back inside. "There's nothing out here. It must have been a trick of the light."

Leo hurried around the front of his car, bending down to look at, or under, the front bumper. His shadow loomed large against the tree trunks, adding to the haunted feeling of the dark, wet night. Cold penetrated her thoughts, and she rubbed at her upper arms to warm herself. Leo straightened and continued around to the driver's door, slipping at one point but catching himself.

The car dipped slightly as he got back in, collapsing against the seat back. "I don't think we hit anything." He noticed Celia's violent shaking. "Here, let me turn the heat on. This baby might not have air-conditioning"—he glanced pointedly at Helen through the rearview mirror—"but it has a good heater. I have a blanket in the trunk. Do you need me to get it?"

"Why would you have a blanket in your trunk, dear brother?"

Leo ignored Helen, looking to Celia.

"No, I'll be fine. Can you drive us out of here, or are we stuck?" Celia asked, doing her best to keep her teeth from chattering. Leo was right—the heater was already helping; but it wasn't just the cold that had Celia shaking.

"I guess we'll find out. Hold on. I don't want you to hit your head again."

Celia braced one hand against the dashboard and held on to the armrest on her door with the other. Leo put the car in gear and worked both the gas and the brake pedals, attempting to get the rear wheels to grab. The car rocked and the engine churned, but the tires refused to bite, the sound of spitting mud doing little to reassure everyone.

Leo dropped his head to his steering wheel, frustrated and exhausted. He looked soaked through to the bone. He'd been out in the rain longer than she had, and she could feel water trickling out of her hair and down her back.

No one said anything as reality sank in. It was late, and no one was likely to miss them until morning. Few would travel this road in the middle of the night.

"Well, ladies, it looks like we're going to spend the rest of our night in the Buick. Not exactly the ending any of us were hoping for." His hand sought his door handle again. "I'll grab those blankets now."

Celia watched him step out again, the elements swallowing him up. He returned quickly, keeping the short stack of blankets as dry as he could. He handed them to Celia. She eyed the bright red blanket on top, handing it back to him before he could climb back into the car. "Why don't you drape this over the back of your car? That way, if anyone comes up behind us in the dark, they're more likely to see us. We're still partially on the road, aren't we?"

Leo held her eye for a moment, then took the blanket and did as she suggested.

When he'd finally settled back into the car, she handed him one of the two blankets she'd kept up front, having handed the two others back to her friends. "You should take that wet jacket and shirt off so you don't freeze. Do you have enough gas to let it run until morning?"

The look he gave her provided the answer she didn't want to hear and he didn't want to say. The windows steamed over inside, a combination of their rain-soaked clothes and bodies, the heat, and the continuing rain outside. She nodded her understanding, offered him what she hoped was a reassuring smile, and then she snuggled down into the one remaining blanket. There wasn't any more talking from the backseat.

"Leo?"

"What?"

"Why *did* you have a stack of blankets in your trunk?" Celia couldn't help but ask. One she might have passed off as good luck. But five of them?

Celia could sense more than see Leo turn his head to look in her direction. "Mother insisted I bring extra in case the ones at the resort weren't to her liking."

"Of course she did," Eleanor whispered from the backseat, and they all got a little chuckle out of Mrs. Nielle's neurotic behavior. At least this time it would help keep them warm through a cold, dark night.

* * *

Celia opened her eyes to a pale wash of light.

It took her a moment to remember where she was, why her shoulder ached and her neck was kinked. She'd spent the night in Leo's car, after nearly causing a serious accident with her irrational reaction to seeing what she now thought might have been a ghost standing in the road.

At least she'd had the sense not to admit that last part aloud. She'd tell no one what she'd thought she'd seen.

Leo stretched beside her, rubbing the back of his neck with a groan. No one stirred in the backseat. He wiped a swath of condensation from the inside of the front windshield and peered out toward the sky. "At least the rain cleared out."

Celia glanced his way and laughed.

"What?"

"You have mud smeared on your forehead," Celia said, pointing.

He angled the rearview mirror so he could see for himself, then rubbed at the dirt with a corner of his blanket. Celia supposed she should feel embarrassed, seeing him sitting there bare-chested, after he'd followed her advice and took off his wet clothes so he wouldn't freeze. But she didn't. It was Leo; she'd seen him this way many times down at the beach.

"I should go for help," he announced, holding his shirt up and slipping it on, shivering against what she could only assume was damp fabric.

"Won't they come find us?" Celia asked, hating the thought of Leo setting out in the dim light of early morning. The clock on the dash read a few minutes after five.

"Eventually. But we probably aren't more than a mile or two from the resort. It'll be faster if I walk for help. You girls will be fine here, won't you? That was a good idea you had last night, to drape the red blanket across the back." He glanced through the back windshield. "It's still there. And now that it's getting light out, there's less likelihood anyone would rear-end us."

Celia shivered. It would feel wonderful to get back to the resort, take a nice hot bath, and crawl under the covers on her bed in the cabin. She wouldn't mind a faster rescue.

"Be careful, all right?"

Leo reached over and squeezed her shoulder again, his touch playful, almost brotherly, but this time he noticed her wince. He dropped his hand. "I'm so sorry, Celia. Did I hurt you? Did you hurt your shoulder last night?"

She waved away his concern. "I'm fine. Just a minor bump."

"Can I look at it?" he asked. His eyes reflected genuine concern.

Celia wasn't shy to show him her shoulder, but she wasn't sure she wanted to look at it herself. It hurt even worse this morning. She nodded, then undid the top two buttons on her dress so she could ease it out of the way. He pulled it down more, his indrawn breath telling her she'd been right. She must be sporting a noticeable bruise.

"That does it. I'm definitely going for help now. We need to have someone look at that shoulder."

Celia worked her dress back into place, careful not to cause herself more pain. "Thank you. And Leo . . . I'm really sorry. I feel responsible for what happened last night. If I wouldn't have screamed like that, we would have gotten back to the resort and had a good night's sleep in a regular bed. Hopefully your car is all right."

"The car is fine. Just stuck in mud. It's you I'm worried about. Sit tight, okay? I'll be back with help as soon as I can."

Celia nodded, thankful he didn't seem to be mad at her. If he'd have let his sister sit up front, none of this would have happened.

Leo left and Celia settled back in her seat, but sleep eluded her.

"Are you all right? That bruise looks ugly," Helen said from her spot directly behind Celia.

"I will be after I go to the bathroom."

"Me, too. It's so stuffy in here. I need some fresh air."

Celia nodded, and they both stepped outside, closing their doors as quietly as possible since both Ruby and Eleanor were still asleep. How they could be was a mystery to Celia. The early-morning melody of birds punctuated the air, along with the dripping of moisture off the leaves and pine needles. The rain had washed away the humidity—at least for the time being—but already a low mist rose from the saturated ground as the sun, still barely visible through the trees, began its slow ascent.

"I don't suppose there's any indoor plumbing out here." Helen sighed, surveying their surroundings. "We are in the middle of nowhere, aren't we?"

Celia nodded. "It feels that way, although your brother didn't think we were too far from Whispering Pines."

"Well, come on then, let's go into the trees. I don't feel like exposing myself to anyone today. Yesterday was enough for me."

They laughed softly as they walked through the tall wet grass.

By the time they made their way back to the Buick, the hems of their dresses were soaked. But they felt better after getting that business out of the way.

"I cannot get back in that car for one more minute," Helen declared.

Celia agreed. The cool morning air felt refreshing and the rising sun had chased away any lingering thoughts she'd harbored about little ghost boys and other scary creatures in the surrounding woods. But the road was too muddy to stand on and the wet grass in the ditch itched her legs. She'd spied a fallen tree when she'd relieved herself.

"Follow me," she ordered, heading back the short distance.

Luckily, the tree was flat on the ground. She doubted she'd have been able to hoist herself up onto anything, given the state of her shoulder. Once settled on the makeshift bench, she patted the wet bark next to her, inviting Helen to take a seat. She ignored the wetness seeping through her dress.

Helen sat, swatting at a mosquito as it tried to make its breakfast from her arm. "Mother would *not* enjoy this."

Celia laughed, unable to imagine Helen's mother sitting on a downed tree, waiting for a rescue party. "Did you have fun last night?"

Helen gave a start and brushed a long-legged spider off the skirt of her dress. "Last night, yes. This morning, not so much. But I'm trying to be a good sport about all of this."

"Say, Helen, I'm really sorry about what happened yesterday," Celia began, feeling the need to clear the air. She'd been dying to say something all this time, and something about the still morning air pushed the moment at her. "I'm sure you feel utterly humiliated after Tripp saw you like that, naked. I know I would. I really wish that wouldn't have happened to you."

Helen said nothing for a moment. When she finally spoke, Celia thought she misheard her friend. She asked her to repeat herself.

Helen vented a heavy sigh. "I said, it's not like he hasn't seen it before."

"Well, maybe he has, but he hadn't seen *you* naked before."

"Actually, he did," Helen confessed, so quietly Celia might have missed it again.

But she heard Helen clearly enough this time. She scrambled for something to say in response to that little bombshell, but failed to before Helen continued.

"Look, Celia, don't judge me too harshly. It happened last year, when Leo brought Tripp home with him from college. We'd just graduated from high school, you and I. Our parents were out for the evening, and Leo had a bunch of his friends over. They were playing pool in the basement, and I know now that I should have stayed away from them. There was drinking, and I guess I was feeling a little lonely. You weren't able to do anything because Beverly was so sick, and Ruby was at her grandmother's. I was bored."

Celia held up a hand to stop the flow of Helen's words. "Wait. Are you telling me that's how Tripp saw you naked? Did you have *sex* with him? With your old family friend?" The revelation hit Celia fully. "You aren't a virgin?"

Helen grabbed Celia's hand and pulled it down, holding a finger over her lips. "Keep it down, Celia, for heaven's sake! I thought you'd be mature enough to handle me telling you this. But I don't want Eleanor to know. She might hate me for it."

Celia had to admit she had a point there. "You may have overestimated my ability to handle news like this, Helen."

Helen turned her head, but not before Celia saw her flick a tear away. She wasn't handling this well at all, her friend's shocking confession. She'd assumed, probably naïvely, that none of them would have sex before they got married. Good girls like them just didn't do that kind of thing.

Do they?

"I'm sorry, Helen. You took me by surprise, that's all. I guess I assumed, you know, that sex wasn't something any of us would do before marriage. And since I'm not sure I ever *want* to get married, I wasn't sure I'd ever *have* sex."

Helen laughed, the bitterness unmistakable. "Well, when someone you've *hoped* to marry since you were a little girl whispers promises of 'forever after' in your ear and lets you sip on his gin and tonic, you might not make the best of choices either. At least I didn't."

"That beast," Celia hissed, squeezing Helen's hand. "Does Leo know?"

Helen snorted. "Absolutely not. Leo can't ever know. He'd kill him. I won't lose my brother over that despicable human being."

Despicable human being.

"So . . . I take it Tripp wasn't honest when he led you to believe he'd marry you?"

"Bingo."

Celia was still trying to process everything Helen had shared. "I'm sorry that happened to you. It certainly explains why you dislike Tripp now."

"I don't *dislike* Tripp. I *hate* Tripp. I swore I'd tell no one what happened to me. I feel so ashamed. Thank goodness I didn't end up pregnant."

A scurrying sound drew Celia's eye upward to where a small squirrel sat high on a branch watching them, chattering down as if to scold them for invading its woods. Or maybe it, too, was sharing a secret with her, one she couldn't understand. "Why did you tell me all of this, Helen? I promise to never tell another soul, of course. But I don't understand."

Helen avoided eye contact as she said, "I told you because I'm worried. I've seen the way Tripp looks at you."

"At *me*?" Celia asked, shocked yet again at Helen's words. "Tripp barely knows I'm alive! I only just *met* him."

Helen shook her head. "Trust me on this. And be careful. Tripp is nothing but trouble. He has a bad temper. I've never actually seen it, but Eleanor said he does, and I can feel it, just below the surface, when he looks at me sometimes."

A new sound drifted down to them from the road above—the slow roll of tires on gravel. Help had arrived. Celia only wished someone could have helped Helen the previous summer, before that bastard Tripp stole something precious from her friend. Helen lost her innocence, and he was to blame.

CHAPTER FIVE
GIFT OF YELLOW ROSES

$\mathcal{T}$heir days fell into a predictable pattern. Heat and humidity would chase the girls out of their cabins by eight in the morning; however, they needed something to keep them busy until they could congregate on the beach—something that wouldn't disturb other guests staying in the cabins nearer the water.

They alternated between canoeing, hiking in the woods, or learning the fine art of fishing from Leo. Helen's brother tried his best to remain patient, but Celia was the only one willing to bait her own hook or remove the occasional fish she'd reel in. The other girls refused to touch anything slimy. Celia's injured shoulder healed quickly, and she naturally took to the casting lessons Leo provided.

By the Friday morning following their near-collision with a tree in the middle of the night, Celia was ready for a break from her three girlfriends. She loved them all dearly, but by now she'd tired of talk about what they'd wear to the dance on Saturday night, who they hoped to dance with this time, and how they could help each other garner invitations from their desired partners.

Celia couldn't help but compare their tittering to their early morning fishing sessions. Her friends were intent on baiting their hooks with showy outfits and perfectly applied makeup. She found their attention to detail dull. Her enthusiasm over the upcoming night at the neighboring resort was waning fast.

Leo was already sitting on the lowest step in front of their cabin when they came outside. He was tying a hook on the string of his fishing pole. "Anyone up for some fishing this morning, before it gets too hot?"

Everyone begged off except for Celia. Since Tripp was still away on business, Celia knew her friends were back to cooling off in the swimming hole where they'd first skinny dipped. There wasn't much threat of discovery now.

Getting naked in front of her friends still held no appeal for Celia. In fact, now that Helen had confided in her about what happened with Tripp the previous summer, she was even less inclined to take part. Given her own lack of experience, maybe she really *was* a prude.

She'd said nothing about Helen's secret, of course, and she had no intention of breaking her promise. But she was struggling to see Helen in the same light as before the confession. It was as if Celia had lost a bit of her own innocence. Suddenly, dancing with strangers made her nervous. If Helen had been willing to have relations with a man so easily, did other girls do the same thing? Would men expect the girls they danced with to be willing partners in things like that?

Celia supposed part of her unease was also because of her disappointment in her friend. Why had Helen done such a thing? No one should have sex before marriage. It was too risky. What if she had gotten pregnant? Tripp didn't want her. Helen's life could have been ruined.

Celia waved at the girls as they paused on the grass in front of the cabin.

Like it or not, they'd all spend the better part of the next afternoon in the cabin, primping and preparing for an evening of dancing. Spending the morning fishing with Leo might help her keep her sanity.

"Celia, why on earth would you rather fish with my brother than take a morning stroll through the woods with your best girlfriends?" Helen asked, her expression one of disdain.

Knowing she couldn't tell them the truth, she uttered the first thing that came to mind. "I'm afraid I may have gotten a touch of poison ivy when we walked on Tuesday morning. My lower left leg will not stop itching. I must be sensitive to that nasty stuff. I'll go next time, after my leg doesn't itch anymore. I promise."

Helen shrugged, spinning away toward the lodge and the promise of a breakfast pastry and coffee. "Suit yourself. I think I'd rather have an itchy leg than play with worms with Leo, but I don't pretend to always understand your thinking. Come on, Ruby, let's go find Eleanor."

Celia gave Ruby a reassuring nod when her friend caught her eye, glancing meaningfully at Leo where he sat on the steps, fishing poles propped up against the handrail. "Go have fun. I'll see you on the beach this afternoon."

Ruby didn't appear to understand Celia's desire to fish either. She obediently followed Helen, glancing back at Celia one last time before rounding the corner of the dirt path and out of sight.

"Now that they're gone, do you want to tell me the *real* reason you'd rather go fishing?" Leo asked, looking up at Celia on the middle step. His eyes were level with her shoes. "Because I don't see a rash on your leg."

Celia turned her foot to inspect the lower portion of her own leg, as if his statement came as a surprise. But Leo wasn't dumb. And she didn't feel like pretending any longer. Groaning, she sank down to sit on the step beside him. "You caught me. My leg is fine."

Nodding, Leo turned his attention back to the hook in his left hand.

"I'm just feeling claustrophobic and thought a couple of peaceful hours on the dock sounded like the better option this morning."

Snagging a barb from the hook in the top eyelet of his fishing pole, Leo grinned. "You picked me over my sister? I'm flattered. You realize I have a girlfriend back home, right?"

Celia reached out with her poison-ivy-free foot and gave him a friendly nudge. "I know that, Leo. Don't go getting all full of yourself."

Patting her foot, Leo stood. "I'm just teasing. Come on, Cee, let's go drown a worm."

* * *

Two hours later, Celia strolled back up the dock and across the sand with Leo. He carried an impressive stringer of walleye and bass and she brought the metal minnow bucket, water sloshing out through small air holes in the top.

"Minnows worked better for bait today," she pointed out.

Leo lifted the stringer of fish higher. "For you, at least. You caught most of these. I think the student is surpassing the teacher."

Laughing, Celia shifted the heavy bucket to her other hand. She didn't dare complain. Leo had his hands full between their catch, a tackle box, and two fishing poles.

It had felt good to sit quietly on the dock, lost in her own thoughts. Leo wasn't one to talk much, which she appreciated today. She'd been going back and forth on the decision she knew she'd need to make soon around a major for school.

Eleanor's comments about building parts for bombers had her thinking. She hadn't dared consider anything so nontraditional. But maybe that's why she'd been feeling stuck. Things like teaching or nursing didn't inspire her. Not that she wanted to make airplane parts, but the war might open up other fields to women, too.

Their host, Eleanor's father, was talking with Mr. Bell when the unlikely pair of fishermen approached the outdoor cleaning station with their catch. Guests weren't expected to clean their own fish. While Mrs. Bell had already proven she could do amazing things in the kitchen with the fish they caught, Celia hadn't met the cook's husband. One of his duties was cleaning the fish.

"Hello, Leo. Celia. It looks like the two of you had some luck this morning," Mr. Whitby pointed out as he stepped aside to allow them access to the small lean-to. "Eleanor told me you girls were going for a hike in the woods this morning. You didn't feel up for the walk?"

Leo nodded a greeting to Mr. Whitby and hoisted the metal

stringer of fish up onto the cleaning station. Celia could hear Mr. Bell and Leo conversing quietly about the impressive size of three of the bass. She gave Eleanor's father her full attention.

She shook her head in answer to his question. She considered using her little white lie about poison ivy again, but decided honesty would be the wiser choice. Eleanor's father would either see right through her feeble excuse or send her to Mrs. Bell for medical help, much as he'd done with her shoulder after they'd returned from their night spent in the woods. "I felt more like fishing than hiking this morning, what with the heat and all."

Mr. Whitby's eyes twinkled. "And I suspect a few hours away from the constant chatter of your group of girlfriends was timely, too?"

Unable to help herself, she grinned, but left it at that.

Mr. Whitby turned to leave, but paused. "Say, Celia. Eleanor mentioned you wanted to possibly help out around the resort. While I expect our guests to relax during their stay, some people aren't comfortable with too much leisure time on their hands. Would you count yourself amongst such company?"

"Most definitely, Mr. Whitby. I grew up helping my mother run our household. There was little time for relaxing. While I appreciate the opportunity to have so much free time on my hands at Whispering Pines, I feel like I'd enjoy my stay even more if I did more than gossip and suntan."

Too late, she realized her host might think she was complaining about Eleanor's hospitality, which wasn't at all what she'd meant. She opened her mouth to soften her blunt comment, but the older man held up a hand to stop her.

"First off, I insist you call me Preston. We don't stand on formality around here. I had too much of that growing up. Second, I admire a young person with ambition and a certain, shall we say, *curiosity* about the world. What is it you are studying at St. Catherine's?"

Celia kicked at a large pebble, reluctant to admit she was still undeclared. She didn't want the man to think she lacked commitment. But still, that honesty compelled her. "Admittedly, I'm still deciding. I haven't found a field that sparks my interest yet. But I'm dedicated to my studies and did well with the general courses I took my first year."

Eleanor's father crossed his arms over his chest, considering her words. "You sound apologetic, but you shouldn't be. I've learned that it's nearly impossible to know what we truly want out of this life until we try a few different things. Take me and this resort, for example," he said, motioning around them. "I never dreamed I'd enjoy owning a place like Whispering Pines, but so far it's the most rewarding thing I've ever done. Not the most lucrative, mind you, but the thing that brings me the most joy."

Celia grinned, allowing her eyes to take in the cabins, beach, and brand-new lodge, looking at it from a fresh perspective. "I suppose a place like this is costly to run. And you don't have nearly as many cabins or accommodations as Grand View. The size of that resort surprised me when we went to the dance last weekend." But again, she felt like she might have offended her host. She really needed to stop saying the first thing that popped into her brain. "Not that I liked that other resort *nearly* as much as Whispering Pines," she quickly added.

He laughed. Clearly she hadn't offended him. "My dear, the two resorts are as different as night and day. My little piece of heaven here would fit into one quarter of the property over at Grand View. Honestly, I prefer the size, the *peace* I feel here at Whispering Pines. I'm impressed that you recognize the lack of cabins here poses certain, shall we say, financial difficulties, though. The cost of running any resort is high, regardless of size."

Celia shrugged. "I suppose you could say I have a bit of personal experience in the hospitality business."

"And how is that?" he asked.

Celia wished she hadn't mentioned her own experiences. Would Mr. Whitby—*Preston*, she reminded herself—understand her family's financial struggles given his vast wealth? But he appeared interested and waited patiently for her to expound on her initial comment.

Taking a deep breath, she gave him an abbreviated version of her younger years. "After my father died, it was just Mother and my little sister and me. We lived in a large house, and my father had investments and such, but much of that evaporated."

"How old were you when your father died?"

"Five."

Celia guessed that Preston was doing the math in his head. She was the same age as his daughter, Eleanor. "Your father died shortly before Black Tuesday."

Nodding, Celia dropped her head in embarrassment. "My mother was much younger than my father. Nearly twenty years. His death left her a widow at twenty-four years old. My little sister, Beverly, has always been sickly. Mother had to get creative so we wouldn't lose our house."

Preston turned, motioning Celia to follow him a few steps away from the fish-cleaning station. He paused under a large pine tree. Someone had trimmed the lower branches away to allow the walking path to pass near it. The shade and the pine-scented air was a relief after the late morning sun and odors emanating from the fish.

"Did you take in boarders?"

His question surprised Celia. "Why, yes, we did. But how did you know that? Do you know my mother?"

"Taking in boarders during the Depression years was something many astute people did in order to hold on to their properties. Never feel shame over your mother's ingenuity. I applaud her for it."

Those words, delivered in such a matter-of-fact manner, lifted a burden of shame from Celia that she hadn't even realized she'd been carrying. He was right. Her mother had done a brave thing, letting strangers move in to their home.

"Did you help, then?" he asked. "With the boarders, I mean."

"I did. Momma couldn't do it all on her own. At first I just helped with the cleaning. But as I got older, she trusted me to collect the weekly rent from the vacationers. She only rented to women. If someone couldn't pay, I'd help them figure out a way to scrape enough money together so Momma wouldn't have to make them leave. I met some amazing women during those years."

Preston held Celia's eye then. "Not only did you meet amazing people, Celia, I suspect those years may have ignited a spark in you. You seem to have an aptitude for figures. I see how proud you are of the ways you helped your mother."

Could Eleanor's father be right? Did she have a head for math or business?

"I'm falling behind in some of my paperwork filing and such here at the resort," he continued. "I could use a hand. Would you have any interest in spending a morning or two with me in the office, helping me get caught up?" With that twinkle in his eye he added, "Unless you'd rather hike or fish, of course."

Celia could hardly believe a man like Mr. Whitby needed her help with anything. Maybe he was just being nice, taking pity on her. Perhaps he thought she was in a tiff with her girlfriends.

When she didn't immediately respond, he looked her straight in the eye. "Celia, do you want to help? I think you might enjoy it. And, no, I'm not offering just to be nice. If you do any work with me at all, 'nice' won't be how you view me. But I may teach you a thing or two. Maybe getting some exposure to the business world will help you decide where to direct your focus at university. What do you say?"

Caught between feeling thrilled and terrified, Celia took a deep breath and took a chance. "I would love to help."

"All right, it's settled then! You start next Monday. You'll spend Monday and Wednesday mornings with me, working on resort business, and we'll see what you can learn between now and when you go home. Now, if you'll excuse me, I should have met the food-delivery man five minutes ago. See you Monday, bright and early."

As she watched her friend's father make his way purposefully back toward the lodge, Celia had the oddest sensation that her life had just taken an unexpected twist.

* * *

Celia climbed out of the backseat of Leo's Buick, now jokingly banned from the front seat—no one wanted to spend another night in the car in the dark woods. Leo dropped them in the same place, but this time air perfumed by the fragrant blooms on either side of the massive lodge entrance wafted over her. Yellow roses bloomed tall, surrounded by a rainbow of other hues. But it was the heady scent of the roses that made her smile the most. Looking around the grounds, she hoped to catch sight of Danny, Eleanor's gardener friend, but no one was about. She could feel the low thrum of musical instruments, even though her friends' chatter nearly drowned out the notes.

They'd arrived at the dance later this time, delayed while Helen argued with her mother over the appropriateness of the low-cut bodice on the young woman's dancing dress. It took plenty of persuasion, but eventually Helen came out the victor.

Celia wasn't at all sure she was up for hours of dancing and small talk. Her mind was back on her meeting with Mr. Whitby—correction: *Preston*—and the work she'd do with him come Monday. She still couldn't believe he wanted to teach her anything.

Ruby caught her by the upper arm and practically dragged her toward the door. "Come on, Celia, the dance has already started. We may have already missed the first set! We need to hurry."

When Celia's feet didn't initially move, Ruby paused, looking back at her in confusion. "Is everything okay? You seem, I don't know . . . *distant* today. Are you feeling all right? I missed you on our walk this morning."

Taking her friend's hand, Celia gave it a friendly squeeze then hurried ahead of her, pulling Ruby through the door. She'd decided not to mention her new work arrangement to anyone. Not just yet. They might not understand her excitement. Vacation was a time to relax. Even Ruby might question her sanity over that one.

"I'm fine! Let's go, before Helen and Eleanor take all the cute boys."

The relief on her friend's face reminded Celia that Ruby didn't feel comfortable at gatherings like this either. Eleanor and Helen thrived in crowds, and on the attention their looks and outgoing personalities garnered. It was another difference that halved their friend group.

"We'll make the best of it," she said, giving Ruby a reassuring smile.

And as so often happens, once she attempted to enjoy herself, Celia had fun. She danced to nearly every song. The dance floor was even more crowded than the week before, although she wouldn't have thought that possible. Her left foot ached; someone in heels had stepped on her big toe three songs earlier. As the tempo slowed and couples paired off to hold each other close, Celia made her excuses and wove her way to the edge of the crowd, slipping through a side door.

Finding herself in a deserted hallway, she slipped out of her shoes, letting them dangle from one hand by the straps. She padded barefoot over the worn wooden floorboards, studying a set of massive photographs lining the walls. Small metal plaques hung below the bottom left corner of the heavy frames, describing the pictures taken at Grand View Lodge. It was a fascinating visual representation of the history of the resort.

There were photos documenting the construction of the building in which she now stood. She could only imagine the massive effort required to hoist the beamed rafters above; to line the foundation with huge fieldstones.

As she wandered, the pictures transitioned to ones of people— many of them staff, based on their clothing. There were also pictures of men holding up impressive fish, and of groups of women and children playing on the grounds.

A voice spoke from behind, causing Celia to jump. "I wonder how long I'd have to work here before I'd have the honor of being included in a photograph in this hallway."

Hand over her heart, she spun around. It was Danny, Eleanor's friend they'd met briefly the week before. The one she'd been discreetly watching for throughout the dance but couldn't find. "I didn't hear you! You surprised me."

He smiled. "Celia, right? I remember. You're one of Eleanor's friends. I'm Danny." He motioned back to the framed photographs. "Aren't these amazing? The photographs, I mean. They capture pieces of history before it's lost forever."

His enthusiasm intrigued her. She'd never really thought about photographs that way before, the way the images, often black-and-white but also sepia-toned, froze time.

Celia continued to meander down the hallway, looking closely at each photograph, and he trailed close behind. "Your flower gardens are beautiful. They should put your picture up here, standing amongst the lovely arrangements."

Her blatant attempt at flattery caused him to laugh out loud, and Celia could feel her cheeks burn with embarrassment. She sounded like someone with a schoolgirl crush, which was ridiculous. She'd only met this boy once, and only for a moment at that.

Or . . . should she consider him a man? He was tall—several inches taller than her—and his shoulders were broad. His clothes were clean. He mustn't have come straight from work. But his outfit seemed too casual to attend a summer evening dance at a fancy resort. She liked the boyish charm in his smile. She wondered how old he was, and if he went to college when he wasn't spending his summer working at this big, fancy resort.

"They aren't actually *my* flower gardens, although I appreciate you saying that. I'm just a lowly assistant, spending my days weeding and chasing vermin away that would like nothing better than to feast on the flowers and plants around here. No, I'd rather be the one *taking* these photos."

Celia could feel his sincerity, his excitement over the prospect of capturing these moments in time.

"But I'm sorry," he said, taking on a slightly more serious tone. "Where are my manners? What are you doing out here, all alone, with your shoes in your hand? Bored with the dance? I can find you a chair if you'd like."

Now she was relatively certain he was younger than her. He spoke to her like an elder. Or maybe like an entitled resort guest, he a lowly employee. Regardless, she didn't care for it. She laughed, hoping to put him at ease.

"My feet were getting sore, and it's awfully crowded in there. I merely stepped out here for a bit of fresh air."

In reality, her toe was killing her, and she hoped she wouldn't lose a toenail over it all, but she didn't want to complain. She'd planned to sit on a bench she'd spied when they'd arrived, strategically set amongst the yellow roses, but the photographs had intrigued her, slowing her progress.

"Here, come through this side door. There's a small garden back here with tables and chairs for the guests. Few people use the area, but they keep it well-lit until after the dance's end. It's a pleasant spot to get away from all the people and the noise. You can rest your sore feet, if you like."

"That sounds nice," Celia agreed.

She followed Danny out the door, careful not to limp. The scent of flowers grew stronger as they made their way around empty tables. As he'd predicted, no one else was in the small seating area. He led her to a small, round table. Its intricate ironwork glowed white in the light cast by lanterns set high on poles. He pulled out one of the two chairs for her to sit.

Smiling her thanks, she took a seat, sighing with relief at taking the pressure off her feet. "This is nice. Thank you."

He bowed slightly, then stepped back. "It was nice to see you again, Celia. Enjoy your evening."

As he turned to leave, she reached out and touched his forearm briefly, surprised by her own forwardness. "Wait . . . can you sit with me for a while? I'd love to hear more about your interest in photography. Unless you were planning to head into the dance?"

"You like photography, too?" he asked, a hint of skepticism in his tone.

Celia shrugged. "I like *those* pictures. Honestly, I've never thought much about photography. But now I'm intrigued."

"So am I," Danny said with a friendly grin, stepping forward and circling around to the other side of the small iron table to pull out the chair across from Celia.

As he sat and inched the chair forward, its feet scraping on the concrete, Celia realized his warm smile might mean he was intrigued by more than the subject of photography.

He began to describe how he'd been fascinated with photographs ever since his father first shared pictures of distant relatives living in what was now called Ireland. Celia was caught up in his enthusiasm, all thoughts of the dance vanishing.

* * *

"I finished the filing you asked me to work on the other day," Celia said as she entered Preston's office early Wednesday morning.

"Already? In one morning?" Preston asked, looking up from the reports he'd been studying. "That's wonderful news! That beastly pile of paperwork has been growing since last summer. What did you learn, going through it?"

The question caught Celia off guard. "Learn? Well, I suppose I'd be a whiz at teaching children their ABCs now. Nothing like four straight hours of filing for a refresher on the alphabet."

Her weak attempt at a joke fell flat. Preston didn't even crack a smile. "Please don't tell me you filed all of that paper and didn't bother to read a single thing on those documents while you worked."

Celia felt her cheeks flush. She stammered, unsure how to respond.

"I won't be mad if you read some of it," he assured her, tapping his pen on the desktop, a hint of a grin teasing the corners of his mouth.

"I wasn't sure if I was supposed to read any of it," Celia finally admitted. "But I couldn't help it. Some of it was interesting."

Preston motioned for Celia to take the seat across from him. He didn't look angry. Maybe she wasn't in trouble.

Preston clasped his hands, peering at her over the top of his spectacles. "I'd have been disappointed if you hadn't read any of it. Celia, sit up straight. Don't cower. I didn't ask you to spend time in here just so you could get my filing caught up or take dictation. I don't need a secretary. I hoped to spur an interest in you related to business."

"All right, sir," Celia said, squirming in her chair. "What would you like me to do today then?"

"I want you to give me your opinion on this," he said simply, handing some of the papers he'd been studying earlier to her. Then he dropped his head again, turning his attention back to whatever he'd been doing when she'd walked in.

Celia quickly realized she was looking at invoices for building materials. There was also a bid sheet for labor and various other documents. Since Preston now seemed to be preoccupied, she took time to study the information he'd handed her.

Eventually, Preston cleared his throat. "What do you think?"

"This is fascinating," Celia said, slowly looking up. She caught a glimpse of the clock on the credenza behind his desk. "Oh my, is it nearly noon already?"

How did I lose all track of time?

"It is. Do you have any advice for me?" he asked, nodding at the papers spread in front of her.

"This is for the new duplex, isn't it?"

"It is," he confirmed.

"I had no idea how much went into a project like that. I'm not sure I have any advice for you, but I did find a five-hundred-dollar error on this bid sheet," she said, pointing at a column of figures as she handed the document back to Preston. "In your favor."

He grinned, taking the paper from her. "I knew you had promise. Now get out of here before my daughter bursts in and insists I let you get back to your vacation. I'll see you in here again Monday morning. I want you to look over the financials for Whispering Pines."

* * *

As Celia handed the last of the heavy suitcases to Leo and he stowed them in the Buick's trunk, a sense of melancholy stole over her. How had a month gone by so quickly?

When they'd first pulled into the parking lot of Whispering Pines four weeks ago, she'd been excited to have such an enticing stretch of unstructured time in front of her. Halfway through the stay, however, the novelty had worn off, and she'd sought opportunities to spend quiet moments on the dock, contemplating what might be next. Time spent with Eleanor's father, learning the basics of running a family-orientated lake resort, had proven to be an eye-opening experience. So much work went into seeing that there was food on the table for three meals a day in the lodge dining room, and cleaning of the cabins happened between outgoing and incoming guests. The lists of expenses were vast, making Celia feel guilty for not paying her own way.

When she'd mentioned as much to Preston, he'd laughed out loud. "Don't you worry about that, Celia. Helen's parents are paying our standard rate for your cabin and meals. If you weren't here to keep their daughter entertained, they might have to do it themselves. Besides, you saved me five hundred dollars and gave me some worthy pointers in regards to the weekly rates I've been charging. Maybe I should pay you!"

Celia had tried but failed to hold in the bark of laughter that bubbled up over his insightful reassurances. She had to admit, his points were valid. She'd earned her keep by helping entertain Helen *and* she'd helped a bit in the office.

Days spent with Eleanor, Helen, and Ruby had, mostly, been delightful. She was heading home with burnished skin, her auburn hair infused with lighter streaks where the sun had left its mark. She could now handle a canoe with flair, had caught almost as much fish as Leo, and nearly perfected her waltzing abilities.

Her only genuine regret was that the summer love she'd dreamed of finding had never materialized. She didn't fancy herself a romantic, but finding a beau might have added an exciting spice to her time at Whispering Pines. Her evening visit with Danny in the side garden, while her friends were off dancing, had spurred her hopes, but their paths hadn't crossed again.

It was probably for the best. She'd be going back to St. Kate's in early September, intent on taking classes that would expand on topics Mr. Whitby had introduced her to. She didn't need the distraction of a long-distance romance. She didn't need a man at all.

Celia would make her own way in the world.

SUMMER 1943

CHAPTER SIX
GIFT OF UNEXPECTED SURPRISES

*C*elia jerked awake at the squeal of brakes. Their bus made a shuddering stop.

"You better wipe that drool off your chin," Ruby advised, pointing at Celia's face with a grin.

Celia ignored her friend. They'd been teasing each other about drool for two years, prompted by exhausting all-night study sessions in their dorm room. "Are we here? Riding in a bus doesn't seem to bother you as much as sitting in the back of a car sometimes does."

Before Ruby could answer, their bus driver stood to face his passengers. "Sorry, folks, we needed to make a quick stop. Take ten minutes if you need to while I have something checked on the bus and then we'll be on our way. We should be in Nisswa by the top of the hour."

He pulled the mechanism to open the bus door; it screeched in protest, sounding as if no one had thought to oil it in a long time. As the driver hurried down the stairs, dust rolled in behind him. Celia wondered if the man was suffering from too much morning coffee. She'd hate to be late arriving in Nisswa. Eleanor promised someone would be there to pick them up and bring them the rest of the way to Whispering Pines.

Helen and her parents were already at the resort. They'd arrived the previous week. Leo wouldn't be joining them this year. Celia's heart lurched, much as their bus had done, when she thought of her fishing buddy, fighting in the big war over in Europe. She prayed nightly for Leo's safe return, as well as that of all the other men Celia knew who were risking so much.

Tripp was fighting in the war, too.

Celia was happy to have the distraction of spending the month of July at Whispering Pines again. Would there still be dances? Or had the effects of the war spread overseas and changed everything?

"Do you want to stretch your legs or use the ladies' room while we wait?" Ruby asked, using her hand to smear condensation from the lower portion of their window. None of the other passengers were getting off, but some opened windows and used anything they could find to fan themselves in the growing heat.

The air was heavy with humidity and the temperature was still climbing. Thank goodness the bus left home before dawn. The temperatures in this metal box would be nearly unbearable by midday. Looking back now, Celia decided their first drive to the resort in Leo's brand-new Buick hadn't been so bad after all.

"No, I'm fine. I just want to get there. Hopefully the bus driver will be back soon and we can get going."

Soon enough, they were back on the road. If anyone checked anything on the actual bus like the driver had said, Celia missed them. The driver was true to his word, however: the minute hand on Celia's watch was straight up when they arrived at Nisswa. She and Ruby gathered their purses and overnight bags, waiting impatiently for the passengers in front of them to file off the bus.

Finally, Celia stepped down onto the curb, discreetly pulling the fabric of her dress away from where it stuck to her thighs. A light breeze played with the material—a welcome relief, to be sure. Even here, in the bustling area surrounding the bus depot, she could smell a hint of pine playing on the breeze. It wasn't as strong as she knew it would be at Whispering Pines, but they were getting close.

Ruby stepped down behind her. "I wonder who's picking us up. Do you recognize anyone?"

Craning her neck, Celia tried to see over the other passengers, but her average height made that impossible. Some passengers barely moved out of the way as they exited the bus, stopping to greet people. Weaving around happily chatting groups, Celia headed toward the Nisswa sign hung high above their heads, attached to a clapboard building. She half expected to hear the blare of a train whistle. But their transportation wasn't nearly as glamorous as train travel.

"Celia!" someone yelled from off to her right. Pivoting, she searched for a familiar face. Her heart skipped a beat when she spied Danny, his arm raised in greeting.

Reaching behind her, careful not to let her pocketbook slip off her arm, she grabbed for Ruby's hand. "Over here. I found him."

"Who?" her friend asked, grabbing tight to Celia's fingers.

Stepping forward, Danny reached for Celia's overnight bag. "Here, that looks heavy. Let me help."

Relieved, Celia dropped Ruby's hand and removed the bag from her shoulder, handing the straps to Danny. The bag was nearly bursting at the seams. Helen's father had collected their suitcases from them two weeks earlier and promised to transport them to the resort on the girls' behalf so they didn't have to deal with them on the bus. Danny helped Ruby with her bag, too. Celia looked him over while his attention was elsewhere. He was taller and even broader in the shoulders than the summer before. His straw-colored hair was even longer now; he kept flipping his head to keep it out of his eyes.

Once he had both women's bags hoisted over his shoulder, he turned back to face them. "Hi, Ruby. It's good to see you again, Celia. According to Eleanor, it sounds like you had another swell year at college?"

Celia was momentarily speechless, something she seldom experienced.

He talked to Eleanor about me?

She'd figured he hadn't given her another thought since their unplanned visit in the garden the previous summer, when her aching toe drove her from the dance hall. She wouldn't have been able to make the same claim. He'd been stealing into her thoughts at unexpected times for months.

Giving herself a mental shake, she tucked a strand of hair behind her ear and smiled back. "We had fun, but my classes were more difficult than the first year, so having a month of vacation at Whispering Pines to look forward to helped. I'm surprised to see you, though. Aren't you still working at Grand View?"

The smile slipped from Danny's face and he turned away. "Why don't we get you loaded into Mr. Whitby's Ford? I'll explain on our drive. Follow me."

Celia glanced over at Ruby and caught the funny look she gave her. Maybe her friend didn't even remember Danny. Ignoring the unspoken question, Celia shrugged and turned to go. "Guess we should follow the man."

The crowd dispersed. Celia and Ruby hurried to keep up with Danny. Celia recognized Mr. Whitby's sedan parked in the back row; she remembered the red stripe rimming the whitewall tires—a small detail she'd noticed the previous summer when Eleanor's father teased Leo. He'd insisted that even though his Ford was older, he'd beat Leo's newer Buick on the straightaway. Thinking about the Buick reminded Celia of how far away Leo was right now. His beautiful car was likely stowed away somewhere, awaiting his safe return.

Danny opened the door to the backseat and Celia climbed in. He set their bags next to her. She'd insisted Ruby take the front seat.

Once settled, she sat back and allowed Danny to maneuver out of the parking lot in silence, waiting until they were on the open road to broach the subject again of why he was the one picking them up.

"It's good to see you both again," Danny finally said, catching Celia's eye in the mirror. "I bet you're looking forward to some fun at Whispering Pines."

"We are," Celia agreed, curious where he'd take the conversation.

"I'm sorry you get me as your driver today instead of Eleanor.

She'd hoped to pick you up, but she was helping my mother in the kitchen. I offered to drive over in her place."

Ruby shifted in her seat to look first at Danny and then back at Celia. "Well, we appreciate that. Are they still holding the dances over at the resort where you work? Those were so fun last year. I've been looking forward to more of them this year."

Ruby did remember him.

Danny tapped his left thumb against the steering wheel, his right hand busy with the manual gearshift. "They've cut back, but I think they're still having one or two dances a month. I'm working at Whispering Pines this summer, though, not over at Grand View Lodge."

"Oh, really?" Celia jumped in, unable to keep the surprise out of her voice. Eleanor's father had sat her down and walked her through the resort's financials the previous summer, teaching her the basics. She didn't understand how Preston could afford another full-time employee this summer, unless they'd somehow expanded their guest capacity.

"Yeah, surprising, I know," Danny acknowledged. "I hadn't planned to make the switch. But I didn't end up having much of a choice. With the war going on, tourism is down. They weren't as busy over at the other resort so there were cutbacks."

"Whispering Pines has stayed busy then?" Ruby asked. Celia knew what her friend wouldn't realize: that even with all the cabins full the resort couldn't support more staff.

"No . . . unfortunately, things are slower at the Pines, too. But Mr. Whitby really needed someone, after what happened this winter."

He didn't seem inclined to comment further. Last summer Danny's parents were the only full-time staff at Whispering Pines. He'd already mentioned his mother.

"Danny," Celia asked hesitantly, "did something happen to your father?"

Celia watched his face in the rearview mirror, could see him squinting, either from the bright sunlight or something else. He took a deep breath. "My father died. Heart attack. In February. He was ice fishing with two of his old codger friends. They told us that one minute he was fine, the next minute, gone."

His words dredged up long buried pain, deep in Celia's heart. Though she'd been a little girl when her own father died, it had been sudden and devastating. She had an idea how he was feeling. "I'm so sorry to hear that, Danny . . . How's your mother doing?"

He sighed. "Thankful for her work at Whispering Pines. But it took both her and my father, working all summer, to save enough to get them through the winter months. When he died, and then I found out they wouldn't take me back at the Lodge, we worried. But Mr. Whitby came to Father's funeral, insisted that if Mother needed anything at all she need only ask. He said he takes care of his best employees. So this spring she asked, and here I am."

While Celia hated the circumstances that brought Danny to Whispering Pines, the prospect of seeing more of him this summer was exciting. She hoped that didn't make her selfish.

* * *

"You two will stay in this cabin this year," Eleanor said, leading them to the smaller structure next to the cabin where they'd stayed their first summer. "I hope you don't mind."

Celia could read the skepticism in Ruby's eyes.

"I know Leo isn't here this year, but will we still all fit in this cabin?" her friend asked.

Eleanor paused, hands on hips. "I guess I assumed, since you're roommates at college, that you wouldn't mind sharing the bedroom."

"That's fine, but what about Helen and her parents?"

Laughing, Eleanor turned and climbed the short flight of stairs to the door of their assigned cabin. "I'm sorry. I should have explained. Helen and her family are staying in one of the other cabins this year, down by the water. Helen really wanted to try one of those. And since there's just the three of them . . ."

Nodding, Celia chimed in as Eleanor's voice trailed off. "And what Helen wants, Helen gets."

Stepping inside, Celia scanned the interior. While it was much smaller than the other cabin, there was a cheerfulness to it. White curtains danced on the breeze; sunlight streamed through the front window. A brick fireplace dominated one wall, its façade graciously free of glassy-eyed bucks that watched your every move.

"We have this cabin all to ourselves?" Celia asked, peeking into the only bedroom.

"You do," Eleanor confirmed with a wink, plopping down on a short sofa. "We didn't think you'd mind."

"Oh, we don't mind," Celia laughed, placing her overnight bag on one of the two twin beds. She spied two large suitcases in a corner of the tiny bedroom. "Thank you for getting our luggage in here, Eleanor!"

"You can thank Danny for that. He made sure this place was up to par for you both."

Wandering back into the main living area of the cabin, Celia took that opening to ask more about Mr. Bell.

Nodding, Eleanor shared how her father had brought Danny in. "Honestly, our cabins aren't full every week this summer, so I wasn't sure we even needed him, but my father insisted. And he was right. Danny is helping with some bigger projects, and his strong young back is a bonus, especially without Tripp here this summer. Not that Tripp ever did anything too useful, but he provided some muscle once in a while."

"Any word on how your brother is doing?" Celia asked, knowing it was the right thing to say.

"Honestly, it's been a while since we've had news. Hopefully it's as they say, and no news is good news."

Ruby pulled open the silver handle on a boxy refrigerator in the corner, swinging the white door open to look inside. Grinning, she pulled out a glass pitcher of lemonade.

Pushing up out of the deep-seated couch, Eleanor took the few steps to the kitchen cupboard and pulled down three tall, slim glasses, matching designs etched into the glass. "Mrs. Bell thought you might be hungry after your bus ride this morning. There's sliced roast beef, cheese, and her special mayonnaise in there, too, and a fresh loaf of bread in the breadbox on the counter."

Celia's stomach grumbled in response, and she joined her friends in the kitchen, opening the breadbox and removing a dense loaf of bread wrapped in white cheesecloth. She caught a whiff of the fresh bread and held it up to her nose, inhaling deeply. "I forgot how yummy Mrs. Bell's bread is! We have to remember to thank her for this."

Eleanor pulled two brightly colored plates off a stack next to the glasses in the cupboard and set them on the counter. Their cheery red and turquoise colors reminded Celia of summer.

"I love these Fiesta dishes. They come in so many pretty colors. Maybe I'll start a set for Mother this Christmas," Celia mused.

"They would brighten up your kitchen back home," Ruby agreed.

Eleanor smiled. "You two make yourselves a sandwich. I've eaten already."

Taking one of the three poured lemonades, Eleanor wandered back to the front window. "I feel like I should warn you both. Daddy . . . he's not quite himself this summer. This war is weighing on him."

Celia laid thick slices of the bread she'd cut on the plates, then reached for the blue-hued jar of mayonnaise, spinning the top off. "I'm sure he's worried about your brother."

Eleanor took a sip of her lemonade and nodded, keeping her eyes on something outside the window. "He is. But it's more than that. He's had to revamp things in the factory, and he's lost many of his shift supervisors to the draft. It's a lot of pressure. A heavy burden."

Ruby added slices of the roast beef to their sandwiches and then ran a stream of water over one of the ruby-red tomatoes ripening next to the sink. "Did your father take your advice and hire women to help on the factory floor?"

Grinning, Eleanor turned back to face them. "He did. And I have news about that."

Both Celia and Ruby paused in their sandwich preparations, curious at the hint of excitement in Eleanor's voice.

"What news?" Celia prodded.

"Daddy has agreed to let me help in his factory this fall."

Celia set the knife she'd used to slather her bread with mayonnaise off to the side. "Wait. This fall? What about school? Aren't you going back to St. Kate's in September? We only have two years left!"

Eleanor drained the rest of her lemonade and joined them in the kitchen, setting her glass in the sink before responding. "I'll go back later. I *really* want to do this. I want to help make airplane parts for the war! With any luck, the war will be over in *less* than two years. This isn't something I can put off. It may be my only opportunity to get in there and prove myself. Once all the men come back, I'm afraid I'll have missed my chance."

Celia took a moment to process Eleanor's big news. Ruby appeared to be doing the same thing. Eleanor watched them expectantly, waiting for a response. Becoming impatient, Eleanor rocked back and forth on her feet. Celia could tell her friend was near bursting with excitement. And she had to admit: it was contagious.

"I admire you, Eleanor. That takes *moxie*. You are one brave woman, my friend. Last summer, you said this is what you wanted to do, and now you're doing it. Good for you!"

Ruby, always the most demonstrative of their group, caught Eleanor up in a congratulatory hug. After giving her a quick embrace, she stepped back with a mischievous grin. "I thought something might be up when you snuck those two engineering courses onto your schedule this last semester."

Eleanor grinned right back. "Daddy wasn't too happy about that, but I think he's finally accepted the fact I'm serious about this. Besides, I'll get to see him all the time again. I think he was awfully lonely with all of us gone."

Celia guessed, from this last bit of news, that there was still no contact between Eleanor's parents. Not that she'd mention that now and chance putting a damper on her friend's big announcement. Instead, she asked the other loaded question that came to mind. "Have you told your roommate about this pending change? I bet Helen will have something to say about it."

The shrug and guilty look Eleanor gave them spoke volumes.

Laughing nervously, Celia flipped the top piece of her bread onto her sandwich, picking it up with both hands. "Be sure to let me know when you plan to tell her. I don't want to be anywhere near the two of you when you drop that little bombshell!"

CHAPTER SEVEN
GIFT OF THE GOLDEN HOUR

*R*uby stared into the crackling flames instead of meeting Celia's eyes. "I refuse to have my picture taken in my bathing suit! It's a *terrible* idea," she insisted.

A log popped, sending a shower of sparks into the air.

"But why, Ruby? You thought it was a brilliant idea when I told you I was encouraging Preston to make up some advertising flyers for Whispering Pines."

Ruby held up her hands, frustration twisting her expression. "That was before I knew you wanted *us* to be on the cover of the brochure, half naked!"

Celia dug her hands into the cool sand on either side of her blanket, feeling it cake under her fingernails. Particles of sand crunched under her heels, too, as she dug them into the scratchy wool blanket beneath her, much as she'd figuratively dug her heels into this day-long argument with her cabin mate. "Since when did you become such a killjoy?"

"A *killjoy?*" Ruby shot back. "*You* are calling *me* a killjoy?"

Another shower of sparks shot into the air, this time from the shovel Eleanor used to turn a log over in the fire. "Yeah, that's a little ironic, isn't it, Celia?"

"What's that supposed to mean?" Celia bit out in frustration, wrapping her arms around her shins and squeezing her thighs to her chest. "If you have something to say, Eleanor, just say it."

"She's too nice to say it," Helen jumped in. "*You* are the prude, Celia. Hell, have you even kissed a boy yet?"

Helen's bored tone reminded them all that she was still sulking about missing the dance over at Grand View Lodge. They'd geared this weekend's dance toward an older crowd. Because they were too young to legally drink alcohol, her mother refused to allow them to attend. Now Helen was taking her disappointment out on Celia.

Still, Celia's cheeks flushed. "That's none of your business, Helen."

Celia tried to ignore Helen. She couldn't understand why Ruby was making such a big deal about her simple request.

Eleanor had been right about her father. Preston wasn't acting like the same man he'd been the summer before when he'd started educating her on running this resort. He was quieter, and when he spoke, there was a bite to his words. Was he worried about things at Whispering Pines? If so, Celia wanted to help. She'd do what she could to increase business, and that included asking Danny to take pictures around the resort that Mr. Whitby could then use to advertise the place.

Celia had gotten the idea from the photographs she'd run across in the long hallway at Grand View Lodge the previous summer. She'd snuck out of the cabin on one of their first mornings back at Whispering Pines, quiet so she wouldn't wake her friend. She'd hoped to sit on the dock and watch the sunrise, but someone had beat her to it. Danny was already there, taking pictures. Celia hung back, unseen. She watched him aim his camera at the rising sun, and then at a pelican as it floated peacefully on the still water in the early morning. From his stance, she suspected his shot would include the quaint white cabins lining the shore behind the bird.

She'd remembered Danny talking about wanting to be the taker of pictures, instead of the subject, when he'd shown her the photos at Grand View. When they'd discussed photography in the garden, while her friends danced the night away inside, he talked about figuring out a way to get a camera of his own. She was happy to see he'd found a way. Now, if she could just get her stubborn friend to agree to some pictures, she'd propose her idea to both Danny and Preston.

"Celia, you know how I feel about wearing swimsuits," Ruby said, pulling Celia's attention back to their late-night bonfire.

"But it'll just be one shot! You know you look pretty in the navy swimsuit you bought in Minneapolis this spring."

Ruby shook her head, refusing to cooperate.

Then Celia remembered. "Oh . . . your grandmother never needs to know."

Ruby jerked her head up, meeting Celia's eyes through the flames —licking higher now thanks to Eleanor's stirring.

"You can't know that for sure."

Dropping the shovel into the sand and sinking back down onto a blanket near Helen, Eleanor sighed. "What are you two talking about? What does Ruby's dear old granny have to do with anything?"

"Ruby used to think her grandmother was a witch," Helen shared, smirking in Ruby's direction.

"Shut up, Helen," Ruby snapped, shooting eye daggers at the other girl. "You don't know what you're talking about."

"Yes, I do. I heard you and Celia talking when we were younger. You didn't know I was there. You said your grandmother was surely a witch, the way she'd curse things and always wore black. She even has a black cat."

"Oh, this is getting interesting!" Eleanor giggled. "Do tell."

"My grandmother is not a witch. She's worn black ever since my grandfather died. Grandmother has never liked photographs. When she was growing up, something terrible happened. A bunch of people in her family got sick and died. I think it was small pox. It was sudden, and young and old alike died."

Celia chewed her lip. She knew what Ruby would say next and hated this part of the story. The macabre nature of it had traumatized them as young girls.

"I don't understand," Eleanor said, looking between Celia, Ruby, and Helen. Celia suspected she felt left out at times, never knowing the stories behind their shared childhoods. "That's terrible and all, but what does it have to do with getting your picture taken in a swimsuit, Ruby?"

"It's not the suit that's the problem," Ruby explained. Earlier, they'd passed a bottle of wine around their circle, and the half-emptied bottle was now stuck in the sand near her feet. She grabbed it, brushed it off, and took a deep swig, as if fortifying herself. Passing it over to Helen to make another round, she looked between Celia and Eleanor, her eyes sad. "Grandma said they propped them up and took pictures of them all, before they buried them."

"What?!" Eleanor shrieked. "You mean when they were sick, right?"

Ruby shook her head. "Not exactly . . ."

Eleanor let out a nervous giggle. "Well, then . . . do you mean they took pictures of them after they were already dead?"

Somewhere off in the distance an owl hooted; a shiver raced down Celia's spine.

"You know that's what she means, Eleanor," Helen said, tossing the bottle of wine, now empty, into the sand.

"Grandma said it was tradition in the old country. She told me there was even a family album that sat on their coffee table when she was young, filled with those kinds of pictures. Pictures of their dead relatives. Once her own mother died, Grandma said she burned the album. Swore she heard shrieks as the pages shriveled and turned to ash."

A rare quiet descended around the bonfire. Celia rubbed her upper arms to dispel the chill brought on by Ruby's retelling of that hated story. The owl, still hidden in the night shadows, let out another eerie cry.

"Grandmother never lets anyone take her picture," Ruby continued, her voice barely above a whisper. "I wish she never would have told me that story when I was a little girl. My mother was so mad at her for scaring me like that. Now I hate to have my picture taken, too. *Especially* in a swimsuit. I know it's silly, but . . ."

"Maybe there's a photo of those dead little boys around here somewhere. You know, the ones that died in that cave?" Helen said, winking at Eleanor.

"You aren't helping, you know," Eleanor said, tossing a harmless bit of sand at her roommate.

Celia's mind flashed back to that terrifying night the previous summer, when she swore she saw something on the road. She'd been so sure in that second that it was a young child, standing behind the distorting curtain of rain. She hadn't ever told Helen—or anyone else —what she thought she'd seen. Had Helen seen it, too?

A low rumble of thunder sounded off in the distance. Either Celia had to shift the mood around the fire or she was going to slink back to the tiny cabin she was sharing with Ruby, crawl into bed, and pull the covers over her head until the morning sun chased the shadows away.

Besides, if she ever wanted to convince her roommate to be part of the picture she was envisioning of the four of them on the beach, she needed to warm Ruby up to the idea.

Eleanor beat her to the punch.

"Well then," Eleanor said, clearing her throat, as if all this talk of dead people was bothering her, too. "What's everyone planning to wear to the next dance?"

Her question pulled their conversation back to their summer plans, and the mood lifted. Celia flashed Eleanor a grateful smile. She didn't agree with Ruby or her grandmother. Photographs should capture happy times, preserve them forever. Their summers at Whispering Pines were special, something she knew she'd want to look back on with a smile. Pictures would help do that.

With Danny's help, she also hoped to use pictures to help with business at the resort, and bring back the jovial mood she'd enjoyed in Mr. Whitby last summer.

* * *

"I like it." Preston nodded. "Can you do it, Danny?"

"Yes, I'd love to put my camera to good use. It was the last thing my father gave me, and we both know how much he loved this place. I think he'd approve, too."

So that's how Danny came to have a camera of his own, Celia realized. She was glad Danny had something special to remind him of his father.

"And you, Celia—I'm impressed with you. I like the way you think. Maybe I should bring you to work in my factory. I could use someone like you in the office."

"Not if I'd have to keep up with your filing. Your pile has grown again I see," Celia teased, nodding at the stack of papers on the corner of his credenza.

Preston's chair creaked as he swiveled to look back at the neglected paperwork. The wheels raised him inches above Celia and Danny, seated across the desk from him. They'd been brainstorming new ideas for the resort all morning.

"Thank you, Preston. Seriously, I appreciate your kind words. But I do plan to finish college before I go to work for anyone."

Unlike Eleanor, Celia had no intention of giving up on college to work before she had a degree in hand. That degree might help level the playing field with men she'd compete against for the jobs she wanted.

He nodded in agreement. "I'd expect nothing less. Now, that daughter of mine, she's a different story. Do you think you could talk her into staying at St. Kate's? She has this hairbrained idea about making airplane parts."

Celia tried to keep a serious expression, but she knew Preston had already given in to his daughter's request. Smiling, she tightened her ponytail, discreetly sending a wink in Danny's direction. "I'm sure she'll go back after the war, sir. She was talking about coming to work with you last summer already, and once she gets an idea in her head, it's tough to change her mind. It really is good of you to let her do this now."

The older man shook his head, then glanced up when Mrs. Bell knocked on his open office door. "What is it?"

"I thought you'd want to see this, sir," Danny's mother said, nodding a greeting to both Celia and her son as she laid a folded newspaper on her employer's desk.

Preston picked his wire-rimmed spectacles off a pile of manila folders perched on the corner of his desk and settled them across the bridge of his nose. He ran his finger down the small newsprint, grunting and harrumphing as he read the cover story on the front page. Celia and Danny stayed quiet, allowing Preston to concentrate on the article. Celia felt a surge of empathy for him. It had to be nerve-racking, having your only son embroiled in a bloody war half a world away. When his finger reached the bottom of the page, he sighed in disgust and picked the newspaper up, tossing it to the side.

"I'll read more later. Although I doubt there will be much in there worth reading. The coverage of this damn war is shoddy."

"I'm sure they're doing their best, sir," Danny offered, nodding toward the discarded newspaper.

"The soldiers?" Preston asked.

"No—well, I mean, sure, the soldiers. But I was referring to the people writing those articles. Taking those pictures. There are brave men and women putting their own lives at risk to bring you the news."

Preston leaned back heavily in his chair, the wood creaking under his weight, as he eyed Danny over the rim of his glasses. Celia feared Danny might have insulted Mr. Whitby. He was unusually touchy with anything related to the war. He formed a steeple with his fingers, considering Danny's comment.

"Pardon me," the man eventually said. "This whole damn war has me out of sorts. You are undoubtedly right, Daniel. Whether someone is holding a gun or a camera or a pen, if they head into that bloodbath as a service to our nation they deserve our respect. I'll keep that in mind, young man."

Danny exhaled, visibly relieved he hadn't overstepped.

Their conversation steered back to the resort, but Celia couldn't help glancing between the photo on the front page of the newspaper, showing military aircraft dropping bombs from their underbellies, and Danny. She'd heard the wistfulness in his tone when he'd mentioned the people documenting the war.

* * *

It was what Danny referred to as the "golden hour"—that time before the sun sank below the horizon, when the sunlight was at its softest.

"Here, look right through there," he said, handing his camera to Celia. "See how the front of the lodge glows, but the shadows aren't too deep yet?"

Celia took the camera from Danny, careful not to drop it or put a finger on the lens. She hadn't understood how complicated capturing a photo could be, what with taking things like lighting and camera settings into account. This was their third informal session of picture taking at the resort. She could hardly wait to see how the pictures themselves would turn out.

Putting the camera up to her right eye, Celia could see how much clearer things looked now compared to when they'd tried shortly after lunch yesterday. Shadows had obscured too many things earlier in the day. Nodding, Celia pivoted, enjoying the view of not only the lodge, but adjacent trees, Preston's black Ford in the parking lot, and, eventually, an extremely close-up view of Danny's nose.

He grabbed the camera out of her hands and shook his head, as if impatient with her lack of professionalism. But he immediately spun the camera on her, snapping off what she'd guess would be a candid, no doubt unflattering, close-up shot of her laughing face.

"Stop!" she insisted, giggling, her hand shielding her face from any more pictures.

"You started it," he said, checking the settings on his camera. "Darn it. I'm almost out of film."

"Oh no," Celia said, hands on her hips. "Do you have more? We still need to get a few shots down by the water."

Looping the long leather strap over his neck, Danny let the camera hang at chest level, freeing up his hands. He brushed his hair back, out of his eyes, and adjusted his cap. Celia wished he wouldn't wear it, as it hid his wavy hair, but she supposed the length of it posed a problem —particularly on evenings like this when the wind sighed through the trees.

"I have two more rolls in my room. I'll load a fresh one tomorrow, and as long as the weather cooperates, we can try to get those shots you talked about."

Which gave Celia one more evening to talk Ruby into participating in the shot she'd envisioned.

"Thanks again for helping with this, Danny. I know Mr. Whitby is excited to have some brochures."

Danny nodded, his eyes roaming over the grounds. "I'm happy to get some practice with my Christmas gift. Father knew of my hope to be a photographer."

Celia considered asking more about Danny's father, but decided against it. If he wanted to talk about the man, he would when the time was right—just as she had now. She changed topics, eager to keep him by her side.

"Are you going to the dance this weekend?"

He shrugged, glancing her way, but the puttering sound of a motor out on the water distracted him. An old, battered fishing boat pulled alongside the dock, filled with laughing resort guests. "I haven't thought about the dance. Maybe. I suppose I might run into some of my old coworkers from last summer. Are you and your friends going?"

"I guess."

He looked at her again, but this time he didn't look away. "You don't sound very excited about it. Not much of a dancer? I seem to recall catching you sneaking around outside the dance hall last year."

Half turning toward the dock and the arriving fishermen, she nodded in their direction. "Come on. Let's go see what they caught."

Stepping toward the beach, Celia peeked over her shoulder to make sure Danny followed her. He undoubtably sensed another photo opportunity. He caught up to her and matched her stride for stride.

"It's not that I don't like to dance," she declared, getting back to his question. "I do. If we could all have fun, and not worry so much about *who* we dance with, I'd enjoy it more."

Danny bent down and picked up a toy, half buried in the sand. It was a white metal bucket with a red interior, and it sported a picture of a young boy and girl on the front. It looked new. A child would be sad when they realized they'd left it behind. He bounced the bucket off the leg of his pants, knocking caked sand off the toy. When they reached the dock, he set it down on a corner of the wooden platform, crouched down, and snapped off a shot of it.

"Hopefully whoever lost this will find it tomorrow," he said, glancing once again at Celia. "So you enjoy the dancing, but not the posturing and primping . . . the *competition* . . . to pull the most eligible bachelor out onto the dance floor? Is that what you're getting at?"

Celia laughed, following him onto the dock. She moved toward the edge, giving the rowdy fishermen room to pile out of the boat and secure the old vessel to one of the supporting poles. The wooden surface was wet and slick with lake water. Danny put a steadying hand on her shoulder to prevent her from slipping.

"That's exactly what I'm getting at," she said.

"I noticed a lot of that *posturing* last year, working at Grand View. Spending most of my time in the gardens gave me an interesting view of things. People seldom noticed I was there. You wouldn't believe the things I heard."

Stepping toward the end of the dock to move farther out of the way, Celia gazed up at Danny. The setting sun bathed her face in light, making her squint. "I wouldn't have pictured you as someone who would eavesdrop."

Grinning at her teasing tone, he lifted his camera again, aiming it back toward the disembarking fishermen. They paid him little atten-tion, too intent on weaving their tales of the big one that got away. As one of them hoisted an impressive stringer of walleye high into the air, Celia heard the clicking of Danny's camera, sure he was capturing fun-filled shots.

Finally, he turned his attention back to Celia. "Believe me. If I could have blocked out their voices and focused on the flowers, birds, and butterflies, I would have. But I've learned that few people appreciate the beauty of silence. I think maybe *you* are one of those rare people."

Holding his gaze, she considered this. "You're right. I'd rather spend my evening sitting out here on the end of the dock with or without a fishing pole in my hand, listening to the hum of insects and the haunting call of a loon, than tolerate the press of all those bodies and loud music. But I've never really stopped to think of it like that. I just thought I was odd, never quite enjoying parties as much as my friends."

"I think they call people like us introverts," Danny offered. "At least that's what my teacher used to say."

"College professor?" Celia asked. She'd been curious whether Danny had ever attended college. It hadn't yet come up in their limited conversations, and she hadn't thought to ask Eleanor.

He snorted. "Hardly. High school. I've never been to college. My folks needed every penny they made to keep a roof over our heads."

The fishing boat banged against the dock. Celia glanced back in time to see the last of the men step out of the bobbing boat. She held her breath as the man wobbled backward. But he mustn't have used all of his luck out on the water, because he grabbed hold of the supporting dock pole before he could topple backward into the water.

"Hey, kid," one of the older men said, motioning to Danny. "We caught ten decent-size walleye. You the one who'll take care of these for us?"

If Celia hadn't been standing so close to Danny, she might have missed the irritated tic of the corner of his right eye at the man's demanding, slightly slurred question. The men had been drinking while on the water.

But Danny nodded, a respectful, if not totally sincere, smile on his face. "You bet. That'd be me, all right. There's a big metal washbasin of clean water in the shack to the north of the lodge. Put the fish in there and I'll be up to clean them in a minute."

Nodding, the group made their way off the dock and across the sand, slapping each other on the backs and congratulating themselves on their catch. The men reminded Celia of Helen's father. They carried themselves with an air of importance, an expectation that the rest of the world existed to serve them. The attitude grated on Celia's nerves.

She guessed Danny tired of it, too.

He turned his attention back to her. "Good thing Father taught me how to clean a fish. But I hate doing it. Mother gets mad if I don't get all the bones." A sudden cloud darkened his expression. "I should have paid more attention to what he was trying to teach me. But I never imagined he wouldn't be here to do it himself this summer."

"Danny, I'm so—"

He stopped Celia midsentence. "Please, don't say you're sorry about my father. I honestly can't take any more sympathy. I don't want to sound unappreciative, but it's done now."

Celia suspected he had yet to learn that losing a parent wasn't something you *finished*; he was still in the early phases of grief. She nodded, offering what she hoped was an encouraging smile. "Can I give you a hand with cleaning the fish?"

A shocked look stole across his face. "You'd help with that?"

Clasping her hands behind her, Celia swayed back and forth innocently. "A girl can't consider herself a legitimate fisherman—or *fisherwoman*—if she can't filet a fish."

"Wait. Don't move," Danny instructed, lifting his camera again. Before she could even react, he snapped another picture of her, standing on the edge of the dock with the lake spread out behind him, the setting sun casting a warm wash of color over the water.

"I thought you were nearly out of film!" she cried, patting self-consciously at her hair as it danced in the wind.

"I am now," Danny said with a sly smile, spinning around and walking back toward the beach. "Come on! Let's go see if you can't teach me a thing or two about the fine art of deboning."

Celia laughed as she skipped along behind him, realizing she was probably the only one out of her group of girlfriends who would ever take Danny up on that offer, regardless of how charming his dimples might be.

CHAPTER EIGHT
GIFT OF CAREFREE SUMMER DAYS

"What's it going to take to get you to smile, Eleanor?" Danny asked, aiming his camera at the group of young women as they waited impatiently to leave for the Saturday night dance. "Are you still pouting?"

Celia grinned as Eleanor, standing next to her, raised her chin ever so slightly and brushed a black curl off her shoulder before putting her arm back around Celia's waist.

"I don't pout, Danny," Eleanor countered, her words clipped; she spoke through a plastered-on smile. "I can't believe you'd even suggest that."

Danny lowered his camera a few inches, motioning for Ruby to stand closer to Helen so he could get all four of them in the shot. They stood two and two on either side of Preston's Ford. "Ruby, relax! You look so stiff."

Celia struggled to keep her eyes open wide as a stray beam of sunshine reflected off the car's black finish like a mirror. Danny had spent the better part of his afternoon polishing it.

"*Please* hurry. We're going to be late for the dance *again*," Eleanor complained.

Apparently satisfied with how he'd finally positioned the girls, Danny raised his camera and snapped off two shots. "Hold your horses. You're just mad Mr. Preston wouldn't let you drive to the dance. Get in the car. I'll put my camera in the trunk and then we can go."

Eleanor dropped her forced smile, scowling as she pulled her arm away from Celia and yanked open the door. "I can't believe Daddy wouldn't let me drive. I have my driver's license!"

"I could have opened that for you," Danny admonished as he came around the side of the Ford, pulling the door open a little wider so Eleanor could slide into the front seat. He swung the back passenger door open, making a sweeping motion with his hand, much as a fancy chauffer would do, inviting Celia into the back. He gave her a wink, but wisely refrained from teasing Eleanor further.

Eleanor set her frustration aside and kept the conversation flowing during the drive to Grand View Lodge. Trees rushed by in a blur as Celia peered into the woods crowding the gravel road. She spied a doe and her fawn, but when she urged Ruby to look, her friend merely grunted. One look told Celia that Ruby was again fighting nausea, sandwiched as she was between Helen and Celia. The cloying scent of Helen's Chantilly perfume wasn't helping.

Celia patted Ruby's knee. "Hold on. It isn't much farther."

"Oh, *shoot*," Eleanor said, spinning in her seat. "I should have let you sit up here, Ruby. I forgot. Will you be all right? You aren't going to be sick, are you?"

Ruby shook her head, offering a weak smile. Celia caught Danny's concerned glance in the rearview mirror and had to grip the door when he punched the accelerator. More speed wouldn't necessarily help Ruby, but it would get them there faster, and Danny didn't want to clean up a mess in the backseat.

"Would you be a dear and drop us at the front entrance, Danny?" Eleanor asked. "That way we can get Ruby inside so she can splash some cool water on her face."

Danny slowed the Ford, easing into the row of cars approaching the impressive entrance to the lodge. "That was my plan all along," he said.

When it was their turn to stop in front of the massive double doors, Danny put the car in Park, got out, and opened the door behind him to allow Helen and Ruby to climb out, proving he was more worried about Ruby vomiting inside the car than acting the proper chauffer. Eleanor did the same thing on the curbside of the vehicle, letting Celia out.

As Celia stepped onto the curb, her eyes swept over the yellow roses that still graced the entrance. They weren't nearly as lush and colorful as they'd been the previous summer. Try as she might, she couldn't catch their scent in the air.

Danny insisted they head into the dance, promising to find them later. Celia wondered if he'd search out any of his old friends. She'd be disappointed if she didn't get to dance with him.

Once Ruby was out of the backseat, she quickly regained color in her cheeks. "I'm feeling better. Boy, Helen, you are wearing a *lot* of perfume! Let's go." Leading the way, Ruby hurried ahead. "The band sounds wonderful, don't they?"

"What is *she* in such a hurry for tonight?" Helen asked, laughing as she struggled to keep up.

Celia wondered the same thing. She'd have to quiz Ruby later, find out if there was someone in particular Ruby hoped to find at the dance. Good thing she wasn't covered in vomit!

* * *

"May I have this dance?"

Celia jumped at the unexpected touch on the small of her back and the words in her ear. The familiar timbre of the voice was a welcome surprise. "I thought I lost you."

Danny held out a hand, acting the part of the perfect gentleman. "And I wondered if you snuck out of the dance again. I had a bugger of a time finding you."

Slipping her hand into Danny's much larger one, she allowed him to lead her from the outer edge of the crowd toward the dance floor. She'd worn the same blasted shoes that pinched her toes last year, but this time she'd avoided getting stepped on. She ignored the ache now, not wanting anything to spoil her time with Danny.

The slow melody of a popular love song filled the ballroom; the singer gave a decent impersonation of a crooning Frank Sinatra.

Danny eased them into a small opening. Celia's heartbeat kicked up another two notches when he turned to her, wrapped his free arm around her waist, and pulled her close.

"I know dancing isn't really your thing, so thank you for honoring me with a turn around the dance floor."

Celia laid her free hand on Danny's shoulder, tilting her head up to meet his gaze. She'd hoped he'd ask her to dance, but had also worried she'd trip or step on his foot. She relaxed in his arms now, more comfortable than she could have hoped. "That isn't true. I enjoy *dancing*. I just don't like the never-ending vying for attention."

"Is that why I found you hiding in the corner?"

She gave his shoulder a friendly slap. "I wasn't hiding. I was catching my breath," she countered.

He let it go, tightening his hand ever so slightly at her waist and then executing a graceful turn without bumping into anyone. It was an admirable feat, given the press of bodies. They danced in silence for a minute, Celia resting her cheek against the starched fabric of his white dress shirt. "Did you lose your jacket?"

"I hope not, since it's Tripp's. Mother would skin me if I lost it."

"Tripp's?" Celia couldn't keep the surprise out of her voice. How did Tripp's jacket fit Danny's broad shoulders?

Grinning, Danny nodded greetings to another couple near them. "I may not come from family money, like most of these gents out here on the dance floor, and I know I'm not one of the eligible bachelors the girls are fighting over, but I can act the part when I have to."

Based on the glances Celia was receiving from other women currently in the arms of those purported "eligible bachelors," she could see they would love to change places with her, regardless of whether or not her handsome dance partner came from money.

She focused her attention back on him. "The flowers don't look nearly as pretty near the entrance as they did last year. I'd say they miss your skills around here."

Danny laughed out loud, pulling additional glances in their direction. "Dear Celia, you give me entirely too much credit. I was a lowly assistant here. It's been a wet summer. The roses thrived last year, when it was drier."

"Well, that may be, but I'll always associate beautiful flowers with your skilled hand."

Something in her words caused Danny's smile to slip away, his arm tightening around her waist, pulling her up against his body. Their steps slowed, and Celia savored the closeness, knowing the song was nearing the end.

All too soon, the last notes faded away. Danny didn't immediately release her. The lights in the large room flared back to life, signaling the indisputable end to the evening. Others jostled into them as they made their way off the dance floor, a few calling out invitations to continue the party at this cabin or that room.

Danny rested his forehead on hers. "Thank you for the dance. I'm glad I caught you this year before you could escape to the hallway again."

Her breath caught as he pulled back, and his eyes dipped to her lips. She was sure he meant to kiss her, right there under the bright lights of the crystal chandelier. But someone bumped into him, hard, and the moment evaporated when the clumsy man dropped a heavy hand onto Danny's shoulder.

"Danny boy, is that really you?" the man boomed, shaking him bodily in greeting.

Reluctantly, Danny squeezed Celia's hand and released it. "Why don't you find Eleanor and the rest of your friends and meet me by the front entrance in ten minutes?"

He dutifully turned his attention back to the man with the ill timing. The flash of disappointment in Danny's eyes over the interruption matched her own.

As she turned to go in search of her friends, she could still smell his aftershave, practically feel his arms around her, and she felt a glimmer of hope that this time around, she'd finally get her summer romance.

CHAPTER NINE
GIFT OF CAPTURED MEMORIES

*D*espite the heat of the day, fewer guests relaxed on the beach compared to Celia's first summer at Whispering Pines.

She pulled the wide brim of her straw hat lower as she reclined in her beach chair. The sturdy stretch of green canvas supported her body, suspending her above the hot sand. Last year they'd spread big woolen blankets out on the sand, letting older resort guests use the chairs. There were plenty of chairs to go around this year.

Eleanor sat in a beach chair made entirely of wood; her elbows rested on wide slats as she battled the wind to hold a newspaper steady enough to read. Celia knew her friend was eager for any news she could find related to her brother's battalion.

Ruby and Helen relaxed on chairs similar to Celia's. Ruby's attention was on something in the water while Helen lay still, soft vibrations emanating from under her sunbonnet.

"Should we tell Helen she snores like her mother?"

Eleanor sighed, giving up on her newspaper. She folded it before tossing it into the wicker picnic basket near her feet. "Not if you value our peaceful afternoon."

"Good point," Celia laughed. "All that dancing last night must have worn her out, poor thing."

"I know it tired *me* out," Eleanor said. "Remind me to throw away those white leather heels I wore last night. Look at this blister! It's as big as my thumb."

"Ew," Celia moaned, turning her head away from the blister splayed across the bottom of her friend's foot. And she'd thought her own shoes pinched.

"It doesn't hurt as much as it did. I think it's more of a callus. Do you think men realize how good they have it, not having to wear things that pinch, like heels, bras, or girdles?"

Celia laughed again, causing Helen to mumble and shift. Her chair tilted precariously, but Ruby grabbed the wooden slat nearest her and prevented Helen from toppling into the sand.

"What's so funny?" Helen asked as she stretched, her voice groggy. "Did I fall asleep?"

Nodding, Celia jabbed a finger in Eleanor's direction. "She's complaining about having to wear a girdle. Who are you kidding, Eleanor? That figure of yours has *never* required a girdle of any kind."

Eleanor rose to her feet and struck multiple poses, reminding Celia of a pin-up girl. Her friend was pretty enough to model, too, if she wasn't so intent on building bombers instead.

"Anyone want to go swim?" the bomber-builder model asked.

Ruby waved an ineffective hand in front of her own face. "It *is* hotter than blazes out here."

Tossing her wide-brimmed hat aside, Helen stood, adjusted her bathing suit, and grinned at her friends. "Last one to that buoy down there has to help Mrs. Bell with dishes in the lodge kitchen tonight!"

Challenge accepted, Celia and Ruby scrambled out of their beach chairs, already steps behind Eleanor and Helen as they all screeched and laughed, kicking up sand in their race to reach the water and the designated buoy.

Floating buoys, anchored to the bottom of the lake with weights and strung together with rope, delineated the area where it was safest for swimmers. Guests were to stay inside the barrier. The girls could only reach Helen's target on the far edge of the safety zone by running through shallow water; the shoreline was too rocky.

Celia nearly caught her friends by the time they reached the water, but Helen was a notoriously fast runner. Celia reached out and snagged her hand, laughing and struggling to hold the girl back. Ruby followed suit, grabbing on to Celia. Eleanor lunged at Ruby. The noisy young women caught the attention of everyone near the water.

Running through knee-deep water, hands clasped, the four drew nearer to the buoy. Not one of them would give up easily, as much for the sheer fun of the race as the threat of a night of dishwashing.

A flash of movement on shore, just beyond the buoy, caught Celia's eye. It was Danny, his camera positioned to capture their antics.

"Let go of me, you goof!" Helen yelled, fighting in vain to free her hand from Celia's.

"Not on your life, Helen! Don't you think it's about time you learned to wash a dish?!"

Celia sensed the moment Ruby spied Danny with his camera. She'd made it abundantly clear she did not want any photographs taken of her in her swimsuit. She stopped short, her hand ripping from Celia's. Eleanor, caught by surprise, slammed into Ruby and they both fell face-first into the shallow water.

When Celia saw them go down, she released Helen's hand and whipped back around, coming to their aid as they struggled to stand back up, snarled hair drooping over their faces and sandy mud dripping from their hands. Helen, oblivious to the chaos behind her, ran on, yelling something about finally getting loose from her deadweight friends.

"Are you all right?" Celia asked, leaning down to glimpse Ruby's face hidden behind her hair. She'd taken the brunt of the fall and appeared the worse for wear. Celia was afraid there were tears amid the lake water dripping off Ruby, but the shaking of the downed girl's shoulders morphed into hoots of laughter.

Eleanor dropped back down into the water—on purpose this time —leaning back to let the water clear her face of hair and to rinse the muck away. Squinting up from her seat in the knee-deep water, she leveled a confused look at the other two losers in their race. "Ruby! What were you thinking? Why'd you stop like that?"

"Because Danny had a camera!"

Ruby's explanation did nothing to clear up Eleanor's confusion. "I know you said you don't like to have your picture taken, but you agreed to a photo last night before the dance. What's the big deal?"

"I told Celia I didn't want to have my picture taken in my bathing suit! I'm too fat."

Celia felt as confused as Eleanor. "Then why are you laughing?"

"Did you see how Eleanor dropped like a rock?" Ruby said, throwing her hands in the air. "Who *wouldn't* laugh at *that* picture?"

"If Danny got that tumble on film, those pictures will never see the light of day," Eleanor threatened.

Ruby squeezed excess water from her hair. "Look, I tolerate pictures sometimes, but I can just hear what my grandmother would say if she ever saw me dressed like this. Celia, did you and Helen set this whole race up just so Danny could get some pictures?"

Celia snorted. "You give us way too much credit, Ruby. We're not nearly that clever. He must have heard all the noise and hurried out here. I promise we didn't plan this. And besides, you aren't fat!"

Ruby glared between Celia and Danny. He still stood on the shoreline, watching them with a mixture of humor and concern.

"Are you ladies okay over there?" he yelled to the three of them. "What happened?"

"*You* happened!" Celia hollered back, but she was all smiles. "Ruby's shy around cameras, and when she saw you she panicked!"

"That was surprise, not panic," Ruby insisted, still wringing her long tresses out over her shoulder and working her snarled hair into a loose braid.

Helen trudged back through the water in their direction, a self-satisfied grin on her face. "You three are *not* worthy opponents. First you cheat and try to hold me back, then you quit! Guess all three of you get to volunteer your services in the kitchen tonight."

She held out a hand to Eleanor, helping her up. Celia caught the glint in Eleanor's eye and knew what was coming. One hard yank, and

Helen ended up face down in the muck, in nearly the same graceless sprawl that she'd missed out on when she sped ahead of everyone.

"We may wash dishes tonight, but you'll be busy resetting your hair!" Eleanor said, hooting with laughter.

After that, they'd all need to wash their hair.

A quick glance toward shore assured Celia that Danny had slipped away with his camera—and, with any luck, snapshots of some spontaneous lakeside fun to use in future advertising for Whispering Pines.

* * *

Despite the girls' offers of help with the evening dishes, Mrs. Bell refused to let any of them into her kitchen. "You girls only have a little over a week left here at the resort, and I won't allow you to waste any of it with dish soap up to your elbows. You young people go—enjoy yourselves! You'll all be tied down soon enough with husbands and babies, doing plenty of dishes of your own."

Horrified at the thought, Celia walked back toward the small cabin with Ruby, her mind still on Mrs. Bell's words. Eleanor begged off early with a headache. Helen was somewhere with her parents, slinking away on the chance her friends would rope her into dish duty, too.

"I can't even imagine being tied down like that yet," Celia said, staring up at the stars as they walked.

Ruby kept her eyes trained on the ground. She remained quiet. The moon wasn't full, and the shadows were deep around their feet.

Celia sensed Ruby had something on her mind. "Are you still mad at me about this afternoon? Because if you really don't want us to use any of the pictures Danny took, we won't."

"Oh. Well, thank you for that, but it's all right. I overreacted. I'm not mad anymore. As long as I don't look ridiculous, use the pictures."

Celia breathed a sigh of relief. She was lucky to be able to call Ruby her best friend. But still, something seemed to be bothering her tonight. She wasn't as chatty as usual. "Is something else wrong?"

Ruby shrugged. "I don't think what Mrs. Bell said tonight sounded so horrible. You always make settling down sound so awful. We don't all feel the same way you do, you know."

Ruby made a valid point. They were all entitled to their own opinions.

"Would you be ready to settle down, start a family soon?" Celia prodded.

"Maybe. If I met the right person," Ruby finally shared, ducking under a low-hanging branch in front of their cabin.

Then Celia remembered Ruby hurrying inside when they arrived at the dance, as if she might be late meeting someone. "And does this 'right person' have a name?"

Ruby climbed the short flight of stairs to their cabin, glancing back down at Celia. "I didn't say I'd met him yet."

But Celia could hear the telltale smile in Ruby's voice, even if she couldn't see her face in the lengthening shadows. "Do you want to talk about this mystery man you *maybe* haven't met yet?"

Pausing with her hand on the doorknob, Ruby shook her head. "Not yet. I don't want to jinx anything." She opened the door. "I think I'll read tonight. I stashed a stack of novels in my suitcase, and I haven't even touched them yet. Would you mind?"

"Not at all," Celia said, holding the screen door and following Ruby inside.

Ruby flipped on a lamp perched under the cabin's front window, flooding the small space with light. Both women changed out of the casual dresses they'd worn to dinner. Ruby settled into bed with her book. A second lamp, this one on the tiny table between the two twin beds, cast a soft glow. Celia didn't feel like reading. She played a hand of solitaire on the petite kitchen table, half listening to voices as they floated in through the open window. The tiny wings of a moth beat against the window screen.

Mrs. Bell was right. She needed to have fun while they were still young. Scooping her playing cards up, Celia peeked in on Ruby. A discarded book lay next to her sleeping friend.

Considering her options, Celia decided to join the laughing voices around the bonfire, the gathering spot they'd always passed on before in favor of a smaller fire on the beach. If she didn't find someone to talk to there, she'd give up and turn in early.

She snapped off the lamp in the bedroom and tiptoed out of the small cabin, not wanting to disturb Ruby. It was nice to share this smaller cabin with one friend this year, instead of staying in the larger cabin with Helen's family. The previous summer had felt like the drama-filled sleepovers they'd shared as little girls.

She nearly lost her nerve as she approached the bonfire, unable to find a familiar face in the group. But a young woman rose with a sleeping child in her arms, saying her goodnights and freeing up a spot. Noticing her in the shadows, an older gentleman waved Celia over, inviting her to sit.

"Come, join us. We may be old, but we promise we're fun," he assured her. "My name is Henry, and this is my wife, Hannah. And you are?"

Celia introduced herself, joining in on the conversation when appropriate. She quickly realized she was the youngest person there by a large margin. The woman who'd left with a sleeping child couldn't have been much older than Celia, but everyone remaining had her by at least thirty years. Despite their age, the group still knew how to have fun. Henry hadn't lied.

Time passed, and Celia laughed along with the rest of the group over stories of botched marriage proposals that still resulted in happy marriages, embarrassing antics of children at the grocer, and even one hilarious recap of a month spent with in-laws during a home-building project. There was an honesty to the conversations, a complete disregard for pretense, that felt refreshing to Celia. None of these people acted as if they cared about social status, and Celia didn't think it was because they were all comfortably wealthy.

The chitchat remained lively, but the fire petered out. Henry stood, offering to go find more wood. Celia noticed how slowly he straightened, one hand braced against his lower back.

Rising to her feet, she offered to go instead. "Please—I need to swing by our cabin anyhow. All of this laughing is dangerous after

Mrs. Bell's fabulous lemonade at dinner. I know where they keep the extra wood stacked. I'll be back in a jiffy."

Henry paused, considering her offer. Hannah reached up and gently tugged his hand. "Dear, let the girl go. There have to be *some* benefits that come with age."

Not waiting for permission, Celia scooted her lawn chair back and stepped out of the shrinking circle of light cast by the dying flames. Henry gave her a grateful nod.

Skipping down the darkened path, Celia hurried right past their tiny cabin, the lamp still glowing in the front window. A soft black canopy of stars twinkled down at her. She didn't need to stop. That had been nothing more than an excuse to soothe Henry's pride. Fetching more wood was the perfect justification for Celia to find Danny on a beautiful summer evening.

CHAPTER TEN

GIFT OF MOONLIGHT

*D*anny's summer home was a tiny cabin, tucked away back in the woods, on the far west side of the resort. He'd pointed it out to Celia when they'd wandered the grounds, searching for photo opportunities that would capture the tranquility of Whispering Pines. He'd admitted the place was little more than a shack, but his mother's homey touches made it livable. It was a place where they could get away from the activity of the resort and put their feet up. Danny didn't mind sleeping on the couch. His mother took the tiny bedroom in the back. There was no indoor plumbing, so in addition to an outhouse, bathing facilities could be accessed in the lodge. There was also a wooden structure to hold stacks of firewood. Danny was responsible for keeping it stocked.

Celia slowed as she reached the edge of the trees. Things looked different at night. The path wasn't as obvious as it wound into the dark woods. If there were any lights glowing in the Bells' cabin, she couldn't see them yet.

The laughter of her new friends reached her from across the grounds, spurring her along. They were waiting for more firewood. Taking a deep breath, she walked into the trees, relying on her spotty memory of the path.

A twig snapped. The pounding of feet, running toward her, pushed her heart into her throat. Should she slip behind a tree, away from the sound of approaching feet, or stay put? She risked a broken ankle if she wasn't careful.

Taking a chance, she ran three steps before a familiar voice stopped her.

"Celia?! Is that you? What are you doing?"

It was Danny.

Of course it's Danny.

Who else would it be back here? It wasn't like Mrs. Bell would run around this time of night.

Dropping her head back in relief, she skidded to a halt, spinning to face him. "You scared me!"

"Why are you wandering around in the dark? Are you alone?" he asked, concern flooding his words. "Is something wrong?"

Very little moonlight penetrated the thick canopy of pines overhead, and Danny had to stand close to see her. A random moonbeam broke through, enough so she could see his worried expression.

"No, no, nothing is wrong," she assured him. "I just came for more wood."

It sounded like a feeble excuse for wandering around in the dark, even to her own ears.

"Where's everyone else?"

"Eleanor had a headache. Ruby was reading, but she fell asleep. Helen is spending the evening with her parents. I wasn't ready to turn in, so I joined a group of guests around the fire. When they needed more wood, I offered to run and get more, since you'd shown me where it was. What are *you* doing? I thought you might be in your cabin by now. It's late."

Celia slapped at a mosquito. Taking her by the arm, he gently spun her toward their shack. She caught a whiff of soap, a glimpse of wet hair.

"Come on, let's get moving before the bugs eat us alive. I'll help you grab more wood."

Her fear of walking alone through the dark woods evaporated, replaced with a different fluttering in her chest. Danny kept a steady hand on her elbow and they hurried through the trees.

"I'm sorry, did you just get cleaned up?" Celia asked. "You probably don't want to carry a stack of dirty wood over to the firepit with me."

He chuckled. "After spending the last five hours putting up the walls on Preston's new duplex, a little firewood will be a piece of cake."

"I'd love to see this project of yours," she commented, already feeling winded. She wasn't sure if it was the fast pace Danny was setting or his proximity. "Preston told me about the duplex. He thinks it was a great idea."

Danny slowed as the little cabin and the lean-to full of wood came into view. No lights glowed inside, but it was getting easier for Celia to see, her eyes having adjusted to the low light.

"Stay here for a second. I'll run inside and grab a flashlight. I'm sure Mother is asleep. Then, if you'd like, I can take you over and show you the duplex after we drop off the firewood."

"That would be great. Go, I'll be fine."

As he hustled away, Celia stood quietly, taking in the night's sounds. Approaching the hulking shadow of the stacks of firewood would have been terrifying by herself, but with Danny only feet away, she relaxed. The cry of an animal echoed through the trees. As she waited, the story of the fabled lost boys wormed its way back into her brain. Luckily, Danny jumped down from the front porch at that moment, his path lit with the yellowish glow of a flashlight.

"I'm glad to see Albert and Arthur didn't snatch you away," he teased when he returned.

"Albert and Arthur?"

"Sure. You know. The two ghosts that roam around out here. The little boys that died in a cave in the woods? Surely you've heard the stories."

Despite his nearness and the welcome glow of his flashlight, Celia couldn't stop the shiver that ran down her spine. Had he read her mind?

Not only had she heard of the ghost boys, she'd swear one of them had stood defiantly in the middle of the road on a rainy summer night last year. But she'd never admit that to anyone. Instead, she laughed. "They waved to me from that thicket of trees over there, but I assured them I'd rather play in the dark with you than the two of them."

Celia felt her cheeks flame. She hadn't meant her flippant comment to come out quite like that. She'd tried to be funny, but what she'd managed to say was loaded with innuendo.

She braced herself for Danny's reaction, but he just grinned, shining his flashlight on the woodpile. The beam did a fine job of pushing back the creepy shadows. "You don't scare easily, do you? Come on. Let's get that firewood."

* * *

They carried the wood back to the firepit and together they revived the smoldering flames. Someone new had settled into her old spot next to Henry, and when he offered to make a new spot for her, she declined as gracefully as possible.

"Henry, leave these two young folks be now," Hannah said. "I'm sure they have better things to do than spend their whole evening with us. Don't you remember when we were young? It's a beautiful evening. You two go on. And thank you for fixing the fire. It chases away the chill."

Celia smiled at the older woman. Hannah winked back at her.

Danny brushed his hands together, set the shovel aside, and bid them all a nice evening.

The two made their escape, heading again into the darkness, but this time toward the other end of the resort.

"They seem like a fun group tonight," Danny noted. "I don't have to show you the duplex now, if you'd rather sit back down with them."

Celia shook her head, her arm brushing against his as they walked. "No. I'm glad I ran into you. Please. Show me what you've been working so hard on."

Their arms bumped again as they walked through the moonlight and the voices faded behind them. When their hands brushed for a third time, Danny wrapped his warm fingers around hers, saying nothing more. They meandered past her cabin, taking their time now that no one was waiting for them. It felt like they were in their own little bubble. No one else was around. It was a Sunday evening, and other than the rambunctious group by the fire, it was quiet.

"Have you enjoyed yourself this summer?"

His simple question reminded Celia she'd be heading home before long. Time was going so fast. "It's been wonderful. I can't believe how quickly this month is flying by. I'm not ready to leave yet."

He gave her fingers a quick squeeze. "I'm not ready for you to leave yet, either."

"Well, we aren't leaving *yet*. We need to make the most of our time here."

They walked along in silence again, Celia contemplating all the things she still wanted to do in the days she had left at Whispering Pines. Most of all, she hoped she'd be able to spend more time with Danny.

As they moved past the lodge, the path wove around two huge old trees. The moonlight faded again, so Danny released her hand and pulled his flashlight out of a back pocket. The beam revealed the skeleton of a large building—much bigger than she'd expected.

"Oh, wow! This is huge!"

"It's pretty neat, isn't it?" Danny agreed, walking ahead of her. "Be careful. I'd hate to have you fall in the basement."

"Basement? There's actually a basement under there?" Celia asked, staring at the large rectangular wooden base, lined on two sides with the beginnings of the walls.

Nodding, Danny helped her up onto what would eventually be the main floor of the structure. "Mr. Whitby is a man of resources. Earlier this summer, he had equipment brought in to dig a basement. When I first suggested he consider building a home back in these woods so his family had somewhere to live other than one of the cabins, he jumped on the idea. He thought to build it with two distinct halves—one side for his family, the other for resort staff. He hates anyone living without indoor plumbing in that old shack, even if it's only for the summer months."

Light from the moon illuminated the worksite. Celia explored the perimeter of the platform, careful to avoid the gaping hole.

"We'll build better stairs down there. Those are just temporary," Danny explained.

"This is really impressive, Danny, but there's still so much more to do. Will you finish before winter?"

Nodding, Danny grabbed hold of one of the partial walls, testing its stability. "Preston has a crew coming in early August to help. We'll get it done."

"How wonderful! Next summer, you and your mother will have somewhere new to live."

Danny bent down to move a discarded piece of lumber onto the pile of scraps, out of the way. "There isn't much more to see," he said, rubbing his hands together. "But I wanted to show you what we'd accomplished up to this point."

"I'm impressed. Now I understand where you disappear to some days."

Grinning, he jumped down to the trampled grass, turning and holding his arms up to her. "Come here. I'll help you down."

She made her way back to him, accidently kicking something metal and sending it in Danny's direction. He stretched to pick up the forgotten hammer, stowing it away in a nearby toolbox. "Thanks. I meant to put that away earlier. I'd hate for it to rust if it rains tonight. You didn't hurt your toe, did you?"

"Nothing it can't handle," she said, thinking of the dance.

He held his hands up to her again. She jumped down with his help. Landing close, she stood her ground. He searched her face, and she held her breath, hoping he'd finally kiss her, but he stepped back, again shining the flashlight on the path away from the new building. "Should I walk you back to your cabin now?"

Had she read it all wrong? She liked Danny, *really* liked him . . . but maybe he didn't see her the same way.

Celia knew going back to her cabin might be the *right* thing to do.

It was late by now. But she didn't want her time alone with him to end.

This might be her only chance to explore her feelings.

"Could we take a walk? It's a beautiful night and I'm not ready to turn in yet. Unless you're too tired. You worked hard while I relaxed all day. If you're ready to turn in for the night, I could do that, too."

He grinned down at her, shifting the flashlight into his left hand and again taking hers with his right. "I'm not tired either. Let's walk."

Their wandering eventually took them to the beach. There were no bonfires burning on the sand. All was quiet. The moon hung high overhead, bathing the surface of the lake and the sand in a white glow. He turned off the flashlight again and they walked down to the water's edge.

"Should we sit out on the end of the dock?" he suggested.

"I'd like that."

Kicking off their shoes, they padded barefoot down the wooden surface, stray sand gritting under their soles. Despite the lateness of the hour, the air still held enough of the day's heat that sitting on the end of the dock and dipping her toes into the cool water below sent a shiver of deliciousness up Celia's arms.

"This is nice. It's my favorite spot at Whispering Pines. The perfect place to sit. To think. I spent plenty of time out here last summer when I fished with Leo, Helen's big brother. I hope he's doing okay. I worry about him, you know?"

Danny settled onto the platform next to her, rolling his pant legs up before lowering his feet to the water next to hers. "I saw Leo over at Grand View a time or two. He was a decent enough fella. Heard he enlisted. Good for him."

"Leo is great. He taught me how to fish. I miss him."

Danny nodded, his eyes scanning the twinkling water. He sighed. "Did the two of you make any promises?"

"What do you mean?"

"Are you still a couple, then? Because, I have to be honest, I really like you, Celia. But I'd never be disrespectful to a man off fighting for our country."

Celia finally grasped Danny's false assumption. She nearly laughed, but something in his tone warned her to take his comment seriously. "Danny, Leo and I . . . we were never more than friends. I've known him all my life. He's like a big brother to me. Besides, he's had the same girl since his first year away at university. Helen thinks they'll marry as soon as he comes home on leave. I worry about him because he's practically family."

"Would you worry about me, if I enlisted?" he asked, finally turning to meet her gaze. His warm brown eyes looked black in the moonlight.

Celia's breath caught. The thought of Danny going off to war caused a hitch in her chest, although his question didn't come as a complete surprise. She'd sensed a restlessness in him when they'd been in Preston's office earlier, discussing press coverage of the war overseas. "I'd hate the thought of it," she whispered, letting her eyes skip away from his, nervously scanning across the water and along the shore, looking everywhere but at him.

Gently, Danny caught her chin and turned her back to face him. "You are an extraordinary woman, Celia. You'd rather help Mr. Whitby here at Whispering Pines or spend an evening learning the history of a place or visit about photography than dance the night away with your friends. I have to admit, I like the idea that you'd miss me."

He let his fingers travel from her chin to the nape of her neck, applying the slightest bit of pressure to pull her toward him, leaning in to place the gentlest of kisses on her lips. If she'd closed her eyes, she might have thought she'd imagined it.

As he pulled back, she smiled up at him, then leaned forward in invitation. She couldn't have imagined a more perfect setting, or a more perfect man, for her first kiss. She didn't want it to end.

* * *

"What had you so restless last night?" Ruby asked, sitting on her bed as she adjusted the strap on her sandal. "I'm not surprised you're still in bed."

"I was restless?" Celia asked, her words distorted by a yawn.

She scooted up so her back rested against the bed's headboard, stretching her arms above her head. It felt like she'd just closed her eyes when the sound of the bathroom door woke her minutes earlier. She'd stayed on the dock, talking and exchanging kisses with Danny until the sun tinged the far horizon a pale pink. When they realized the time, he'd quickly walked her home. She'd changed into her pajamas and eased into bed as carefully as possible, wanting to keep their magical night to herself.

Pink was now her favorite color.

"Your tossing and turning woke me up. You were muttering something about the war . . . I thought you were maybe crying, but I couldn't see any tears."

Celia didn't remember any dreams. Frankly, she doubted she'd slept long enough to fall into one, but she wouldn't say as much to Ruby. "I'm sorry if I woke you."

Ruby waved away her apology. "Don't be. I fell asleep too early last night. I think all the dancing on Saturday tired me out, and then spending the entire day out in the heat yesterday. I'm sorry I was such a fuddy-duddy last night. Did you turn in early, too?"

For a moment, Celia considered telling Ruby about her near perfect night. Sitting on the end of the dock in the moonlight, talking and kissing with Danny, had exceeded any of her girlish dreams. His question about whether she'd miss him if he enlisted still nagged at her, but she wouldn't think about that now. She wouldn't let anything, or anyone, diminish her inner glow of happiness.

Celia gave a noncommittal shrug as she swung her legs out of bed, deciding to keep her own secret. "Not nearly as early as you."

Padding barefoot to the bathroom, she could still feel the grit of sand between her toes. She closed the door behind her. Morning light streamed through the small window, high above the tub. Leaning over the sink, Celia examined her face in the mirror, touching her lips with her index finger. Her face looked the same as it always did.

How can that be, when my world changed overnight?

CHAPTER ELEVEN
GIFT OF A PRIZED POSSESSION

*C*elia made the most of her remaining days at Whispering Pines.

She said nothing about her evolving relationship with Danny to her friends, careful to spend enough time with them every day that they wouldn't become suspicious. After three weeks together, all four women were ready for some time to themselves. No one mentioned Celia spending an inordinate amount of time with Danny. She wasn't sure they noticed.

She liked keeping the budding relationship with him to herself. Her friends would want to pick it apart and examine it from all angles, maybe pressure her to seek a commitment she wasn't even sure she wanted.

Danny had a long list of tasks to accomplish on the duplex before the larger crew would arrive in a week, so Celia spent time at the partially built structure on the edge of the resort, handing nails and various tools to him as he climbed up and down ladders. The process intrigued her, and Danny was more than willing to explain the steps.

"But how do you *know* these things?" she'd asked, holding one end of a tape measure so he could mark the width and length of the rooms on the main floor.

He shrugged. "My father was a handy guy. Over the years, he more than doubled the size of the house we lived in. I helped. He taught me the basics. There's plenty I don't know, and things I can't accomplish alone, but I know enough to keep this project moving for Preston while we wait for the next crew. Men are harder to come by this summer, given the war efforts."

Celia soaked it all in, both the fundamentals of home building and time with Danny. One never knew when such practical knowledge would be useful—or when she'd have time with him again.

The two of them also spent time with Preston, learning more about the mechanics of running a resort like Whispering Pines. Eleanor's father had also taken Danny under his wing, now that Danny's own father was dead and Tripp was off at war.

Late nights became their time to spend together. Once everyone else was asleep, they'd sneak outside under the cover of darkness, often ending up at the end of the dock again. They discussed everything, from their childhoods to their thoughts on the current war raging overseas to the kinds of things they'd always dreamed of doing.

Their relationship was still so new, yet it was strange how the dreams they shared were starting to include each other. They talked about how life might look, years down the road, but they never talked about how things would play out over the next few months when they were apart, or even next summer.

As her time at the resort drew to a close, nothing mattered more than spending time with Danny. The two of them watched the sun begin its predawn ascent on the day Celia was to leave, wrapped in each other's arms at the end of the dock. Silent tears streamed down Celia's face.

"I can't believe I have to go home today," she whispered, feeling a thin, jagged crack in her heart that would ache until she could see him again.

"I'll miss you like crazy," Danny agreed, swaying gently with her and dropping soft kisses all over her face.

She loved how safe she felt inside his firm embrace.

When will I see you again?

It was a question she was afraid to ask out loud.

A rowdy trio of men clamored across the sand in the predawn light, headed for one of the resort's fishing boats anchored near the buoy she'd raced toward with her friends. That sunny day felt lightyears away now. Danny dropped his arms, and they stood.

The men were strangers, but their intrusion broke the spell.

* * *

Bang!

Celia jumped at the slam of their door, nearly dropping the heavy textbook she'd been balancing on the armchair while scribbling notes on a steno pad. She scowled at Ruby. "What has you in such a tizzy?"

"We got mail!"

Happy for the distraction, Celia snapped her book shut and tossed her study materials onto their dorm room floor.

"Did your grandmother send a batch of her sugar cookies again?" Celia asked, mouth watering at the thought. "I swear, they melt in my mouth. She's going to make us fat."

Laughing, Ruby shook her head. "Not this time. I received two letters. But look, a package came for you."

Surprised, Celia pushed out of her uncomfortable chair. "Did Mother send something?"

Ruby held a box behind her back, a mischievous smile on her face. Celia caught a glimpse of the box: it was slightly bigger than a shoebox and wrapped in brown paper. "It's not from your family. I'm surprised at the name on the return address . . . but it might explain a few things. You aren't nearly as sneaky as you think, you know."

Celia smoothed her skirt down, pushing up the sleeves of her cardigan and sauntering closer to her friend. With a grin, she lunged for the box, but Ruby was faster, spinning away to skip to the far side of her bed.

"Come on, Ruby," Celia cried. "Quit messing around! You're acting like a child. Who sent it?"

Ruby checked the return address again, tapping the side of her chin as if deep in thought. "Now why would you get a package from Whispering Pines? Did you accidentally leave something there that Mrs. Bell might have mailed back to you?"

"Mrs. Bell sent that?" Celia asked, motioning toward the box. Ruby held the package at an angle so she still couldn't read what it said. She was trying not to appear too excited, but she was failing miserably.

Her friend shrugged. "Maybe. If her first name starts with *D*. It says 'D. Bell,' and I can't imagine who *else* that could be . . ."

Celia dove across the bed, grabbing Ruby by the wrist. Surprised, her friend loosened her grip.

"Jeez, you must think there's gold in there or something. I think you broke my nail," Ruby complained, sticking her thumb in her mouth.

Rolling away from Ruby, Celia examined the return address on the front of the box, testing the weight of the package. She could hardly believe Danny had mailed her something. He'd hinted at sending her the pictures they'd taken at the resort, once he got them developed, but she'd doubted he'd go to the trouble. They'd said their goodbyes, making no promises to each other. She'd tried to put on a smiling face to mask the ache in her heart whenever she thought of him, and she'd held on to the hope that she'd see him again the following summer at Whispering Pines. She'd doubted he'd be the letter writing type, so she hadn't suggested it during their goodbyes.

That was two months ago. She'd spent the month of August at home with her family, monitoring her little brothers to give her mother some much-deserved time off. She'd helped her sister Beverly get ready for her senior year of high school. Labor Day weekend, she headed back to St. Catherine's with Ruby and Helen, and now it was already late September.

She was dying to open the box, but didn't want to do so in front of Ruby.

"I'm going out, but I'll be back," she declared, clutching the box against her chest. "Please don't lock me out."

She didn't even look Ruby's way as she closed the door on her way out. Ruby had to know "D. Bell" was Danny. Her roommate was likely putting two and two together and feeling hurt that Celia hadn't been more open about her feelings for him.

I'll deal with her later, she thought, hurrying down the stairs, one hand on the smooth wooden banister so she wouldn't tumble in her haste. Her saddle shoes made a racket on the stairs, but no one was around.

Once outside, she paused, inhaling the crisp autumn air. An apple tree, its limbs heavy with fruit, added a tang to the air. A golden leaf drifted down and landed on her shoulder. She wondered how the air smelled at Whispering Pines in late September.

Glorious, she was sure.

The lawn was littered with other students, some in groups, others sitting alone with their schoolwork. Some gathered in knots of three or four girls, debating or laughing about things important to college-age women. There was only the occasional male instructor or visitor.

A grassy spot under a large oak beckoned and Celia hurried over, sinking down to sit on the leaf-strewn lawn, leaves crunching under her. They would cling to the navy wool of her skirt, but she didn't care. All she cared about was the contents of her surprise package.

She shook it carefully. Something rattled inside. It held more than papers or pictures. She tried not to rush, but she felt heady with anticipation.

She ran a finger over the bold letters of her name, imagining Danny sitting down to address the package. Sliding her finger under the folds in the end of the wrapping, she broke the seal, careful not to tear it. The paper was easy to remove, but he'd sealed the box with more tape.

Her fingernails were short and ineffective against the tape. She should have thought to bring a letter opener. Or her keys.

Glancing around, she noticed a girl she knew from her advanced typing class walking on the sidewalk nearby, a pencil stuck behind her ear.

"Gretchen, can you come here for a minute? Please?" Celia shouted, and the girl smiled in her direction, crossing the grass to her side.

"Hello, Celia. Did you get your typing done for tomorrow?"

Thankful she'd stayed after class that morning and finished it, Celia nodded. "Yes. But I have a bit of a dilemma here," she explained, holding up the sealed box. "Would you mind if I try to open this with your pencil?"

Her classmate slid the yellow pencil out from behind her ear, handing it to Celia. "Try it. If it breaks, I've got plenty more."

Taking it with a smile of thanks, Celia braced the stubborn box on her lap and attacked the tape. The sharp pencil pierced the stubborn adhesive, but the lead broke before she'd made much progress. Luckily, however, it was enough. She could get a finger in and break the seal.

"Cookies?" Gretchen asked, taking her pencil back. "I've gotta run or I'll be late for English Lit, but if that box is full of chocolate chip cookies, bring me a few during class tomorrow."

"Will do," Celia assured the girl as Gretchen skipped away.

Taking a deep breath, Celia removed the cover, setting it in the grass. She recognized one of the navy linen napkins from Whispering Pines, wrapped around something. Curious, she lifted the object out and unwound it, gasping as Danny's camera rolled into her hand.

Danny loves this camera! Why in heaven's name would he mail it to me?

Carefully, she turned the camera over in her hands. It appeared to have weathered its trip inside the box without damage. There was even film in the camera. Peering through the lens, she aimed it at the façade of her dormitory. Beautiful ivy, turning a deep crimson in the fall air, clung to the sides of the building. She snapped a picture; it sounded like she thought it should.

Relieved, but still confused as to why Danny would send her one of his most prized possessions, she gently set the camera aside, on top of the napkin. Next was a manila envelope, sealed shut with a metal clasp. He'd scrawled her name across the front. She bent the tiny metal brackets out of the way.

The envelope contained a stack of glossy photographs. The black-and-white pictures, all nearly the size of the large envelope, made an impressive collection of shots, all taken at Whispering Pines.

There were pictures of the cabin she'd shared with Ruby, a bonfire on the beach at dusk, and another of the row of white cabins that hugged the shoreline. He must have taken the shot from the dock.

From *their* dock; the spot where they'd spent hours talking about both their separate histories and their potentially joined futures . . . and the place where he'd first kissed her.

Behind the picture of the white cabins was a progress shot of the duplex, nearly complete.

There was a photo of herself, laughing. It was a closeup, and she remembered when he'd snapped it.

Then there was the shot he'd taken of the four girls, standing around Preston's Ford the night Danny had driven them to the dance. The same night they'd danced together for the first time. She studied the faces of her and her friends. They were all so happy, so carefree. Eleanor had even managed to hide her pout behind a realistic smile.

Finally, she reached the bottom of the stack and sucked in a breath. He'd done it. He'd captured them, running through the shallow water, hand in hand, their faces gleeful, the way a person should feel while on a summer vacation at a Minnesota lake resort.

Danny's talent was undeniable.

But there were no pictures of him.

She remembered him saying, the first night she'd met him, that he preferred to be *behind* the camera, not in front of it.

She flipped through the pictures again, enjoying all of them. She hoped he'd given a similar set to Preston to use at the resort. She'd cherish these.

One last envelope remained in the box. She leaned back, resting her spine against the stately oak, and opened the letter, unfolding the single sheet of paper. Danny's bold handwriting covered the piece of stationery, front and back.

September 9, 1943

Dear Celia,

I suspect you're surprised to receive a package from me. But remember, I promised to send you photographs. I'm a man of my word. I hope they'll make you smile, as they did for me. I knew you'd be photogenic. You made my work easy.

And, yes, I'll give copies of some of these to Mr. Whitby. But not the one of you laughing. That one is for me. That is how I want to remember you— smiling and having fun.

Things have been busy at Whispering Pines since you left, which is good, because it helps me forget how much I miss you, at least for a little while. The duplex is coming along. We will enclose it before the snow falls.

Speaking of snow, it won't be long before we have to winterize things here at the resort. Mother and I will go back home to Wisconsin when the resort closes for the season. Mr. Whitby is going back to Chicago. The summer went by too quickly, but you made it magical for me.

With any luck, my camera made it to you in one piece. I trust you remember how to use it? Now, to be clear, I'm not giving you my camera. I want you to hold on to it for me. Keep it safe. Use it to document your life, so when I see you again, you can show me what you've been up to.

I won't need that camera for a while. I have news, although I'm not sure how you will receive it.

You see, after my father died, I had to stay with my mother, until I was sure she would be all right. I needed to help save money, for her sake. She assures me she'll be fine. She's adjusted to being alone, as much as a person can, I suppose.

So I've enlisted.

By the time you read this, I will probably be on a boat, heading over to where I'm most needed. My hope is I'll contribute to the war efforts by holding a camera instead of a weapon. I'll be talking with my superiors about that when the time is right. I want to be a photojournalist. The rest of the world needs to know what is really happening over there. Mr. Whitby needs to know what is happening with his son, Tripp. Your friend Helen and her family, and you, need to know about Leo.

I wish things were different. None of us want to go off to war, but our country needs dedicated men, and I'm able-bodied.

I know we'd hoped to see each other again, to sit on the dock together at Whispering Pines, but I doubt I'll be back soon.

This is something I have to do. I hope you understand, Celia. I'll miss you terribly, and I'll tuck a copy of your smiling picture in my breast pocket.

Live your life, dear Celia. There are too many unknowns for you to wait for me. Move on, but keep my camera safe. Take pictures to show me some day and know that you'll forever hold a special place in my heart.

All my love,

Danny

Slowly, the sounds of the lively college campus ebbed back into her consciousness. Her heart felt shattered into a million tiny slivers. He left. She might never see him again. Suddenly, the dangers of war felt much more pronounced. Could she do as he asked?

Fingering his camera, she committed to take the pictures. She'd have stacks of them to share with him when he came home. He'd *have* to come home. He'd have to find her. She had his camera.

How had the simple wish for a summer romance blossomed into so much more . . . only to come crashing down with the words scribbled on a single piece of paper?

SPRING 1944

CHAPTER TWELVE
GIFT OF CONFIDENCE

*L*etters continued to arrive throughout Celia's junior year of college, but most were from Eleanor. Her friend stood by her commitment to build airplane components to serve the war efforts, and her letters often included a unique mixture of hilarious snippets and stories of blatant discrimination from the floor of her father's factory. Celia missed Eleanor's energy at school.

She heard nothing more from Danny, but her sister, Beverly, wrote often. Beverly's letters guaranteed an entertaining read. The girl was born with an innate talent for spinning amazing stories. According to their mother, Celia's sister took after their father in this way.

Celia remembered one evening in particular, shortly before their father died, when he'd set her on one knee and Beverly on his other. A bright fire burned in the hearth; the flames reflected in his round spectacles as he told his two young daughters a colorful story of dragons, a kidnapped princess, and a prince who rode in to save her. They'd laughed when their mother tried to shush him, worried he'd scare them.

It was the most vivid memory she'd managed to hold on to of her father.

Their mother was right about Beverly. She could weave an intricate tale. A heart defect weakened her body, but her imagination was boundless. The letters she sent Celia often contained made-up stories of classmates, always including kernels of truth but exaggerated to the point they morphed into something beyond the realms of actual life.

Celia saved all the letters. When she was feeling blue, or worried about Danny fighting on foreign soil, her sister's stories often provided the boost she needed.

Celia wasn't the only one struggling.

Most nights, Helen slept on the couch in Ruby and Celia's dorm room. With Eleanor gone, Helen had a new roommate. She had little in common with the young woman: Lois was more interested in debating politics and pushing women's rights than dating or fashion. Helen may struggle to relate, but Celia liked Lois. She found her views fascinating and her outspoken nature refreshing.

The weeks and months clicked by as they focused on their classes.

Helen insisted she and Ruby come to Whispering Pines with her family again for a third time, though Celia worried it wouldn't be the same. In a previous letter, Eleanor had warned them she'd have little time to spend at the resort. The factory was having a hard time keeping up with demand. She also hinted at family discord but didn't elaborate.

The most magical part of the previous summer—and the one before that, for that matter—had been the times she'd spent with Danny. She knew he wouldn't be there, but maybe spending time with his mother would help ease some of Celia's loneliness.

One afternoon in early May, as Celia arrived at the library to study for final exams, Ruby caught up with her, breathing hard from the rush.

"We need to talk," Ruby said. Her eyes were bright with unshed tears.

Warning bells chimed in Celia's mind—Ruby wasn't one to cry easily. "What is it?"

Nodding toward a carved wooden bench in front of the majestic old building, Ruby hurried over and took a seat. Celia joined her.

"Has something happened?" Celia pushed.

Setting her heavy pile of textbooks onto the bench opposite Celia, Ruby wrung her hands. "I'm afraid so. It's Grandmother."

Celia gasped and put a supporting arm around her friend's shoulders. "I'm so sorry, Ruby. Did she pass?"

Flicking a lone tear away that had escaped down her cheek, Ruby snorted, a hint of amusement flitting across her face. "No, she didn't *pass*, Celia. Grandmother is much too stubborn of a woman to *die*." Ruby paused, covering her mouth for a second. "I'm sorry . . . that was crass. No, she's alive. But she fell. She broke her hip. Mother is with her now."

"I hope she'll be all right. It's good your mother is there so she isn't alone," Celia said—although, based on the way Ruby was reacting, she suspected there was more.

"Mother is insisting I go to Duluth to stay with Grandmother for the summer. And she's right, Celia . . . she reminded me I wouldn't even *be* in school without Grandmother's help, so it's the least I can do."

Selfishly, Celia's first thought was how this would impact her own plans for another summer at Whispering Pines. No Danny, no Eleanor . . . and now no *Ruby*? Maybe she should make other plans for her summer, too. Whispering Pines without any of them would surely be a bore. And lonely.

"I'm so sorry, Celia," Ruby went on, clearly thinking the same thing. "I know this messes with our summer. I was *so* looking forward to Whispering Pines again. This will probably be our last summer out there, regardless . . . and now I can't go."

Feeling guilty over how transparent she must be, she tried to give Ruby a reassuring smile, squeezing her shoulders. "The important thing is that you help your grandmother. Family first, right?"

While Celia did believe her own words, Ruby was like family, and summer wouldn't be the same without her. But then something else Ruby said registered. "What did you mean, our 'last' summer out there?"

Ruby checked her watch and gave a start, extricating herself from Celia's arm and standing. "Darn. I'm going to be late for class."

Scooping up her books, she turned back to Celia. "By this time next summer, we'll be graduating from college. Don't you suppose we'll start acting like honest-to-goodness *adults* by then? You know, settling down, finding actual jobs, that kind of thing? I was looking forward to one last summer at Whispering Pines, but now I have to spend it playing bridge and hiding from that devil cat."

Celia's face must have registered displeasure as the truth in Ruby's words settled over her. Ruby gave her shoulder a reassuring squeeze and offered a half-hearted smile. "I really am sorry, Celia. I have to run, but I'll see you back at the room later."

As Ruby hurried away, Celia remained seated, any ambition to cram for exams deserting her. Her excitement over their summer plans had evaporated. She envisioned Helen's reaction if she canceled on her, too. It would be too ugly.

* * *

Celia made room on the dining table for one last plate of goodies. Stepping back, she surveyed their handiwork, pleased with the outcome. There was a nice variety of party foods, and the graduation cake her mother had created was truly a work of art. The painstaking number of hours in their hot kitchen had been worth it.

A flash of movement on the far side of the table caught her eye. She grinned as a chubby little hand reached up, felt around blindly, and plucked a cookie off the plate nearest the edge.

"George, you know Mother said you couldn't have one of those cookies because you didn't eat your carrots at lunch."

She laughed out loud as the stolen cookie came back into view, her youngest brother trying, but failing, to return the cookie to where he'd found it. He stayed low, slinking out of the room. She'd scold him later, after she finished up a few last details for Beverly's graduation party. Guests would arrive soon.

Circling the table, she picked up George's discarded cookie and stuck it in her own mouth, brushing crumbs off the white linen table-cloth and into her hand and then pushing the platter farther back on the table—out of reach of grubby little hands. She'd assigned Gerry, her six-year-old brother, to watch the three-year-old, but Celia knew that wasn't an easy job for anyone. She'd give them both a break this time—as long as they behaved once the party started.

The deep clang of their doorbell, its toll much like that of an ocean liner cutting through fog, surprised her. One glance at the grandfather clock told her guests shouldn't arrive for another twenty minutes. She hoped Beverly was ready to receive them. Maybe it was Ruby, stopping over early to help.

Celia skipped to the door and pulled it open.

But it wasn't Ruby. It was Preston Whitby, Eleanor's father. Celia didn't have to review the guest list for Beverly's high school graduation party to know Preston wasn't on it. He'd never even met her sister.

"Mr. Whitby? What are you doing here?"

Before the man could reply, the sound of heels click-clacking on the wooden floor echoed behind her. "Celia, dear, can you go tell your sister her guests are arriving?"

Stepping back slightly from the doorway, Celia motioned to her friend's father. "Actually, Mother, this is Mr. Whitby, my friend Eleanor's father. The man who owns Whispering Pines, the resort I go to with Helen's family every summer."

Stepping forward, Celia's mother nodded a greeting. "Preston Whitby. It's been a long time. Celia's said so many pleasant things about your resort. What brings you by today?"

Celia glanced between Preston and her mother, shocked to learn the two had met before. Neither had ever mentioned as much to her.

Preston noticed the balloons and streamers lining the banister of the open staircase behind Celia and her mother. "Hello, Maggie. I apologize. It appears I've dropped in at a most inopportune time. I should have called first. I have something important to discuss with your daughter. If you'll pardon the intrusion, I'll try to stop by later today, before my train leaves."

"Nonsense. I've kept Celia busy all day, preparing for her younger sister's graduation party. Everything is ready and no one else is here yet. There's no need for you to leave and come back. You two take all the time you need. It was nice to see you again, Preston. If you'll excuse me, I need to finish up a few things."

Celia nodded to her mother, then turned back to her unexpected visitor. "I had no idea you knew my mother. Would you like to come in?"

"If you don't mind, why don't we take a brief walk?" Preston suggested. "I don't want to interfere with your sister's party, and it's a beautiful spring day."

A car pulled up to the curb in front of their house. The party was starting.

Celia nodded and stepped down onto the front stoop, noticing the wider streaks of silver at Preston's temples and deep smudges under his eyes. With a start, Celia realized something was likely wrong for him to show up on her doorstep unannounced. "Is Eleanor all right? Tripp?"

Preston offered his arm to her along with a weary smile. "My children are fine—at least as far as I know. But I have a request. Come, let's walk."

Slipping her hand into the crook of his arm, Celia proceeded down their front steps with him, curiosity overtaking her initial sense of dread.

Car doors slammed. Celia nodded a greeting to three girls she recognized from Beverly's class, then turned her full attention back to Preston. "You have me curious. Anything you need, you know I'm happy to help, although I can't imagine what that might be, Mr. Whitby."

"You really must call me Preston, Celia," he said, patting her hand where it rested on his arm. When their steps brought them to the end of their walk, Celia took them to the left. "I find myself in a bit of a bind. But before I explain, you *were* planning on spending a month at Whispering Pines this summer, correct?"

Celia nodded, reminded of her doubts regarding her summer plans. "Helen's invited me to accompany her family for the month of July again."

"How would you feel about coming sooner? Now that you're home from school for the summer, do you have plans for June and August?"

She glanced up at him with curiosity as she gave it thought. "Nothing in particular. Mother and Clarence can always use a second set of hands around here. My youngest brothers keep all of us busy. Have Helen and her family changed their plans?"

"No. And I hope they won't have to. But that all depends on you."

Checking the side street as they came to a corner, Celia's intrigue mounted. "I don't follow."

"Look, Celia, I know what I'm about to ask is a lot. But I find myself in a predicament. Let me back up for a moment. As you know, my . . . wife . . ." He paused, as if searching for the right words. "My wife took our youngest daughter and went back to live with her family in England."

He glanced her way, and she nodded to show she was following. At least so far.

"Word has reached me that she—my wife, that is—has fallen ill. Her health is failing quickly."

Celia stopped walking and pulled her arm back, clasping her hands together. Concern for both Preston and Eleanor flooded through her. Eleanor put on a brave front, but she'd made enough comments for Celia to know she still held on to a glimmer of hope her parents would someday rekindle their relationship so their family could be whole again.

"Does Eleanor know?"

"She does," Preston confirmed, blowing out a sigh as he massaged his right temple. "And she knows I stopped to see you today. In fact, she'll be monitoring things at the factory for me. I have a supervisor in charge, but I feel better having family watching things. You see, I must travel back to England. There are things that need taking care of, and . . . and my youngest will surely need me. She's not strong. Not like Eleanor or Tripp. Not like you."

Celia's heart went out to Preston. She could see how this was weighing on him. "I'm so sorry. What can I do to help?"

"Well . . . with Eleanor needed at the factory, and Tripp off fighting this damn war, there's no one to run Whispering Pines this summer. I hate the thought of turning our vacationers away. Some of them are regulars, coming for nearly two decades now, since well before I took over the resort. I'm booked for the summer, thanks to the marketing I developed using some photographs you and Danny provided. That was a stroke of genius you had."

The compliment passed her by as she felt a pang in her heart at Danny's name, but she tried to stay focused on Preston. "That is a dilemma. Will Mrs. Bell be working there this summer?"

"Yes, thank goodness. But she can't do it all herself. I need someone who can handle the money, at least until I can get back. That's why I'm here. Can I hire you, Celia, to run Whispering Pines for the summer?"

Conflicting emotions flooded through her at the question. The sense of panic and uncertainty was the strongest, but there was also an undercurrent of excitement. She felt utterly unprepared, but flattered.

"Oh, Preston, I don't see how I could . . ."

He held up a hand to stem her words. "Celia, stop right there. Two years ago, I saw a spark in you. A curiosity. You were a quick study. Then, last summer, you added value to my business. I know it won't be easy, but I have faith in you. I need someone to attend to the most critical financial items. Mrs. Bell has agreed to take responsibility for as many of the logistics around housekeeping and meals as possible. I've also hired someone to do the things her husband used to do, and that Danny took care of last summer. That covers everything except the financial aspects. I need someone capable—someone I *trust*—to handle the business end of things."

Celia struggled to process it all. She turned and resumed walking, head down and hands clasped behind her back as she thought back to the many things he'd taught her. Could she do it? Was Preston naïve to think she could?

He followed her but stayed silent, as if he understood her need to think through the huge undertaking he was asking of her.

Their steps brought them to a small, parklike area that the local

Ladies Auxiliary VFW had developed. Beautiful spring flowers bloomed, and a concrete bench provided seating within the perfumed air. Her feet carried her across the cobblestones that branched off from the sidewalk and she sank onto the perch. Preston followed her lead.

Before this, she'd considered canceling her visit to Whispering Pines this summer. It wouldn't be the same without Eleanor, Ruby, or Danny to help her fill her days. But Mr. Whitby's request shifted everything. She was tempted, and she could see he truly needed her help. Plus, she could save the money she earned. She'd need it to set herself up after her college graduation.

But what about her own family? It was like she'd said to Ruby—family first.

Glancing down the street, back at her own home a few blocks down, she could see additional guests arriving to celebrate her sister's graduation. There had been times throughout the years when they'd all worried Bev wouldn't live to see this point in her life.

An idea blossomed.

"Preston . . . if I agree to do this, I would need something from you."

A slight smile softened the worried expression on the man's face. "I taught you well, Celia. I haven't even laid out the details of how I'll compensate you, and you're already looking to negotiate with me. And therefore, I know you're the man—I mean, the *woman*—for the job. What do you have in mind?"

"Helen's father is generous. He normally pays for me and Ruby to come along. I'm sure you won't charge him this year, if I'm working for you?"

"That is correct," Preston nodded. "Go on."

"Ruby can't come this year. She's spending her summer in Duluth, taking care of her grandmother. If I were to spend my entire summer at Whispering Pines, instead of just July, I'd miss spending time with my sister Beverly and my little brothers. This is my last summer before I graduate from college. Next summer I'll likely be working, maybe somewhere far from here."

"I'm not sure bringing your little brothers to Whispering Pines would work."

Celia laughed—she could see by the twinkle in his eye he didn't really think that was what she was about to suggest.

"What would you think if I brought my sister with me to Whispering Pines? I couldn't afford to pay to have her there, but she could share the small cabin with me. I'd be able to help you, and I think the fresh air and change of scenery would do Beverly a world of good. She has trouble with her heart."

The smile on Preston's face grew to a full-fledged look of both relief and satisfaction. "I knew you had a good head on your shoulders, young lady," he said, rising to his feet and placing a hand on her shoulder. "Your sister is more than welcome at Whispering Pines. We'll work out all the details, but first: Do we have a deal? Would you feel more comfortable if I discussed this with your parents?"

Celia stood and extended her hand. "That won't be necessary. My parents consider me an adult. I'm nearly done with college. I'm guessing Beverly will be delighted at the opportunity to spend her summer at Whispering Pines, but of course I'll ask her to make sure. You've got a deal."

Preston beamed. "I knew you'd help me keep Whispering Pines going this summer. You can see how special the place is, too, can't you?"

"Absolutely," she replied without hesitation. "And I promise to always help you look out for it, no matter what."

They shook on it, and Preston insisted she get back to her sister's party.

After that, she'd need to pack.

CHAPTER THIRTEEN
GIFT OF FOREBODING

*C*elia sucked in a deep breath as she strolled from her cabin to the lodge, enjoying the cool, pine-scented air. She'd only ever spent time at Whispering Pines in July, and while she loved the heat and didn't mind the humidity, the light breeze of the early June morning felt invigorating.

The crisp air helped clear her head, which she certainly needed.

Today, the actual work would begin.

Beverly had jumped at the chance to spend her summer at the resort, swearing that it was the best graduation gift ever. The trepidation in their mother's eyes had been obvious, but Celia assured her Beverly would benefit from the slow pace and fresh air.

Preston left his Ford at the resort for Celia to use in his absence, but they had still needed to get to Whispering Pines. Their parents, Maggie and Clarence, decided a day trip was the best option. All six of them, including young Gerry and George, squeezed into her stepfather's tired old Chevrolet for the drive.

Despite a high temperature of only seventy-two degrees and a lake that had not yet warmed following the Minnesota winter, Celia's two little brothers headed straight for the beach, impervious to the chill. Clarence sat with them while they waded into the icy water up to their knees, and then built sand castles away from the lapping waves. Maggie helped Beverly get settled in the same cabin Celia had shared with Ruby the summer before.

Celia remembered feeling a sense of pride as she'd given her family a tour of the grounds. It was still hard to believe Preston trusted her to run Whispering Pines by herself for the summer.

Well, she wasn't running the resort *entirely* on her own. Mrs. Bell would handle most of the guest interactions. Nevertheless, the summer would test Celia's abilities.

Celia and her sister had accepted their mother's hugs as their family piled back into the car. The two waved goodbyes until the car turned out of sight, down the gravel lane.

Chuckling to herself, she remembered how Beverly had clapped her hands together then raised them and spun in circles, motioning to the skies above. She'd caught Celia up in a big hug. "Cee, I've never ever been away from Mother in my life. Thank you for giving me this summer. I know we'll have a grand time."

She hoped Beverly was right. Celia's pulse tripped with nervousness as she let herself into the lodge through the front door. The hallway was dark, though she could hear someone back in the kitchen. Running a light hand along the wall, she felt her fingertips brush across what she remembered to be two framed pictures, hanging on the wall next to the front door and across from Preston's office. She flipped the light on and studied the two pictures. Both were old—blurry black-and-white shots—one of a grizzly old man holding a large fish, the other of a hunter standing next to a downed bear.

She wondered who'd hung them, and as she thought back to the impressive gallery in the hallway at Grand View Lodge, she decided one of her goals for the summer would be to add to this collection. Maybe Preston would follow her lead in the future and build their own gallery here at Whispering Pines.

Liking the idea, she snapped the light off and made her way to Preston's office through the gloom. Maybe she'd need to think of it as *her* office—at least for the summer.

Standing beside the old scarred desk, she rested her palms on its wooden surface, her mind swinging back to the previous summer when she'd sat in this small room with Preston and Danny. They'd discussed press coverage of the war overseas. Now Danny was there, in person, and Preston was embarking on what could also be a dangerous trip, traveling to Europe during a time of worldwide upheaval. Suddenly her task of keeping the doors open at Whispering Pines didn't seem so monumental.

"Here are the invoices from the laundress and the food delivery," Mrs. Bell announced as she bustled into the room, giving Celia a start. Grinning, the older woman handed the loose sheets of paper over. "Sorry, dear, didn't mean to startle you."

Celia accepted the paperwork, smiling, and shook her head. "Don't apologize. Thank you. Hopefully I'll remember what to do with these."

Mrs. Bell dropped her hands into the pocket of her crisp white apron, a gesture Celia noticed often. She wondered what the woman kept in those pockets. She also wondered how she kept the aprons so clean, working hard cooking and cleaning as she did.

"If Mr. Whitby has confidence in you, so do I. He's not one to trust easily. I think he saw something in you from that first summer."

Celia rolled back the heavy oak chair and sank into it, resting her elbows on the desk and clasping her hands together. "Don't you mean *we'll* do fine, partner?"

A pleased look crossed Mrs. Bell's face, but the clang of a timer echoed from the kitchen on the back side of the lodge. "And that would be today's bread!" The woman spun and hustled out of the room with a wave. "Get to work there, *partner.*"

They settled into a routine. Celia would be in the resort office by seven and spend the first few hours of every day there, paying bills and reacquainting herself with all other manner of bookkeeping. The occasional jingle of the telephone brought word of new reservations, a rare cancelation, and interactions with suppliers.

Once, it was Preston himself on the other end of the line, checking in to make sure things were going as expected. The connection was terrible, and she thought she could hear exhaustion in her mentor's voice, but he brightened a bit when she had only good news to share. There had been no hiccups yet—at least not significant enough to mention to Preston; he had his hands full.

Beverly thrived in her newfound freedom. Never an early riser, she was often still puttering around the cabin in her robe and nightgown when Celia returned from her morning in the office.

Unlike the previous summer, when Celia snuck out and spent her nights walking or sitting on the dock, talking with Danny, she got into the habit of turning in early. Beverly did the opposite, often composing stories or writing poetry in her journal at the kitchen table until well past midnight.

"Are you ever going to let me read any of what you've been writing since we arrived?" Celia asked. They were setting the table for a light lunch of sandwiches and potato salad that Mrs. Bell had pressed into Celia's hands as she left the office. "You used to let me read all your work, but you've been more secretive about it this summer."

Beverly shrugged. "I doubt it's anything worth reading. I'm experimenting with something a little longer than I usually do, and with a slightly older bend to the storyline."

Celia glanced at her sister. She noticed for the first time that Beverly was dressing older than she had when they'd arrived at the resort a few weeks earlier. Maybe it was the pretty yellow sundress she wore, instead of the denim pedal pushers and T-shirts that made up her normal summer wardrobe at home. The bright color contrasted nicely with Beverly's dark hair and blue eyes. Her sister's hair reminded Celia of dark chocolate, and she'd always envied the richness of its deep tones. Her own hair was lighter, bordering on a distressing shade of red.

"Is that a new dress?"

Holding the skirt out and spinning in a circle, Beverly nodded. "It is. Do you like it? Great Aunt Middleton sent it for my graduation."

That would explain the quality of the fabric, the stylish cut. Their paternal great-aunt never spent time with her two great-nieces, but she did occasionally surprise them with generous gifts. Celia knew Beverly couldn't remember meeting the woman. She'd only come to visit one time, following their father's funeral. He'd been the woman's eldest nephew. Celia was only five when their father died, Beverly just two years old. Celia had never understood the strained relationship with their father's only living relative, and their mother refused to discuss it.

Not that it mattered. Clarence made up for any shortcomings of their biological father's family. He wasn't a perfect stepfather, and Celia worried he was overly strict, but he'd saved their little family when things were at their darkest. Maybe his tough disciplinary ways were necessary with his two rambunctious young sons.

"Earth to Celia. Where did you go, sis? Do you like my dress?"

Celia grinned. "You know I do. I wish I could wear yellow."

Laughing, Beverly filled their glasses with iced tea from the refrigerator. "And I wish I could wear pink, but there you go."

"Back up a minute," Celia said. "What do you mean, your story has an older 'bend' to it?"

Sinking into her chair with a sigh, Beverly picked at the crust on her sandwich. She'd always hated the crust. "If you must know, I'm trying to write a novel. A romance, actually. But I'm afraid it's rubbish, what with having absolutely no personal experience myself with matters of the heart."

"What about Peter?" Celia asked, trying to keep a straight face. "You've been sweet on him since you were a little girl."

"Ha-ha. You can be such a brat sometimes, Cee. You know how I despised that boy. Thank goodness they moved away before school started last year. He wasn't there to torture me my senior year."

Indeed, they'd all been relieved when Peter and his family moved out of their neighborhood. Peter's mother had died years earlier, and his father was a bully, passing the tendencies on to Peter and his two brothers. Peter teased Beverly mercilessly for years. Celia suspected it was because he'd had a crush on her sister, but Bev could never stand the boy.

Beverly used her knife to cut the crusts from her sandwich and then took a bite. "This is delicious. Who knew leftover meatloaf tasted so good on bread?"

"You better get outside and get some exercise. Mrs. Bell is a splendid cook. She'll fatten us up if we aren't careful."

Nodding, Beverly took a sip of her tea. "What about you, Cee?"

"I get plenty of exercise walking all over this place monitoring things."

Shaking her head, Beverly set her glass back down, her expression suddenly serious. "No, I'm not talking about *exercise*. Have you ever been in love? You never talk about boys, but you must date at college, don't you?"

Surprised, Celia wiped her fingers on her napkin, avoiding Beverly's gaze. "I go to an all-women university, Bev."

"Come now, Celia. Why won't you share with me? I have this feeling there's someone, but you never talk about him."

She could hear the sincerity in Beverly's voice, her desire for a glimpse into her big sister's life. Ruby and Helen knew a bit about her feelings for Danny—they'd talked her into showing them the contents of the package he'd sent her the previous fall—and maybe Eleanor suspected, but no one else had any idea how deeply she cared about him.

Her and Beverly's three-year age gap, coupled with Bev's health issues, had resulted in a relationship between the two sisters that felt more like a mother–daughter bond. But Beverly didn't need a second mother, and Celia could use someone to confide in. It was harder than she'd expected, being at Whispering Pines, seeing Danny's mother every day. She missed him terribly. She'd only received the one letter from him and had yet to muster up the courage to ask Mrs. Bell if she'd had any news from her son.

"All right . . . I'll admit there was someone. Last summer. But I suppose it's over now."

Beverly's eyes brightened with curiosity. "Really? Do tell."

Celia considered how much to share, now that she'd opened the door on the topic. "What do you want to know?"

"Everything!" Beverly laughed, as though it were obvious.

Celia decided it might help to talk about it all. "All right. But let's finish eating and put our suits on. Save your pretty dress for later. It's a beautiful day outside, and I have a few hours until I need to go do some more work. We'll talk on the beach. Deal?"

Bev positively beamed. "Deal!"

* * *

Celia sat beside her sister on a wood-slatted lounge chair, the hot summer sun beating down on their heads. With one leg on either side of the foot rest, she dug her toes into the sand, through the heated top surface to a cooler layer below. Her fingers played with the towel draped modestly across her lap, and she smiled at her memories of the grit that had lingered between her toes on that fateful morning following the night of Danny's first kiss.

Beverly gave Celia's hand a reassuring squeeze. "I'm sorry you didn't have more time with him. He sounds amazing."

Celia returned her sister's squeeze then pulled her hand away, adjusting the wide straw hat she'd hoped would protect her fair skin. Freckles already appeared across the bridge of her nose. "He was amazing. *Is* amazing, I mean. I just can't help but worry about him. I have no idea how he's doing. I'm sure nothing terrible has happened, or Mrs. Bell would have said something."

"I don't understand why you don't just ask her," Beverly said, raising her face to the sunshine. "She knew the two of you hung out together last summer, right?"

Shrugging, Celia considered Beverly's question. "Well, sure, I guess. But she might have thought we did that because we were both helping Mr. Whitby."

Beverly was skeptical. "Mothers can sense these things, Cee."

"She's mentioned nothing about him."

"Maybe she's waiting for you to ask," Beverly countered. "Or maybe he asked her not to say anything, in case he wants you to move on. He sounds like the kind of guy who'd want the best for you."

Celia sighed, leaning forward to adjust the back of her wooden chair so she could recline. She kicked the sand off her feet and situated herself flat on her back, rested her hat atop her face, and closed her eyes.

"All right, I take it this is your subtle way of telling me you don't want to talk about it anymore," Beverly said, and Celia gave her a thumbs-up. "Fine. I'm going to go cool off in the water, then."

"Don't swim out too far," Celia said from beneath her hat.

She heard Beverly shuffle away. Maybe talking to her sister about Danny had been a mistake. It felt good to talk about him, but it also made her ache with loneliness. Sitting here, on this beach where she'd spent so much time with him, made his absence even more real. Maybe Beverly was right and she should ask Mrs. Bell about him. What if Mrs. Bell thought she was rude or self-centered for not asking about her son?

She let the warmth of the sun sink into her skin. She'd been so busy since they'd arrived, she hadn't allowed herself time to relax. The voices of guests busy having fun swirled around her, along with the squawk of a bird. Eyes closed, she let her mind wander.

The brilliant red of the strong sunshine behind her eyelids and thin hat faded to black as a cloud obscured the sun and a chill blew across her sun-warmed body. The shadow quickly passed and warmth returned. She may have dozed off for a time. Shouts and laughter continued to punctuate the peacefulness. It felt good to relax.

Something snagged her attention then, the tease of a familiar voice. She tensed, listening intently, hoping it was her imagination playing tricks on her.

Her sister's sunny laugh came from the direction of the water. Celia let herself relax again. She was so glad she'd thought to bring Beverly along for the summer. Her sister had blossomed, matured, right before her eyes. Maybe she *would* be ready to try college in the fall. Celia had suffered doubts, as she knew her mother had.

But then she heard it again. That voice. Scrambling up, she tossed her hat onto the sand and pulled the back of her beach chair up. Blocking the glare of the sun with a hand, she scanned the beach, sure she'd been mistaken but bracing herself. While there were smatterings of men here and there, she didn't see his face.

Letting her eyes travel along the water, she did her best to identify the swimmers. There weren't many, despite the heat of the day. She saw Beverly standing in water up to her waist, facing in Celia's direction. A man stood in shallow water between the sisters, his back to Celia. Beverly was talking with him, trailing her fingers through the water as she spoke.

Hairs stood on the back of her neck. It had been nearly two years, but there was no mistaking the man.

Jumping to her feet, she scooped up the loose-fitting sundress she'd worn over her bathing suit for their walk down to the beach and pulled it on. She knocked sand off her bonnet, jamming it back on her head as she hurried to the water's edge.

Beverly laughed again, and there was an underlying quality to it that Celia had never heard from her sister. It sounded flirtatious, and given who was standing in front of Beverly, Celia's stomach flooded with dread. She pulled up, needing to collect her wits.

Damn. What is he doing here?

He shouldn't be here. But she needed to be careful.

Continuing on at a more measured pace, she came within a few feet of him. His shoulders tensed and she could tell the moment he felt someone there.

Beverly shifted when she noticed her. "And this is my big sister, Celia."

Those same shoulders, beneath a white cotton T-shirt, visibly relaxed. He nodded, his hair so similar in color to Eleanor's. He turned slowly to face her. Celia fought the urge to take a step back as her eyes met his. There was even more intensity in that look than she remembered.

"Tripp. This is a surprise," she said, allowing herself one quick scan up and down his body. From behind, she hadn't noticed the massive bandage at the end of his left arm, or the jagged scar down the front of one thigh. The scar was fresh, not yet fully healed. "We weren't expecting you."

"Celia. It's nice to see you again," Tripp greeted her, although his voice held little warmth—and there was certainly nothing nice reflected in those eyes that bore down on her. "I have to admit, this day is *full* of surprises. I expected to find my father in his office. Instead, I ran into Mrs. Bell in the lodge. Imagine my astonishment when she told me where my father is spending his summer—and who he left in charge here."

It was obvious he didn't appreciate either surprise.

Beverly waded toward shore, coming to stand next to Tripp in the ankle-deep water. Celia spared her a glance and wished her little sister was wearing more than her swimsuit. Tripp was the last person she wanted ogling Beverly. How had she not noticed how much curvier her sister had become? So much bustier than Celia would ever be.

"I take it you two already know each other then?" Beverly asked, smiling between the two of them.

Tripp didn't acknowledge Beverly's question. "And what is this I hear about Eleanor working at Father's factory? Dropping out of school? Has the world gone mad?"

"I'll take that as a yes," Beverly said, a perplexed look on her face. "I think I'll dry off now."

Her movement caught Tripp's attention, and Celia hated the glimmer she caught in his eyes as Beverly walked back up the beach to their chairs. She remembered when she and Helen had waited in the woods after the car got stuck in the rainstorm, the story she'd shared. Beverly was roughly the age Helen had been when Tripp took advantage of her.

That would not happen this time.

Speaking of Helen—her family would arrive in two days. Her friend wouldn't be happy that the prodigal son had returned.

Turning her attention back to Tripp, she crossed her arms over her chest, meeting his eye again. "Yes—actually, Tripp, the world has gone slightly mad. People have to do things they'd never normally do, take chances they'd never planned on, when a country is at war. But I shouldn't have to tell you that, should I?"

His right hand touched the massive bandage at the end of his left arm, although she doubted he was even aware he'd done so. "I don't need a lesson in madness from a sheltered college girl, Celia."

A shiver ran down her spine at the bite of his words. She knew he'd have witnessed madness close-up. For the first time, she felt a twinge of pity for him. Had he lost a hand? "I'm sorry you were injured."

He looked put off by her comment, as if the unexpected sympathy were completely foreign to him. He nodded, but stayed silent for once. She needed to remember this was Eleanor's big brother, and Preston's son. They were both important people to her, with big hearts and strong loyalties. There had to be redeeming qualities to Tripp, too. He'd been through hell overseas, given his injuries, and his mother must have hurt him emotionally when she deserted them.

She'd start over with Tripp and try to remain civil. He'd been out of the loop, and arriving here at Whispering Pines, expecting to find his family but finding her in charge, had to come as a shock. He was probably still in pain. His stance was unnatural, as if he was trying to keep his weight off his injured leg.

Spinning around, she motioned for him to follow her. "Let's sit down, then, and I'll tell you what I know."

An empty chair sat a few feet from where she'd been sunning with Beverly. Her sister watched as Celia dragged the extra chair closer and reclaimed her own seat. Tripp's expression remained stoic as he trudged through the sand and sat.

Once settled, Celia explained how Preston had visited her the day of Beverly's graduation party. The man was in a terrible bind with little options. She felt more than saw Tripp's body tense when she mentioned the dire state of his mother's health. It had to be awful, the realization that it was likely too late for his family to reconcile.

"And Eleanor?" he prodded, quickly moving past the situation with his mother and younger sister.

Celia couldn't help but laugh. "Oh, yes . . . Eleanor. I don't think you need to worry about her. She told us two years ago that she wanted to put her nursing career on hold and help build bombers. I remember my shock when she'd suggested it, but I never really thought she was serious. Turns out she meant every word. Last fall she finally convinced your father to let her come to work for him on the factory floor. She promised she'd go back to school after things go back to normal."

Tripp snorted. "I'm not sure I know what 'normal' is anymore."

Celia nodded—she couldn't disagree. "Anyway, now she's helping your father monitor things at the factory. He left a foreman in charge, but I think he was glad to have her there, having to leave like he did."

She waited then, giving Tripp time to process the updates she'd shared. Beverly was listening, but remained quiet. Tripp left his right leg angled straight out and slightly to the side, but he dug the toes of his left foot deeper into the sand much like Celia had done, almost as if trying to ground himself.

Watching him, Celia remembered someone mentioning the purported healing powers of Whispering Pines. While she still felt a huge dose of animosity toward the man sitting next to her, she hoped the legends were true. Tripp could use plenty of healing—in both body and soul.

They sat in silence for a few minutes. Despite herself, Celia was curious where he might take the conversation next. Maybe now he'd understand the predicament his father had found himself in, why Preston had taken a chance and asked her to help at Whispering Pines.

Eventually he leaned forward, resting his injured arm on his strong leg. "Well, the good news for you is I'm back now, so you can stop worrying your pretty little head about working this summer and spend the rest of your time here"—he gestured around them—"relaxing on the beach. It's what you were doing anyhow, so it shouldn't be much of a stretch. Now, if you ladies will excuse me, I'm going to go try to ring my father, update him on my arrival. I'll see you at dinner."

Stunned into silence, Celia watched him stand, find his balance, and then hike through the sand in the lodge's direction. When she realized her mouth was hanging open, she snapped her jaw closed, glaring after him.

Once he was out of earshot, she turned to Beverly. "Can you believe the nerve of that man? Who the hell does he think he is, showing up here, out of the blue, and patronizing me? Preston left *me* in charge. Tripp can't just dismiss me like that!"

Beverly glanced between her sister and back over her shoulder at the building Tripp had disappeared into, her expression guarded. "Celia, understand what a shock it must have been to come here expecting to find his family, only to find them all gone and you here. And he's obviously still suffering from his battle wounds. Maybe helping his father out with Whispering Pines until Mr. Whitby can get back is just what Tripp needs right now."

Celia knew she was doing it again: staring at her sister, mouth agape.

Does she honestly think Tripp is equipped to run the resort? She doesn't even know the man.

As far as Celia knew, Preston had never taught Tripp any of the bookkeeping for Whispering Pines. Instead, he often sent his son off on factory errands. Tripp should probably leave the resort and go help there instead. But then, would Eleanor end up feeling just as Celia did now? Dismissed by an egotistical man?

Celia took a deep breath. She needed to rein in her temper. "Beverly, you need to be careful around that man. Don't assume for one minute that Tripp is anything but dangerous."

Even as she uttered the words, she could see they fell on deaf ears. Beverly waved her warning away dismissively. How could she make her sister see she was right, when even Celia had a momentary lapse in judgment, giving him the benefit of the doubt? Not that her sympathy lasted long. Tripp had a way of bringing out the worst in her.

"I'm serious, Bev. Watch yourself. That man is a taker. Keep your distance."

Beverly settled back in her beach chair and raised her face to the bright sunshine. "Whatever you say, Cee. You always know best."

Snorting with disgust, Celia pushed up out of her chair and mean-dered over to the old wooden dock, drawn there by an overwhelming sense of dread. Her bare feet carried her out to the end of the deserted platform and she sat, planting her feet and pulling her sundress down over her knees. She did her best thinking out here. She wished either Leo or Danny were here with her now, to give her advice on how to handle Tripp. But both were far away, fighting in the blasted war that had chewed Tripp up and spat him out, sending him back here, wounded and bitter.

How could she protect herself and Beverly from the demons he carried?

CHAPTER FOURTEEN
GIFT OF A RIVAL

"*W*hat do you mean, Tripp is *here*? That's impossible."

"I wish," Celia said. She'd pulled Helen to the far edge of the parking lot the minute she arrived with her parents.

"But I don't understand," Helen whispered, glancing around as if Tripp might be standing right behind her. "You told me Preston left you in charge out here—which, by the way, was an enormous leap of faith on his part. But he wouldn't have done that if Tripp was home."

Celia ignored Helen's comment about Preston's *leap of faith*. They could argue about that another time. The important thing was to determine if she had a staunch ally in Helen. She needed to feel like *someone* was on her side in all of this.

"Be prepared, Helen. Physically, Tripp's in rough shape. I suspect he lost his left hand. And he walks with a limp, although that seems to be getting better. I assume he came home because of his injuries. Preston couldn't have known this would happen. Besides, if the Army sent any advance communication about his condition, they'd struggle to locate Preston, since he's traveling right now."

The slam of a trunk cut into their hushed conversation. "Helen, dear, please grab your suitcase and follow us."

"I'll be right there, Daddy," Helen called over her shoulder. "You go ahead. I know the way."

"All right then. Don't forget your suitcase. Hello there, Celia. Nice to see you," Mr. Nielle said before turning away, his arms loaded with luggage. Helen's mother was already out of sight. She'd slipped off, no doubt empty-handed.

Once they were alone, Celia continued, feeling breathless. "I'm so glad you're here. I've been feeling out of sorts since Tripp got back two days ago. He ordered me to stay out of the office, claiming he'd handle everything, but I know for a fact he hasn't stepped foot in there himself, other than to call his father on the phone. Mrs. Bell has been watching and keeping me up to date. Helen, you and I both know Tripp doesn't care about Whispering Pines. And Preston left me in charge. What should I do?"

Helen rubbed her temples, overwhelmed by all the news. "Honestly, Celia, I don't know what to think. It's been two years since I've even seen Tripp. Maybe he's grown up. Shouldn't war turn even the most obnoxious of boys into men?"

Celia nodded. She'd harbored similar hope upon Tripp's surprise arrival. But his surly attitude had already dashed such optimism. "He has no doubt suffered. But Helen, he's so bitter. And I have a terrible feeling. Not only does he want to handle everything here at Whispering Pines, but he seems to have his eye on Beverly."

"What?! But she's a child!"

It was Celia's turn to rub her face in frustration. "I know that's how *we* think of her. But Helen, she's eighteen. The same age as you were when . . . you know. She graduated, and she's all curvy and pretty now. You came to her graduation party. You saw her. When Tripp first got here, he ran into Bev on the beach. He was flirting with her, turning on the old charm, until I stepped in."

"She looked pretty at her graduation party," Helen acknowledged, pacing away from Celia. "But I still think of her as your gawky little sister. How is she feeling?"

Celia knew Helen was referring to Beverly's heart. Bev could go months with no trouble, but then she'd catch a cold or some other physical stressor, and she'd suffer a terrible setback. The spells with her weakened heart were scary—dangerous, even. Celia lived in constant fear of losing Beverly.

"She insists she's feeling great out here. She's resting, writing, and enjoying the beach. Everything was wonderful until *he* showed up."

Helen, of all people, would understand Celia's concern. Beverly was young and naïve, and understandably curious about men, intrigued by romance.

"What worries you more?" Helen asked. "Beverly or Whispering Pines?"

Celia appreciated that Helen was taking her concerns seriously, and gave the question some thought. "Honestly, both."

The front door to the lodge swung open, catching Celia's eye.

"Oh, thank goodness. There you are, Celia," Mrs. Bell said from the open doorway. "Hello, Helen. Celia, it's Mr. Whitby. He's on the phone. He needs to talk to you immediately."

Stepping back toward her suitcase, Helen waved a greeting to Mrs. Bell. "Go. See what Preston has to say about all of this. I'll go get settled. We'll talk at dinner."

Celia nodded to her friend and ran toward the lodge.

Maybe Preston could clear this up for them.

* * *

Mrs. Bell had outdone herself with the evening's meal. The man Preston had hired to help with the maintenance-type tasks at the resort, things Danny and his father always handled in previous summers, caught plenty of fresh walleye to help feed the resort's guests. Mrs. Bell prepared the catch with a light crust and almonds, serving green beans and wild strawberries on the side.

But even the delicious food wasn't enough to settle the unease in Celia's stomach.

As expected, Preston's shock over his son's unexpected arrival at Whispering Pines had matched her own. He'd told Celia that he'd already talked with Tripp when he called; Preston had explained to his son that he had faith in Celia's ability to manage the resort's business affairs.

"I assured him you have things under control and he should focus on healing," Preston had said. He'd then asked for her honest assessment of the extent of Tripp's injuries. She'd shared what little she knew—all based on observation, since Tripp refused to discuss any of it with her.

"Celia, my son is a proud man. I know his arrival puts even more of a burden on you. Tripp can be . . . *difficult* . . . but you handle people well. Please be patient with him. I agree that you need to be the one to keep Whispering Pines going in my absence. He's struggling with his own issues right now."

Celia wondered if those issues extended beyond Tripp's war experience.

When she'd asked Preston when he might be back at Whispering Pines, he'd sighed. "She's bedridden and comatose, but alive. I'm not sure how long this will go on. My youngest is having a terrible time with it all. We won't be able to leave until after my wife passes. I'll keep you apprised. I know this is hard on Tripp, too . . ." Preston paused, then continued. "He misses his mother, though he'll never admit it. We all carry scars, Celia—some obvious, some hidden. Never forget that. And thank you again for being such a godsend this summer. I assure you I will reward your dedication."

She toyed with the delicious food on her plate. Her conversation with Preston hadn't soothed her jangled nerves in the slightest. In fact, it only served to reinforce the struggles she was likely to face over the next two months.

Her sister's laughter pulled her attention back to the dinner table.

She and Beverly sat with Helen, her parents, and Tripp. Mr. Nielle was questioning Tripp about general things related to his time overseas, but veered away from any talk of actual battles or Tripp's specific injuries. Celia tuned in, finding herself fascinated. They all were. She supposed Helen's father was especially curious, given his own son was still over there. Celia worried about both Danny and Leo. How much longer could this go on? Would they both make it home? And if they did, would they also suffer physical and emotional scars?

Eventually, Helen's mother insisted they discuss something more uplifting. Celia suspected the table talk had to be killing her inside. Despite Mrs. Nielle's many faults, she loved her children.

Celia glanced around at the half dozen tables in the lodge's dining area, taking in the smiling faces and soft conversations, evidence of how much their guests were enjoying their stay. It made it hard to believe a bloody war raged in another part of the world, but one look in Tripp's direction, where he'd pushed back from the table and rested his injured arm in his lap while visiting with Beverly, was a grim reminder of reality.

She didn't like the way her sister was hanging on Tripp's every word.

The crash of glass and metal, coming from the kitchen, tore Celia's eyes away from her sister and brought her to her feet. "If you will all excuse me, I'll see if Mrs. Bell could use some help."

Hustling through the swinging kitchen door, Celia looked for Mrs. Bell and the source of the crash. The older woman was on her knees, cleaning up a mess of broken china and crumbled cake. A large silver tray, probably previously supporting the dessert plates stacked high with slices of chocolate cake, lay off to one side.

Hurrying over, Celia reached out a hand. "Here, get off the floor. Let me do that. Are you okay?"

Flustered, Mrs. Bell tittered about the mess she'd made.

"Don't worry about that," Celia insisted. "It's nothing a broom and dustpan can't handle. But I don't want you to cut yourself."

Nodding, Mrs. Bell accepted Celia's hand, slowly lifting one leg and bracing herself on her knee. "I'm so sorry. Look at this mess."

"Don't worry about that," she said again. "Here, sit down on this stool. Are you sure you're all right?"

Celia steered the woman over to the stool. A second chocolate cake sat, untouched, on the counter. There was still plenty for the guests. She'd dish out a new set of servings and deliver them to the tables while Mrs. Bell caught her breath. The mess could wait, as long as no one ventured too close to the sharp shards sticking up amongst the smears of thick chocolate frosting. It would take a mop, in addition to a broom, to clean it all up.

Taking a fresh knife from the utensil drawer, Celia quickly sectioned off the sheet cake so there would be a piece for everyone.

An envelope, sitting on the counter near the cake, caught her eye. Written across the front was Mrs. Bell's name, along with the Whispering Pines address. The handwriting was unmistakable.

She froze, the knife embedded in the cake.

"Mrs. Bell . . . what is that?" she asked, eyeing the envelope. She already knew it had to be from Danny.

"That's what has me so distracted. It's a letter. From Danny," Mrs. Bell replied, pointing. "My son. But, silly me, you know who Danny is."

"And is he . . . ?" Celia couldn't bring herself to finish the sentence, fear clenching deep in her gut. Thoughts of Tripp, with his mangled hand and scarred thigh, raced through her mind.

"If he's telling me the *whole* truth in that letter, then yes, he's fine."

Expelling a sigh of relief, Celia went back to her cake cutting, dying to know what was in the letter. "Do you hear from him often?" she asked, trying to sound nonchalant.

Stretching across the counter from her perch on the stool, Mrs. Bell scooped up the envelope. "Not nearly often enough. This is only the third letter in all this time. There was Whispering Pines correspondence in the mail for you today, too. It's in on Mr. Whitby's . . . I mean *your* desk."

She'd deal with the mail in the morning. All she cared about right now was Danny's letter. "Tell me . . . What did Danny have to say?"

With a sigh, Mrs. Bell got down off the stool and set the envelope near the refrigerator, out of the way. "Let me help you with that cake. At the rate you're going, our guests will be ready for breakfast before we get it out to them." Taking the knife from Celia, she pointed at another drawer. "Get one of those clean spatulas out."

Celia did as she was told and searched the drawer, ladles and spatulas clanging.

"I was wondering when you'd get around to asking me about Danny, child. Do you think a mother doesn't know when her son is smitten with a pretty girl?"

Spying a pie-shaped spatula that should work, Celia held it up in front of her, spinning back to face Mrs. Bell. "What do you mean?"

"Don't play coy with me, dear," the woman warned as she wagged her knife at Celia. A dollop of frosting flung off, landing with a plop on the countertop. She tried but failed to hold a stern expression. "I know you and Danny were sneaking around most of the time you were here last summer. The boy wasn't himself after you left. A little of his spark faded. But when he started talking about enlisting, to see if he could somehow work his way into reporting on the war, the spark was suddenly back. The opportunity excited him. It pained me to see him go, but it was what he wanted."

Celia handed the woman the spatula, caught her eye for a split second, and then turned to pull another stack of dessert plates from an upper cupboard. She placed a hand over her own heart after setting the plates next to the second cake. It was beating so hard, Celia worried Mrs. Bell would hear it.

"He mentioned you this time," the woman offered. "He asked if you'd come back this year, to Whispering Pines. I'll write him back, but it can sometimes take months for my letters to reach him, if ever. I'd told him about Mr. Preston having to leave, but our correspondence must have crossed. His letters are brief. My Danny would much rather talk through pictures than words."

Celia laughed. That sounded like the Danny she knew. "Did he send pictures?"

"Oh, no. But it sounds like he is getting the chance to document some things with a camera. Nothing official yet, but he's optimistic."

Celia thought about the camera Danny had left in her care. She'd brought it back to Whispering Pines with her, just as she brought it everywhere, but it was still tucked deep inside her suitcase.

Helping Mrs. Bell plate the dessert, Celia was hungry for more news, but the woman let the subject drop. Maybe, like Mrs. Nielle, talking about her son off at war was too difficult. Celia knew how gut-wrenching it was for herself; she could only imagine how a mother would feel.

She retrieved the silver platter from the floor and stacked plates on it again, offering to serve the dessert herself. Mrs. Bell, now sporting a large smudge of chocolate on her normally pristine apron, looked relieved.

"And leave that," Celia said, nodding to the mess on the floor. "I'll clean it up in a minute."

Making her way back out to the dining area, she hoped now that they'd had an initial discussion about Danny, she'd be able to talk to Mrs. Bell about him more. Scanning the tables, she could see most of the guests remained, relaxing after the main course. But one glance at the table she'd eaten at earlier revealed, in addition to her own, two open spots.

Celia bit her lip. She hurriedly handed cake to those who wanted it, exchanging dessert plates for the guests' empty dinner plates. Her tray got heavier as she went. She wished, not for the first time, that they could afford to hire dining room help.

When she finally reached their table, she snagged her friend's eye. "Helen, where did Tripp and Beverly disappear to?" She hoped Helen's parents wouldn't notice her clenched teeth.

Helen's expression revealed a shared concern. "I stepped away to use the bathroom, and when I returned they'd left. Mother said Beverly complained of a headache and Tripp graciously offered to escort her back to your cabin."

Celia nearly groaned out loud, forcing herself not to grill Helen on why she hadn't gone after them. Her friend's parents likely saw Tripp's response as completely appropriate.

Celia quickly served the Nielles their dessert but declined to join them, explaining that Mrs. Bell needed a hand in the kitchen. Hurrying back, she attacked the mess on the floor while the other woman started in on washing the dishes. All Celia really wanted to do was run out the back door and find her sister—but she couldn't leave Mrs. Bell to clean up the cake and china mess alone.

Beverly is fine. I have to trust her. What could possibly happen in the ten minutes it'll take me to clean this up?

Her internal pep talk did little to settle Celia's concern over her sister's welfare.

Is this how parents feel when their daughter goes out on her very first date with a boy? Unfortunately, Tripp is no boy.

Celia forced herself to focus on the task at hand or risk slicing a finger. Mrs. Bell needed her help tonight. It was an enormous job to serve these groups of diners each evening, not to mention keeping lighter fare available throughout the day. Celia wasn't sure how Mrs. Bell did it.

But Celia remained distracted, her mind conjuring up all the inappropriate things Tripp might do with her naïve sister. She needed to finish and go find them.

"Heavens, girl, what has you so uptight?" Mrs. Bell asked, wiping her brow. "Was it our talk about Danny? I'm worried about him, too, but we have to keep the faith."

Celia shook her head as she dumped a dustpan full of slivered china and cake crumbs into the large garbage can. "Honestly, it relieves me to hear he's doing all right. It's been weighing on me, but I didn't feel comfortable coming out and asking. I'm not sure why."

"I understand," Mrs. Bell said, plunging her hands into the soapy water again. "If it's not about the letter, what is it? You're wound up tight as a watch."

Celia debated how much to confide in Mrs. Bell about her concerns over Tripp. It would certainly be nice to have another ally. "It's my sister. She complained of a headache. Tripp offered to walk her home."

"Ahh . . . yes. Tell me, is it the headache or the escort, then, that has you concerned?"

Dropping to her hands and knees, Celia used a wet cloth to finish cleaning the floor. A mop would have worked better, but that would take too much time. "Honestly? Both. Beverly was born with a weak heart, so we're careful where she's concerned. But Tripp . . . I don't know . . . he makes me nervous."

Mrs. Bell turned to face her, wiping her dripping hands on a dish-towel. "Nervous how?"

Celia finished scrubbing the floor, allowing herself a few seconds to figure out how to best articulate her thoughts. She stood and shook her rag off over the garbage then tossed it in the basket for soiled linens, turning to face Mrs. Bell again.

"I'm not exactly sure. But there's something about him . . . some-thing, I don't know, unsettled, maybe? I noticed it before, that first summer. Maybe it's his eyes. The way they look at you. And now that he's back, he's even more intense. When he looks at me, I feel funny. Almost like he's a hunter and we're all the prey."

Her concern mostly stemmed from what Helen had shared with her about Tripp, of course, but she'd never betray that confidence.

"Does he ever make you feel like that?" she asked Mrs. Bell, holding the older woman's gaze, hoping for guidance.

Mrs. Bell sighed. "I never like to speak ill of anyone, and Mr. Tripp, he's sacrificed a lot, fighting for our country like he did. And Mr. Preston has been *so* good to us," the woman said, seeming to struggle to keep a balance between loyalty to Tripp's family and being open with Celia. "But . . . it's not a bad idea to keep a closer eye on your sister. Men like Tripp, with their good looks and deep pockets, they can sometimes turn the heads of young women more easily than we'd prefer."

Celia nodded, understanding what Mrs. Bell said . . . and didn't say. She sensed the woman harbored reservations about Tripp, too.

And Beverly was alone with Tripp at that very minute.

Celia took one last glance around the kitchen. "I hate to leave you with all these dishes, but would you mind if I went to check on my sister? I can come back after I'm sure she's settled."

Waving away Celia's offer, Mrs. Bell turned back to the pile of dirty dishes. "Don't be silly. I've got this. Won't take me more than an hour and I'll be back at the duplex, enjoying a hot bath and a delightful book. Go. I'll see you bright and early tomorrow morning."

Celia doubted the woman would be done in an hour, but her

concern for her sister overpowered her desire to help in the kitchen. "Thank you for understanding."

Mrs. Bell picked up another stack of dishes from Celia's cake tray and set them into her hot, soapy water. "Get a move on, girl. It's getting dark out there, and Tripp was away fighting for a long time. Don't give him a chance to give in to any temptations he may have harbored."

Hating that Mrs. Bell was likely spot-on with her concerns, Celia rushed out of the kitchen through the back door, into the deepening dusk. She paused, giving her eyes a second to adjust. The air felt thick with heat and humidity—even worse than inside the kitchen. A storm was brewing.

Celia jumped at the hoot of an owl; the cry echoed through the still night.

She hurried toward their cabin. She desperately hoped she'd find her sister stowed safely inside, preparing to turn in early in deference to her headache, with Tripp long gone. A flash of lightning off in the distance illuminated the tops of the tall pines lining her path. As she approached their cabin, its dark windows concerned her. She rushed up the stairs and through the front door, snapping on the lamp. She didn't need to walk through the tiny cabin to know it was empty. It *felt* empty.

Beverly wasn't back yet.

A rumble of thunder filled Celia with dread.

"Don't overreact," she counseled, the warning echoing through the empty cabin. Beverly was an adult.

Kind of.

She *was* an adult. And more importantly, she wasn't stupid.

Celia needed to think. Where could they have gone?

Another flash of light, chased by more thunder, meant the storm was getting closer. The beach would have been an obvious choice for an evening stroll, if the weather weren't so threatening. Celia knew Danny and Preston had completed the duplex on the edge of the property, and Tripp was staying on one side while Mrs. Bell lived in the other. Would he have taken Beverly there, under the guise of showing her the recent addition to the resort?

Spurred on by a sense of urgency, Celia grabbed the flashlight she'd stowed under the kitchen sink, kicked off her low heels, and shoved her feet into Beverly's tennis shoes, discarded by the door. Rushing outside, she hurried toward the duplex, trusting but dreading the feel in her gut.

She groaned as her flashlight flickered off. The batteries must be weak.

As she jogged around the curve in the path where it skirted around two broad trees, she slammed into a warm body. Her hands shot out, dropping her flashlight and grasping the arms of the other person. By a stroke of luck, neither of them tumbled at the impact, and the flashlight flared back to life again in its tumble.

Celia knew in an instant she'd found her sister.

"Whoa, is everyone all right?" came the deep timbre of Tripp's voice. He stooped down and collected the flashlight.

The beam stung Celia's eyes, temporarily blinding her.

"Celia?! What are you doing?" Beverly cried out. "Are you crazy? You almost knocked me over!"

"What am *I* doing?" Celia shot back, her system overwrought with jumbled feelings of dread and relief. "What are *you* doing? Wandering around out here in the dark when a storm is coming? Tripp, quit shining that light in my face!"

The blinding light swung away, creating a pool of light around their feet. "Sorry," he muttered.

"You scared me," Celia bit out, hating to admit it.

"Scared you? Why?" Beverly asked, the irritation so quickly gone from her tone. "Tripp was nice enough to offer to walk me home when my head began to throb, and you were busy in the kitchen."

Celia hesitated. *Had* she overreacted?

"But this isn't the path to our cabin, Beverly," she pointed out, still unsure what to make of it all.

The flashlight blinked off again. Tripp shook it.

"I know that, Celia. Jeez, I'm not dumb. Tripp was telling me about the new building his father had built, and he offered to show it to me. We were going to go back there, but as soon as it thundered, he insisted we turn right around. He wanted to see me home before the rain started."

If what Beverly claimed was true, it stood in stark contrast to the vivid images Celia had conjured up in her own mind of Tripp's nefarious motives. Bev made him sound like the perfect gentleman.

"Well, I'm here now, and it's starting to rain," Celia said, glancing up when a big raindrop plopped onto her nose. "We'll be fine, Tripp. Thank you for escorting my sister. You better head back home or you'll get wet."

She held her hand out to Tripp for her flashlight, and when he handed the barrel to her, the beam glanced off his face. Did she only imagine a self-serving smirk there, before the beam angled away, lighting up the trees to their right?

"If you're sure you'll be all right, I'll bid you both goodnight then. Hurry on back to your cabin. The wind is picking up, too. And Celia, be responsible and replace the batteries in that flashlight. I'll see you both tomorrow."

With that, he left them, the clacking sound of his shoes on the paved walkway punctuating his retreat into the darkness.

Beverly grabbed Celia's arm, turning her toward their cabin. "You really have to stop treating me like a child, Celia. Do you know you interrupted a perfectly romantic walk? How am I ever going to write about love if I never get to *experience* it?"

That was when Celia knew she'd been right to hurry to her sister's side. She doubted Tripp was interested in the same type of "romance" Beverly had in mind. She opened her mouth to lecture the younger woman, but then snapped it shut. Warnings might drive Beverly straight into Tripp's arms.

Celia would need to find a better way. All she had to do was keep Beverly away from Tripp for the rest of the summer, and everything would be fine.

She had her work cut out for her.

CHAPTER FIFTEEN
GIFT OF SISTERLY CONCERN

*C*elia missed absolutely everything about her previous summers at Whispering Pines. She'd felt a sense of freedom while staying in the tiny cabin with Ruby, and other than helping Preston in the office, her time had been her own. There had been few responsibilities. Now, Helen was her only girlfriend at the resort, and with Danny gone, she split her time between work and keeping Beverly away from Tripp.

She should have recognized those earlier summers for the special transition periods that they were: a time of magical possibilities, free from worry, for both her and her friends. Adulthood brought new layers of responsibility.

Poor Eleanor hadn't gotten enough time away from the factory floor to make the trip to Whispering Pines, and still she waited for news of the potential death of her estranged mother. Ruby was taking care of her ailing grandmother, an eccentric old geezer who acted as though she cared more for her cat than her own granddaughter. Worst of all, Celia worried, were the horrors of war that Danny and Leo were surely facing. Interacting with Tripp was a daily reminder of what was at stake for so many young men.

As the weeks passed, Tripp's limp became less noticeable. He'd left the resort for a few days and returned with an artificial hand in place of the bandage. The prosthetic looked stiff, and he masked it with a glove. He refused to discuss his injuries or his recuperation with Celia.

She spent the first half of each day working in the office, during which she'd asked Helen to watch her sister. Beverly maintained her routine. She stayed up late writing in her journals, and usually slept in, but on those days when she left their cabin before Celia returned from the lodge, Helen tried to keep her occupied and out of trouble.

Tripp didn't act as if he felt the same sense of responsibility as Celia when it came to Whispering Pines. He'd stop in the office occasionally, boss Celia around, then leave to spend hours sitting quietly on the beach or back at the duplex. Sometimes she didn't know where he'd disappeared to. But as long as Tripp stayed away from her vulnerable younger sister, Celia didn't care where he went.

By late July, it wasn't looking like Preston would be back for any part of the summer. His wife lingered, clinging to life. They, all of them, were in limbo. Waiting for loved ones to return. Waiting for others to die. Waiting for life to get back to something that felt more normal.

Celia suspected she'd never again find those carefree days she'd relished the previous summers.

* * *

Helen had troubles of her own.

"Do you think it's because she's worried about Leo?" Celia asked her friend as they strolled along the main walkway that crossed through the heart of Whispering Pines. She felt bad that Helen was feeling smothered by so much time spent with her parents. Her mother insisted Helen spend her time socializing with the elite at both Whispering Pines and the larger Grand View Lodge resort.

Helen shrugged. "Without a doubt. She constantly brags about his exploits on the battlefield. I'm sure the other women are tired of hearing about him. Some of them have sons over there, too. Since

Leo's a pilot, and his name has made it into the newspapers a few times, she acts as if he's doing so much more than anyone else. But I've also overheard her crying in bed at night. She's sick with worry."

Celia thought back to the quiet times she'd spent fishing with Leo on the dock that first summer. He was so mild-mannered, so kind. She struggled to reconcile the memories of her friend with the image of a battle-worn man. Would he be hard and jaded when he returned, like Tripp? She'd read stories of Leo's involvement in more than one major battle. Was it all propaganda, meant to sway support of the war efforts at home? Flashy pictures in the newspaper and the sensationalist headlines might not be a fair representation of what the soldiers faced—what *Leo* faced.

She'd have loved to discuss all this with Danny. The war coverage had fascinated him last summer. Was he the one taking pictures now, she'd often wondered, documenting actual stories behind the lines? She prayed Danny was holding cameras instead of guns. She'd heard that photographers were sometimes spared from the worst of the atrocities of war. Sometimes.

"I miss Eleanor and Ruby," Helen was saying, and Celia pulled her attention back to her friend. "It isn't the same without the four of us here."

"I've been thinking the same thing," Celia admitted. "This summer feels so different. We haven't even gone to a single dance. And when we get back to school, it'll be our last year. Have you made any plans yet? For after graduation, I mean."

Helen snorted. "If Mother has her way, I'll marry by the end of next June." There was a hard edge to her tone.

"But, Helen, is that what *you* want? Whatever happened to your dream of going to Paris to be a fashion designer? Remember our picnic during our first summer out here, when you said that was your dream?"

Laughing, Helen clasped her hands behind her back. "Those were mere musings of a silly young woman."

Celia hated when Helen talked like that. "Now you sound like your mother. Are you still drawing?"

Ducking off the path, Helen wandered over to a sunny patch in the grass and sat down, leaning back on her hands. Celia followed.

"No. I left my sketchbooks at school when I moved home this spring. I regret it now, but it would have made Mother even more anxious if she caught me drawing. It wasn't worth the hassle. Besides, I suppose she's right. It's silly to think I can do anything other than marry and start a family after college. I enjoy the finer things in life. I'll never have those things unless I marry rich."

Celia plucked a long blade of grass from near her feet, wrapping it around her finger in contemplation. They'd had this discussion many times through the years. She'd hoped college might awaken Helen to more possibilities, other avenues, but her mother's influence was clearly still too strong.

"You know I want more for you out of life," Celia reminded her friend.

Helen collapsed onto her back, draping an arm over her eyes. "I hate it when you do that."

"Do what?"

"Take that tone with me, Celia. Why are you so intent on carving a different path for yourself? And why do you feel it's your duty to drag all of us along with you?"

The bitterness in Helen's words caught Celia by surprise. But she supposed it was a fair question.

"I'm not sure," she admitted, settling onto her back next to Helen. She took a deep breath, noting the crisp smell of freshly cut grass, the blades under her prickly. "I suppose it's because I never want to find myself in my mother's shoes. You can't understand how terrifying it is to live in a nice house but have no food for the table. We were practically destitute."

Helen let her arm drop to the grass above her head. "Why do you think Mother insists I marry into money? Seriously though, Celia, those were terrible times for everyone."

"Not for your family," Celia pointed out.

"You don't know that."

"Did you ever wonder where your next meal would come from?" Celia challenged.

"Well, no, but I remember how worried my daddy was. I don't think we'll ever see the economy fall to pieces like it did back then."

Celia tracked a fluffy white cloud as it scudded lazily across the sky. She sighed, not feeling the same level of confidence in the economy as Helen. And she didn't want to give up on her friend. Or rather, she didn't want Helen to give up on her own dreams. She opened her mouth to argue her point, but a flash of red on the walkway caught her eye.

"I hope she's just going to get coffee and fruit from the lodge for breakfast."

"Who?" Helen asked, scanning the area.

"I just saw Beverly on the path. She put on her red sundress this morning."

Helen crossed her legs. "I can't hold a candle to your sister in the wardrobe department this summer. Does she *ever* wear anything but dresses? I don't remember her taking so much time with her appearance back home."

Celia sat up, pulling her knees to her chest. Since she wasn't working, she'd opted for soft cotton shorts that morning. "Beverly has always worn dresses when she's not at home. Even when we were little. When Mother was running the boardinghouse, she'd play dress-up with the women's cast-offs. She didn't care that they were too threadbare to salvage. She said dresses made her feel like a princess."

Helen shuddered. "She wore other people's clothes? How awful."

Glancing sideways at her friend, Celia shook her head. Helen couldn't understand how terrifying true poverty felt. Worry may have plagued her father during the darkest days of the early thirties, but Celia's mother nearly wound up on the streets with her young daughters, without so much as a roof over their heads. Maybe if Helen had experienced a bone-deep fear like that, she wouldn't have been such a snob.

Celia hoped the poverty she'd endured had given her a sense of empathy for others. She didn't ever want to be blind to the pain and despair that came from not having enough to eat.

"Where'd she go, then?" Helen asked.

"Beverly? I'm not sure. I better go find her. If she was heading for the lodge, she'd have come by us by now."

"Come on. Let's go see," Helen suggested, jumping to her feet and brushing the grass off the seat of her pedal pushers. "Maybe she snuck off to see Tripp again."

Celia's heart leapt at the suggestion. It had been a close call when Tripp slipped out with Beverly after the walleye dinner to walk her home, but she hadn't caught them spending time together since. She'd tried to convince herself there was nothing to worry about, that Beverly would heed her warning. Had she been wrong?

"Don't even joke about that. But you're right. We should make sure that's not where she's going."

"She might have been heading over to that new building you told me about. Isn't that where Tripp is living now?"

The thought of Beverly alone in the duplex with Tripp terrified Celia. Her sister was gullible and desperate for her naïve idea of romance. Tripp might not have any qualms about taking advantage of her.

Celia worried Helen was right. She rushed toward the path.

"Celia!" Helen hissed, catching her by the elbow. "Slow down! We don't even know if she's back there. And if she is, she might be helping Mrs. Bell with something. She lives back there, too, right? Just because Tripp can be sneaky doesn't mean *Beverly* is."

Celia considered Helen's words, slowing. If they were wrong, and her sister was simply out for a morning stroll—or there was any other explanation other than Tripp—Beverly would see right through any excuse Celia might offer for running down the path in her direction.

"You're right. But we still need to hurry."

Rounding the curve just past the lodge, Celia and Helen approached the duplex more slowly now, their soft-soled shoes soundless on the path. The front of the duplex came into view. Celia wondered if Danny saw the building through to completion, or if he'd gone off to war before. Had he smiled at the bright red paint someone had used on the two doors? The contrast between the color of the doors and the yellow siding made her smile.

Slipping behind the enormous tree that pushed the path to the right, she pulled Helen with her.

Helen giggled. "I feel like a *spy*."

"*Shhh!* Can you see her?" Celia asked, peeking out from behind the tree.

"There!" Helen pointed.

Celia's heart sank as she watched her sister climb the front stairs of the duplex. Her first instinct was to run to her side, but Helen grabbed her arm.

"Wait. See what happens first. We don't want to embarrass her if it's nothing. You can't treat her like she's ten, you know."

Celia begrudgingly stayed put. Helen was right: she had to give Beverly a little credit. She hoped this wasn't a clandestine meeting on a hot summer morning, away from prying eyes. But Beverly would kill her if she embarrassed her again.

"Fine," Celia bit out. "But one wrong move and I'm done waiting."

"Fair enough."

Celia watched intently as Beverly stepped up to the right-side door and knocked.

Her muscles tightened, ready to spring.

Beverly waited, then knocked again.

"If that's Tripp's side, maybe he's not home," Helen whispered. "Or he's still asleep. It's only nine, and I doubt he's an early riser."

But still Beverly waited. Did she know for a fact he was home? Was that why she hadn't turned around and left when he didn't immediately answer the door?

A crow squawked, high in the tree above Celia's and Helen's heads.

"I think he's scolding us for spying on your sister," Helen whispered, her words tinged with laughter.

"Or he's warning us she's in danger." Glancing up, Celia found the large black bird amongst the pine branches. It tilted its head down at her, squawked one more time, then flew off, its wings batting heavily at the air.

"Look!" Helen whispered, pointing. The red door swung inward. Even from their hiding spot, they could see Beverly fidgeting, her pretty red skirt, a shade brighter than the door, swirling slightly around her knees. She was either nervous or flirting—Celia wasn't sure which.

"Wait to see what they do."

Celia followed Helen's advice, but stood poised to bolt. There was no way Beverly was going into that unit alone with Tripp.

They were talking, but their voices didn't carry. Beverly stepped back and Tripp came out to stand on the small porch next to her. He pulled the door closed behind him, and Celia expelled a sigh of relief. Tripp wore beach clothes. Since it was Saturday, this wasn't unreasonable. Celia wasn't working either—unless you count spying on your eighteen-year-old sister work.

"What are they doing?" Helen whispered.

Celia shrugged. "Don't know."

As they watched, the two on the porch strolled over to the top step and sat down. They were still talking, and while Celia couldn't hear the words, Beverly appeared calm. Maybe she'd overreacted. It wasn't a terrible thing for Beverly to be friends with a man. She might even welcome the idea, if the man she was sitting next to weren't Tripp.

Had Celia been too quick to judge Tripp? He'd been through trauma of his own. But when Helen bumped into her arm as they both tried to stay hidden behind the tree, Celia remembered what Tripp had done to her once innocent friend. He'd lacked scruples before the war. Had the war made him even more dangerous?

"She's handing him something," Helen reported.

Celia nearly giggled then, despite her nerves. Helen was enjoying their spying. Suddenly, she wondered if Helen might be jealous. Celia had never doubted the story her friend had shared with her in confidence, but she hadn't considered the possibility that Helen might have feelings for Tripp. Feelings other than hate.

Glancing at the couple, Celia could see Tripp reading something Beverly had handed to him. A sheet or two of paper, maybe.

"She spends most nights writing, long after I go to bed. Maybe she wrote him a story," Celia suggested. "Or a poem."

Helen made a gagging sound. "I doubt Tripp would appreciate poetry."

Either her friend was a fabulous actress or she truly held only contempt for Tripp. She'd never known Helen to fake anything, so she suspected she was wrong and there was no jealousy on Helen's part.

The two on the porch sat side by side, conversing for a while longer, and then Beverly stood. Tripp remained seated, catching her right hand and bringing it toward his face.

"Ew, did he just kiss her hand?!" Helen bit out in disgust.

"Shh!"

Celia watched her little sister skip back down the stairs, her face glowing. She had to admit the gesture looked innocent enough—romantic, even. The fact Tripp had remained on the porch with Beverly, sat with her, and then given her nothing more than a chaste kiss goodbye . . . it certainly had Celia wondering. No one was around —at least as far as Tripp knew—and he could have just as easily swept her inexperienced sister inside. But he didn't.

As Beverly neared their hiding spot, Celia pressed up against the far side of the tree, holding a finger to her lips. She prayed Helen wouldn't give away their hiding spot.

She needn't have worried that her sister would see her. Beverly skipped right past them, lost in her own little world, the hint of a smile on her face, one hand on her chest.

Celia's own heart skipped a beat. Beverly usually rubbed her chest when her heartbeat fluctuated. It was often the first sign of trouble—something her sister might not notice immediately. Was her habitual gesture now because of complications with her weakened heart or something entirely different?

As the red of Beverly's skirt disappeared from view, Celia glanced back toward the porch. Tripp stood slowly, using his good hand to hoist himself up. Then, to Celia's dismay, he raised his gloved hand in their direction, flashing a knowing smile at them.

"That bastard!" Helen spat. "He knew we were watching."

Celia couldn't stop the shiver of apprehension that raced down her spine. She'd do well to remember that Tripp was not someone to trifle with, and Beverly needed to be more careful.

But how could Celia convince her?

* * *

"Are you glad you're spending the summer with me at Whispering Pines, Beverly?"

Her sister glanced up at her, smiling, as she pulled plates off a stack of dinnerware Celia held and placed them on the dining tables in the lodge. Mrs. Bell was sick, so Celia volunteered to get the room set for the evening meal. Beverly had been happy to help.

She probably hopes she'll run into Tripp.

"I am glad. Thank you again for inviting me," Beverly said, taking the last plate from Celia. "I'm only sorry you have to spend so much of your time working."

Celia retrieved a wooden box of silverware from a sideboard, balancing it against her hip. She placed forks, spoons, and a knife next to each plate, the proper order ingrained in her from a young age.

"I don't mind," Celia said. She noticed a large water spot on one spoon. Tossing it back into the box, she chose another. "Normally, I'd relax for the month of July. This way I get to stay for the *entire summer*, and I earn some much-needed cash. Besides, I still get some time to relax. It's hard to believe I only have a year of college left, and then I'll get a place of my own. I'll need money, and I don't want to have to ask Mother and Clarence for it. That wouldn't be fair to them."

This surprised Beverly. "You mean you aren't coming home after graduation? I guess I just assumed you would, until, you know . . ."

Celia followed her sister's train of thought, even though she stuttered through the last of it. "No, Beverly, I will not come perch at home until I find a man to marry and then move into a house with him."

"But why not? Isn't that what most women do?" Beverly asked, her tone innocent as she watched Celia place the silver.

Celia pulled out a nearby chair and set the box of silver upon it, items rattling around inside. She spun on Beverly.

"Do you truly think that's our only option, Beverly? I'm not spending four years of my life at college, just to find a man. A single mother raised us! You *know* women can be self-sufficient. Remember how Mother figured things out, after Daddy died but before Clarence came along?" Celia knew frustration was causing her voice to raise, but the lodge was empty.

Beverly crossed her arms, every bit as stubborn as her big sister. "Yes, it's true Mother raised us all by herself for a long time, but those were *hard* times—and *unavoidable* after we lost Daddy. You make it sound like things were so wonderful back then. That's not how *I* remember it. I recall going to bed with an empty stomach more times than not. And I *hated* giving up my room to share a bed with you and Mother just so she could rent my bedroom out to a total stranger. I never want to live like that again."

An antique English clock chimed the top of the hour from its perch on the ornate sideboard. There were three more tables to set, and they were running out of time. "I don't want to live like that either. Grab those plates." Celia scooped up a pile of linen napkins before turning her attention back to their discussion. "You think the answer is to rely on a man to take care of you? You saw firsthand how that turned out for Mother."

Beverly counted out another eight china plates from the stack on the sideboard and continued setting the tables. "That was different. There was an accident. That rarely happens. And besides, things got easier for Mother again once she married Clarence."

"I still don't think a woman should ever be completely reliant on a man," Celia argued, absently folding the linen napkins into fancy little cones and propping them up on the plates, exactly how Mrs. Bell had taught her. "Look how many women are fending for themselves now, with their husbands away at war."

"Aren't most of the soldiers single?" Beverly countered.

"Many, but not all. Look, Beverly . . . I just want what's best for you. You're different. Special. I never want anything bad to happen to you," Celia said, finally voicing the thing that was bothering her the most. Beverly's health was fragile, and if a man ever treated her poorly or left her without resources, she'd be more vulnerable than most. She'd much rather her sister had at least some skills of her own to fall back on.

"But what if I found the perfect man? Someone who would never leave me? Who understands me and all my quirks. What would be the harm in relying on him?" Beverly asked.

"Because, frankly, little sister, those types of men are few and far between. And," she added, "even perfect men can die unexpectantly."

Beverly didn't reply, instead picking up the last of the plates to finish setting the tables. Celia followed behind her with napkins and silverware, neither speaking as they considered the other's point of view.

"I'm short one plate. I'll be right back," Beverly said, disappearing into the kitchen.

The front door to the lodge opened and closed, the sound of uneven footsteps causing Celia's pulse to skip. Despite his efforts to hide his limp, she recognized the rhythm of Tripp's gait.

"Where's Mrs. Bell?" he demanded as entered the dining room.

"Hello to you, too, Tripp," she muttered, not feeling inclined to tell him Mrs. Bell was ill.

"Why are you setting the tables? I didn't know *that* was in your job description, too. Did you already rake the beach and mow the grass?"

Celia truly thought she'd be loving her summer at Whispering Pines if it weren't for Tripp. The man was so irritating.

"I'm giving Mrs. Bell a hand. What do you want with her?"

Celia was learning how to handle Tripp. He enjoyed riling her up, but if she didn't rise to the bait, he bored of her quickly. "That's none of your business. Is she in the kitchen?"

Without waiting for an answer, he brushed past her and disappeared behind the swinging doors.

"Wait, she's not in there," Celia cried, failing to stop him. She followed Tripp into the kitchen. The mouthwatering scent of roasting meat assailed her senses, along with the warmth of the ovens.

Beverly kneeled in front of a large cupboard in the corner, her back to the door. "Celia, I don't want you to worry about me. You need to trust in my ability to know when I've found a man who will take care of me. I'm not strong like you. I don't have as many options as you do."

Her sister clearly hadn't heard Tripp's voice. "Beverly, look who wandered in!" she said, loud enough to cut off her sister's ramblings.

She watched as Beverly glanced over her shoulder, her face registering surprise when she took in the man standing next to Celia. "Oh! Hello, Tripp. I didn't hear you come in."

Stepping forward, Tripp scanned the room. "What are you doing down on your hands and knees, Beverly? Is Mrs. Bell here?"

Beverly rocked back onto her heels and stood, smoothing her sundress into place. "No. Didn't Celia tell you? Mrs. Bell is feeling poorly. We're helping get the tables set up. She'll be in shortly to make the final preparations for dinner."

Tripp sent a questioning glance at Celia. She supposed she could have told him where the cook was, but he always brought out the worst in her. If she wasn't careful, she'd start acting as immature as Tripp.

"Let me help you," Tripp insisted. "What are you doing?"

Shaking her head, Beverly laid a hand on Tripp's forearm, the gesture far too familiar for Celia's liking. "I can manage. But thank you."

Beverly bent back down, pulled out a plate, then stood again. Tripp would have had trouble bending down like that, but Beverly's insistence saved him from embarrassment.

"All right then, Beverly. Will you do me the honor of saving me a seat next to you at dinner tonight? I feel like we've so much to talk about."

Beverly caught her lip between her teeth, looking between Tripp and her big sister. She was now painfully aware of the animosity between the two.

"I'm afraid that can't happen tonight, Tripp," Celia interjected. "Helen and her family have invited us to dine with them, and an acquaintance of Mr. Nielle is joining us. I'm sorry to say the table is full." Though she wasn't sorry in the slightest. "Perhaps another time."

"Since when?" Beverly asked.

Despite the flash of anger Celia caught in Tripp's eyes, he kept his mask of pleasantry in place and nodded. "That's a shame. I'm afraid we're running out of time to become better acquainted, Beverly. Perhaps tomorrow. Please be sure to let Mrs. Bell know I need to speak to her. I have a message for her. From my father."

And with that snub, Tripp breezed out of the kitchen, pointedly ignoring Celia. If he had a message from Preston, she wanted to know what it was. Had his wife, Tripp's mother, finally passed? But if that was the case, wouldn't Tripp be more upset? Unless he was that masterful at hiding his emotions.

"You see, Celia?" Beverly huffed. "Some men are good through and through. I'm not as naïve as you seem to think I am."

Throwing her hands up in defeat, Celia headed back to the dining room.

Had she ever been as headstrong as Beverly?

* * *

Celia's ploy to keep Beverly away from Tripp during dinner fell apart. Helen's parents had other plans for the evening, so when her friend showed up alone, Beverly was on to Celia.

"I can't understand why you don't want me to spend time with Tripp. He's perfectly nice! Besides, his family is wealthy. I could do worse than sitting next to a handsome, eligible bachelor for dinner. Is it because he lost his hand? Is that why you don't approve?"

"Of course not! How could you even suggest that?" Celia shot back.

"Beverly, you should listen to your sister. I've known Tripp most of my life. He has a dark side, a temper, he doesn't let everyone see," Helen said. "But trust me. It's there."

With an immature snort, Beverly picked up her fork and poked at the pasta on her plate. "You two are no fun at all."

That evening set the tone for the last few weeks of their summer at Whispering Pines. Undeterred, Tripp sat next to Beverly each evening at dinner. God only knew what they talked about. They kept their heads bowed close, their voices low.

Sometimes Helen and Celia sat with them, other times they shuffled the tables. Celia helped in the kitchen more often. Mrs. Bell never complained, but Celia could see she was struggling to get her strength back following a bout with a stomach ailment.

At last, a few days before she and Beverly would leave, Preston made it back to Whispering Pines. His wife had finally slipped away in her sleep, and since he'd had time to make all the arrangements before her death, he could return to his resort before summer's end.

Helen and her parents, having stayed nearly a month longer than they usually did, left for home. As Celia said goodbye to her friend in the parking lot, Helen caught her up in a hug and whispered in her ear.

"I think I've taken care of that little problem. I'll tell you everything when you get back to school. See you in a few weeks."

The lodge door opened and shut behind them while Helen hugged Celia. Celia waved as Helen climbed in the back of her father's car, then she noticed Tripp standing on the sidewalk, watching the Nielles' departure. He didn't acknowledge Celia. She wasn't even sure he saw her standing there, he stared so intently as the car drove away. Without a word, he turned and rounded the corner on the far side of the lodge, out of sight. His actions set little warning bells off for Celia. The animosity rolling off him had been palpable.

Behind her, the grating of a window caught her attention, and Preston's voice floated out to her.

"Celia, can you come in here for a moment, please?"

"Be right there," Celia called back, still watching as the taillights on Helen's family car disappeared around the bend.

What had her friend meant about taking care of a problem?

She'd have to wait to find out. She needed to update Preston on how the summer months had gone during his absence. And then she and Beverly would leave soon, too. Where had the summer gone? She hated for her time at Whispering Pines to end again. This time, she didn't know when she'd be back. With any luck, she'd head straight into employment somewhere following graduation next spring.

Would she ever again spend time at Whispering Pines?

EARLY SPRING 1945

CHAPTER SIXTEEN
GIFT FROM THE HEART

"I'm back!" Celia yelled.

She struggled to remove her muddied rain boots without making a mess inside the front door. That done, she inhaled deeply, appreciating the familiar scents of home. Where had nearly four years gone? She could hardly believe her time at college was nearing an end. She'd graduate in a month, and then she better get serious about finding a position somewhere. If not, she might find herself right back here on a more permanent basis.

She shook the water droplets from the umbrella—which had kept her only semidry in her dash from Helen's car to her front door—and stood it up in the corner to dry. She dropped her overnight bag onto the nearby bench, noticing suddenly how still the house felt. Normally, George or Gerry would come running to greet her. They'd probably both grown inches since she'd been home at Christmas. Boys did that at ages seven and four.

She hung her damp raincoat on an empty hook above the bench, fluffed her hair, and smoothed the skirt of her dress before wandering through the living and dining room areas in her stockinged feet. In the kitchen a large black kettle bubbled on the stovetop, steaming the glass on the windows. No one was there either.

"They can't be far," Celia muttered. Her mother would never leave food unattended on a hot stove.

A *thud* from above gave her a clue. It wasn't quite five in the afternoon yet, so Clarence was likely still working. Maybe her mother and siblings were upstairs, cleaning up after a busy day.

Whatever was boiling on the stovetop smelled good enough to make her stomach rumble. She pulled a ladle out of a nearby drawer for a sample taste, blowing on the broth so she wouldn't scorch her tongue.

"I'm sorry, honey, I didn't hear you come in!"

Celia jumped, spattering hot soup on the front of her pale green dress. Setting the ladle on the countertop, Celia grabbed a dishcloth from the sink. "Don't sneak up on me like that, Mother! Look what I did. I hope this'll come out . . ."

Dabbing at her soiled top, Celia turned toward her mother. She froze at the sight of her sallow complexion and rumpled clothing.

"What's wrong? Is it Beverly?"

Her mother's tired smile was fleeting and didn't reach her eyes.

"Mother. Tell me. Why is it so quiet in here? Where is everyone?"

Crossing the floor of the kitchen with her arms extended, Maggie pulled Celia into a welcoming hug. "I'm glad you're home. We'll have a nice Easter now."

Celia allowed her mother to hold her despite the fear coursing through her. Something was wrong, and Celia's instincts shouted *Beverly!*

For years, together, Celia and her mother had maneuvered the trials of Beverly's illness. Her sister had nearly died at birth, entering the world blue and lifeless. The midwife massaged the newborn back to life, but Beverly suffered all her life because of her weak heart. Given how well her sister felt during their summer at Whispering Pines, it had lulled Celia into a false sense of security.

"How bad is it?"

Still in an embrace, she felt her mother's chest quiver with a deep breath, and then the older woman stepped back, gripping Celia's upper arms. "It's been a tough couple of months, honey. The doctor has told us to keep her comfortable."

"No!" Celia cried. The anguish in her own voice cut through the quiet of the main level of the house. She shook off her mother's grip and ran for the stairs, taking them two at a time, her stockinged feet a whisper on the wooden treads.

The door to her brothers' shared room was shut tight. The thresholds to both her room and the master stood open, but Beverly's door was closed. Celia rushed forward, sliding past Beverly's door in her haste and grabbing the doorknob to slow her momentum. Taking a fortifying breath, she tapped softly. When there was no response, she tried one more time, fully intending to burst in if Beverly didn't speak up. But finally she did, her voice muffled.

"Mother, I told you, I just want to rest. Will you please leave me be so I'm ready for Celia when she gets home? I don't want her to worry about me!"

Celia felt an uptick of optimism at her sister's words, her tone suggesting annoyance versus terminal illness. But the second she opened the door and spied Beverly, propped up against the massive headboard with its heavy carvings that nearly reached the ceiling, her hopes plummeted. The stately bed always dwarfed her sister, but the contrast today was striking, as were the girl's sunken cheeks and the dark circles under her eyes. It didn't look like she'd combed her hair in days.

The room was hot enough to be positively stifling. A low fire crackled away in the fireplace, chasing away the dampness.

"Too late, sleepy head!" Celia said, plastering a smile on her face that hopefully masked the shock coursing through her system at her sister's sickly appearance. "I'm already home and it's nearly dinnertime. What are you still doing in bed? And why is it so stuffy in here?"

Making her way to one of the multipaned windows, Celia slid it open a crack to allow a small stream of fresh air into the room. The pitter-patter of the rain ebbed inside.

"I'm still in bed because I'm dying. At least that's what old Doc Reynolds says."

Plopping down on the side of the bed nearest the door, her knee brushing against Beverly's thin arm where it rested on top of the coverlet, Celia waved her sister's words away. "Beverly, we both know that old albatross has been saying that since the day you were born. He's a man of little faith when it comes to the resilience of us Middleton women."

Beverly lifted her arm and dropped her hand on Celia's stocking-covered knee. Even through the thin nylon of her opaque tights, Celia could feel the icy chill of her fingers. Her sister might as well have wrapped her cold fingers around Celia's heart, they chilled her so.

"I'm afraid he might finally be right this time," Beverly replied with a weak smile as she squeezed Celia's knee. "Much as I hate to oblige him, I can't seem to find the energy lately."

Celia looked away, hoping to hide the devastation she felt, staring instead at Beverly's rosary beads, dangling from the top of the ornate mirror on the vanity that matched the bed. The reflection of the beads made it look like two sets. Celia wondered if this was a sign it would take twice the prayers to bring Beverly back to health this time.

She dropped the banter. The seriousness of the situation was sinking in.

Clasping Beverly's icy fingers, Celia enveloped them within her warm palms. "How long has this been going on? Why didn't Mother call? I could have come home to help. I can't believe she kept me in the dark about this."

Pulling her hand back, Beverly boosted herself higher on the bed. "I told her not to."

Celia stood, expelling an exasperated sigh, and then she pulled the covers back to crawl in next to Beverly. While the bed sported an impressive headboard, it was narrow, making it a tight squeeze, even though Beverly appeared to have lost considerable weight.

"Why in heaven's name would you do that? Beverly, it's always been the two of us against the world!"

Beverly grinned, then bent in front of Celia to tuck the blanket tight under her sister's thigh. It reminded Celia of the many times she'd done the same for Beverly.

"Celia, you're a grownup now. Watching you take charge at Whispering Pines this summer taught me that. You have too much going on right now to worry about your silly little sister. You have your final exams soon, and then your college graduation. I figured we could manage here without you for a couple of months and then you'd be home. *Then* you can be at *my* beck and call, waiting on me—all day, every day."

Celia felt a spasm of doubt pass through her at Beverly's teasing words. She wasn't sure whether it was guilt because she hadn't intended to live at home after graduation, or if this stemmed from a darker fear. Celia sat quietly, letting her head rest on Beverly's bony shoulder. They sat like that for a time, each lost in their own thoughts. Celia noticed Beverly's shallow breathing even out, but couldn't tell if her sister had dozed off.

The sound of a door opening and closing down the hallway caught Celia's ear, followed by the scampering of feet. Two toe-headed boys peeked in through the crack in the door she'd neglected to shut when she'd entered Beverly's room.

"Hi, Celia!" Gerry whispered, nearly as loud as a shout. "Is Bevvy sleeping? Momma said we had to be quiet so she could nap."

George stepped around his big brother and pushed the door open. The creaking of its hinges reminded Celia of years gone by. "I don't get why Bevvy *wants* to take a nap. She's a big girl." He didn't bother to whisper.

Celia giggled at the four-year-old's slight lisp. Naturally, taking a nap voluntarily sounded atrocious to him.

Beverly sighed and raised her head from where she'd rested it against Celia's, smiling at the intrusion. "You two did great, entertaining yourselves and staying quiet. I would have sworn you'd gone to work with Clarence, it was so quiet in here."

George put his hands on his hips and puffed out his chest. "See, Gerry, I told you I wasn't being too noisy." Turning his attention back to his big sisters, he grinned. "Daddy isn't home from work yet, you silly girls."

Celia pretended to check the thin watch on her left wrist. "Well, would you look at that? You're right, George. But he'll be home any minute, and I bet you two haven't washed up for dinner yet. You better go wash your hands and then run downstairs to help Mother set the table. Hurry!"

Gerry grabbed George by the shoulder and tried to pull him toward the door. Little George angrily shook him off. "Just a minute, Gerr! Bevvy, can you come down to eat at the table tonight? I miss you. You never sit by me down there anymore, like you used to."

Celia's heart cracked at his earnest request.

"Scoot now," Celia instructed, waving them out the door, but softening her words with an encouraging smile.

"Okayyy," George said, shoving tiny hands into his pockets and leaving the room, head bowed.

"I hope you feel better, Bevvy," Gerry said. He caught Celia's eye as he turned to leave. She could see her own fear reflected in his.

Once the boys left, she turned her attention back to Beverly. "What do you say? Do you want me to help you get cleaned up for dinner and come downstairs? Or would you rather I bring a tray up to you?"

Beverly gave her the ghost of a shove. "First, get out of my bed. I'm too tired to come down tonight. I just need a brief nap, and tomorrow will be a better day. I'm sure of it, now that you're home. Go. Please. I'm tired of everyone fawning over me."

Celia rolled off her sister's bed, tucking the coverlet back under Beverly's left side. "Fine. I'll bring you a tray. And tomorrow, I'll help you bathe and set your hair. We need to look pretty in our Easter dresses on Sunday."

Beverly smiled then, motioning toward her vanity. "That reminds me. I have something for you. In the top drawer. Will you get it, please?"

"For me?" Celia asked, surprised. She did as Beverly asked, even though she could hear her mother downstairs, hollering for the boys to come set the table. It was nearly time to eat, and she wanted to get Beverly that tray.

Celia smiled at the framed family photograph perched on top of her sister's vanity. She remembered how badly the boys squirmed while sitting for the photographer at Christmastime. She hoped their mother had gifted her with a similar framed picture. Perhaps a matching one was waiting for her in her room.

Sliding open the shallow middle drawer, Celia grinned at the plethora of stubby pencils and loose papers inside. She shuffled her hand through the top layer. "What am I looking for? Did you write something for me?"

Beverly sat up taller in the bed, trying to see into the drawer. "No. I crocheted you something."

"Since when do you crochet?"

Beverly shrugged. "Since I asked Mother to show me how to do it. I had to find something to keep me busy in this bed. I couldn't write *all* the time. My brain gets too tired."

Celia glanced back at Beverly. She'd never heard her sister say she was too tired to write. Searching again, her hand fell on something soft, up against the left wall of the drawer. "Is it wrapped in satin?"

"Yes. Good, you found it! Don't unwrap it yet. Bring it over here, please. It probably needs an explanation."

Scooping up the compact bundle, Celia followed her sister's instructions, taking a seat again on the side of the bed and facing Beverly.

Taking the fabric-wrapped item, Beverly laid it atop the coverlet. "You may think these are silly, but hear me out. These past couple months have served as a painful reminder that, despite all our hopes and prayers, this old ticker of mine probably won't last much longer."

Celia moved to argue, but Beverly silenced her. "No. Hear me out. Let me say this, Celia. Even if I rally again, I've had to accept the fact that I may never grow old alongside you. I may not even live long enough to meet the children you'll have someday, and I'll surely never have babies of my own. I wanted to give you something for my future nephews or nieces. Turns out arguing with you about me finding the perfect man to marry was probably a moot point."

She picked up the bundle and unrolled the slippery white silk.

Celia gasped at the intricate set of crocheted baby booties resting in Beverly's hand.

"You *made* these?"

Beverly laughed then, seeming almost like her old self. "You don't have to sound quite so surprised."

Taking them from Beverly's outstretched palm, Celia ran a light finger over the pale blue yarn that rimmed the top and created a bow on the tiny white set. She could feel tears welling in her eyes.

"I plan to make you a pink set, too. These just took me longer than I expected, so I wanted to give you them now."

Celia could feel Beverly watching her closely. She was battling a wave of potent emotions over her sister's thoughtfulness—and the vast, nearly unimaginable implications behind the gift.

"Did I do good?" Bev asked, grinning sheepishly at Celia.

Celia leaned forward and hugged Beverly tight, giving up her fight against the tears. Beverly rubbed her back in comforting circles.

"All right. Enough of that now," Beverly announced, leaning back against the headboard again, dry-eyed. "I hear Clarence downstairs, and you know he doesn't like to wait for his dinner."

Celia straightened. "I'll bring you up a tray right away." She was still incredibly moved by Beverly's gift and felt at a loss for words.

"That's not necessary. You eat first, enjoy your time downstairs with the family," Beverly insisted, covering a yawn with her hand. "All this drama has worn me out. You don't need to rush right back up here."

Celia nodded and pushed off the bed, still clutching the booties. At the door, she turned back to her younger sister. "Thank you, Bev. They're perfect. I'll cherish them forever."

"Just don't let your baby poop on them and stain them. I worked hard on those," Bev chided as she crawled under the covers.

Her laughter followed Celia down the hallway.

Stopping for a second in her own room, she tucked the precious gift inside her girlhood jewelry box for safekeeping. Just as she'd hoped, next to the jewelry box a new family photograph sat waiting for her. Trailing one finger along the silver lines of the frame and then the chill glass covering Beverly's smiling image, Celia smiled back.

Keep the faith, she reminded herself.

She'd faced the possibility of her sister's mortality more than once through the years, and Beverly always rallied back. She'd do it again.

"Easter is a time for miracles," she whispered.

Feeling better, she skipped back down the staircase. Gone was the quiet that greeted her when she'd first arrived at the house. Clarence hugged her, reminding Celia that he wasn't nearly as gruff as he pretended to be, and George grabbed her by the hand to pull her toward the table, insisting she sit in Beverly's chair, right next to him. The seat Celia normally sat in remained empty, much as she supposed it had for the past four years.

She chatted with her parents and brothers throughout the light meal of chicken dumpling soup and early spring berries. The three adults exchanged concerned glances, but no one wanted to burden the boys by putting their worries into words at the dinner table.

When Celia moved to go prepare a tray, Clarence stopped her.

"Let me take her dinner up to her," he insisted. "I haven't popped in to say hello yet today. The boys are enjoying catching you up on things."

Clarence was right. Her brothers hadn't stopped talking long enough to eat their own dinners yet. She'd barely touched her own soup, her appetite deserting her after witnessing Beverly's condition. She remembered Beverly's high energy level and optimism while spending the previous summer with her at Whispering Pines. The contrast with the girl upstairs was striking.

Celia smiled at Clarence as he left the table to prepare Beverly's tray, then turned her attention back to her brothers.

George was still going into vivid detail, describing exactly what he was expecting the Easter Bunny to hide for them on Sunday morning. When Celia asked if the Bunny would bring her anything, both boys laughed and laughed like that was the funniest question ever.

The sound of crashing glass cut off their laughter. It sounded as if Clarence had dropped the entire tray of soup and berries on the floor.

A pregnant pause followed, stretching on for an interminable length of time, finally broken by Clarence's anguished cry.

"Margaret!"

CHAPTER SEVENTEEN
GIFT OF NEW AND OLD HEIRLOOMS

*C*onflicting emotions bombarded Celia as she gazed down on her sister's casket in the open grave. She'd survived their mother's gut-wrenching sobs during the solemn, ritualistic service at the church. Her stepfather kept Maggie from collapsing, physically holding her on her feet with a strong, steady arm. Celia suspected he dug deep for the fortitude to stand there respectfully, supporting his wife, given how he detested organized religion. He'd never attended a single church service with them in the past, claiming pompous men in clerical robes shouldn't dictate how he worshiped God. He attended now for his grieving family.

Celia remained dry-eyed, holding Gerry close as the young boy's eyes flitted between the casket, the priest who droned on about things unrelated to their beautiful sister, and to their distraught mother. It was all too much for a boy his age. They spared George from the ordeal, leaving him at home with a family friend. During the service, she'd searched for the words to help Gerry understand what was happening, but how do you possibly explain something you don't understand yourself?

Despite the ever lingering threat of death in the darkest corners of their home ever since Beverly's birth, Celia had steadfastly refused to acknowledge the possibility.

Her refusal had done nothing to alter reality.

The crowd was dispersing behind her, but she couldn't leave yet. Would the tears come now? Would they ever?

As she stared into the gaping black hole, she felt a deep rage instead of the grief she'd expected. Rage over the unfairness that George didn't get his Easter morning, rushing around the house to beat his big brother to the hidden eggs and chocolate. Rage over the fact that her mother had to bury her beautiful daughter. Rage that Beverly would never turn nineteen or have the chance to hold a baby of her own in her loving arms.

What is the point of it all?

Celia jumped at a light touch on her shoulder. Glancing back, she saw her dear friends, Ruby, Helen, and Eleanor, all gazing at her with pity.

Spinning to face them, she raised the black netting away from her face. It cascaded down from the black pillbox hat she'd pinned to her head that morning. Despite its elegance, the black ensemble was a bitter stand-in for the Easter bonnet she'd planned to wear. She struggled to focus on what they were saying. Worst of all, she fought her compulsion to yell at them for staring at her with so much pity.

"Celia, honey, people are leaving," Helen said. "Do you want to visit with any of them? Or can we take you home? It's been a terrible week. You look dead on your feet."

Ruby slapped Helen's arm over the insensitive comment. Celia felt a tugging at the corner of her mouth over the slip. Leave it to Helen to tell her she looked dead as she stood in a graveyard.

But she couldn't. Leaving meant Beverly would be all alone.

Is this how I'm supposed to feel?

It was all so terribly confusing.

Helen stepped forward, grabbing both of Celia's gloved hands in her own, the black silk that separated their fingers only adding to the surreal feeling. "Celia. Come on, girl. You can do this. You've nearly made it through the worst of it. Let us help you."

The worst of it? No—never, *ever* seeing Beverly again would be the worst of it.

"I can't," Celia whispered.

"You can't what, dear?" Helen asked, squeezing Celia's fingers even harder. "Because the Celia I know can do anything she puts her mind to. I understand how awful this must be for you. None of us can believe she's really gone. But you know she'd expect you to act the role of the proper big sister. Now, go thank people for coming, listen to the condolences they need to give you, and push through it. Think how brave Beverly was to live the way she did, getting up every morning without knowing if she'd see the sunset, and draw on that strength."

Helen's directive finally broke through the fog she'd been lost in for days. Nodding, she squeezed her friend's fingers then pulled out of Helen's grip. "You're right. I can do this. Mother needs me to be strong now." She turned to Eleanor, who'd made the long drive from Chicago along with her father and brother. "Thank you for coming, Eleanor. It means a lot."

Eleanor hugged her. "I'm sorry I never met Beverly. She sounds amazing. Why don't you come talk to Father for just a minute? I know he'd want to speak with you before we leave."

Celia allowed her friends to lead her away from the graveside, but a piece of her heart stayed behind. They slowly made their way over to the mourners cloistered around their vehicles, parked on the gravel ribbon of a road that wove through countless headstones. She spied her parent's automobile pulling away. Gerry locked eyes with her as he stared forlornly out the rear window.

"Your mother was feeling poorly," Ruby explained when she followed Celia's gaze. "I suggested she head home to lie down. I insisted we'd bring you home when you were ready. I didn't want you to feel rushed."

Eleanor's father pushed away from his Ford at their measured approach, somber in his black, custom-tailored suit. "My dear Celia, I'm so sorry. My condolences to you and your family. Your sister was a delightful young woman, and I'm honored to have met her this past summer."

Celia nodded at his well-meaning words, too emotionally drained to muster anything more than a thankful smile. She allowed Preston to pull her into a solicitous hug. Looking over her mentor's shoulder, her eyes snagged on Tripp. The man's jaw was clenched so tightly, Celia wondered if his teeth would crack. He stood with his arms crossed, one tucked up under his armpit in a gesture she'd become familiar with over the previous summer. His red-rimmed eyes pulled her toward him when Preston released her.

"Tripp."

He gave her one curt nod but maintained his standoffish posture, simply uttering, "I'm sorry for your loss."

"I appreciate you coming. You didn't have to do that," Celia said, and she started to turn away, Tripp's presence unsettling her.

He straightened and relaxed his stance, dropping his arms to his side. She tried not to look, but the motion drew her eyes to his left arm. He'd turned the sleeve of his black suit coat under, pinning it over the stump of his forearm. It was the first time she'd seen him without the stiff, artificial hand. He looked vulnerable, more human.

"Wait. Celia. You need to know that I couldn't stay away. Your sister was an amazing person. I'm not sure I would have survived last summer without her. I can hardly believe she's gone."

Celia paused, turning back to fully face Tripp again. His words captured the devastation she felt.

How could Beverly leave me? Forever?

It was as if he'd read her mind. She wondered again if she'd misjudged him. Someone who recognized the beauty of her sister's soul couldn't be all bad.

She'd watched Tripp so carefully during their time at Whispering Pines, convinced he was intent on deflowering her sister for sport. She'd never considered that Beverly was helping *him* heal from his devastating war wounds. But now it seemed so obvious: What else would Bev do but think of others over herself?

The man standing in front of her now had changed. He wasn't the cocky young boy who had come upon them as they swam naked in the woods that first summer.

"I wish I'd never listened to you, Helen," he spat out, pinning Celia's friend with a glare. "Maybe things would have turned out differently. But now I guess we'll never know, will we?"

And with that parting blow, Tripp spun away. He rounded the back corner of his father's automobile without a backward glance and climbed into the front seat. Celia stood there, unsure of what he'd meant.

Helen fidgeted beside her.

"Helen? What did he mean by that?"

But she shook her head. "I'll explain later. Now isn't the time."

"I hate to interrupt, ladies, but we have a long drive ahead of us yet, Eleanor, so we best be going," Preston said, placing a fatherly hand on Celia's shoulder.

She'd forgotten he was there.

The older man squeezed her shoulder and took a step toward his car, then paused. "Celia, dear, now is not the time or place, but I want you to know you've earned my eternal gratitude. I know you are finishing up at college. Please, take your time, but when you're ready, ring me up. I want to discuss your future with you."

Although any future without Beverly nearly brought Celia to her knees, she thanked Preston and his family again for coming and watched as they left the cemetery.

While she'd been visiting with the Whitbys, others had taken their leave. Perhaps she'd shirked her duties by failing to greet them all individually and thank them for coming, but she couldn't bring herself to care.

Now only Helen and Ruby remained.

"Can we take you home now?" Ruby asked, her voice calm and low.

Celia considered Ruby's beat-up sedan, its hood obscured by a grand headstone. A frigid gust of wind blew the netting of her hat back down over her face. "Can I take another minute with my sister first?"

Stepping back, Ruby nodded and motioned to Helen to follow her to her car. "Take all the time you need."

Appreciating the patience of her friends, Celia walked back to the deserted area flanking the still-open grave. She plucked a glorious ivory rose from a flower spray beside the grave, kissed the petals, and dropped the stem into the hole. The silky feel of the petals against her lips reminded her of the white satin wrap around Beverly's last gift to her. Had it only been four days since her sister gave her those precious baby booties? Four days since she'd come home?

Inhaling a ragged breath, Celia yanked the offending mourning hat from atop her skull, ignoring the pain as hairpins pulled at her hair.

"Beverly, I swore this day would never come . . . but you knew differently, didn't you, my dear sister? I don't think you ever feared your own death nearly as much as I did. But I promise you, Bev, as I stand here today, that I'll work hard to face life head-on, without fear, just as you've always done. You taught me that there is no room for fear. All it does is steal our joy. I'm going to make you proud, little sister. I'm going to live a life big enough for both of us."

The sigh of the wind was Celia's only answer.

If Beverly could see her now, she'd laugh and insist she stop being so dramatic, to crawl into her best friend's car and go home to check on their family. She'd tell her to get back to school, finish her final exams, and get on with her life.

So that's exactly what she'd do.

That advice Celia imagined Beverly giving her, as she'd stood over her grave on the day of her funeral, was so much more difficult to follow than Celia could have imagined.

It wasn't until she'd muscled her way through the rest of the week at home, sat stoically in Helen's vehicle for the drive back to St. Catherine's, and walked back into her stuffy dorm room, alone, that the tears finally hit. They gushed out of her like a broken dam.

Ruby studied in the library to allow her some privacy, and for the first time since Beverly died, no one was close enough to hear her sob into her pillow.

She cried for hours. She cried until she felt wrung out and empty.

She muddled her way through the last two weeks of her college career, ignoring the pitying looks her professors and fellow students shot her way. She couldn't bring herself to study for exams. What did they matter? She even considered skipping her college graduation ceremony, but she knew Beverly would have hated for her to do that. Knowing it was what her sister would have wanted, she stood with her class, flipped her tassel from the left to the right as she crossed the stage, and accepted her diploma. The only tears she shed came when a girl resembling Beverly accepted her diploma.

Poor Beverly never even had the chance to experience college life.

After that, Ruby entertained Celia's little brothers while Clarence and Maggie helped her move out of her dorm room. The day turned out to be tolerable, but it was void of the joy they all should have felt over Celia's accomplishment.

When she walked back into her childhood home again, her arms full of spare pillows and bedding, the atmosphere felt different. Empty somehow, even though everyone was home—everyone who could be. Trudging up the stairs, she turned directly into her bedroom, eyes downcast and purposefully avoiding Beverly's room farther down the hall.

Dropping the bedding from her dorm in a corner, she pulled off her lightweight sweater in deference to the warmth of the early summer afternoon.

Now what?

So much had changed since Easter.

She glanced around her bedroom, noting her favorite doll; she'd worn most of the hair off the doll's head, she'd played with it so often. A threadbare blanket, in a paler shade of blue than the summer sky outside, draped over the end of her bed. She'd rescued the blanket from the garbage once, after her mother claimed it was no longer fit for use.

It was the room of a child.

Her childhood was in the past. Beverly's death had whisked away any last remnants of childhood glee she might have felt.

A passing car honked on the street below. The sound drew Celia to her window. She slid the bottom sash open—much as she'd done on Beverly's final day in this house, to freshen Bev's stuffy room—and welcomed the soft breeze. A bird twittered on a branch nearby, its red plumage a stark contrast to the bright green leaves. A red cardinal, Celia mused, thinking how Gerry, their resident bird expert, would love spotting a bird like that.

As if her imagination conjured him up, the boy appeared in her doorway, knocking hesitantly.

"Hi, Celia . . . Can I talk to you about something? It's important."

She couldn't help but smile at his serious expression and careful pronunciation of the words. *This must be important,* she thought. "What's up?"

"Momma told me you're moving to . . . Chic—Chicker— Wait, where are you going?"

"Chicago."

"Right," he said, snapping his fingers. "Chicago! Momma said you're moving there in a few weeks and that it's a long way from here."

Celia chewed the inside of her lip. She'd been dreading this conversation. She couldn't help but feel she was abandoning her family when they needed her most. But she needed a fresh start. She couldn't live in this house now. Not after what happened.

"I am. Does it bother you I'm moving away?"

Gerry shrugged. "I kind of wish you weren't. But you haven't been here much, not since I was little. So I guess it'll be okay. You're a grownup."

Relieved, Celia prodded him. "Was there something you needed?"

He shuffled from foot to foot. "Kind of. I have a question for you. But you can say no if you want to."

Sweet Gerry, she thought. Never pushy. Not like younger George could be.

"I won't know until you ask me."

He nodded and scratched at the side of his jaw, his actions mirroring Clarence's when the man had something to discuss. She waited.

"Can I have your room?"

Celia blinked. "My room?"

"Yeah, can I move my stuff in here? I mean . . . not yet . . . but after you're gone? George is messy, and he won't keep his hands off my stuff, even though I tell him to. It would be nice to have a room of my own," he pleaded, looking around longingly. "I know Bevvy's room is empty, too, but . . ."

Celia nearly shuddered at the thought. She couldn't even bring herself to look toward her sister's room. She'd never expect Gerry to move in there.

"I'll tell you what," she said, tamping down her instinct to pick up the young boy and hold him like she used to. He was growing up and wouldn't have appreciated it. "As long as you promise you'll be okay sleeping with George when I come home for visits, you can have my room."

Throwing himself against Celia, her brother wrapped his arms around her waist and hugged her tight. The top of his head nearly reached her chin, surprising her. "Thank you, Cee-Cee," he mumbled into her shirt. "I can do that. I know you wouldn't want to sleep in Bevvy's bed either."

* * *

"Honey, will you come down in the basement with us for a moment?" Maggie asked, popping her head into Celia's room.

Sighing at another interruption, she tossed the skirt she'd been folding onto her bed, wondering if she'd ever finish packing in time to catch her train the next day.

Following her mother downstairs, however, her curiosity peaked. There wasn't much down there, just cold storage for her mother's preserves and an area Clarence had taken over as a small woodworking shop. He liked to putter. She'd noticed he'd spent more time in his shop since they'd lost Beverly.

The tang of freshly cut wood and paint fumes wafted out when Maggie pulled the basement door open.

"What did you want to show me, Mother?"

Motioning for Celia to continue down the stairs, her mother laughed—a sound Celia had missed over the past two months. "Be patient."

Lights were on down there, and she heard the tinny sound of the old radio Clarence always played while he did his woodworking. As they entered the shop area, Celia smiled at her stepfather, standing there with a goofy smile on his face.

"Happy graduation, dear," he said, stepping aside to reveal a wooden trunk, painted a glorious blue. The color reminded her of her favorite blanket, before umpteen washings had bleached away much of its color.

"Oh my goodness! It's so pretty! Did you make it?" she asked, awestruck at the notion.

"I did," he said, color blooming in his cheeks. Celia loved how easily he blushed. "Come around to this side. This is the front. It's called a hope chest. Your mother tells me girls like to save important things in these."

Doing as he asked, she came around to stand next to him. An intricate lock gave a decorative element to the piece. She loved the graceful simplicity of the trunk.

He turned the key that protruded from the lock and lifted the lid. A pungent, not unpleasant smell enveloped them, overpowering the lighter smell of cut wood. "All cedar-lined. Nothing beats it for storage."

Celia bent over to examine the variegated hues of red and brown in the cedar lining. "Even the inside is pretty!"

The trunk wasn't empty. White tissue paper covered whatever filled its bottom portion.

"If you'll excuse me, I'll run upstairs now, make sure the boys aren't destroying anything. I believe your mother has a few more things to show you."

Celia hugged him, a tear escaping down her cheek as she thanked him. She'd be forever grateful to this man who came into their lives and saved her family. He slipped away, and Maggie stepped forward, dropping to her knees in front of the trunk.

"I'm going to have to show you these quickly, and please excuse me if I seem to rush this, but I think you'll understand how difficult it is for me to talk about these things right now. Hopefully that will get easier with time."

Celia didn't need her mother to add that this was difficult because Beverly wasn't standing in the room with them, and she never would be again. If this was going to get emotional, Celia was all for making it quick.

Maggie pulled back the white tissue. There, on top, was an exquisite little dress of lace and ivory silk. There was something vaguely familiar about it.

"It's a christening gown. We baptized both you and your sister in it as newborns," Maggie explained. "Your father wore it, too. It's a family heirloom."

"You saved this for us?" Celia asked, her voice cracking on the last word.

Nodding, Maggie took it out of Celia's hands. "I did. Your little brothers never wore it. You know how Clarence feels about that kind of thing. Besides, it passed down through the Middleton family. I hope that someday your own children will wear it."

Biting back tears, Celia understood why Maggie had said this would be difficult.

"Beverly gave me a set of beautiful baby booties, too, with the same wish."

"I know she did, honey. Put those in here, too. For safekeeping. But wait, there's one more thing."

Celia turned her attention back to the next layer of white tissue. This time she pulled it back as her mother held the christening gown. More lace and silk, in an even brighter white, lay beneath. With a sigh,

Celia allowed herself the sensation of running her fingers over the creamy silk.

"Pull it out of there," her mother encouraged.

She didn't have to be told twice. Carefully removing the garment, she let the folds fall out of it. "It's a wedding gown," she said, the awe she was feeling coming through in her words. "Did you wear this when you married our father?"

Maggie laughed. "I did not. No one has worn this dress. Your father's mother had it made for you, before she died. You were only two, but she was very ill, and very rich, and she wanted you to have something special, even though she knew you'd never remember her. She hoped you would someday wear it as a bride."

Celia turned it around and held it up to her chest, imagining what she'd look like in something so spectacular. "She died before Beverly was born, didn't she?"

"She did. She had this made especially for you, honey."

"Does Clarence know?" she asked, feeling somehow unfaithful to her stepfather, allowing her mother to store the two beautiful gowns in the hope chest he'd made for Celia.

Maggie laughed. "He knows. And he approves. He's going to have to move it out of here, though. It's taking up too much room in his shop, and if he doesn't get started on a new project soon he may drive me crazy. It'll need to go into your bedroom."

Celia nodded, but then realized what that might mean. "But Mom, Gerry wants to move into my room after I move. There's no way I want him messing with these dresses!"

"He won't. He won't be able to open that lock. Your treasures will be safe inside. Just warn him to be careful not to damage the outside of the trunk. He'll listen to you. He doesn't want to lose the chance to move into your room."

Celia was still skeptical, but the only other alternative she could think of was putting it in Beverly's room. She didn't want to do that. It didn't feel right.

"Promise me you'll keep an eye on my trunk when I'm gone. And thank you. For all of this," Celia said, wrapping her arms around her mother.

I used to tell Mother to keep an eye on Beverly, she thought as she hugged her mother tight.

She loved the trunk and the dresses, but she couldn't wait to board that train.

She needed to get away, or she'd go mad with grief.

WHISPERING PINES
SUMMER 2019

*B*y the time Renee rounded the corner of the lodge, her sister was already sprinting to the water's edge.

A puff of smoke hung in the air above the old aluminum fishing boat floating three feet from shore. Nathan stood in waist-deep water behind the boat, while Robbie crouched inside, fiddling with the motor.

"What happened?" she yelled, shielding her eyes from the sun.

Nathan threw his hands up in frustration. "No idea! But I think this old motor might be toast!"

Jess yanked the front of the boat onto the sand, sending Robbie toppling over, upending an open tackle box.

Renee couldn't hold back a grin as she watched the mayhem from her perch beside the lodge. As the white smoke floated higher and dissipated, like a ghost at sunrise, she supposed she should worry about the cost of replacing a boat motor. Instead she felt a flood of relief that no one was hurt—unless Robbie strangled Jess for tipping him over.

Renee wouldn't be any help with the motor, so she headed inside to work on the stacks of photographs. Taking her seat again, she picked up the picture Robbie had commented on earlier. She doubted he and Nathan would catch a similar stringer of fish today, with the boat out of commission. There was a boat in the photograph, too, and Renee squinted, trying to make out the details. It wasn't the same one as had just given up the ghost. The one in the picture looked larger, but there was something else about that motor . . . Snatching up her reading glasses from the table, Renee studied the details.

"You don't suppose . . ." she whispered, wishing the photo wasn't black and white.

"You don't suppose what?" Jess asked, nearly causing Renee to drop the frame.

One hand on her racing heart, Renee looked up to see her sister standing in the doorway. "God, you scared me! Everything all right out there?"

Jess shrugged. "They're mad. Can't get the motor started again. Nathan mentioned calling Dad. He might have more luck. He loves tinkering on those old motors."

A glance at the clock on the kitchen stove confirmed Renee's suspicion: the boys wouldn't get in any fishing unless they waited until evening. The temperature would be ninety by midafternoon. Not exactly prime fishing weather.

"Speaking of old motors, look at this," Renee said, handing the photograph she'd been studying to Jess. "Is it the same one, you think?"

Jess squinted, holding the picture at various distances, then gave up, pointing at her sister's glasses.

"Welcome to the club," Renee laughed, handing her younger sister the readers.

Jess tried again. "Wow. You might be right. If the picture is from 1943, that means the motor is over seventy years old. Guess it doesn't owe us anything. The boat is different, though."

Setting the frame down but leaving Renee's glasses perched on the end of her nose, Jess scooped up the stack of photographs she'd dropped minutes earlier when the motor backfired. Renee watched her flip through them, the crease between her sister's eyes deepening.

"What are all of those?" she finally asked when she couldn't take the suspense any longer. "And why would someone put a bunch of photographs in one frame?"

Jess shrugged. "I think the top picture is of Celia with some friends. I recognize her. Believe it or not, someone penciled 1943 on the back of it, same as the one Robbie was looking at with the stringer of fish earlier. There must be a dozen pictures in this stack. Look at this one."

Renee took the picture then wiggled her fingers at Jess. "You really need to get your own pair."

"No, I don't. If I borrow yours, it means I don't really need them. It's like when Aunt Letty used to bum cigarettes off Celia. She claimed she wasn't *really* a smoker if she never bought them for herself. But seriously, Renee, do you recognize that?"

Renee shoved her glasses back on, examining the photograph. "Oh my God! Is that the sand bucket we found on the beach when we were kids? When Val or somebody got sand in their eye? It has to be!"

"I think it is. What are the odds?"

"Can I see the rest of those, please, or are you going to make me beg?" Renee asked.

Jess handed them over, then sank into her chair again. "It's quite the assortment. They're all black-and-white, all have the same year on the back."

Renee nodded, flipping through the stack. "I love these shots of Celia. This close-up where she's laughing, and the one on the end of the dock with the lake in the background. Why have we never thought to have a bonfire down on the beach? That would be so fun."

Jess started shuffling through the stacks of frames, nodding as Renee commented on the pictures she'd already looked through. "I didn't think the duplex was quite that old. And I wonder how long ago those white cabins came down. Now I'm curious if any of these other frames hold more than one photograph. Maybe we need to dismantle all these frames to see what we're dealing with if we want to figure out how to rearrange everything."

"I love this one!" Renee exclaimed, flashing the picture now on the top of the stack at her sister. "It's the same set of girls as the one by the car, but this one screams 'summer' to me. Couldn't you just see this on one of those vintage-looking signs, advertising old lake resorts? I see them on Pinterest all the time."

"That's my favorite, too," Jess agreed. "I—"

The slam of the screen door and her nephew's noisy entrance cut her off.

"That sucks," Robbie declared, heading straight for the refrigerator. He helped himself to a bottle of water and a bowl of grapes. "Guess we won't be earning our place on your Wall of Fame today."

"I'm sorry about that, Robbie," Renee offered. "I know you were looking forward to going out with Nathan. Maybe your grandfather or uncles can get it going again."

Robbie shrugged as he downed half the contents of his water, the plastic crackling as he squeezed the bottle. Then he moved on to the fruit, popping a red grape into his mouth. "Maybe," he agreed, talking out of the side of his mouth. "Nathan's on the phone with Grandpa now. It's so flippin' hot out there, we might have cooked in the boat if we'd gone out."

"Don't choke on that, Robbie."

"Mom, I'm not three."

"Well then, don't act like it. Even your little cousin doesn't talk with her mouth full."

Robbie grinned. "Yes, she does. You just can't understand what Harper's saying most of the time yet."

"What are we going to do with this mess, Renee?" Jess asked, pulling her attention back to the task at hand.

Renee considered the question. It *looked* like a big mess: mismatched frames spread out from one end of the twenty-foot table to the other. She sighed. "I think you're right—our best bet would be to take all the pictures out of the frames. Then we'll know exactly what we have to work with. We could put them in some kind of order, probably by date, and decide what goes back on the wall. We'll know how many matching frames to order that way. Plus, we'll want to add some newer pictures, like we talked about earlier."

"That probably would be best," Jess agreed. She lifted her dark, shoulder-length hair away from her neck and fanned herself. "Maybe Robbie's idea of a beer to cool off isn't so bad. It's getting hot in here. It might make this job less painful."

"What would your husband say if he heard you busting on the idea of spending time with these old pictures?"

Jess laughed. "It wouldn't surprise him. Maybe I should call him to come help. He'd get a kick out of this."

"I'm happy to offer my services for the low price of a beer or two," Robbie tossed in, but the sheepish grin on his face told Renee he knew there was zero chance she'd take him up on his offer. "No? All right then. I'm going to go see if Grandpa gave Nathan any suggestions on how to get that old hunk-of-junk motor started."

Robbie made a quick exit, leaving the bowl of grapes out. Renee shook her head. "How many times do we have to tell them?"

Jess laughed again, stood, and grabbed the bowl off the island, bringing it over to the table. She rearranged the stacks and set the bowl down between them. "Save your breath. And help yourself. Where do you want to start?"

Renee popped a grape in her mouth and ripped the backing off the closest frame, much as Jess had done before.

"Be sure to transfer any information on the back of these frames to the actual pictures," Jess said, searching between the stacks for a pen or pencil.

"Now you sound like your hubby."

"I've gone along enough times now when he pulls apart an old building. I know the drill. It's all about the notes."

"History is a bit of a puzzle," Renee said. "Each of these pictures is a piece of the puzzle behind what Whispering Pines was like back in the day."

Getting in on the action, Jess peeled the backing away from another frame. "Maybe we'll even uncover some mysteries belonging to Aunt Celia."

Renee clapped her hands together. "Wouldn't that be fun!"

SUMMER 1951

CHAPTER EIGHTEEN
GIFT OF WEDDING BELLS

"*I* remember when *my* waist used to be tiny like that," Helen sighed, nodding toward Celia and Ruby as she tugged at the pink sash of her bridesmaid dress. "Now this white tulle makes me look like a marshmallow."

Celia checked over her shoulder to make sure Eleanor hadn't come out of the bathroom in her wedding gown yet. She didn't want to offend the bride. "Personally, I think we all look like marshmallows, or cotton candy, but it's her wedding, and we do as she says *without* complaint. At least we don't look like sunny egg yolks for this wedding."

Giggling, Helen nodded. "Looking back, I should have found something in a more flattering shade for blondes and redheads. Be honest, can you tell I'm pregnant? I had no intention of getting myself into this condition again so quickly. Little Gloria Jane isn't even two yet!"

"Only when you move your bouquet away from the front of your stomach," Ruby teased. As the smile slipped off Helen's face, Ruby laughed. "I'm kidding! That little baby bump is barely noticeable in this style of dress. Just keep the sash up high and the skirt will hide it.

Warren must be awfully proud of himself, knocking you up again so quickly."

"My husband is hard to resist," Helen admitted. "Wait until you see him in his tuxedo. Have you found a wedding dress yet, Ruby?"

Celia stepped away from her two friends, pretending to search for lipstick in her white beaded handbag. She was tired of all this talk about weddings and babies. Six months from now, she'd be the only single woman left in their group. Since moving to Chicago six years earlier, she'd made time for dating but had yet to find anyone special. Not that she was actively looking for a spouse. Work consumed most of her time, and she loved it. Her vacations were little more than a few days here and there to run home to see her parents and brothers. She kept those trips short. It was still too difficult for her to spend much time in that house.

She'd been excited to make the trip back to Whispering Pines for Eleanor's wedding. Initially, she'd planned to stay for the weekend, but Preston insisted they all make a week-long vacation out of the celebration. They'd arrived that morning. She was looking forward to lazy days on the beach, late nights around the firepit with her old friends, and sleeping in. She couldn't remember the last time she'd slept past seven.

She'd be a good sport about the day's wedding festivities, although her heart wasn't in it. Romance felt foreign to her.

Helen and Ruby gasped. Celia snapped her purse shut and spun around to see an elegant Eleanor enter the room. Her gown's silhouette was like that of her bridesmaids, but no one would outshine the bride today. The sweetheart neckline, made of creamy ivory silk, sparkled with tiny seed pearls and crystals against her skin. A diamond solitaire hung suspended on a fine gold chain, adding the perfect touch of sophistication. Matching diamonds sparkled at her ears. Exquisite lace encased her slender arms.

"Oh my," Celia exclaimed, giving Eleanor a nod of approval. "You certainly don't look like the girl who built bombers on the floor of her father's factory."

"You're never going to let me live that down, are you?" the bride asked as she executed a quick spin, her full skirt lifting off the floor. "It's been a few years since I held a rivet gun. Ruby, Helen, I'd like you to meet Iris. My younger sister."

Eleanor stepped aside to reveal a young woman standing behind her in a dress matching theirs. "Iris, say hello to Ruby and Helen. And you've met Celia before."

Iris offered them all a tentative smile, but nothing more. Celia couldn't remember ever hearing the girl say more than a word or two. Years ago, Eleanor had mentioned her sister suffered from an anxiety or social disorder. Celia knew the girl seldom left the home she still lived in with Preston. Her mother's death had to have traumatized her.

Since Iris was in the wedding party, that meant Tripp was, too. Celia couldn't get away from him, even on vacation. They worked closely together in the office, and while their relationship was civil, they barely tolerated each other.

A woman Celia didn't recognize stuck her head into the room. "Ladies, we're ready for you."

"We'll be out in a minute," Eleanor assured her.

"Here, let me get your veil," Iris said, shattering the record for the number of words Celia had heard her utter in one sentence. As the girl carefully pulled the netting down over Eleanor's face, she lowered her voice, but Celia stood near enough to hear. "Momma would be proud of you today, Eleanor. I'm sorry she couldn't be with us."

The heartfelt comment hit Celia hard. The words reminded her that her dear Beverly would never stand in front of Celia on her wedding day, giving her advice. If such a day ever even happened. Celia had a gown, but no sister and no suitor. Maybe the gorgeous dress her grandmother had so thoughtfully provided for her special day would never come out from the white tissue in her blue trunk.

"Thanks, Iris," Eleanor said, hugging her sister gently. "Now hush or you'll make me cry, and Daddy will kill me if I get mascara on this dress."

Helen took charge. As a wife and a mother of a stubborn two-year-old, she knew how to keep things moving. The ceremony would be on the grassy expanse of lawn in the heart of the resort. Helen prodded them in the right direction. A long white swatch of velvet stretched from the edge of the grass, cutting down the center of rows of white chairs, each festooned with white bows, to a white archway covered with flowers.

Iris would walk in first, followed by Ruby, then Celia, based on height. Helen, as the matron-of-honor, would enter right in front of the bride. Iris took her first steps onto the velvet, and the haunting strains of a harp filled the air. Tall pines swayed in the light breeze, almost as if they were moving with the melody.

Guests filled the chairs. Perhaps Celia would recognize a few business associates. She caught sight of Harry, the groom, standing near the priest at the front, flanked by a man she didn't recognize. Maybe Harry had a brother. As expected, Tripp was there, along with Leo and Helen's husband, Warren. It had been wonderful to see Leo, her old fishing buddy, upon their arrival. She hadn't run into him since he'd returned from the war. He was married and a father of two now.

As Celia walked down the aisle, she wondered if Leo's wife was in the group of guests and if she might allow Leo to go fishing with her. She'd loved fishing with Helen's brother during their first summer at Whispering Pines.

She noticed Leo smile at someone to her right, and Celia glanced in that direction, trying to guess if one of the women wearing pretty summer dresses was his wife.

In her search for Leo's wife, her eyes picked out a familiar silhouette. Mrs. Bell sat next to the velvet-covered aisle, fanning herself. The woman's face lit up as Celia came alongside her, and Celia nodded a quick greeting. The day had just gotten much brighter. Not wanting to delay the processional, Celia kept walking, but her step was suddenly lighter. She couldn't wait to catch up with Mrs. Bell. What had the woman been up to in the years since Celia had left Whispering Pines? Had Danny come back to visit her?

Celia proceeded to her assigned spot and turned to watch Helen. She nearly laughed at how stiffly her friend held her spray of summer roses in front of her. The notes from the harp faded away and the graceful melody of a violin filled the air. Preston stood beside Eleanor at the start of the runner, looking proudly over the crowd and then back down at his daughter. The guests rose to their feet in unison, turning slightly to admire the bride and her proud father as they made their way toward the groom.

As the bride reached the area near Mrs. Bell, Celia froze. The sound of the violin faded away. Maybe she even swayed, because Ruby poked her in the ribs with her bouquet.

"Celia? Are you okay?" she whispered. "Don't lock your knees."

Ruby's warning snapped Celia back. She gave her right leg a discreet shake, catching her breath.

Then she dared to look again. It was him. She'd recognize him anywhere.

There, standing next to Mrs. Bell, was her son. The years had been kind to him. He'd grown taller and filled out. It was obvious he'd been watching her, and now, when their eyes met, his warm smile made her heart skip a beat or two. She realized Eleanor was already in place and everyone had shifted slightly to face the bride and groom except her. Pivoting, she allowed her eyes to drift to the priest, but she couldn't concentrate on what he was saying.

Ruby poked her again, this time in the back. "Is that *Danny?*"

Her whisper caught Helen's attention, and the matron-of-honor shushed them both over her shoulder.

Ignoring her, Celia nodded. "Can you believe it?" she whispered back.

* * *

The air filled with sounds of champagne flutes tinkling together in toasts of well-wishes for the happy couple. The wedding party then mingled with the guests, moving between round tables covered in white linen. All the while, catering staff kept glasses topped off and platters of fancy appetizers at the ready.

Celia circulated amongst the guests but kept a close eye on Mrs.

Bell and Danny, both of whom sat at a table on the perimeter of the reception chatting with Preston.

Ruby bumped her elbow, then took a sip from her champagne, eyeing her meaningfully. "It's been years since I've seen that expression on your face."

"What expression?" Celia asked, not attempting to mask her curiosity over the man talking with her boss.

"The one that says, *I'll follow you to the ends of the earth and bear your children*," Ruby teased, motioning toward Danny with the stem of her glass.

Celia laughed and gave Ruby her attention, lowering her voice. "Don't be ridiculous. I'd never follow a man anywhere. And as for bearing children, I'd have to have sex first."

Making a *tsk-tsk* sound, Ruby shot Celia a pitying look. "Twenty-eight years old and still a virgin. Don't you think it's about time you did something about that?"

"Ruby, be quiet! I told you that in confidence," Celia whispered, horrified should someone overhear. "You don't have to go announcing that to the world. You know I haven't found the right man yet. Not like you and your Edwin." Something suddenly occurred to her. "Wait —are you saying you've already *slept* with him? I thought you said you wanted to wait until your wedding night!"

Ruby shrugged, seeking her fiancé in the crowd and giving him a finger-wave. "I decided a ring on my finger was close enough."

Celia smiled as light glinted off the princess-cut diamond on Ruby's left hand. The ring was more modest than either Helen's or Eleanor's, but Celia knew the man, a fellow teacher at the school where Ruby taught, was perfect for her friend. The couple often talked of visiting the great art museums of Europe for their honeymoon.

Until today, Celia had nearly given up on anyone ever making her heart flutter the way Ruby claimed hers did anytime Edwin walked into the room. She'd forgotten how she'd felt, all those years ago, when Danny did something as simple as smile at her. She'd even convinced herself it didn't matter. Her career was her life, and it took all of her energy to prove herself in a company full of men—men who held their own business skills in higher regard.

She watched Tripp approach the table where his father sat laughing with the Bell family, whispering something in Preston's ear. Tripp was the guiltiest of them all when it came to an overabundance of self-confidence. She would admit—but only to herself—that there were rare days when Tripp impressed her, but most of the time he was just annoying.

With a nod, Preston stood, shaking Danny's hand and patting Mrs. Bell's shoulder before leaving to attend to whatever issue Tripp had brought to his attention.

"Now's your chance," Ruby encouraged. "Get over there, before that gaggle of women surround him."

Celia had been so busy watching Danny that she hadn't noticed the trio of women, approximately her age, eyeing him. "Not today, ladies," she said, her mock haughty tone and snooty expression causing Ruby to crack up. Helen had taught them well. "Go talk to your fiancé, Ruby. I'm sure he's lonesome. I have an old friend to greet."

"Enjoy!" Ruby said, the sparkling sound of her laughter trailing behind her as she turned to do as Celia suggested.

Taking a swig of her champagne for a shot of liquid confidence, Celia approached the Bells, stepping more quickly when she saw one of the three women break away and head in the same direction. What was it about weddings that made everyone bolder? The woman didn't yet know she wouldn't stand a chance with Danny. Celia would see to that.

Danny stood at her approach. Their eyes locked. This time he didn't smile like an excited teenager. His gaze was intense, as if he were drinking in the sight of her. She felt drawn to him in a way she'd never experienced before, not even during that summer they'd shared.

But she had learned a few things about men through the years, and so she'd try to play it cool, get his story before letting him see how much his presence was affecting her. Besides, he'd gone off to war and, other than the one package, she'd never heard from him again.

He'd left with no apparent regret. Maybe he'd forgotten all about their time together. She'd do well to remember that.

She gave him a brief nod, but immediately turned her attention to his mother. "Mrs. Bell! It's so wonderful to see you! You look well." She rested a hand on the back of the woman's chair, causing her to spin in Celia's direction.

Danny sat back down. Celia could still feel his eyes on her. She grinned as the other young woman who'd been approaching the Bells shot Celia a haughty look as she passed right on by their table.

"My stars, child, you are a sight for sore eyes," the older woman said in greeting, patting Celia's hand affectionately. "I so hoped I'd see you today. It's been too long! We missed you here at Whispering Pines."

Celia glanced around them and inhaled the earthy scent she associated with the resort. "And I missed both you and Whispering Pines. How have you been? Do you still work here?"

Pulling out the chair Preston had recently vacated, Mrs. Bell gestured for Celia to sit. "Sadly, no. Mr. Whitby was so good to me. I worked here in the summer months for a few more years after you left, but it got to be too difficult for me physically. Besides, I needed something year-round. Danny saw the invitation for Eleanor's wedding on top of a pile of mail when he came for a visit. He insisted we come."

She swiveled in her chair and reached back to pat her son's cheek. He didn't flinch at the gesture, smiling patiently at his mother and sparing her a glance before again settling his gaze on Celia. Try as she might to keep her attention on Mrs. Bell as she spoke, she was finding it difficult to ignore him.

"It's so fun to see all of you again. Say, my dear, I was so sorry to hear about Beverly. She was such a wonderful girl. When Preston told me of her passing, I cried for you. Are you doing all right? How are your parents?"

The woman's words caused a stabbing pain deep in Celia's chest. She knew Mrs. Bell meant well. People generally did when they uttered what they thought were necessary words of condolences, no matter how much time had passed. But it didn't dim the ache the words caused. She doubted it ever would.

"I'm sorry, Mother, did you say Beverly? Celia, didn't you have a sister named Beverly?" Danny asked. The timbre of his voice, a full octave lower than she remembered, coursed through her.

Celia nodded, blinking quickly and tilting her head back to stare up at a pillowy cloud as it temporarily obscured the hot summer sun. It stemmed the pesky tears elicited by the sympathy in his voice.

"I'm so sorry," he said, reaching around his mother for her hand.

Without thinking, she took it; his hand was so much larger and warmer than her own.

"I had no idea."

And she believed him. Maybe if he'd known, he would have reached out to her at some point. She squeezed his hand, then released it, the fluttering his touch created making her uneasy. She needed a distraction.

"I wonder if they had enough of those plates left to serve cake to all the guests," she said, winking at Mrs. Bell and gesturing to the china plate holding the slice of wedding cake the woman had been about to taste when Celia first approached.

Mrs. Bell looked confused for a moment, but then she laughed, long and hard, slapping her knee. "Goodness, child, I forgot all about that! I'm lucky Mr. Whitby didn't fire me over that one."

Shaking her head, Celia assured her Preston would never have fired her, even if she broke every plate in the set. They continued to reminisce about that last summer when they'd worked so closely together to keep things going in Preston's absence. Danny listened with interest to the humorous events he'd missed after enlisting.

Tripp wandered by, reminding Celia of how he'd battled to heal after his injuries that summer. How Beverly had helped him during that dark time. She never gave his missing hand a thought anymore, she was so accustomed to it, but he had to have suffered. She supposed she should have been more patient with him.

Danny continued to watch her as she caught up with his mother.

Celia declined a passing server's offer to refill her champagne. Danny's presence made her jittery enough.

"My heavens, is that our old delivery man?" Mrs. Bell asked, her attention diverted when she spied a balding man talking with Eleanor next to the table holding a crystal bowl of pink lemonade. "I believe I could use another glass of punch. If you'll excuse me, I must say hello. Danny, keep our girl company."

Grinning, Danny helped his mother scoot her chair back, and together he and Celia watched her hurry toward her old friend, arms outstretched. "I always suspected Mother had a thing for that guy after Father died."

His words surprised Celia. She'd never thought of Mrs. Bell in that light. But as she watched her now, she had to admit Danny was probably right. The woman was practically skipping.

Turning his attention back to Celia, Danny's expression grew more serious. "It's good to see you, Celia."

"It's good to see you, too, Danny. The years have been good to you."

"And you're as beautiful as I remember," he said.

Flustered by his words, she tore her eyes from his, feeling the heat rise in her cheeks. There was so much she wanted to ask him. Where had he been? What had he witnessed in his travels? Was he still taking pictures? Was he *married*?

He stood then and offered her his hand. "May I have this dance? I remember dancing isn't exactly your favorite pastime, but I'm hoping you'll make an exception this time."

A string quartet had taken their seats next to the wooden platform put in place to allow for dancing. How had she not noticed before? She didn't know how long they'd been playing, but a handful of couples were swaying to the classical tune.

She didn't dislike dancing, but she remembered their ongoing banter on the subject that started that first night she'd met him at Grand View Lodge. She'd been roaming a hallway alone, giving her sore feet a break while admiring the photographs on the wall. It had been the beginning of their brief friendship.

Slipping her hand into his, she allowed him to lead her to the dance floor. At that moment, she might have allowed him to lead her anywhere.

* * *

The rest of the celebration passed quickly. When she'd stepped into Danny's arms on the dance floor, it had felt like a blend of her past and her present. She'd relaxed against him, and his warm hand at the small of her back felt right. She wouldn't remember later how many songs they'd danced to, but at some point Preston had asked to cut in. After that she'd danced with all the groomsmen except Tripp, who didn't dance at all. It was fun to spend a few minutes catching up with Leo; he promised to go out fishing with her, as long as his four-year-old son could join them.

She kept a discreet eye out for Danny, but he'd disappeared. Had that woman from earlier gotten him out for a dance?

As the sun set, the musicians packed away their instruments and the caterers cleared the remaining food. Eleanor and her new husband slipped away to the tiny cabin Celia had previously shared with Ruby and then Beverly. She loved that her favorite little cabin would be a quaint bridal suite for the week.

Celia and the rest of the wedding party took over the white cabins nearest the water. The party wasn't over yet.

Danny had mentioned they were staying in one half of the duplex. He and his mother weren't leaving immediately following Eleanor's special day. Celia felt a tiny thrill at the possibility of more time with him.

Dared she hope this visit to Whispering Pines, after so many years away, could once again be a magical time?

CHAPTER NINETEEN
GIFT OF A SECOND CHANCE

"*I*t'll feel so good to get out of this itchy dress." Ruby sighed and glanced over her shoulder at Celia. "Unzip me, will you?"

Changing out of their wedding finery, Celia and her friends donned comfortable clothes and met on the beach for a bonfire, reminiscent of their first summer at Whispering Pines. As Celia molded the sand beneath her blanket and scanned the familiar faces circled around their makeshift firepit, she couldn't help but reflect on how much they'd all changed. Helen with her husband, their young daughter at home with Warren's parents, giving them a free week. Ruby and Edwin, laughing as they wrestled with a toasting marshmallow over the flames using a limp stick.

Tripp sat across from her, staring moodily into the fire. She wondered what he was brooding about.

Her mind flashed back to Beverly, laughing and playing in the water on this beach all those years ago. How she missed her sister. She suspected Tripp missed her, too. They'd grown close that summer.

Celia now knew, with the benefit of hindsight, that the crash of glassware above their heads when Clarence discovered Beverly's lifeless body had been a turning point in her life. The door to her younger self slammed shut that day. The magic fled. She wondered if George had felt a touch of that, too, when his dreams of the Easter Bunny withered. He'd been much younger, but she could see how they'd all changed that day, even the younger ones.

"Do you want to make one, Celia?" Ruby asked, interrupting her thoughts. Celia shook her head at the stick poking in her direction. Sighing, Ruby tossed the wimpy thing over her shoulder into the darkness, giving up on it.

The soft whisper of footsteps through sand reached Celia's ears, and she half turned.

"Is this a closed party, or can I join you?"

Celia turned back to face the flickering flames at the sound of Danny's voice, and she caught the wink Ruby tossed in her direction before encouraging him. "Come! Join us."

A round of boisterous greetings and introductions followed as Celia's old friend dropped onto the sand next to her, as if doing so were the most natural thing in the world. His presence kept her mind firmly tied to both the conversation and the knowledge of him next to her. She let thoughts of that dreadful day recede.

Celia noticed Danny inch his way closer to her as stories were told and retold. He didn't know the stories, but he had a relaxed way about him, and his occasional contributions to the conversation spurred more sharing.

Tripp, however, remained withdrawn, leaving an hour after Danny joined them.

Not long after Tripp's departure, Celia noticed Helen leaning back against her husband. Warren sat directly behind her, providing a backrest. Her friend sat with a protective hand over her midsection, and the gesture struck Celia. One of her oldest friends was now a wife and mother, building a family with a man she'd eyed ever since her big brother Leo had brought him home for a college visit. The couple traveled to Paris for their honeymoon, and while Helen's life was absent of designing, it seemed to be playing out much as she'd always imagined.

Ruby was on a similar path, though a bit behind Helen on the whole wife-and-mother timeline. Celia couldn't remember a time when Ruby was ever this happy.

Maybe Celia had been wrong to focus all her attention on her job, working hard to make a name for herself in Preston's company. She battled to get the men around her to take her seriously. Why was it that everyone expected her to handle the domestic tasks in the office when she was better at project management and sales than most of the men working there?

With a groan, Helen swung her feet under her, rising as far as her knees before Warren stood and gently boosted her to her feet. "It was a fun day, everyone," she announced, "but my bed is calling."

As the couple disappeared beyond the light cast by the fire, Ruby and Edwin rose, too. "Will you be up soon?" Ruby asked, locking eyes with Celia from across the fire.

Celia turned questioningly to Danny, so close now that his arm was behind hers.

"We have lots to catch up on," Danny offered, sending Celia's pulse racing.

The satisfaction in Ruby's smile at his answer was unmistakable even in the dark.

"Don't wait up for me," Celia said, grinning at Ruby. "Let's plan to take that hike in the morning. It'll be fun! I'm not fishing with Leo and his son until Monday."

Ruby nodded, taking her fiancé's hand and leading him toward the cabins. The cabin she shared with Ruby had two bedrooms, but she suspected her friend would appreciate some privacy, especially after the bombshell she'd discovered at the wedding. She doubted Edwin would head back to the cabin he was sharing with two of Eleanor's elderly uncles.

Soon, all that remained was the sound of waves, gently lapping against the shoreline and the crackle of the fire. And Danny.

"I still can't believe you're here," she said, holding herself upright, although all she really wanted to do was to sink back against his strong shoulder, directly behind her own.

As if sensing her apprehension, Danny slipped off his light jacket and gently placed it around Celia's shoulders, using it as an excuse to touch her, to rub her upper arms for a moment, as if to warm her.

She shivered, but it wasn't from cold.

"I can't quite believe I'm sitting here, next to you, on our beach, after so many years," he whispered, echoing her words. "Are you still chilly?"

Pulling his jacket more tightly around her, she shook her head, inhaling the scent of him. "I'm fine. But I want to know everything. Everything you've seen and done since you left."

"Since *I* left?" he asked, a teasing note in his voice. "I was still here when *you* left to go back to college."

"You know what I mean," she insisted. "Thank you for the pictures you mailed to me, by the way. If I'd have known you were going to be here today, I could have brought your camera back to you."

Silence passed. When he spoke again, she could hear the smile in his words, even though she continued to stare into the fire. "Keep it. I have more. Do you use it?"

"The camera?"

"Yes. I'd hoped someday you would show me your life in pictures. I didn't know if we'd meet again in a year, a decade, or half a lifetime, but something told me that our one short summer wasn't the end."

She caught the huskiness in his voice. He sounded as if he'd missed her nearly as much as she'd missed him. "I'd hoped we'd see each other again someday, too," she acknowledged.

"Celia, lean back. I just want to feel you against me. I want you to tell me everything you've been doing in the past seven years."

With a sigh, she relaxed against him, letting his large, warm body support her as she rested her eyes on the fire. Mesmerized by the flames, she let the years play out like a film reel in her mind. She shared everything that popped up from her memories, from the heartbreak over Beverly's death, to making a home for herself in her tiny Chicago apartment, to both the satisfaction and the frustrations of her work.

"I'm relieved I didn't find you here with a husband, married with children like Helen. Or engaged like Ruby. Does that make me self-ish?" he asked, his words warm in her ear.

She grinned as his breath tickled her skin, causing more shivers. "If it's selfish of you, that puts me in the same boat. When I saw you there, standing next to your mother, my first prayer was that there wasn't a wife sitting on your other side."

"I'm not exactly the marrying type," he said, his left hand gently caressing her arm, his lips brushing against her ear.

"What type are you?" she asked, her words sounding hoarse to her own ears. "I've told you all about my life. Now it's your turn."

"I'd rather just kiss you," he admitted.

But she wouldn't allow him to distract her. Not yet. "I'm serious, Danny. I think of you often, wondering whatever became of you, if I'd ever see you again . . . I want to know everything."

With a sigh, he shifted behind her, moving so she sat between his thighs. He eased her against him again, until they both sat comfortably, still facing the fire. "All right. If it's that important to you."

"It is," she assured him, holding his forearm where it still rested lightly across her chest.

What if someone sees us sitting so close? Like a couple. Would they assume Celia was loose?

No one else, except maybe Ruby, would have any way of knowing that she'd always felt this man, sitting comfortably behind her after so many years, was *the* one. He was likely the real reason she'd chosen a path different from so many other women her age. Or at least his absence cemented her earlier desires to put career first.

She focused her attention on what he shared, not caring what anyone might think.

Danny spoke of the two years he'd spent overseas at the tail end of the Second World War. The recollections he shared made the time sound both terrifying and exhilarating. Learning he'd escaped unscathed—and that he'd spent more time behind a camera than a rifle—allowed her to release a deep-seated worry. There were likely horrific experiences he'd omitted from his retelling, but that was all right. Her own life experiences had taught her that some things were easier to keep bottled up inside. Bringing them out into the light of day—or the light of the bonfire—only served to keep the pain alive.

Danny talked about how he built his career as a photojournalist once the war ended. His work took him on travels around the world.

"Don't you miss your mom?" Celia asked when he mentioned he'd gone years without seeing her.

"I do miss her when I'm gone so long. But I can't avoid it. I hated how hard she used to have to work to support herself. Americans are hungry for news from foreign places like Europe, Africa, even China. Foreign correspondence is more lucrative than work in the States. I can support her now. Besides, I love the travel."

"Tell me all about the places you've been," Celia encouraged, trying to envision the things Danny had experienced firsthand. Her own life suddenly felt incredibly boring next to his.

He talked of the castles he'd toured, the feeling of being surrounded by other entities, long dead. "If only I could capture them on film," he joked.

He'd climbed rugged mountains and walked in warm ocean waters. There'd been a safari he documented for a diplomat's biography. He even shared about visiting his ancestral home and a family graveyard in Ireland.

"It all sounds glorious," she sighed, dropping her hands to rest on his thighs.

He grunted. "Trust me, I'm sticking to the high points. There are plenty of ugly stories, too, but you might not be as impressed to hear about the nights I slept on floors with nothing more than a threadbare blanket, or the weeks we'd go without clean water or decent food. My entire goal tonight is to *impress* you."

Celia laughed. It felt amazing to spend what felt like stolen time, held in the warm cocoon of his arms. She twisted so she could see his eyes. "*You* want to impress *me*? Why?"

"All I've ever wanted to do was impress you."

His simple answer spoke volumes. Maybe she *had* been on his mind through the years. Or maybe they weren't so different, both throwing all their energy into their careers when no one else came along to make them question their priorities.

In her years without him, she'd convinced herself their one short summer had been the only time she'd ever have with him, and that it had been enough. As she stared into his warm, toffee-colored eyes reflecting the firelight, she realized it hadn't been nearly enough.

His eyes roamed over her face, falling to her lips, and her body responded. She leaned into him, brushing her lips against his, and the years fell away. His hands found their way into her hair, tangling her auburn strands around his fingers.

How many hours had they spent on this beach kissing like this, hidden by a cloak of darkness, when they were younger?

A log hissed and popped behind her, reminding her she wasn't that kid anymore. And anyone looking toward the beach, despite the late hour, would see their silhouettes. That felt wrong. This was a private moment. She finally had her Danny back, even if it was only for the night. But their reunion was no one else's business but their own. She pulled back.

His eyes drifted open. "What's wrong?"

Celia shrugged, wondering if she was being silly. It had to be well past midnight. They were likely truly alone, but she still didn't feel comfortable. She admitted as much to him.

He caressed her cheek, dropping one quick kiss on lips already swollen from his attention. Then he stood, offering her a hand up, much as Warren had done for Helen earlier. "Why don't we take a walk?" he suggested, his voice barely above a whisper, still holding tight to her hand.

Relieved, she used her free hand to collect her blanket, shaking sand from the wool. She'd grinned earlier when she'd noticed the pink stain on it, barely visible now after undoubtedly countless washings. They'd stained a blanket with spilled wine—she and her girlfriends— on a summer picnic when she'd first visited Whispering Pines. It had to be the same one.

Danny released her hand so he could kick sand over the fire, dousing what remained of the flames. It took a moment for Celia's eyes to adjust. It was as if he'd flicked a switch. The stars above glowed brighter, the moon a brilliant white crescent over the water.

"Here, let me carry that," he offered, taking the wool blanket from Celia and giving it a more vigorous shake. More sand tinkled to the ground.

"Where should we go?" Celia whispered, looking around them. "It's so dark."

"The dark never used to scare you," he teased. "Have you gone soft on me?"

Playfully, Celia took a step forward, well into his personal space, setting her fingertips onto his chest. "Not yet," she whispered, before stretching up to kiss him, feeling bolder now that the beach was dark.

He half laughed, half groaned, taking his fill of her mouth before stepping back, groping for her hand in the dark. "Come on. Remember how magical the woods are in the moonlight?"

* * *

Danny pointed out the fireflies as they danced along a faint path stretching out in front of them through the grass. The moonlight cast intricate shadows over a fallen tree trunk, transforming the woods into something otherworldly.

"I always knew you'd be a fabulous photographer," she whispered, drawing a curious look from the man walking next to her.

"Because I notice fireflies?"

She squeezed his hand. "Partly, I suppose. But it isn't just fireflies. It's the light. It's the beauty in the smallest of things. You never stop looking for things worthy of capturing in a photograph, do you?"

"I suppose it eventually became second nature to me," he conceded. "Would you mind if we check to see if that old cabin I lived in with Mother is still standing?"

Celia paused to get her bearings. "It's over this way, isn't it?"

Nodding, Danny turned slightly to their left. "If it hasn't fallen down yet."

They picked their way through dark shadows. If not for the moon, they'd never have managed it without a flashlight. "Careful, you're going to have to duck down so you don't hit your head. It's more overgrown back here than I remember."

Celia followed his lead, and together they cut through the woods, their path less direct than if they'd headed straight for the old building from the main lawns of the resort. At one point, a cloud obscured the moon, dropping a black curtain around them.

"Hold up a minute," he said, pulling back on Celia's hand.

She obliged, turning back to him. "It seems spookier out here without the moonlight," she said, settling against him, her words muffled against the fabric of his shirt. Remembering he was coatless, Celia felt a twinge of guilt. "Oh gosh, I'm sorry, Danny, are you freezing? Here, why don't you take your jacket back? I'll be fine."

She started to pull the coat off, but he stopped her. "Why don't I just slip my arms in here, like this, and it can keep us both warm?"

He unzipped the jacket, draped the blanket over his right shoulder, and slid his arms into the front of the coat, wrapping them around Celia's waist. He held her tight against him. Her mind registered the itchy feel of wool against her cheek.

Danny's body felt different from that of the young man he'd been at twenty. His arms were thicker, stronger, although he was gentle with her. As they kissed again, his hands explored places on her body he'd never dared touch when they were younger.

"Stop me if this makes you uncomfortable, Cee," he whispered against her mouth, a new huskiness to his tone.

Instead of stopping him, she followed his example, letting her hands reach up to test the width of his shoulders and then travel down to hover at the small of his back. With a groan, his hands cupped her bottom, pulling her lower body flush with his. While she'd never been intimate with a man, despite her age, she'd read plenty of books and listened to her more experienced friends talk about sex. She felt no shame, and saw no reason to. There was no one she'd rather do this with.

The cloud scuttled away and white moonbeams, weaving through the tall pines above, shone down on the path again just as a clanging noise, off in the distance, broke the spell.

"What was that?" Celia whispered, squeezing her arms tighter around Danny. Tales of the two ghost boys purported to roam these woods flooded her mind.

"I think it's our old cabin," he said, his white teeth flashing in the moonlight.

"But is there someone out here?"

Keeping her close, he guided them in the sound's direction. "I'm sure it was a racoon or something. We probably scared it. He might have heard you moan."

Feeling the heat of a blush steal up her cheeks, Celia elbowed Danny in the chest.

"I'm kidding, I'm kidding," he assured her. "Whatever it was, we've probably scared it away."

His sure steps led them to an opening in the trees. "By God, the old girl is still standing. Would you look at that?"

Celia peered ahead, taking in the cabin's outline. She'd visited here a few times with Danny, but that was all. Nothing had changed much, other than the vines and brush growing up and over it, as if the woods were trying to reclaim the area as its own.

"Do you think it's locked?"

Shaking his head, Danny pulled her toward the cabin. "Not unless someone installed a lock."

Sure enough, the door opened when he tried it, hinges grating in protest.

"Stay here for a second," he instructed, dropping her hand and passing the blanket to her. "I want to make sure the floor is safe. Maybe there's still a lantern on the kitchen table."

"Be careful, Danny," she hissed into the darkness, hearing the sounds of his rummaging in the dark.

A match flared and light glinted off a sooty chimney flute. "Some things never change," he said, holding up a box of matchsticks. The old lantern still sat in the middle of the rickety old table. The glow spread, chasing the shadows into the far corners of the kitchen.

"Is that safe?" Celia asked, eyeing the table with concern.

"Probably not."

He picked up the lantern, and together they headed toward the other small rooms of the cabin, of which there were only two. The living room looked as if Mrs. Bell just walked out of it, except for the heavy layer of dust covering everything. She'd never have allowed a dirty home. A forgotten pile of *National Geographic* magazines lay on a small end table between a couch and rocking chair. Celia remembered Danny used to sleep on that couch, leaving the bedroom for his mother.

Keeping an eye on the floor, she watched Danny walk into that bedroom. Should she follow him? Was there still a bed back there? She wanted to follow him. But she stayed where she was, her hand poised on the back of the rocking chair, pushing it back and forth.

The light shifted and Danny came back out without the lantern. He walked straight to Celia's side, took the blanket from her arms, and kissed her softly. "Celia. I want you to come back in the bedroom with me. I want to make love to you tonight. I've dreamed of this moment for years. I thought it would never be more than a dream, but now that we have the chance, I don't want to let it slip away. Is that what you want, too?"

Despite the gloom of the shadowed, dingy room, Celia felt light suffuse her body. A man wanted her. And not just any man. This was Danny. He was the real reason she'd held all men at arm's length. She'd worried she'd grown cold. Now she realized her soul had been patiently waiting for this precise moment in time.

"It's what I've always wanted," she whispered, reaching out to take his hand.

* * *

Celia would look back on that magical day, from the moment her eyes clashed with Danny's from her spot at the front of the wedding ceremony, all the way through until the sunrise the following morning, as one of the best of her entire life. Danny had been both surprised and humbled to realize he was her first. She hoped he'd also be her last. They'd spent the following days getting to know each other again, not caring if others noticed their stolen kisses or whispered conversations. They were both single adults; old friends becoming something else.

More than once, Danny suggested she quit her job, give up her flat in Chicago, and come travel the world with him. They'd become famous, their photography earning them enough to keep their bellies full and the next plane ticket in their pocket. His concept of a nomad existence tempted Celia. She sensed he was serious, but that kind of lifestyle felt so foreign to her. She was loving her time at Whispering Pines, but his impractical invitation made it all feel surreal, like stolen moments in time that would soon dissolve, once again, into nothing but precious memories.

Patterns have a way of repeating themselves, she knew. She should have remembered that, instead of giving her whole heart to this man again. Destiny would cut their time together short once again.

* * *

They sat together on the end of the dock, talking—the same dock where Danny snapped pictures of Celia so many years before—when footsteps pounded up the wooden planks behind them.

"Celia!" Ruby cried, the skirt of her blue-and-white polka dot sundress streaming out behind her. "Celia, honey, something's happened. We need to get you home right away!"

Celia yanked her feet out of the chilly lake water. Danny scrambled to stand, helping Celia up. "What happened, Ruby?" he demanded, still holding Celia's hand, his other resting protectively on her shoulder.

Celia laid a hand on top of Danny's, drawing strength as a sense of dread flooded through her at Ruby's pained expression. Drama wasn't Ruby's normal reaction to things.

"A phone call came through for you. There's been an accident. It's bad, Cee, really bad. Edwin is pulling his car around. You need to get home as soon as possible. Do you want to go grab your things?"

Celia struggled to process Ruby's words. Her limbs wouldn't move, as if stuck in quicksand. "An accident? Who?"

"Your parents," she replied, her eyes awash with fear.

Danny pulled Celia into his arms and held her close. "You need to go. Let Ruby and Edwin get you home. I'll pack your things and bring them to you. Don't worry about anything here."

Celia, still feeling unhinged, tilted her head back and stared into his eyes. The good times never lasted. She was terrified to step out of his arms. Would she ever see him again? Immediately on the heels of that thought came terror for her parents. Were they okay? What about her brothers? She couldn't take more loss.

"Celia, babe, you need to go with Ruby now," Danny coaxed, squeezing Celia's shoulders. "They'll get you home to your family. I need to talk to Mother, change some plans, and then I'll come. Very soon. I promise. Now go."

Danny took Celia's hand and physically handed her over to Ruby. Ruby placed an arm around Celia's waist and hurried her down the dock and onto the sand. She waved a hand to Edwin. He'd pulled his car forward in front of the lodge, letting it idle as he waited for his fiancée and her friend.

Their sense of urgency finally penetrated the fog of dread that had descended over Celia. She spared one last glance at Danny, who still stood at the end of the dock; she waved back at him then broke into a run, leaving Ruby to run along behind her.

Her mother and Clarence needed her. She could feel it in her bones.

CHAPTER TWENTY
GIFT OF A FATEFUL SUNSET

*G*erry and George waited on the front step of Celia's childhood home. George fiddled with a red ball, tossing it lightly into the air and catching it. Gerry sat motionless, his hands clasped over his knees. They didn't stand when Edwin pulled up at the curb.

Celia burst out of the back passenger door and sprinted up the walk. Their expressions lodged a sharp blade of fear in the middle of her chest. Skidding to a stop at the bottom of the steps leading up to the carved front door, Celia gulped for air. She felt as if she'd been holding her breath since Edwin pulled away from Whispering Pines. Placing her hands on her hips and allowing herself a split second to compose herself, she sent up a silent prayer.

"What happened?" she demanded, attempting but probably failing to keep the panic out of her voice. Her question finally caused George to look her way, missing his ball as it fell back to earth, the red rubber sphere bouncing down the stairs and rolling right past Celia. She didn't stop it as she stared at her brothers.

"A car accident," Gerry replied, repeating what Ruby had already told her. He wasn't crying, but he looked bewildered, as if either he didn't yet know the details or, worse, he didn't want to accept the truth.

She glanced over their heads at the front door, wondering if anyone was inside. As if reading her mind, Gerry shook his head. "They're in the hospital."

A door slammed nearby. "Celia! Celia, is that you, dear?"

A neighbor, an elderly woman Celia met shortly before moving to Chicago, hurried in their direction. She'd bought the house when Ruby's parents moved away.

"Yes, it's me. Hello," Celia replied, forgetting the woman's name but too concerned about her parents to bother searching her memory for it. She waited impatiently for the hobbling woman to reach them.

"Oh, Celia. It's just dreadful. The police arrived a few hours ago. They pulled in front of your house, knocked on your front door. Your brothers were across the way, playing ball at that house over there. I was watering my begonias, you see. When no one answered your door, they came over and—"

"Why? What's happened? All I've heard so far is a car accident. Are Mother and Clarence all right?" Celia hated to be rude, but she needed answers, not a full play-by-play.

"They refused to tell me much, only that your parents were taken to St. Vincent's. They offered to take the boys to the hospital . . . they both ran over here when they saw the officers talking to me after leaving your house . . . but the children insisted they wanted to wait for you. Gerry had the good sense to give the officers the emergency contact numbers you'd left in the house."

Celia felt a rush of gratitude for her mother insisting she keep her informed of her general whereabouts, even though Celia moved away years earlier. She'd told her mother about Eleanor's wedding at Whispering Pines. "Do you know any more about what happened?"

The woman shook her head, checking her watch. "That was almost four hours ago now, dear. Take your brothers down to the hospital right away, check on Maggie and Clarence. They are such delightful people. I've been praying for them for hours. Do you need to borrow my car?"

Celia glanced back toward Edwin's car, idling by the curb. Ruby and her fiancé stood beside it, watching with concern. "No, my friends will take us. Thank you."

* * *

Celia had spent more time in hospitals growing up than most children, visiting Beverly during her various heart procedures and health scares. Bursting through the doors now, the unmistakable combination of industrial cleaner, overcooked food, and something else, something she refused to consider, hit her. She battled the memories the smell evoked as she rushed to the front desk.

"My name is Celia Middleton. There's been an accident. My parents, Clarence and Maggie Richter, were brought here."

The nurse, approximately Celia's age, stood and whisked out from behind the desk on silent white shoes. "Follow me, please," she said, turning toward the hallway to their left. George and Gerry rushed up behind Celia. "And these are?"

"My younger brothers."

"And they are?" the woman asked again, nodding toward Ruby and Edwin as they hurried in.

"My best friend and her fiancé. They brought us here."

"I suggest the boys stay out here with them for a bit." The nurse held Celia's eye for a beat, her gaze speaking volumes.

Turning to face her brothers, Celia laid a hand on their shoulders. A recent growth spurt had pushed thirteen-year-old Gerry to within an inch of Celia's height, but George, having just turned ten, was shorter and still pudgy. "Guys. Only one of us can go back at a time," she fibbed, not wanting to alarm them even more before finding out exactly what was happening.

What is waiting for me behind that swinging door?

Would this turn out to be yet another horrifying, life-defining moment for her family, or merely a dark day that would eventually end with all of them finding their way home safely?

Forcing herself to meet the eyes of each of her brothers, she squeezed their hands. "I need you to stay here with Ruby, all right? I'll come tell you what's happening as soon as I know more."

George moved to protest, but Gerry grabbed his arm. "Let Celia get some answers for us."

"It'll be okay," she promised, but even as she uttered the words, she felt a stab of regret. She couldn't know that for sure.

The nurse led her down the hallway on her eerily silent shoes. Celia focused on the woman's white cap, looking so professional atop her tight knot of black hair. She remembered how Eleanor had talked once about becoming a nurse. They trained nurses and doctors to take care of people. Her mother and Clarence were in expert hands.

Her internal pep talk didn't help. An awful feeling, deep in the pit of her stomach, warned her something was terribly wrong.

The nurse swung right and then left, finally pausing in front of an open doorway. She glanced back at Celia, then entered. "Mrs. Richter, your daughter has arrived."

Rushing into the room at the mention of her mother's name, Celia stepped around the woman and hurried forward, desperate to see Maggie. Her mother's eyes were closed, but they opened slowly, a tiny smile lifting one side of her mouth. The smile looked odd to Celia, off-kilter somehow. A white bandage encircled the top third of her mother's head, but it couldn't completely hide a purplish bruise that spread down from her right temple onto her cheek. A sling supported her right arm and another bulky white bandage fully encased one leg. Clarence was nowhere in sight.

"Momma, what happened?" Celia whispered, dropping to her knees and resting her elbows on the bed. She took Maggie's good hand in her own, seeking to both give and draw comfort with the connection. Her mother's fingers, normally so warm and capable, were cool and limp. "Are you all right?"

"I will be, dear, I will be," her mother replied, her voice stronger than Celia would have expected.

"Where's Clarence?" Celia asked, glancing around the room again, hoping to spot him sitting in a corner, keeping his injured wife company.

Maggie squeezed Celia's hand, pulling her attention back. Her mother's eyes lacked their familiar spark. Celia had attributed that to the pain, but a flash of insight conveyed a bleak truth. Celia had witnessed that look in her mother's eyes before. She tried to shield herself from the words she feared were coming.

Her mother drew a ragged breath. "He'd run me to the market. I needed a few things, and I'd planned to walk, but it started to rain. When he realized the weather would prevent him from starting his work day, he offered to take me. We never even saw the truck. Maybe it was the rain."

"Momma, where is Clarence?" Celia asked again. Her mother wanted to tell her the entire story, but all she wanted to know was that her stepfather, the man who had lifted her family up out of despair, was okay.

"They tell me he's gone, honey," Maggie finally said, shooting a hate-filled glare at the nurse, still standing by the door, before her eyes drifted shut.

Celia felt her world tilt. She wanted to rage against the news. It couldn't be true. But when she stood and looked to the nurse, the woman confirmed it.

How was this happening again? First her own father, a man she barely remembered, then Beverly, and now Clarence? So much loss.

Worst of all, she'd have to tell her brothers their father was dead.

* * *

The tree sheltering Beverly's headstone, and their father's older marker, had grown taller in the years since her sister's death. Celia knelt in front of the newer stone, laying a bouquet of yellow roses tied with a red ribbon on the grass. Her fingers traced the dates that marked the beginning and ending of Beverly's short life.

"I'm sorry I haven't been back, Beverly. It was too hard. I thought maybe if I stayed away, it would make the finality of this less true. But I was wrong," Celia whispered, flicking a tear away. "And I'm sorry to have to tell you we buried dear Clarence today. But maybe you already know that. Maybe he's already found you, up there among the stars. Tell me, dear sister, how does this work? When we leave here, what's waiting for us? Are you all alone, Bevvy, or can we somehow find each other again? Can you help Clarence find his way?"

Celia jumped when a hand touched her shoulder.

"I like to think we find each other again," Danny said, rubbing her shoulder. "I wondered where you'd disappeared to. Is this your sister's grave?"

"It is. My sister and my father. He died when we were little girls. Clarence . . . he was like a father to us, too. He helped us so much. We'd barely been scraping by, hardly holding on. He treated us like we were his own, and if it weren't for him I wouldn't have my brothers."

Danny nodded. Celia had already told him most of this before, but he let her go on.

"It seems strange that he's buried in another part of the cemetery, but they designate this older section for families that founded the town. That's my grandmother's grave, next to my father's."

Celia's mind flitted back to the day Clarence had surprised her with the blue trunk he'd crafted for her college graduation. He'd been so proud, and she so touched. She thought of the gorgeous wedding gown her grandmother had so thoughtfully provided her, hidden away at the bottom of that trunk. She almost mentioned it to Danny, but he'd shied away from the subject of marriage during their animated discussions at Whispering Pines, so she didn't. They'd talked about the possibility of her leaving everything behind to go away with him, but there had been no specific talk of marriage.

Her knees began to ache and Danny helped her to her feet.

"Thank you for coming, Danny. I'm glad you met my mother and brothers."

The hot summer wind blew a piece of Celia's auburn hair over her eyes. She'd opted not to wear her black hat with the fancy netting for the funeral today. She would forever associate it with the bitter memories of Beverly's funeral.

Danny tucked the stray lock behind her ear. "I'm sorry I wasn't here for you when your sister died."

239

She managed a small smile. "You would have come if you'd have known."

She wasn't entirely sure that was true, and he glanced away at her words, but she let the subject drop.

"Thank you for helping Gerry and George with Mother's wheelchair. I hate that she's stuck in that thing for the foreseeable future. I pray her leg heals properly."

"Speaking of your mother, she sent me to find you. People are leaving, and I think she's ready to go home."

Celia was ready to leave, too. She'd felt gutted, hollowed out, standing near her stepfather's coffin, an arm around each of her brothers. She hated the bleak pain reflected in their eyes as they'd said their last goodbyes to their father. At least they hadn't had to endure the pain of a lengthy funeral inside a church. Clarence wouldn't have wanted that. He would have approved of today's brief ceremony, outside in the open air.

Taking Danny's arm, Celia allowed him to lead her away from Beverly's grave. Her eyes traveled up the tree that now cast its shadow over her family's headstones below. Its bright green leaves danced in the summer breeze, life over death.

A flash of red suddenly surprised her. She stopped.

"Look," she said, pointing up.

"Well, I'll be," Danny whispered. "It's a red cardinal."

"It's so pretty," Celia whispered. "Beverly liked red."

"My mother always says red cardinals are actually our loved ones, coming back from heaven with a message for us."

"Really? I've never heard of that before."

Danny patted her hand where it rested on his arm. "Maybe it's Beverly, coming to tell you she'll keep an eye on Clarence for you."

Tears filled Celia's eyes, and she let them fall, smiling up at Danny. "I like that idea."

* * *

Celia found herself at another crossroads in her life. Her shrinking family needed to piece their lives back together. While she felt compelled to run away from the pain of it all again, to slink back to her flat in Chicago and lose herself in her work, or even to escape with Danny, she knew she shouldn't do that this time.

Maggie's leg suffered extensive damage. Her arm healed quickly, and the headaches she'd suffered since the accident slowly subsided, but her future ability to walk without pain was questionable.

Celia enlisted her brothers' help to revamp the main level of their house so their mother could navigate it all from her wheelchair. Thank goodness for the bathroom on the main level. They converted a small room in the back, initially meant as a study or library, into a temporary bedroom. Her brothers were again sharing a bedroom upstairs to give Celia a place to sleep. They were all optimistic that Maggie would be able to use the master bedroom again, after she had time to heal. Celia knew it was foolish to still be averse to using Beverly's old room, but she couldn't help it.

Picking up a hairbrush from the top of her dresser, Celia studied the white bristles. She'd used this same brush as a child. Her heart caught when she noticed dark strands of Beverly's hair, tangled with her own brighter strands. They used to play beauty shop as girls, taking turns being the patron and the hairdresser.

With a sigh, Celia sat on the edge of her bed, running the brush through her hair.

Now that she'd addressed her mother's immediate needs, it was time she made some decisions about her own life. Their situation wasn't much different from her younger years after her own father had died. She wondered how Maggie would support herself and her children. This time it was Gerry and George instead of her and Beverly.

Her stepfather had worked hard and provided a comfortable living, but there'd been little left over at the end of each month to tuck away for darker times such as now.

Celia stood and crossed her room, tossing the hairbrush down with a thud. She'd resigned herself to what she needed to do, but still she feared the hard conversations she faced with both Danny and Preston.

The familiar chime of the doorbell rang out below. She checked her reflection one last time, wanting to look nice for her dinner out with Danny. He'd given her time after the funeral to be with her family, but then called the previous day asking if they could talk.

She needed to speak to him, too.

As she descended the stairs, her heart did its customary little lurch when she spied the man talking with George. The ten-year-old must have let him in.

Her brother heard her on the stairs. "It sounds like Danny is taking you some place fun for dinner, sis. Promise me you'll bring me your leftover dessert?"

Smiling, Celia ruffled George's hair as she reached the two. "Are you implying I don't need dessert, George?"

George smacked her hand away with a grin. "Well, you aren't as skinny as you used to be, but you aren't fat yet either. I just like dessert."

Both Celia and Danny laughed at George's honesty. She envied him the innocence of the world he still lived in. She'd worried his father's death would change that.

"Take care of Mother, will you?" she instructed. "Gerry's at that baseball game with his friends. I won't be late."

"We'll be just fine, Celia," came her mother's voice from the kitchen. "Go, have fun."

"Thanks, Mother. We will," Celia hollered back.

Danny was the perfect gentleman, holding the door for her as they left the house and again when she climbed into the late-forties-era pickup truck he'd borrowed from a friend. Danny didn't own a vehicle of his own; his transient lifestyle made it impractical. Celia noticed a large envelope on the dash as he pulled away from the curb and drove toward the restaurant.

"What's that?" she asked, curious.

He glanced toward the envelope, then back at the road. He looked as tense as Celia felt. "A little something for you" was all he'd say, and silence fell again within the cab.

Celia already missed the carefree nature of their time together at Whispering Pines. Those special days between Eleanor's wedding and the dreadful phone call had been like nothing she'd ever experienced. Her heart was breaking, knowing they may never experience that freedom again.

"Danny, we don't have to go sit in some fancy restaurant and make small talk."

"Aren't you hungry?" he asked, reaching for her hand.

"Not really, not for a heavy meal. I'd rather go somewhere we can be alone, where we can talk. I think we need to."

Bringing her hand up to his mouth, he kissed her fingers. "We do."

He wasn't familiar with her hometown, so she directed him to a nearby park where they could sit outside and enjoy the summer day without being surrounded by others inside a busy establishment. They found an empty picnic bench, poised in the shade and near the river that provided the perimeter for the city park. Celia peeled off the lightweight sweater she'd worn over her sundress in anticipation of a more formal atmosphere.

Grinning, Danny nodded at her feet. "You might want to take those heels off, too. Who cares if you're barefoot in the park?"

Who cares indeed, she thought, following his advice. It felt freeing, after the heartache of the past two weeks, to walk barefoot through the grass and feel the hot sunshine on her bare shoulders.

Danny left his suit coat and tie in the truck, too, rolling his sleeves above his elbows and opening the top button on his dress shirt. He kept his shoes on. "In case I have to carry you over broken glass," he'd joked.

As they settled on the top of the battered green picnic bench facing the flowing river, their feet on the lower bench, Celia considered where to start.

"Danny . . . we should discuss some things."

He nodded, again capturing her left hand and holding it against his chest. "Yes, I know we should."

"What's happened with Mother and Clarence, I'm afraid it's changed everything," she said in a rush, getting right to the point. She felt a sting on her shoulder and slapped a pesky mosquito away with her free hand.

Danny didn't immediately respond, his eyes on the swirls and eddies of the river, swollen by recent heavy rains—rains that likely contributed to her parents' fateful car crash.

Eventually, he sighed. "I understand, Celia. I do. But I need you to be honest with me about something."

She met his eyes and nodded, encouraging him to continue.

"If this hadn't happened, would you *really* have given up your life in Chicago to travel the world with me, or was that all just a fantasy?"

Taking her time to consider his question, knowing he deserved the truth, Celia bent down and used her fingernail to peel back a sliver of green painted wood that was poking at her big toe.

Would I have left with him?

"Honestly, I do think I would have gone with you, Danny. You painted such a vivid picture for me in my mind, and I loved the idea of experiencing the world with you. Maybe I'd never have been the photographer you are, but I would have tried. I never could get your old camera to work."

Danny rubbed the back of his neck with his free hand, his other still holding tight to hers. "And now?"

"Now I'm afraid all of that is impossible. At least for the time being."

He sighed again. "I suppose it is."

She'd been prepared to argue the point with him, but while Danny might live an unconventional lifestyle, he'd always been a realist. He pulled a small pocketknife out of his pants pocket and flipped open the blade. He released her hand and jumped down off the table. Turning, he leaned forward and dropped a soft kiss on Celia's lips, then sat down properly on the bench. From this position, they could see each other's faces, side by side, as they contemplated their futures.

Celia took a deep breath, detecting a hint of evergreens in the air—a scent that would always remind her of Whispering Pines, even when the resort was far away. It gave her the strength to share her thoughts. "I can't go back to Chicago, either. Preston is coming to town tomorrow and we're having dinner. I'm planning to resign. I need to find a job here, move back home. I'll live with Mother and the boys, at least until she heals. She'll need my help, both financially and with my brothers. I hear teenage boys can be a real handful."

Danny scratched at the green surface of the picnic table with his knife. When Celia saw what he was doing, she grinned. "Maybe *men* can be a real handful, too. Are you going to vandalize this picnic bench?"

"I'm not vandalizing anything. This thing has seen better days. I feel compelled to leave something behind, to memorialize us here."

Boys, she thought.

She watched as he carved into the wood, taking more time with the rounded portions of the letters.

C.M. + D.B. '51

He didn't speak as he carved, and she suspected he was gathering his thoughts. She was already relatively certain she knew what he'd say. They each had their internal makeup that drove their external worlds. He blew the shavings away from his creation and set his pocketknife to the side, his finger tracing their initials. It reminded Celia of doing the same thing with the dates on Beverly's headstone.

"I've loved our time together, Celia. More than anything. I need you to believe me."

Leaning over, she dropped a kiss on the top of his head, his hair warm from the sunshine. "I believe you, Danny."

"And you deserve complete honesty, too," he continued as she straightened. "I've thought long and hard about this. I've considered giving up my work, looking for something around here, and asking you to marry me. But deep down, I think settling in one place, giving up my camera and my travels, would kill me. Maybe not right away, but a bit every day, until I was a broken, hollow man, just going through the motions. And you deserve so much more than that."

His words weren't a complete surprise, but hearing him say them out loud still stung. He watched her closely, as if trying to gauge her reaction.

"I can't leave. You can't stay," she whispered, feeling the truth of it deep in her heart. She remained dry-eyed, despite the pain. She would cry later.

"It would have been easier if I'd just stayed away from that damn wedding," he said, placing his warm hand on her knee.

"Easier, yes," she agreed. "But I learned a long time ago that the easy things in life aren't where the colors are the brightest. I'll never regret this extra time we've found together. Will you?"

Their eyes locked, and Danny got back to his feet, moving to stand between her legs. He kneeled on the bench, taking hold of her waist and pulling her forward so their torsos were flush against each other, their pounding hearts aligned.

"No regrets," he said, his eyes still holding hers as he leaned in, only allowing them to drift shut when their lips met.

They stayed that way, kissing, lost in their own little world, neither of them wanting it to end, until the blare of a horn and catcalls from a car full of teenagers rolled by behind them—kids out on a joyride.

Danny pulled back, laughing, and kissed the tip of her nose. He then reached for the envelope she'd forgotten about and handed it to her, standing back just far enough to give her space to open it but keeping both his hands on her knees.

Blinking quickly to clear the fog from her overloaded senses, she tore the top of the envelope open, careful not to harm anything inside.

"Pictures," she said, pulling a small stack of eight-by-ten colored photos out. She should have known. On the top was a candid of her laughing with her friends on the dance floor of Eleanor's wedding. "I didn't see you take this!"

He shrugged. "I'm discreet. It's my job."

"You, sir, are good at your job."

There was another of Celia with her friends, gathered around the fire on the beach the evening following the wedding, before the sun set. He must have quietly approached them, snapped the photo, slipped away with his camera, and then returned later to join them.

An early morning shot of what she thought of as her little cabin, a quirky white tissue bell hanging over the door, dew on the grass, made her heart ache for Whispering Pines. The bell marked it as Eleanor's private wedding retreat, if only for that weekend.

Next was a photo of the rickety old cabin where they'd made love under the moonlight for the first time. Instead of the deep, mysterious shadows of night, he had taken this picture in the light of day. "What's that?" Celia asked, squinting her eyes at something.

"That, I believe, might be the same racoon that made all the noise the night we were searching for the old cabin."

"No way!"

Danny shrugged, smiling at her amazement.

There were a variety of other shots, each one sure to be precious to her in the years to come. Her favorite was a picture she actually remembered posing for. Danny had asked Tripp to take one of the two of them, and he'd grudgingly complied. The focus wasn't as clear as the others, but it captured their smiling faces as they stood next to each other on what she considered their dock, making it priceless to Celia.

"Oh, Danny," she whispered, holding the stack of photographs to her chest. "I can't imagine my life without you."

He stepped forward again, careful not to crease the photographs, and leaned his forehead against hers. "You managed just fine for the seven years between our time together at Whispering Pines."

She shook her head lightly, not wanting to break their point of contact. "But that was before."

"Before?"

Laughing, she leaned back, playfully punching him in the shoulder. "You know what I mean."

"What if we agree to spend a week together, once every seven years?" he asked, cutting off her laughter. "Don't look at me like I'm crazy. I have no plans to settle down and marry. And I can't picture traveling the world with any woman other than you, so I'm thinking this bachelor life might become a permanent state for me. And you . . . you've told me more than once that you'd rather perfect your skills in a boardroom than a kitchen."

Celia searched his eyes, still not entirely sure he was serious. He *looked* serious, and his eyes challenged her. "I know I said that, but it would be highly unusual for a woman to do anything more substantive than serve coffee in a boardroom."

Danny shrugged. "My dear, if any woman can do it, it'll be you."

"Do you really have that much faith in me?" she asked, amazed that he'd listened when she talked about how much she enjoyed her work. Most men assumed she was working until she gave it up to start a family. "And what if I meet someone someday? Maybe I'll change my mind."

Taking the photographs from her, he slid them back into the protective envelope and set them to the side before capturing both her hands in his. "I have no doubt that you will accomplish anything you set your mind to. I also know there *will* be men that try to change your mind. If you find someone else, I want you to know you have my blessing."

"You're crazy. You know that, don't you?" she asked, shaking her head yet intrigued by his preposterous suggestion of meeting at set intervals of time.

"I'm crazy about you," he countered, giving her hands a playful tug and catching her when she came up off the picnic table. He kissed her deeply, then set her feet down on the ground. "I seem to be getting my appetite back. How about you?"

"I always seem to be hungry when you're around," she answered, knowing exactly what Danny was implying. The sun was setting and the mosquitoes were swarming. She turned toward the pickup, took three steps, then winced when a sharp rock poked her bare foot.

Laughing, he swung her up and over his shoulder, a muscular arm around her thighs, holding her in place. Her auburn curls tumbled out of the loose bun she'd worn.

"You better hope those kids don't come by again!" The back of his shirt muffled her warning and giggles.

When they reached the vehicle, he opened her door and deposited her onto the seat, swinging her legs in before closing the door. She watched him walk around the front of the truck, wishing the vicious mosquitoes wouldn't prevent them from making use of the pickup box.

"Where to?" he asked, turning over the engine.

"Are you leaving tomorrow?" she asked, fearing she already knew his answer.

The light ebbed from his eyes. "I have to catch the train at ten tomorrow morning."

"Then take me to your room."

"At the hotel?" he asked, surprised. "Are you sure?"

"If I have to wait another seven years to see you after tonight, there's only one way I want to spend our last hours."

He drew her to him for a deep kiss. Then he shifted into gear, his timing on the clutch off enough to cause the truck to jump before it settled and eased down the road. "You won't have any dessert to take home to George," he pointed out, grinning at her in the dimming light.

She shrugged. "I'll just tell him it was too good to save until later."

"I'm going to miss everything about you, Cee."

And she'd miss him terribly. But tonight, she'd put that out of her mind.

CHAPTER TWENTY-ONE
GIFT OF HOMETOWN OPPORTUNITIES

"*I*'ll be moving into Beverly's old room after lunch today," Celia announced. All eyes swung in her direction.

"Cool, I get my room back," Gerry said around a mouthful of bologna sandwich.

"Don't talk with food in your mouth," Maggie scolded. "Celia, are you sure? The boys are fine sharing a room. Or you can take mine. Heaven only knows when, or if, I'll be able to sleep upstairs again."

But Celia had made up her mind. "No. It'll be fine. It's a perfectly good bedroom, and it's silly not to use it. The room has sat empty long enough."

Despite the six years since Beverly's death, it still felt too soon. Based on the look on her mother's face, she no doubt felt the same, but Celia needed a distraction. As the clock in the living room chimed twelve times, Celia pictured Danny rocking slightly in his seat on the train as it sped away from her. Their parting had held a romantic, almost mysterious quality the evening before, but now his leaving left another gaping void in her life.

"Will you help me move my blue trunk into my new room, Ger?"

Gerry stuffed the remaining quarter of his sandwich into his mouth and washed it down with a gulp of lemonade. "Really? This keeps getting better and better."

"No kidding," George agreed, taking another bite of his peanut butter and jelly sandwich. He hated bologna. "I get *my* room back, too!"

"Celia, honey, we probably need to talk about all of this," her mother said, her voice weary.

"Yes, we probably do, Mother, but not right now. I have dinner plans with Mr. Whitby. He's coming to town to visit, and then we'll talk. Tomorrow. Today, I need to keep busy."

"I don't like this, Celia. Your life is in Chicago." Guilt swam in her mother's eyes.

"We'll make the best of it, Mother. We always do. Gerry, if you're finished, let's go move that trunk. George, finish your lunch, and then clear the dishes."

He started to protest, but Celia frowned. "Do you want your room back or not?"

"Fine. But I wish you'd brought me that dessert you promised. Gerry ate all the cookies last night."

"Yes, well, we can't always get what we want, little man," Celia said, tossing her napkin onto her luncheon plate and heading for the stairs.

It's time he learned that, she thought, although she regretted uttering the words when his face fell. Hadn't she hoped Clarence's death wouldn't force the boys to grow up too quickly? And now here she was, reiterating the hard facts of life to him over sandwiches.

"Are you sure there's enough space in Beverly's room for the trunk?" Gerry was asking as he plodded up the stairs next to her.

"We'll make room."

The trunk wasn't overly heavy, but it was awkward to carry without handles. Celia cringed when they banged the side of it against the crystal doorknob of her new room. "Be careful, Gerry! Why are you in such a hurry?"

"Sorry, sis. I'm supposed to meet the guys at the field at one. Where do you want this?"

Celia mentally judged the distance between the foot of the bed and the vanity, where Beverly's rosary still hung, draped over the mirror. It would be tight, but there weren't many options. The large bedroom furniture already filled the decent-size room.

"I guess this will have to do," she said, nodding to the spot and positioning her end. Once it was in place, she ran a hand over the wooden top, saddened by the nicks and scratches its once pristine surface bore. She'd hoped it would remain that way, but she supposed it had been too much to hope for. "Gerry, why is this top so beat up?"

Guilt stole over the thirteen-year-old's face. "I'm sorry about that, Celia. I guess I should have been more careful."

He sounded sincere, and in the scheme of things, a few scratches weren't a big deal. She was starting to feel like the trunk looked, showing early signs of wear, even though neither were very old.

"You can go. Thanks for the help. Don't keep your friends waiting. I have plenty of work to do in here."

Glancing around, Gerry nodded, then quickly left the room. Did it still spook him, this room where their sister had slipped away from them in her sleep? How much of that time did he remember?

Truth be told, it still bothered her. But what choice did she have?

She opened the closet, dismayed to see Beverly's dresses still hanging there. Her mother couldn't bring herself to clear away her sister's things after all these years.

"It's time," Celia announced, as if saying the words out loud could help convince her heart it was true.

She'd use these hours before dinner with Preston to go through Beverly's personal items. Maybe if the room was a blank slate, Celia could make it feel more like her own. Pulling the clothing out of the closet, she laid it all out on the bed, considering what to do with each piece. Did she want to keep any of it? Could she? Should she discuss it with her mother? Celia never let herself sit in indecision for long. Her mother could have dealt with all of this a long time ago, but she hadn't. Now the woman would need to deal with her husband's personal items. Celia could take care of Beverly's.

She found a few empty boxes in the basement and brought them upstairs. Going through the pile of clothing, she neatly folded most of the dresses, skirts, and blouses away. She'd donate them. Her early years, during the Depression, had taught her there were always people in need.

She set three dresses aside, unable to part with everything. Beverly had worn all three of them during their summer at Whispering Pines. The yellow sundress had been a high school graduation gift, the red one was Beverly's favorite, and the pretty white one with a smattering of flowers across the skirt embodied summertime for Celia.

There was a hanging rack in the attic where their mother kept the most special items of clothing as they'd outgrown them through the years. Celia would put these there. She couldn't get rid of them, but she didn't want to see them every day either. It would be too painful.

The hours flew by, her focus intense as she forcibly kept the memories of the many ghosts at bay. When George rapped on her door, the time shocked her.

"Wow, it looks different in here," George said, taking in the boxes and bare walls.

"I suppose it does," Celia agreed, looking around her. She'd accomplished what she'd set out to do.

"Mother made me come up to see if you were getting ready for dinner yet. You're making so much noise up here, she thought maybe you'd lost track of time."

Celia thanked him for the reminder as she pushed wild tendrils out of her eyes. She couldn't go out for a nice dinner looking like she'd been battling demons all afternoon—even if those demons only existed in her mind.

She hoped it wouldn't take long for her to start thinking of this as *her* room.

"Go watch for Mr. Whitby's car, will you? He has a new Thunderbird. Black. Very sharp. You'll like it."

George's eyes lit up. "Cool! Does it have red leather inside? Those are the best."

"I believe it does." Celia grinned. "Maybe he'll even give you a quick spin around the block if you ask nicely."

"Yes!" George shouted, clapping his hand against the doorframe.

"I'll let you know the minute he gets here. But if you aren't quite ready, I'll keep him busy."

Celia laughed, her own spirits buoyed by his youthful enthusiasm. So much about their current situation was awful, but she'd missed her brothers and mother.

It was finally starting to feel good to be home.

* * *

"Celia, I won't accept your resignation. I can't."

"What do you mean, you can't? Look. Preston. I've explained my situation. I can't stay in Chicago. My family needs me here. Surely you understand that. I appreciate *all* the opportunities you've given me over the years. I've learned so much, working for you. I'm hoping you'll give me a letter of recommendation. I need to work. We need the income. I just can't live and work in Chicago. I could never uproot my family, and they need me," Celia repeated. "Our home is here."

Preston nodded as he dabbed at the corners of his mouth with a gold linen napkin. The nearly ten years since she'd first met the man had leached most of the color from his thick head of hair, but beyond that, he'd changed little. His brown eyes still gazed warmly at her. She'd never been sure what he saw in her, why he'd taken her under his wing and taught her so much. He'd always treated her as if she was qualified to do anything the men did in his office settings.

"Your commitment to family is one thing I've always admired about you, Celia. I understand you can't stay in Chicago. To be honest, I didn't drive all the way over here just to have dinner with you. I had other business to attend to in town."

This surprised Celia. "Did you find a new supplier nearby to work with?"

"Not exactly," he said, nodding at the server as the smartly dressed man discreetly removed their plates. "You know I've been interested in expanding for some time."

She did. Competition was fierce in Chicago. Preston had already opened a satellite office in a small town in Nebraska. Initially, Celia questioned why he didn't opt for Omaha, but Preston would have faced similar competition in a city of that size. He was experimenting with midsize towns.

"Preston . . . are you considering opening an office here?"

If it were true, she may not have to resign after all. She held her breath, waiting for his reply. Her future hinged on it.

He didn't keep her waiting. "Yes. In fact, everything is already in place. We open in a month. We've secured space and have a rough opening plan. Hiring still needs to happen. I want you here. You'd be a tremendous asset for me. For the company."

Celia could hardly believe what she was hearing. "You want me to run your new office?"

He faltered, a wary look flooding his eyes. "Well . . . not exactly."

"Well, what then? I don't understand."

"Establishing an office here was Tripp's idea. He's been working on it for months."

At the mention of Tripp's name, Celia narrowed her eyes. "How did I not know about this?"

Preston shook his head. "My dear, while you are well versed in the inner workings of the company, there are some things we need to keep under wraps while we're still investigating their viability."

Celia fidgeted, hating the condescending tone of his words.

He must have read her body language. "Don't misunderstand me, Celia. There may come a time when you'll take part in these types of decisions. You just aren't quite there yet. But regardless, I want you in the office here."

"Working for Tripp," she spat out, unable to hide her dismay over the idea. The events of the past few weeks left her too overwhelmed to hide her genuine reaction.

He chuckled. "Yes. For Tripp. As distasteful as the idea may sound to you, the two of you make a good pair. My son does a masterful job working with customers and suppliers, but he lacks attention to detail. You, my dear, let nothing slip through the cracks. I need both of your skill sets here, in order to make this work."

"You need us *both*, but you want *me* to work for *him*."

"Correct," he agreed, and Celia knew from his tone that there would be no room for negotiation on the point.

Celia's mind flashed back to her conversation in the park with Danny about women in the boardroom. He'd buoyed her confidence. She needed to remember this wasn't a straightforward path she'd chosen for herself—to make her way in a world dominated by men. She'd never succeed if she didn't keep her foot in the door.

She'd tolerated Tripp to this point; maybe she could again, even if she'd now be working for him directly. What choice did she really have? Starting over, somewhere new, without Preston's mentorship, held even less appeal. Besides, her family needed the money. They were her responsibility now.

"Fine. I accept. But I'll need a week to move my things back from Chicago."

"Of course, Celia. Take your week. And then I expect to see you back here, ready to help us get this new office off the ground."

* * *

Celia's mother was waiting for her in the living room when Preston dropped her off, no doubt eager to hear what had transpired.

"Oh! Hello, Mother. I'm surprised you're still up," Celia said as she opened her pocketbook, pulling out a small bundle wrapped in a gold linen napkin before dropping her house key back into the purse.

"Let me guess. Extra dessert for George? Will the restaurant come knocking, looking to take their napkin back?"

Laughing, Celia shook her head. "I peeked at the bill as Preston was paying. Believe me, they shouldn't miss it. Let me go set this in the refrigerator."

"Then come tell me how the discussion went," Maggie instructed, her voice trailing after Celia.

When she opened the fridge, Celia frowned. It was nearly empty—a poignant reminder that her mother couldn't keep the household running on her own, at least not until she healed. Celia needed to make a trip to the grocery store.

She sighed, shutting the door. Despite her reservations about working so closely with Tripp, it was her only option for the time being. She wouldn't share her concerns with her mother. Besides, if it wasn't Tripp causing her difficulties at work, it would be some other man. Her presence made many of them feel threatened.

She forced a smile as she rejoined her mother. "Hopefully George likes Boston cream pie," she said.

"I doubt he's ever had it, but if it has sugar in it, he'll like it. Now, I want to hear all about your evening. You seem to be in a pretty good mood."

Nodding, Celia shared the stroke of good fortune around Preston's plan to open a local office. Her mother sat quietly, tears glistening in her eyes. It wasn't the reaction Celia had expected.

"Mother, what's wrong? I thought you'd be pleased that I won't have to find other work."

Taking a deep breath, Maggie sat taller in the wheelchair. "*Pleased* would be an understatement. After everything that's happened, losing so many wonderful people, it's hard to believe this is something that turned out in our favor."

"So why the tears?"

"Foolishness, I suppose," Maggie claimed, brushing at her cheek. "I just worry about you giving up your exciting job and the home you've made for yourself in Chicago to come back here to take care of us. And what about that nice young fellow who took you out on a date last night? Danny? He doesn't live here, does he?"

Celia felt a pang in her chest at the mention of his name. "No, Danny doesn't live here. But he doesn't live in Chicago either. He does most of his work abroad, so even if I was still in Chicago we wouldn't be able to see each other nearly as often as we'd like."

"Could he find work here?"

She shook her head, considering how best to steer the conversation in another direction. "Don't worry about Danny, Mother. I'm afraid there's no future for me with him. I'm not too terribly sad about giving up my apartment, and this new role at work, here in town, may be my chance to prove myself, versus staying in

Chicago where Preston already has a strong management team in place."

Maggie sighed. "How did I get so lucky to have you for a daughter? You've always been here for me, through all our tough times."

Standing, Celia reached for the handles on her mother's wheelchair. "You might not still feel like that, six months from now, when you're tired of my cooking. You know how I despise the kitchen."

Maggie reached over her shoulder to pat Celia's hand. "I've already thought of that and started instructing Gerry on some basic dishes. He may be our only hope, if I want to have any decent help with meals around here."

WINTER 1955

CHAPTER TWENTY-TWO
GIFT OF THE WORLD

*C*elia yelped in pain, grabbing her foot as she dropped onto her blue trunk. She *really* needed to get Gerry and George to haul the hope chest up to the attic before she broke her big toe on it. She'd lost count of the number of times she'd banged into it over the past four years.

She'd have to remember to ask them to do it tomorrow. Gerry was too busy in the kitchen now, and if the mouthwatering aroma of roast turkey wafting through her open bedroom door was any indication, her brother was helping their mother create a prize-winning Thanksgiving meal. Celia felt a twinge of guilt over not helping, but then she reminded herself she'd *bought* all the food. Gerry was seventeen, handy in the kitchen, but likely to consume a vast quantity of the meal himself. Between her two brothers, she doubted there'd be much for leftovers, despite the jaw-dropping amount of groceries she'd brought home.

As she rubbed her aching toe, Beverly's rosary caught her eye. It was the one thing Celia never touched in the room. Seeing it there sent her mind back to earlier Thanksgiving meals: Clarence, seated at the head of the table, jabbing the air with his fork as he shared a funny story gleaned during his work as a handyman; Beverly's laughter, light and musical, skipping up and over everyone else's. She remembered how a young George would try to sneak olives from Gerry's plate when he wasn't looking, and how one silencing look from Clarence would squelch their bickering.

Celia missed those early days, when she'd had nothing more to worry about than if anyone would invite her to prom or if she'd get a decent grade on a test. So much had changed since those earlier holidays. Now Gerry was the senior in high school instead of Celia.

A gust of wind rattled her windowpanes, blasting icy pellets of snow against the glass. Maybe Old Man Winter had his holidays mixed up. Celia inhaled, smiling at the delicious scent of this year's Thanksgiving dinner. Celebrations looked different now, but she still enjoyed them.

She flexed her foot, testing it, to be sure she'd again avoided breaking her toe, then stood and smoothed the skirt of her dress. Her eyes fell on the newspaper. She picked it up and unfolded it, still amazed to see a picture of herself staring back.

The piece had been Preston's idea. Celia knew nothing about it until he'd called to instruct her to go down to the local newspaper office. "And wear something nice," he'd said, although he offered no further clarification.

The article highlighted Celia's ten years working for the Whitby Company, beginning after her college graduation, first working in Chicago and then locally. Preston described her significant contribution to the success of their new office. His quote praised Celia as a "rising star" in the company.

The purpose of the article was to enhance their overall reputation in the community, to position the company as forward-thinking and innovative. Other small hometown construction businesses touted the fact they were "local" while Preston's company was headquartered in the "big city." Since Celia was a local girl herself, Preston wasn't afraid to use this to his company's advantage.

Tripp had mumbled something about it being a fluff piece, but

Celia suspected he was jealous his father hadn't featured *him* in the article. Maybe it was fluff, but Celia was choosing to view it as a victory for working women.

She'd felt a twinge of guilt when the reporter specifically quoted her desire to "never depend on a man after seeing her own mother suffer badly, not once, but twice, having lost two husbands." While it was the truth, Celia never wanted to hurt her mother's feelings by shining a light on her personal tragedies.

When she'd admitted as much to Maggie, the older woman waved away her daughter's concern. "If I had it to do all over again, I'd probably feel the same way you do, honey. I'm so proud of you." Maggie even brought home ten copies of the newspaper, confirming how proud she was of her daughter.

Celia put one copy of the article into the scrapbook she'd started a few years earlier. Whenever she'd spot a photo in a newspaper that either specifically listed Danny as the photographer, or that she suspected he might have taken because it matched his style, she added it to the scrapbook. Danny was finding success in his chosen profession. His work was popping up in newspapers and magazines from around the country. Celia was proud of him.

"Come and get it!" George yelled upstairs.

Celia's stomach rumbled with hunger. She refolded the newspaper, considered grabbing her shoes from her closet to complete her holiday outfit, but changed her mind when she flexed her toe. She could still feel a faint throb where it had connected with the corner of her trunk.

With any luck, Maggie wouldn't notice her stockinged feet at the table. Her mother expected them to dress for dinner on holidays.

After Clarence died, Celia started sitting at one end of the table, across from her mother. The boys grabbed their chairs on opposite sides. They said grace and started passing dishes.

"This stuffing is so good, Mother. I wish we'd have it more than twice a year," Celia said, nearly moaning over the delicious side dish.

"You can thank your brother for that," Maggie said, grinning across the table at Gerry. "I think the student has surpassed the teacher with this one."

Smiling, Celia tipped her head to Gerry. "Mother's right. This might be the best yet."

Gerry shrugged, but Celia could tell his nonchalance was an act. She'd overheard him mention to George that he might like to go to culinary school.

Their conversation flowed easily around the table. George teased Celia about using the newspapers their mother had brought home to line his rabbit cage out back (to which Maggie said he better not). Celia countered with the suggestion they try rabbit stew for their upcoming Christmas dinner this year.

Maggie had just excused herself to fetch the pumpkin pie when the doorbell chimed. Curious who might visit on Thanksgiving, Celia stood to answer. Gerry and George barely glanced her way, never missing a beat in their debate over whether Green Bay or Detroit would win the upcoming football game. They were eating later than was common, so perhaps whoever was at the door had assumed they'd already finished celebrating. Hopefully their visitor wouldn't take offense at her stockinged feet.

Celia swung the door open—and froze. Icy air rushed in, surrounding her. She wondered if her eyes were playing tricks on her. Dusk had fallen while they were eating, though true sunset wouldn't fall for another hour.

"Hi," he said, his simple greeting doing little to clear up her confusion. "I hope this isn't a bad time."

"Danny," she finally managed. "This is a surprise."

"I always knew you could do it," he said, holding up a newspaper she hadn't noticed he was holding; her own eyes stared back at her in black-and-white. "I knew you'd make it to the boardroom."

A laugh puffed out from her lips, forming a cloud in the frosty air. "I've hardly *made* it."

He shook his head. "Celia, you're only thirty-two years old. You're on the front page of your newspaper. I'd say it bodes well for your career."

"How did you even see that?" she asked, still confused over his sudden appearance on her doorstep after a four-year absence. There'd been no correspondence between them in all that time, just as before.

"My mother showed it to me."

Footsteps sounded behind her. She didn't need to look to know it was her mother. Though Maggie had healed, she now walked with a pronounced limp. "For Heaven's sake, Celia, invite the poor man in and close the door. We could feel the chill back in the dining room."

"I'm sorry, where are my manners?" Celia stepped back out of the way, motioning Danny inside.

He nodded appreciatively, and as he brushed past her, Celia inhaled the scent of him: a heady mixture of cold, tobacco, and a subtle cologne with a woodsy undertone. She nearly laughed when the scent of him reminded her of Whispering Pines.

How was it this man could walk back into her life and send her pulse racing like no one else? She'd dated over the past four years, but no one had held her interest.

"Mother, you remember my friend, Danny?"

Nodding, Maggie smiled warmly at this man who was actually so much more, and somehow less, than a friend. "We were just sitting down for a bit of coffee and pumpkin pie. Would you care to join us?"

A stricken look settled on Danny's features. "I'm so sorry. I shouldn't have stopped by unannounced like this and interrupted your holiday celebration. Mother and I ate earlier, I never dreamed . . ."

As his voice trailed off, Maggie laughed. "We're eating fashionably late because the pilot light on the stove went out, and I failed to notice right away. Don't apologize."

"Mother, give us a moment, would you?"

"Certainly. Take all the time you need," Maggie said, backing away. "I'll save you a piece if you prefer."

They remained silent as Maggie rejoined her sons in the dining room. When they were alone again, Celia turned back to her unexpected visitor, now standing just inside the closed door.

"Danny, what are you really doing here? It's been a long time."

But not seven years.

He sobered. "It has. In fact, I have a question for you first. Is anyone else celebrating Thanksgiving with you? Other than your mother and brothers?"

Realizing he couldn't know for sure whether she was with someone now, she considered how best to respond. The newspaper article he held in his hand spoke to her single status, but that didn't mean there wasn't someone special in her life. She sensed Danny's hope that she dined alone, although they'd parted under the understanding that they each wanted the other to move on.

Celia had never truly done that. But could she admit as much to Danny?

They'd never played games with each other. She wasn't about to start now.

"No. It's just the four of us."

Danny's shoulders visibly relaxed, but he still wore a pensive expression. "Is it fair for me to say how happy I am to hear that?"

"Not even a little." She wanted to play it cool as Danny's eyes held hers, but she feared that would be a fruitless effort. She still felt that all-too-familiar pull toward him.

"Would you like me to join you for dessert?"

Celia considered this. The small talk they'd both have to endure when all she really wanted to do was find out why, after all this time, Danny was back. And how long would he be here? She'd learned it was never for long enough.

"Let me grab my coat," she offered instead.

He smiled then, his eyes traveling down to her stockinged feet. "It's cold. You won't make it far in only a coat."

She'd forgotten all about her lack of shoes and her sore toe. "If you have time, I'll just run up and put on something warmer. I wasn't expecting to leave the house."

"Of course."

As she ran upstairs and down the hallway, she nearly slid past the bedroom she'd finally come to consider her own. The wooden floorboards were slippery, and she was still in shock. Hurrying inside, she closed her bedroom door and collapsed against it, catching her breath.

"Bev. He's back. Why is he here? What should I do?" she whispered to the silent room. The muffled voices of her brothers floated up to her, but there was no response from her long-dead sister, nor did Celia expect one. But as she let her eyes drift shut, a memory of her sister, forever the idealistic eighteen-year-old that sought romance despite her pained life, floated to the surface, laughing and encouraging her.

Grab this opportunity and don't be afraid to take a chance, Beverly would have said.

Celia may regret opening her heart yet again to the man standing downstairs, but after losing so many people, she didn't want to miss out on anything more.

* * *

"I still can't believe you showed up on my doorstep on Thanksgiving!" Celia said, tilting her head back to meet Danny's eyes. She was in his bed at the hotel, and while part of her mind screamed at her over the impropriety of it all, a stronger part silenced that judgmental inner voice. She was a grown woman, and she'd loved this man for over ten years. Their relationship wasn't typical, with the trappings of tradition and rings, but it didn't make it any less real.

His arm tightened around her shoulders and he kissed her forehead. "When I boarded that train four years ago without you, I was terrified. I worried I might never have the chance to hold you like this again. Was I walking away from the best thing that would ever happen to me?"

Celia placed her hand on his bare chest, feeling his heartbeat under her palm. "That was a dark time for me, Danny . . . It nearly killed me to let you go, but I didn't feel like I had any choice."

"And now? Do you still feel you made the right choice?" he pressed, laying his hand over hers, holding it over his core.

She considered his question. What if she'd have made a different choice that day? What if she would have boarded that train with him?

Shifting, she propped herself up on her elbows and held his gaze. "I guess we can never know if one choice is better than another. We can only see how our lives evolve following the choices we *do* make. We can never really know what might have been."

Danny leaned forward, kissed the tip of her nose, and fell back on the bed, never breaking eye contact with her. "I suppose you're right. We'll never know how things might have turned out if I'd have stayed, or if you'd have come with me. Do you regret coming here with me tonight?" he asked, lightly running his finger over her heart.

She laughed. "What, can you hear the little angel on my shoulder, scolding me for letting you seduce me so easily again?"

But this time he didn't smile back. "Is that what you think I'm doing here? Seducing you? Celia, it has never been just about the sex with us. At least for me. I love you. I'll always love you. We just can't be together all the time. The things we want in life are too different."

She felt her own smile slip away at his declaration. "I know, Danny. And I love you, too. We aren't kids anymore. And we've both stayed true to our own paths. I'm not naïve enough to think that this changes anything. You'll leave again, won't you?"

Nodding, he pushed up so his back rested against the headboard. The sheet covering him slipped down to his waist, but he adjusted it to keep Celia modestly covered.

For the first time, she noticed a scar running from his left shoulder down to his navel. She reached up and traced the line.

"Danny," she whispered. Even she could hear the fear in her voice.

He caught her hand as it reached the top of the sheet. "My job isn't without risks."

Her heart physically hurt at the thought of him injured, lying in a hospital in some foreign country, alone and hurting.

"Celia, I'm fine," he assured her, kissing her fingers.

"For now," she sighed. She sat up and wrapped her arms protectively around his midsection, not caring that she was naked, uncovered. She had nothing to hide from this man. She'd found her soul mate in him.

"I have something for you," he said, his tone taking on the light-heartedness she'd missed.

"For me? Why?"

He twisted, opening a top drawer in the bedside table. He removed a long, rectangular box wrapped in red paper, a gold bow on top. "Think of it as an early Christmas present."

Grinning, she accepted the gift. "But I have nothing for you."

Danny laughed out loud. "Celia, don't be ridiculous. I show up on your doorstep, unannounced, after four years, and you think I'd expect you to have a gift all picked out and wrapped?"

Playfully, Celia set the gold bow on top of Danny's head, then tore the paper away, ignoring the red curls of paper as they fell onto the white sheet. Removing the top of the box, she pulled back a length of white cotton. Nestled below, strung from one side of the narrow box to the other, was a gold bracelet dotted with unique charms.

This wasn't a gaudy, childlike charm bracelet. Each charm was dainty and exquisitely crafted. "Oh, Danny. It's so pretty."

"Here. Let me put it on for you." He took the box from her and carefully removed the piece from the tiny clasps at each end, then wrapped the delicate gold chain around her right wrist, opposite the silver watch she wore on her left.

She slowly touched each charm one by one. "Tell me the story," she whispered, her gaze shifting between the piece of art she now wore and his eyes.

And he did, describing where he'd picked up each of the charms over the years. There were miniatures of the Eiffel Tower and the Colosseum in Rome, speaking to his international travels. There was also a tiny replica of both the Golden Gate Bridge and the Statue of Liberty. "You couldn't travel the world, so I thought I'd bring the world to you."

Celia thought her heart might burst.

"And this one?" she asked, her finger buoying up a charm that

looked like a Christmas tree. But she already knew what it represented to Danny.

"You know what that is," he said, smiling into her eyes. "That signi-
fies our special place."

"And this?" Celia asked again, this time touching a tiny gold heart.

"That's mine," he said, "and I gave it to you years ago."

There were a few more charms, but as he leaned in to kiss her,
they forgot about the jewelry.

CHAPTER TWENTY-THREE
GIFT OF A FAITHFUL MENTOR

"Ou look pretty, dear," Maggie complimented her daughter as Celia walked across the living room in search of her purse.

"Thank you. Did the boys find the last box of Christmas decorations in the attic yet, the one with the tree skirt?" Celia asked, the black spikes of her heels clicking across the hardwood floors. She smoothed the red velvet of her form fitting dress over her hips.

Maggie turned back to her task of hanging strands of tinsel from the boughs of the balsam fir they'd stood in the corner of their living room earlier that day. "Hopefully not. I need a few more minutes to finish with this tinsel before they come back down. You know what a mess they make of it when they try to help."

Celia nodded with a slight smile, admiring their Christmas tree. She'd helped her mother string the fat, colorful lights before heading upstairs to get ready for her holiday office party. The star the boys placed on top was slightly off-kilter—not enough to warrant fixing but enough to bring a smile to Celia's lips. They'd hung many of their favorite ornaments from the boughs while she'd been upstairs, trying to force her unruly red curls and pale face into a presentable ensemble for the evening's festivities.

The cheerful sight gave her spirits a boost. She wasn't excited about the party, and would have preferred to call her date and cancel for the evening, but Preston and Tripp expected her to make an appearance. This was work. Not fun.

She hoped the man Ruby set her up with for the evening wouldn't bore her to tears. As she reached for her purse next to the sofa where she'd dropped it after returning from tree shopping, her gold bracelet caught in the black lace of the wrap she'd donned over her dress. Try as she might, she couldn't untangle it with one hand. She heard a car pull up outside.

"Mother, can you help me with this?"

Glancing her way, Maggie nodded, finished applying the strands trailing from her fingers, then made her way to her daughter's side. Taking her wrist, she examined the bracelet. "Celia, this is exquisite. Where did you get it?"

"From Danny," she said, trying to keep the resigned sigh from her voice. She hadn't been able to bring herself to wear the bracelet since he'd dropped her back at home in the predawn hours following their Thanksgiving reunion.

Maggie frowned, the disapproval on her face clear. Her mother hadn't said a word about her unexpected visitor, or even her sneaking back into the house at such an ungodly hour. Celia swore the woman had the ears of a bat. She knew her mother didn't understand the bond she shared with Danny. She probably blamed him for her daughter's ongoing single status. But her relationship with Danny wasn't something she felt compelled to discuss with her mother.

"Come here, closer to the light, so I can see what I'm doing."

Like an obedient child, Celia allowed her mother to pull her by the wrist. It took Maggie only seconds to untangle the wayward strands of her shawl from the bracelet. Years of sewing and mending made her adept at dealing with tiny, twisted threads.

"There you go. Now, enjoy your evening. And Celia, give this boy a chance," Maggie said, her tone resigned.

Turning toward the front door and the sound of footsteps on the stairs, Celia nodded. Her date was far from a boy, and she was approaching the evening as more of a business arrangement than the beginnings of a romantic entanglement. Ruby hinted the man would like to come to work for their company, and Celia's heart was too bruised, once again, to even think in romantic terms about anyone.

* * *

Ruby's friend served his purpose, and Celia noticed his eyes lit up more at the prospect of an introduction to Tripp than they had when he'd first laid eyes on her. He wore his dark suit well and displayed the expected social niceties toward her. The only thing that gave her pause was the possessive way he kept a hand at her waist. She'd have preferred to walk into the gathering on his arm and then mingle with fellow employees and invited guests on her own. She didn't need or want a chaperone.

When her date offered to fetch her a glass of champagne, she took it as her chance to slip into an adjoining room. She spied one of their biggest customers mingling next to the dessert table. Glancing around, she saw her date making a beeline for Tripp, now that she'd made the initial introduction, and Celia could only hope Tripp would engage the man in conversation for a while.

"Mr. Fletch, it's delightful to see you this evening," Celia said, her hand outstretched in greeting to the squat, balding man whose eyes were level with her chin, thanks to the black heels she'd chosen. "And this must be your lovely wife."

The man beamed at the attention Celia offered him. Her current small town celebrity status stemming from last month's newspaper article gave her extra clout in the eyes of some of their clients. She knew it wouldn't last, but she'd gladly capitalize on it for now.

Preston caught her eye from where he stood with another small group of customers and local officials, giving her a discrete wink. He'd taught her the importance of mingling and building relationships with customers and prospects.

The short man was introducing his portly wife to her, and she turned her attention back to the couple, but the fishy smell wafting off platters of shrimp and salmon pâté hit her with unexpected force. Struggling to smile and at least pretend to listen to the man expound on his plans for expansion in the coming year, Celia snapped open the clasp on her black velvet clutch that hung from her wrist. She pulled out a tissue and held it under her nose, trying in vain to pay attention to what the man was saying.

"Joseph, dear, I believe this dear woman may need to hear about your plans later."

The man stopped midsentence, confused when his wife cut him off so abruptly, and looked between the two women.

"Please be a dear and go get me one of those delightful glasses of eggnog, would you?" the wife asked, although her tone left no room for argument.

Nodding, the man turned away with a promise to be back in a moment. Once he was out of earshot, she turned back to Celia. "My dear, you look positively green. Go. Quickly. Before he comes back. I think you may need some air. I remember feeling that same way when I was expecting my first. But don't worry, the sickness will pass."

Horror flashed through Celia's mind at the woman's words, and she felt rooted in place.

"Oh, I'm so sorry, I just assumed— It was always the smell that got to me . . . but if I misjudged . . ." the woman stammered, ashamed at the conclusion she'd jumped to.

But Celia couldn't even summon the energy to reply. The tissue helped block the stench, but her stomach still roiled. A wave of self-preservation washed over her and she spun in the direction of the door, hurrying across the room and down the hallway as quickly as her ridiculous shoes would allow, nearly upsetting a silver tray of stuffed mushrooms carried by a server in a white jacket.

Bursting through the outer doors into the dark night, Celia gulped the cold, crisp air. Lanterns mounted on either side of the door cast pools of yellow light on the concrete, freshly dusted now with snow that fell while she'd been inside.

She stepped aside as a late-arriving couple approached from the street, willing her stomach to settle as the pair nodded a greeting to her and let themselves in through the front entrance. The heavy door swung shut, cutting off their voices, and once again she was alone in the quiet of the dark night.

Her stomach refused to cooperate, and she hurried out of the circle of light toward a hedge of evergreens, low to the ground and twinkling with tiny holiday lights. Bracing her hand on a low wall, Celia emptied her stomach into the bushes, horrified at her inability to control her body.

She remained bent over, still heaving even after her stomach was empty. Tears tracked down her face, hot against the icy feel of her cheeks. Her shoulders were bare. Her shawl was inside with the coat check.

A warm hand touched her shoulder, resting there for a moment before strong fingers urged her upright and thrust a soft handkerchief into her hand. It reminded her of the hanky Clarence used to keep in his back pocket, always handy to dab away a spot of blood when he nicked a finger at work or to wipe a snotty nose on one of his sons.

"Celia, are you all right?" came Preston's deep baritone. "I saw you run out, and when you didn't return, I thought I better check on you. Are you ill, dear?"

Gripping the cloth against her mouth, the white glow of it like a flag of surrender, Celia slowly nodded her head. The pieces of a puzzle clicked into place. The woman's advice, gleaned from personal experience, still echoed in the back of her mind.

Danny had taken precautions, as he always did, but maybe this time that hadn't been enough. Had they gambled one too many times? Condoms weren't foolproof, but Celia had always steadfastly ignored the potential risk of an unplanned pregnancy.

As if he could read her mind, Preston's eyes widened, and even in the dark she could see the disappointment register. He'd never looked at her like that before. In that single moment, it felt as though everything she'd worked so hard for over the past ten years might evaporate in a flash.

"I'll send my car around for you. Go home. Clean yourself up. We can't have our guests seeing you like this. I'm not leaving until Tuesday. I expect to see you first thing Monday morning. We'll figure this out, Celia. I'll tell your date you felt ill and I sent you home. Is there anything else you'd like me to tell him?"

Celia held his gaze, this mentor of hers who had taken so many chances on her, and she felt a deep sense of despair settle over her. She'd never wanted to disappoint him. She shook her head. "No, I just met him for the first time tonight."

Nodding, as if she'd answered his unspoken question, he turned back toward the lavish holiday party he was hosting. "Wait on the curb. I'll send my driver right out."

Celia did as he instructed, tossing the soiled handkerchief into the bushes and straightening her red velvet dress before walking away from the hall. Inside, the people she'd worked so hard to impress for a decade mingled and sipped champagne. She should be in there with them right now. Instead, she was banished to the curb, never more aware of the unfair biases the world erected against women. She suspected that Tripp, Preston's own son, married less than a year to the daughter of a powerful politician, had a nasty habit of infidelity. But since he was a man, she doubted his actions would ever negatively impact his career.

But she'd known the risks. And unless she was suffering from a severe case of food poisoning, she'd face the consequences.

* * *

Monday morning dawned gray with the threat of their first blizzard of the season. The air felt heavy, expectant. Growing up in Minnesota, Celia recognized the calm before the storm.

The weather matched her mood.

She'd driven to the office, but had arrived forty minutes early. Only Tripp's car was in the parking lot, and he was the last person she wanted to exchange words with this morning. Instead of pulling into a spot, she gave in to her desire to keep moving. She eased back out of the parking lot—taking care, as the roads already had a light coating of ice on them; it must have rained during the night while she slept, and the temperature was dropping fast.

A tin of saltine crackers sat on the passenger seat. She pulled one out to nibble on. While sitting in the back of Preston's rented limousine on her way home from the party, she'd put the pieces together. She should have started her cycle two weeks earlier, but hadn't, and didn't even notice she was late in the busyness of the days leading up to Christmas. They planned to kick off a new advertising campaign in January, and she'd been spending extra time on it, intent on helping the company start the new year off strong. She'd been too busy to notice her lack of appetite, or even how tired she'd felt every day as she dragged herself home from the office.

She didn't need to see a doctor to know what was happening. She was thirty-two and had never been late with her cycle. She'd watched first Helen, and then Ruby, suffer through the early stages of pregnancy.

She'd just never expected to find herself in the same boat.

Lost in her thoughts, she drove slowly through the deserted park where she'd come with Danny, back before he'd left on the train after Clarence's death. The bare branches of the trees were skeletal against the white of the heavy clouds. The dormant grass bore a gray haze. The only spots of color were the deep green of the tall pines and the picnic tables sprinkled throughout the park. Celia wondered why the tables were still outside instead of in storage, away from the elements. She rolled to a stop next to the table where she'd sat with Danny years ago. Walking over to it, she noticed a fresh coat of paint. The table didn't look as shabby as it had that day, but Danny's handiwork remained, carved deep into the wood. She likened the table to her own heart. He'd also carved his initials there, and she doubted they'd ever truly fade.

"Danny, what do I do now?" she asked out loud.

Her only answer was the twittering of a bird, hidden somewhere in the treetops above.

She'd considered reaching out to him but had decided against it. At least for now. When they'd parted again, it was with the same understanding as before. They were both to go on living their own lives. This parting had felt more permanent, and she'd felt heartsick ever since, but they'd made their choices long ago.

If Danny knew she was pregnant, would he come back to her? Yes, she thought he would, out of a sense of responsibility and love. But she didn't want him to feel trapped. He was so talented, living the life he'd always dreamed of, traveling the world and documenting it for others.

Because she'd always loved him, she couldn't steal that dream from him.

She'd considered other options. She knew there were age-old ways to make the problem go away. But she couldn't bring herself to do that either. They'd conceived the child in love, even if it was an accident.

Could she give up her career to raise the baby? Women were making strides in the working world, but the company where she was building her career wasn't *that* forward-thinking—Preston's dark expression the other night was proof enough of that. Maybe they wouldn't fire her, but she'd never be able to keep her executive position.

She was at yet another crossroads.

Celia turned, startled, at the sound of tires rolling up behind her. She'd been so lost in her own thoughts that she hadn't heard a car approach. The black-and-white body of a cruiser stopped directly behind her own vehicle where she'd left it in the middle of the road. She hadn't expected anyone else to drive through the park on a blustery Monday morning.

"Everything all right, miss?" A young officer watched her through an open window. She could see his partner, an older man, behind the wheel. The two were likely munching on donuts as they patrolled the local parks, expecting little in the way of trouble.

"Yes. Everything is fine, Officers. I apologize for parking my car in the way. I'm heading in to work now," she explained, stepping carefully back toward her own car in deference to the ice underfoot.

The man eyed her skeptically but nodded and started to roll up his window. "Be careful. There's a storm blowing in. I'd hate for you to get caught in it."

She watched as the car inched around hers, leaving wheel tracks along the road's edge in the icy grass, and slowly rolled out of sight. She climbed into her vehicle and drove slowly back toward the office. She'd figure this out. Women had been rearranging their lives around surprise pregnancies since the beginning of time.

* * *

Preston waited for her behind the enormous desk in the corner office. She knew Tripp wanted to claim that premier spot for his own, but the old man made it clear the office was his alone. No one else was to use it, even though he was seldom in town.

She'd left her jacket and other things in her own small office before making her way to Preston's. She'd felt a sense of pride when they'd screwed a nameplate for CELIA MIDDLETON into the wall outside her office. The office wasn't fancy, but it was hers, and she'd earned it. They hadn't relegated her to a desk in front of the ring of offices, an accomplishment that made her proud, and she'd vowed to never take it for granted.

"I trust you're feeling better this morning," Preston said as she entered his domain. "At least your cheeks have some color today."

Celia nodded, shutting his door securely to ensure their privacy. Thankfully, the brisk air during her walk in the park gave her the appearance of health, despite the tendrils of morning sickness still stirring her insides. "I'm fine. Thank you for your kindly offer of a safe ride home on Saturday night. Please know how sorry I am."

Preston squinted at her, catching the loaded meaning behind her words.

"You need to deal with this situation quickly and carefully. You realize that, don't you?"

"I do," Celia agreed, taking a seat across from him. She sat back in her chair, crossed her legs, and rested her fisted hands together in her lap. She'd keep her back straight during this pivotal discussion, and under absolutely no circumstance would she allow herself to cry.

"Can I assume you weren't suffering from a stomach bug?"

If he wanted to talk in code, she was good with that. "That would be a correct assumption."

"Does the man know about this?"

Celia refused to break eye contact with Preston. She wouldn't cower in shame. "He does not. And I plan to keep it that way."

She wondered what Preston would think if she told him Danny was the baby's father. They knew each other, and she knew the older man liked Danny. Preston had been good to Mrs. Bell and Danny when Mr. Bell died unexpectantly. But she'd never tell Preston who the father was.

She didn't plan on ever telling anyone.

Only her mother and brothers knew he'd come by on Thanksgiving, and she doubted her brothers had paid any attention. She hoped she'd earned her mother's discretion.

"Do you plan to carry it to term?"

"I do."

Celia thought she saw Preston's shoulders relax at her confirmation. He was a practical man and would have considered this from all angles, too. Maybe she'd earned back a point or two of respect in his eyes. She had no way of knowing how he felt about the controversial subject of abortion, but he appeared relieved. That path wasn't right for her.

"Will you keep it?"

Celia nearly grinned. Preston avoided using the word *baby*. What was it about pregnancy that made men so nervous?

"That is the one question that isn't so easy to answer." She relaxed her hands, letting her gaze break from his. She looked to the scene beyond the large windows behind him. From this vantage point, the view of Main Street was impressive, even if it couldn't compare with the skyline of downtown Chicago. "I decided years ago that I wanted to choose a different path than most women. Part of it was out of necessity, but part of it was because I wanted to be something other than a homemaker. Maybe, someday, it'll be easier for women to have both children and a career, but we aren't there yet. At least I hadn't planned to learn how to juggle both."

Preston watched her but didn't interrupt. She shifted in her chair, trying to keep her tenuous grip on what she thought she wanted.

"I plan to have this baby. I know there are couples out there who want children but can't have them, so I've decided to give my baby up. I may not be the mothering type, but that doesn't mean I don't want what's best for this child."

Preston leaned back, crossing his arms over his chest. The desk lamp next to the blotter in front of him was on, despite the time of day, given the dreary weather outside. The light glinted off his cuff links; it was as if the universe were reminding Celia of what this man had accomplished in his own life. He'd made sacrifices, too, and now he had the power to make things happen.

Taking a deep breath, she leaned toward him. "Can you help me with this? And let me keep my job? You know I've earned my position here. If I were a man, we wouldn't even be having this conversation. Men's personal lives are just that. Personal. But because I'm a woman, and I won't be able to hide this pregnancy, I can't keep it private."

"You realize you've put me in a delicate position, don't you, Celia?" he asked.

"Because of the newspaper article, you mean?" Celia thought back to the comments she'd freely made to the reporter about her choice to forgo motherhood in deference to the less traditional choice of pursuing a career.

"Yes."

"I apologize for that, Preston. It wasn't intentional."

He sighed and uncrossed his arms, resting his forearms on his desk, and held her gaze. "I've thought of little else since Saturday night. I think I've come up with a plan that might work. But you have to trust me. And you have to do as I say. Then, a year from now, this can all be behind us, and we can pick up where we left off."

His words raised more questions than answers, but she realized she had little choice if she wanted to keep her job. And that was precisely what she wanted. She doubted any of her close friends, or her mother, would understand her thought process. Since they were all mothers now, she'd probably seem coldhearted to them. Unnatural, even. But she wasn't any of those things.

"I'll do exactly what you say," she agreed.

Celia watched as he pulled out a paper and pen. This was classic Preston. He'd lay out the plan for her, and together, maybe they could put all this behind them.

SPRING 1956

CHAPTER TWENTY-FOUR
GIFT OF HIDDEN TRUTHS

*C*elia wanted to smack Tripp right between the eyes and wipe that smug look off his face. She'd never hit anyone before, but today might be a first.

"Rein it in, girl," she muttered to herself, pushing the door open to the ladies' room for the umpteenth time that day. If she wasn't careful, people would notice.

She cracked the window open next to the sink to freshen the stale air. Since she was one of only four women in the office (if you didn't count the cleaning woman), she seldom encountered anyone else in the bathroom. She scowled at the ashtray stashed between the inside window and the outer screen. It held two discarded butts smeared with the bright red lipstick Tripp's secretary wore. No one was supposed to smoke in the restrooms. The stale smell of old cigarettes curled around her, carried deeper inside on the light spring breeze. Her stomach rolled—something it had done less often in the past two months. Turning sideways, she checked her profile in the mirror. Between her many trips to the bathroom and her expanding midsection, people were going to get suspicious.

Since her pregnancy was becoming more obvious, she and Preston had met with Tripp that morning to inform him that Preston was sending Celia to Whispering Pines for the upcoming summer season. Celia could understand the confusion on Tripp's face. If she wasn't painfully aware of the *real* reason Preston was banishing her to the resort, she'd be confused, too.

"But, Preston"—Preston expected Tripp to call him by his given name while in the office—"how am I going to service all of our accounts while she's gone? You know I do better out in the community, drumming up business!"

"Lucky for us you've been doing plenty of the 'out and about,' as you like to call it, since January. Our schedules are plenty full for the better part of this year. I can afford to have you *inside* for a few months."

Celia bit her lip to keep from smiling. Tripp didn't notice the sarcasm dripping from his father's words. Ever since she'd agreed to Preston's plan, she'd worked extra hard to secure several new, lucrative jobs scheduled for the summer months. Tripp couldn't take all the credit for the uptick in business, although he'd try.

Preston mentioned devoting too little time to the resort in recent years, and he worried he may need to dispose of it soon if someone didn't turn things around out there. This was a contrived excuse, of course. Preston had solid bookings and staff lined up for the summer already, but Tripp wouldn't know that. It had been years since he'd set foot out there. Tripp's wife, Sofia, preferred city life, insisting on trips to places like New York City and Los Angeles, even London once, instead of vacationing "out in the woods," as she liked to refer to it. Sofia had never even been to Whispering Pines.

Celia hadn't been back to the resort in five years herself. Eleanor and her husband, living in Chicago and raising kids of their own, never visited the resort anymore. Helen and family didn't go either. The staff was all different. She was nervous about her imminent return.

She was leaving the Monday after Easter. Preston claimed he needed her attention on some early season issues. She'd remain there until it was time to close up in the fall.

If Celia had thought he was serious about possibly selling Whispering Pines, she'd have been heartbroken. Despite the years since her last visit, it was still her favorite place on earth.

Tripp knew better than to argue with his father. But Celia's plans would put a damper on his lax summer schedule. Later, after Preston left to return to Chicago, he'd stopped by her office.

"I know what this is really about," Tripp said, standing in her doorway with his legs wide and his arms crossed over his chest, his stump tucked in his armpit. He'd given up on the prosthesis years earlier.

She glanced up from the note she'd been making, her heart skipping at his words. Had he guessed? She worked to keep her expression neutral. "What do you mean?"

"You need a break. I always knew it would come to this. The pressure. It's too much for you." He scoffed. "Typical."

She nearly recoiled as spittle shot from his mouth. For reasons she could never figure out, he still held her in contempt. She didn't know what she'd ever done to deserve it. Maybe he thought her existence threatened his position in the eyes of his father. Or maybe he was still bitter that she tried to keep him away from Beverly all those years ago.

"Excuse me?" she hissed, carefully setting her pencil down instead of zinging it at his face like she wanted to.

He relaxed his stance. "You heard me. You can't take the pressure, so you need a break. Can't say I'm surprised. Women aren't really cut out for the real world."

"The real world?"

"Yes, Celia, the *real* world. Where deals get made that keep the world going round. But don't worry. I'll set some of my typing aside, and you can take care of that when you get back next fall."

Pleased with himself, he spun on his heel and headed for the door, probably off on another of his two-martini lunches.

Knowing the thin walls of her office offered little protection from the curious, and that anyone in the office likely overheard Tripp, she'd escaped to the bathroom to catch her breath, shocked over his audacity.

"Someday, Tripp . . . *someday* . . . I promise you'll pay for how terribly you've treated me all these years," she promised, eyeing her reflection in the bathroom mirror. Her words, fueled by the rage over years of indirect abuse, settled into her soul.

Someday she'd make good on her promise.

* * *

Her mother had doubts about Celia's spring and summer plans, and she tried to articulate her concerns while they waited for the boys to join them at the table for Easter brunch.

Celia had noticed Maggie stealing glances at her when she thought her daughter wouldn't notice. Perhaps her mother suspected the real reason she was leaving town for a few months. It was nearly impossible to hide her condition from the woman who knew her best, but Celia refused to discuss it. She'd gone above and beyond in providing for her mother and brothers. She figured she'd earned the right to handle this her way, in private.

Her brothers rushed in, cutting off any further discussion between mother and daughter about her upcoming departure. Both had changed back into jeans and T-shirts the second they'd gotten home from morning Mass. After Clarence died in the accident, Maggie started attending church again—a practice Celia normally appreciated, although the cloying scent of incense had her practically swaying on her feet that morning.

"When are you leaving, Cee?" Gerry asked.

"In the morning," Celia said, setting the roll she'd been buttering back down onto her plate. "I'm so sorry I'll miss your graduation."

Gerry shrugged. "Like I said, it isn't a big deal. Heck, if I had the chance to go spend my summer at a lake resort, I'd take it. Are you sure they don't need any more help out there? It sounds cool, and I need a job."

She shook her head. Unfortunately, that would defeat the purpose of Celia hiding away for the final few months of her pregnancy. "Sorry, bud. Not this year. We're all staffed up. Maybe next year."

"Don't forget about me, Celia. I could use a job next summer, too. I'll be sixteen and needing to work."

Wagging her fork at both brothers, she promised she'd keep them in mind.

"And you should probably skip the desserts, maybe do some hiking out there, Celia," George said, grinning at her. "You're getting a little thick."

He ducked, but not fast enough, and the roll Gerry threw at him bounced off the top of his head. "Jesus Christ, George, I told you not to talk to girls like that, even if it's just Celia!"

"Boys!" their mother bit out, her eyes locking on Celia's. "That is enough!"

CHAPTER TWENTY-FIVE
GIFT OF SECLUSION

"If George thought I was thick in April, he should see me now," Celia murmured, crawling out of her bed and waddling to the tiny bathroom in the cabin she'd practically hidden out in all summer. She felt as big around as a house—or at least the cabin.

She'd spent time in the resort office keeping up on paperwork, but the tasks didn't challenge her brain anymore the way her normal duties did. She missed the hustle and competing priorities she encountered daily at the office.

Celia told staff and guests she was a widow, spending the rest of her pregnancy at Whispering Pines, nursing her broken heart after the untimely death of her husband. Preston expected her to uphold this charade they'd created. Unwed mothers were not well received, but widows were something else entirely.

The new cook wasn't as gifted in the kitchen as Mrs. Bell, but she made sure Celia ate plenty of healthy meals and snacks each day. The woman's young son often stopped by Celia's cabin to drop off food. Guests invited her to join them for evenings around the large campfire, giving her a reprieve from her solitary existence, but they deferred to her wish for privacy when she refused to discuss what happened to her husband.

Telling fewer lies meant a lower risk of getting caught in one.

A midwife checked on Celia throughout the summer, more frequently as her time drew near. When the baby kicked and turned in her belly, Celia couldn't help but feel pangs of doubt. Was she making the right decision? Could she give up this baby, the one she'd created with Danny? Was it fair of her not to reach out to him, to tell him what she was doing?

These questions and more plagued her as she watched the sun dip below the trees from the rocking chair in front of her little cabin. She liked to relax here in the evenings. She didn't have an unobstructed view of the lake, but she'd watched enough sunsets from the dock to know how quickly the sun disappeared.

She slapped at a mosquito; the little buggers were even more of a pest than usual this past summer. Maybe it was all the extra blood her body needed to grow this little human inside of her.

"Those things carry disease, you know," the young son of the cook said as he wandered up to where Celia rocked. He handed her a piece of cake wrapped in a napkin. "Mother thought you'd like this."

"And your mother also told you to check on me, didn't she?"

The boy nodded, a shy smile on his face.

"What were you saying? About diseases?"

"Oh. Yeah. We learned that in school. Bugs carry disease. Like malaria. You probably don't want that. Not when you are going to have a baby."

Celia doubted malaria was anything to worry about in Minnesota, but his concern touched her. He'd impressed her over the past few months, dutifully monitoring her but never getting in her way or bothering her. "Thank you. I'll keep that in mind. And I'll be careful."

He nodded and turned to leave.

"Wait," she said, hungry for human interaction. "Do you like school?"

He shrugged. "I guess."

"Do you plan to go to college someday?"

He held his hands out. "I'm ten. I don't know."

Celia chuckled at this and rocked again, her hands resting on top of the mound that used to be her flat stomach. "It's never too early to plan."

He stared at her like she was crazy. "Sorry, but I need to get back. I have a sink full of pans to wash. Father is taking me back home tomorrow because school starts next week. I have lots to do."

Consumed by her own situation, Celia hadn't thought about having to say goodbye to this precious young boy who'd kept her quiet company over the summer months. She felt a twinge of sadness, followed quickly by the realization that it was for the best. She'd have this baby soon, but she wouldn't keep it. How would she explain that to this young boy? Early on, Preston insisted she claim the baby died if anyone were to ask. That contingency plan was easier to agree to before she felt the baby kick. Her due date fell after most people would be gone for the season, but babies don't always arrive on schedule. It was good the boy was leaving. "Will you promise me you'll work hard in school? Maybe you'll want to be a doctor someday."

The boy grinned. "You don't think that's crazy?"

"No," Celia answered honestly. "You can be anything you want to be. At least that's what I've always believed."

He nodded and waved goodbye. As he turned to go, she sensed a new level of confidence in the set of his narrow shoulders. He reminded her of her own brothers, once so young, now nearly grown themselves. As she watched him go, a sudden pain stabbed her midsection. It wasn't like the false labor pains she'd discussed with the midwife earlier in the week. This was different.

"Wait!"

He paused, turning back to her. "Is something wrong, Mrs. Celia?" he asked, using the name she'd insisted on, instead of a fictitious surname.

She waited for the pain to ebb away and then smiled as calmly as she could. "Go get your mother, please?"

* * *

The next twenty-four hours passed in a blur. The midwife arrived, but when Celia's body didn't progress through the expected stages of labor, the elderly woman insisted they take Celia to the nearest hospital. There was pain, followed by oblivion. Then Celia woke to bright sunlight shining through a hospital window. The bed beside hers was empty. She was all alone in a world of white: white walls, white bedding, white floors. Even her arm looked washed of color where it lay limply over her midsection.

Gone was the familiar flutter she'd become accustomed to. Without having to be told, she knew she was, once again, utterly alone. Her fingers went automatically to her belly. A soft nothingness replaced the rigidity. Her baby was gone.

She lay quietly with this knowledge, struggling to come to terms with the vast gulf of emptiness. Tears leaked silently down her cheeks.

Eventually, exhaustion overtook her. She dozed, imagining the feel of a tiny warm body in her arms, clothed in the white christening gown hidden for years at home in her blue trunk. The infant kicked, revealing tiny feet encased in delightful, handcrafted booties. The last gift Beverly would ever give her.

A hand gently nudged her awake.

"Take this. It will help with the pain," a kind voice whispered in her ear.

Celia fought to open her eyes, expecting to see her sister standing beside her, but it was a stranger in a white nurse's uniform, smiling kindly at her while holding a paper cup in front of her face.

"It's all right. I know it hurts. You were so restless, I could tell your incision was causing you pain, so I brought something in that should help."

Celia hadn't felt the physical pain until the nurse mentioned it. The pain in her heart overshadowed everything. She'd tried to prepare for this time, knowing giving up her baby would hurt like hell, but some things you just can't prepare for.

"My baby?" she whispered, locking eyes with the young nurse.

The woman faltered, her smile slipping for a split second. "Is fine.

The doctors encountered some complications. You had to have a cesarian section. But you'll be fine, and so will the baby."

"Was it a boy?" Celia remembered the blue-rimmed booties, but her muddled mind was having difficulty distinguishing between what was real and what wasn't. "Or a girl?"

The woman shook her head. "The doctor will be in to speak with you later. Take these now. You need to rest."

* * *

Celia floated in and out of consciousness for another day. The hospital staff kept her for three more days. It was a lonely time. Her heart ached at the cries of a baby down the hallway. A beautiful arrangement of yellow roses arrived, compliments of Preston. His note wished her well, adding that he was eager to see her upon her return to the office.

She stopped asking the staff about the baby. Maybe it would be easier not to know if she'd had a girl or a boy. Preston took care of the adoption details, and she trusted his integrity. The baby would be in excellent hands. Her mentor would see to it.

As she sat quietly in the hospital bed, watching the rays of sunlight stream from one corner of her room to the other, she had ample time to think. She wished her mother was sitting beside her now. She missed her smiling face and knew Maggie would have helped her on this journey if Celia would have allowed it. She might have even approved of the decision Celia made. But Celia had been too stubborn to ask for help.

She missed her brothers and her friends. A month before Easter, Celia had finally confided in Ruby. While Preston graciously handled the adoption arrangements, he wasn't someone she could talk to about her firestorm of emotions. Ruby had begged to be by Celia's side when the baby arrived, but Celia wouldn't hear of it. Now she wished desperately that Ruby was in the room with her.

Finally, the day before her release, she called her oldest friend.

"Celia!" Ruby nearly shouted through the phone. "You made me sick with worry! Are you all right?"

Celia took a deep breath, the sound of Ruby's voice like a balm to her haggard soul. "I will be."

"And the baby?"

"I'm told the baby is fine, too."

There was a pause. "I take it you went through with it, then? You gave the baby up?"

A lone tear rolled down Celia's cheek. "I did. Honestly, Ruby, this is probably the hardest thing I'll ever do in my life. But I still feel it's for the best. For the baby. And for me."

Maybe if she kept saying it, someday she'd believe it.

"Then I support you, my friend, one hundred percent."

Celia played with a loose string from a snag in the coverlet draped over her stomach. She fought the urge to touch her deflated midsection. There was nothing there anymore. Nothing.

"Do you think I made a mistake, Ruby?"

She heard a telltale sniff. Ruby was losing her battle against tears, too. "Celia, this wasn't a decision you made lightly. I know you. You thought through this from every side. You came to peace with it. I know your heart is in pain. That's unavoidable. But remember, you did what you thought was best for everyone. You knew it wouldn't be easy. But that doesn't mean it wasn't right."

Celia nodded. Maybe someday she'd believe it.

CHAPTER TWENTY-SIX
GIFT OF PROTECTION

*C*elia held Ruby's words close as the car Preston had arranged for her dropped her back at Whispering Pines. She stood on the sidewalk in front of the lodge. All was quiet. With the Labor Day weekend behind them, no guests remained. Preston had avoided any late fall bookings in deference to her solitary return.

She'd never been alone at the resort before. Nash, the caretaker, should still be around somewhere; he wouldn't leave for the season until he'd completed all the upkeep and shuttered the cabins in October. But Nash's truck wasn't in the parking lot, so for now, she was still alone.

The extra days in the hospital had given her back some of her physical strength, but she still felt emotionally fragile. Despite the date on the calendar, the sun shone down on her with a strength more typical of midsummer. Without conscious thought, she found her feet carrying her out onto the dock instead of back to her cabin, and she sank down on the end, dangling her feet over the edge. The previous dry summer meant the water level was low, and she had to stretch to dip a toe in the water. She recoiled at the iciness of it. Sunlight or not, chilly nights had already stolen some of the summer's warmth.

She willed herself to relax, allowing her mind to drift where it wanted to—a luxury she seldom allowed herself. She couldn't have said how long she sat. It was as if her mind wouldn't clear completely, stuck in a light fog.

Eventually her stomach rumbled with hunger. She'd worn no jewelry to the hospital, so she didn't know the exact time, although it had to be approaching midafternoon. Dark clouds had emerged on the horizon, and the previously calm lake rolled with an angry energy.

Late summer storms were not uncommon here. Celia remembered Preston mentioning a September hailstorm years earlier that left broken windows and damaged cabin roofs in its wake.

Acknowledging her hunger, she swung her legs back up onto the platform and stood. She wobbled as a gust of wind buffeted her. She needed food and her incision ached. And she should probably get inside in case the weather turned.

She hadn't noticed the caretaker's return. He'd parked in front of the lodge.

Why do I feel so shaky?

Taking a fortifying breath, she let her feet carry her up the dock, across the sand, and down the path to her cabin. The brisk wind wove its way through the trees, dislodging tiny sticks and pine cones, and the first yellowing leaves of fall fell to the path before her.

Things felt off the moment she opened the door to her cabin. A clean yet empty feeling.

Someone had left a note propped up on the table.

Dear Celia,

Welcome back! I hope you are feeling better. I asked Nash to move your things to the duplex. You'll have more room there, and I want you to be comfortable for the rest of your stay. Don't worry about any of the fall duties. Nash will take care of everything. You need to take time to heal. You'll find plenty of excellent food, some wine, and even some of those nasty cigarettes you seem inclined to enjoy.

. . .

Celia paused in her reading, laughing at Preston's words. How could someone who smoked cigars call cigarettes nasty? She enjoyed a cigarette occasionally, but hadn't smoked since the early days of her pregnancy, when they'd tasted vile. She read on.

I suspect this is an emotional time for you, but you are a strong woman and you'll get through this. Never doubt yourself, Celia. I've never doubted you. You are like a daughter to me. I appreciate everything you've done for our company. Your future is bright, my dear.

Sincerely,
Preston Whitby

Preston's kindness touched her, and she laughed at the formal way he signed his full name.

She'd been perfectly content in her cabin—after all, it was the one she'd shared years ago with Ruby and then Beverly—but it was kind of him to insist she move into the larger duplex. The newer building would surely be warmer as the nighttime temperatures dipped low.

She stuffed the note into her pocket and checked the bathroom and bedroom. None of her things remained. She pulled the cabin door tightly shut and made her way over to the duplex, glancing up at the darkening sky.

Nash, who'd lived in one half of the duplex over the summer, sat on the front step, whittling. He nodded a greeting to her, then turned his attention back to his knife and the stick he was scratching away at. "Mr. Whitby mentioned you'd be back any day," the man said, still looking down. "I trust you're feeling all right?"

"I'm getting better every day, thank you."

He nodded. The man, who looked to be somewhere in his fifties, had been respectful but quiet around Celia during the summer months. This conversation likely amounted to more words than they'd exchanged in all the months up to this point. His quiet nature reminded Celia of Tripp and Eleanor's younger sister, Iris. His silence didn't make Celia nervous. Instead, she found it comforting. She was glad she wouldn't be entirely alone for her last few weeks at Whispering Pines.

"Better get on inside now," he counseled, curls of thin wood falling to the steps at his feet. He pointed to the sky with the knife's blade. "This here is a nasty storm brewing. If it gets too rough, head on down to the basement. We should be fine."

Another gust of wind hit Celia's back, pushing her toward the stairs.

"What about you?" she asked. "Shouldn't you be going inside too, then?"

He looked up from his whittling again, a grin lifting half his face. "I'll just sit out here for a spell. Keep an eye on things."

She suspected that was exactly what Preston had ordered him to do, to monitor things, and to make sure Celia could heal in peace. She sensed Nash would have done so regardless of their boss's directives.

A fat, cold raindrop plopped on top of Celia's head, causing her to duck and laugh. The cheerful sound felt foreign as it squeaked out of her. She hadn't laughed enough lately. Not nearly enough. As heavier rain began to fall, she skirted around Nash to rush inside, smiling the whole way.

* * *

Later, after she'd eaten her fill of cold chicken and potato salad she discovered in the refrigerator, she poured herself a small glass of wine and headed upstairs. A cigarette no longer sounded as disgusting as it had during her pregnancy, but she was so exhausted she feared she'd fall asleep and start the mattress on fire if she dared light one now. Killing herself in a self-induced house fire would have negated the need for all the effort Preston had gone through for the past nine months to hide her pregnancy—and she wasn't one to waste hard work.

She forced herself to take a quick shower before collapsing into bed, washing away the lingering stench of the hospital she still smelled on her skin. Lightning illuminated her new bedroom as she slipped a flannel nightgown over her head. Thunder rumbled, its vibration deep enough that she could feel it through the floorboards.

She drained the last of her tepid wine and crawled under the covers, delighting in the smell of freshly washed linens, soft against her skin; the sensation was a stark contrast to the bleached and starched sheets in the hospital. Her eyes drifted shut. She was hungry for the oblivion of sleep. Celia was finding her way through the hours, day by day, eager for the time when her heart might ache a little less over the loss of her baby.

As the storm gained strength outside, she welcomed the protection of the four walls surrounding her. Danny was the one who had brought her to this duplex, all those summers before, when he'd helped with the initial framing. It felt appropriate for his work to offer her protection now.

Later, a banging sound pulled her up from the oblivion of deep sleep.

Maybe taking her last pain pill, along with the wine, had been shortsighted. She couldn't form a cohesive thought.

The ruckus continued downstairs. Was that yelling now, too?

The howl of the storm had subsided.

"Mrs. Celia, are you all right?!"

The noise finally morphed into something her brain recognized.

Nash?

Tossing the covers back, Celia climbed out of bed. Grabbing her robe from the back of a chair, she pulled it on over her nightgown as she walked gingerly down the stairs. No outside light streamed in through any windows. The sun wasn't up yet.

Celia flung the door open, surprised to see a wild expression on Nash's face. He sagged against the doorframe, limp with relief at the sight of her.

"Thank God," he said, rubbing his eyes.

"What the hell is the matter, Nash?" Celia asked, looking beyond him into the darkness. It was then she realized it wasn't pitch black, but a hazy gray, like the minutes immediately before the dawn of a new day.

Is that a tree limb down in the yard?

"I've been banging on your door for ten minutes!" he exclaimed, his voice still holding a note of panic. "I wondered if you'd wandered off somewhere. Maybe you couldn't sleep or the storm kept you awake."

The light outside brightened ever so slightly as he spoke, and now she could see that an entire *tree* was down. "I must have been more exhausted than I realized. What happened?"

He straightened, then followed her line of vision, turning to face the yard. "The storm was terrible. The howling of the wind woke me. Don't tell me you slept through it?!"

"Afraid so," she admitted. She didn't mention the pain pill and wine combination that helped her find the oblivion she'd needed.

He shook his head, as if sloughing off the fear he'd felt on her behalf. "I suspect we have plenty of damage to deal with. You go back inside now. Stay there until the sun comes up. I'm going to go check things out. I'll let you know what I find."

Celia knew he meant well, but his words rubbed her the wrong way. An image of Tripp's sneering face floated up from her memory, along with his condescending words, and she shook her head. "No way. You aren't going out there alone. Give me a moment to find my shoes and a jacket. I'm coming with you."

Something in her tone—a tone she'd been honing for a decade working with men who underestimated her—caught his attention. He sighed, clearly frustrated at the delay, but he agreed to wait, suggesting she also take the time to slip on pants. Minutes later, she popped back into the doorway, more appropriately covered for inspecting storm damage.

He huffed down the stairs in front of her. "Don't you go getting yourself hurt now, Mrs. Celia, or Mr. Whitby will have my ass."

Despite the chaos she suspected they were about to walk into, Celia laughed. She liked this man.

* * *

Storm damage at Whispering Pines was extensive. Local law enforcement stopped to check on them the following day, making sure there were no injuries. They reported a tornado had ripped through resorts and small towns along the water's edge.

It horrified Celia to learn two people had died in the town that housed the hospital she'd only just left. She'd grabbed a deputy's arm as he'd turned to leave. He'd stared impatiently down at her hand where it clenched his shirt sleeve.

Realizing her mistake, she backed away apologetically. "I'm sorry. Were any children, or babies, hurt?" she asked, fear washing through her at the possibility. Her baby was out there somewhere.

"No, ma'am," the deputy replied, his features softening. "The fatalities involved an elderly couple inside a vehicle, probably out for a joyride. Mustn't have been able to sleep. They should have stayed home, where it was safe."

She'd breathed a sigh of relief as the men climbed back into their cruiser and drove away, both relieved and horrified over their report.

Preston had arrived just an hour before. "Show me," he directed, his take-charge nature on full display.

Nash nodded and headed toward the beach. Preston followed, with Celia close on his heels.

"Damn," he muttered as the white cabins along the shore came into view. Or what was left of the white cabins. "Thank God the guests were all gone."

Would there have been people in there, if not for my predicament? Celia wondered.

Nash and Celia stood there while Preston took in the surrounding damage. They'd had more time to come to terms with the devastation.

"There's damage, but at least there weren't injuries," Celia eventually offered.

Preston squared his shoulders. "Agreed. Is this the worst of it?"

"Mostly," Nash confirmed. "A couple trees fell on that old shack back in the woods. The one you didn't use anymore. That'll have to come down. The two cabins butting up against the woods, plus the lodge and the duplex, all had some minor damage, but nothing some new shingles and a few panes of glass won't fix. Lots of trees down, though."

Celia felt a pang in her chest at the mention of the old cabin where Danny and his mother lived before the duplex was inhabitable. It would soon be gone, too.

"Do you think these cabins are going to have to come down, too?" Preston asked the caretaker, motioning to the jumbled mess near the shoreline.

"I suspect that would probably be your best option," Nash confirmed. "But if you rebuild, I'd move back from the water next time, away from the worst of the elements."

Preston turned from his caretaker to the damaged cabins. "Thank you, Nash."

A semi hauling a trailer loaded with equipment pulled into the parking lot.

"If ya'll excuse me, those fellas are here with the boom truck. I needed help with all these busted trees."

"Of course," Preston agreed.

The older man hurried away. Nash had impressed Celia with what he'd already been able to accomplish in the day since the tornado hit.

Once it was just the two of them, Preston glanced down at Celia.

"How are you?"

"I'm fine."

"Really?"

She shrugged. "I'll *be* fine. Eventually."

He dropped a hand on her shoulder, the weight of it comforting after everything she'd been through.

"I know you will be." He squeezed her shoulder before allowing his hand to drop back to his side. "This is going to be expensive to rebuild."

"Is that what you want to do?" she asked, feeling like the tables were turning—now it was Preston seeking guidance.

He pivoted slowly, his eyes traveling from one end of his small resort to the other. Celia suspected Preston funneled more money into this place than he ever pulled out of it. But she knew that wasn't really the point of it all for him. It was more than a profit (or loss) center for Preston. Time spent at Whispering Pines had helped him heal when he lost his wife. Celia knew it would always be a special place for him.

Just like it was a special place for her. She'd lived some of the best days of her life beside this lake.

"Do you think she deserves a second chance?" he asked, turning back to look at Celia.

Celia tilted her head up to let the warm sunshine fall on her face and smiled. She knew he meant Whispering Pines, but he could have been referring to her, too.

"I think we all deserve second chances."

CHAPTER TWENTY-SEVEN
GIFT OF RESOLVE

*U*nder any other circumstances Celia would have helped with cleanup at Whispering Pines, but Preston wouldn't hear of it. He insisted she wasn't ready for strenuous physical activity. Arguing hadn't worked.

"Celia, Nash will bring in the help he needs. You need time to heal. Take the rest of the month. It's beautiful out here in September. If you go home now you'll create suspicion, since you aren't ready to return to work yet. I'll come back on the first of October, check the progress here, and bring you home. I'll need you back in the office by then, before that son of mine runs it into the ground."

Reluctantly, Celia agreed. She'd spent the summer doing little more than relaxing. But she soon realized Preston was right. The weather was glorious and peaceful throughout September. She took long walks, enjoying cooler days and the brilliant colors of fall as leaves transitioned to brilliant golds, oranges, and reds, made even more vivid in contrast with the persistent green of the tall pines. She watched the heavy demolition work arranged by Preston and Nash. They cleared away debris from the storm before winter snows would arrive. They'd scheduled a construction crew for early spring. It was important to replace the white cabins, as Preston didn't want to give up the entire season next summer.

Her physical strength returned, and the scar from her cesarian faded. She worked to come to terms with the decision she'd made to give up her baby. As promised, Preston returned for her at the end of the month. Celia felt stronger, both emotionally and physically, ready to return to her life.

When her boss pulled up in front of her house, Maggie was outside clearing spent vegetation from the flowerbeds in their front yard. Preston insisted on transferring her luggage from his trunk to her front door. She'd left home months earlier, and since she'd needed a range of clothing for her changing body shape *and* the seasons, Celia had used her full set of bags.

Maggie hugged Celia but eyed her daughter with suspicion. Celia never stood back to let any man wait on her. Even though nearly a month had passed since she'd given birth, Preston was still treating her like she was breakable—but she couldn't tell her mother that.

Preston drove off with her promise she'd be in the office bright and early the next morning. They'd discuss their strategies for the rest of the year before Preston returned to Chicago. She would spend her Sunday unpacking, catching up with her family, and helping her mother ready the house and yard for winter. Celia looked forward to getting back into her routine.

"How was your summer?" Maggie asked, shielding her eyes from the bright afternoon sun.

"Busy. But also relaxing. You know how I love spending my summers at Whispering Pines."

"What's not to love?" her mother joked, and Celia remembered how she and Clarence had toured the resort when they'd picked her and Beverly up after their summer at Whispering Pines. "We have lots of catching up to do, but you look beat. Why don't you go on inside? Your brothers will both be home for dinner tonight. They can help you take your luggage up to your room."

Celia nodded, then hugged her mother a second time, holding on for a beat longer than she normally would. She felt a new sense of kinship with this woman, her own mother, now that she'd carried and birthed a baby herself. When she pulled back, she avoided Maggie's concerned gaze.

"Good, I'm glad Gerry and George will be here," Celia said, patting her mother's upper arms before turning away. "I can't wait to hear what kind of trouble they found this summer."

She could feel her mother's eyes on her as she went into the house, but Celia kept moving. If she wanted to keep her secret—and she did —she'd need to find a firm footing again with her emotions.

Grabbing two of the lighter bags from the pile Preston had left inside their front door, Celia plodded upstairs. The house was quiet. Breathing deeply, she took in the familiar scents of lemon furniture polish, old wood, and food cooking in the kitchen. She recognized the smell of roast and looked forward to a home-cooked meal. Her own cooking over the past month paled compared to her mother's skill in the kitchen.

She dropped the bags on her bedroom floor, pulled off her jacket, and collapsed onto her back on the bed. "I had a baby, Beverly," she whispered, touching her stomach. This room was where she always felt closest to her dead sister. "Please don't be ashamed of me for giving it up. Love created it, but neither I nor Danny ever planned on having children."

She folded an arm under her head, eyes on the ceiling, but instead of seeing the pink-colored glass of the light fixture above, she imagined she was looking into her sister's face. "I have to work. Mother needs me. Ever since the accident her leg has bothered her, and I don't want her to have to worry about money. Gerry doesn't live here anymore, and George is sure to move out soon, too. Women don't work in jobs like mine and have a husband and children, too. Sometimes I wish that were possible. But it isn't. At least not yet. Maybe someday."

The opening and closing of a door below brought Celia up and off her bed.

Why am I trying to explain myself to a ghost?

Unzipping the first suitcase, Celia flipped the lid back and pulled out the dress on top. As she rounded the bed, her toe caught the edge of her blue trunk. Again.

"Dammit!" she hissed, dropping to the floor and squeezing her wounded foot. She leaned her back against the blue-painted surface, cursing herself for failing to get the trunk moved upstairs, where it would be out of the way and the risk to her toes eliminated.

The pain in her foot subsided much faster than the pain in her heart. She heard a door again downstairs, and Celia felt the emptiness of the house once more. She knelt before the trunk and tried to open it, forgetting about the lock. Celia felt compelled to touch the items inside, especially the crocheted booties and christening gown. She'd thought of them often throughout the summer. She hurried over to her jewelry box and fished out the key. It was underneath the charm bracelet Danny had given her that fateful night . . . the night their love had created something real, something that felt more tangible than their relationship ever had.

She'd left the bracelet behind when she'd gone to Whispering Pines. Just like Danny always left Celia behind.

Ignoring it now, she took out the key and opened her trunk. The lid squealed open on seldom-used hinges. There, sitting on top of a fold of white tissue paper and next to the black-and-white newspaper article Danny had used as an excuse to seek her out on Thanksgiving Day, were Beverly's booties.

Celia hiccupped with emotion at the sight of them. She pressed the fingers of her left hand against her mouth as her other hand touched the blue trim. She reminded herself that Beverly gave them to her in love, never meaning for the little slippers to bring her heartache.

"Celia?" Maggie's voice floated up from the base of the stairs. "You have a visitor!"

"Crap!" Celia muttered. She hurried over to snatch a tissue from a box on her nightstand and wiped at her tear-streaked face. Steady footsteps ascended the stairs. "Just a minute," she yelled, doing her best to sound upbeat.

"Cee, it's me," a familiar voice said, and Celia felt a wave of relief.

Her oldest friend in the world stepped into her room and closed the door tight behind her. With just one look at Celia's face, Ruby opened her arms wide. She gave up on her effort to stem the tears and rushed into her friend's arms. Neither woman spoke. Celia let the tears and sadness flow out. When her sobs finally subsided, Ruby gently nudged her to sit down on the edge of her bed. Ruby glanced inside the open trunk, sighed, then gently closed the lid.

"Beverly made me those," Celia whispered. "She said they were for my babies. Babies she knew she'd never get to meet. Little did I realize I wouldn't get to hold my baby, either."

She barely got the last word out before dissolving into tears again. Ruby sat on the bed next to her and put a comforting arm around her waist, giving her time to cry. When Celia got her tears under control for a second time, she stood and grabbed another tissue, blowing her nose before sitting back down next to her friend.

"I know it's hard to believe," Ruby finally said, "but it will get easier. After I had little Jack, I was a wreck. My mood swings were crazy. I know what you're going through is more than just the 'baby blues,' but your body is trying to adjust, too."

Celia nodded and blew her nose. "How long did they last?"

Ruby considered Celia's question before answering. "I'll let you know when they stop."

Celia smiled, appreciating the humor. "So I can look forward to this emotional rollercoaster for another four years?"

Her friend shrugged. "Things felt more normal after a few months."

"Normal would be good," Celia conceded, dabbing at her eyes with the sodden tissue.

"Are you still comfortable with your decision?" Ruby asked.

Celia nodded. "As comfortable as I think anyone can be with something this monumental."

"How much more time are you going to take off?"

Celia tossed her tissue into a nearby wastepaper basket, bracing herself for a lecture. "I go back Monday."

"Monday? Are you crazy, Celia? You need time! Your body just endured the miracle of life. You need time to heal."

Despite Ruby's fiery words, her presence was helping Celia to regain her sense of calm. She stood and walked over to the window, eyeing her mother down below, who was still clearing out her flowerbeds. "I'll heal better if I keep my mind busy at work. It's not like I have a hungry newborn waking me up at night. My body is healed. My heart is coming around."

Ruby sighed. "I don't know how you do it, Celia. You are so strong. You came back here, after your stepfather died, and took care of your mother and little brothers. And now, after this, you want to get right back to work."

Celia touched the glass of the window separating her from the outside world. She could see both hers and her friend's vague reflections in the glass. "But don't you see, Ruby? We're women. *All* women are strong. We're the caregivers of this world. We take care of our families. We survive. Men don't always stick around to do that."

Ruby got off the bed then, too, and walked over to the vanity. She unwound the rosary beads from the graceful wooden arm supporting the vanity's oval mirror, letting the beads drip from her fingers. "Not all men leave, Celia."

All the men in my life do, Celia thought. First her father, then her stepfather. And Danny waltzed in and out of her life every few years. In Celia's world, men didn't stick. Women did.

She watched Ruby finger the rosary beads and wondered if her friend was silently asking the Virgin Mary to help Celia move through this incredibly difficult turn in her life. With a sigh, Ruby returned the beads and turned to Celia, arms crossed over her midsection.

"I need you to make me a promise, Celia."

Ruby had proven throughout a lifetime of friendship that she always had Celia's best interest at heart. Celia owed her for that loyalty. "All right. What do I need to promise you?"

"You need to promise me you're done with Danny," Ruby said. "I know you feel a special connection with him. You always have. But you need to have more self-respect."

Celia grunted, but then quieted at Ruby's intense look.

"I'm dead serious, Cee," Ruby insisted. "That man, and whatever it is the two of you have, it isn't good for you. If you aren't careful, you are going to end up alone."

"There are worse things in life than a woman who doesn't marry," Celia insisted, unable to keep the defensiveness out of her voice. "I have a lot of responsibilities here, and I like my work. I have a good life. I'm not alone."

Ruby shrugged again. "I never meant to imply otherwise. Lots of women would love to have a job like yours. You get to dress up every day, work at a job that challenges your mind, and come home to a hot meal on the table. I just want you to protect your heart. I don't want Danny to take advantage of the feelings you still have for him."

Celia knew Ruby harbored regrets over her extremely short career as a teacher before giving birth. Her friend had dreamed of getting lost in the world of art and sharing that world with eager students, but she'd given it all up when she'd married and gotten pregnant with their son.

Why did women have to choose between a career and a family?

Ruby had never tried to hide her feelings about Danny from Celia. The relationship she'd shared with Danny through the years was so foreign to Ruby that her friend couldn't understand it. When someone doesn't understand something, they assume it's wrong, and Ruby was no exception.

"Celia," Ruby said, pulling her attention back to their discussion. "Promise me you won't let Danny put you in this position ever again."

She needn't argue with that point. Celia would never again face an unplanned pregnancy with any man. Her doctor had broken the news in the days following her baby's birth: There would be no more babies for Celia. The complications she'd experienced had stolen that option forever. This added to her emotional struggles, but it was something she wouldn't even share with Ruby.

"I promise I will never again allow Danny to impregnate me and then hop on the next train out of town."

Snorting with disgust, Ruby walked to the door and flung it open. "You are impossible. I'm glad to see you haven't totally lost your sense of humor. Now, I have to go home and get supper on *my* family's table."

As Ruby disappeared down the hallway, Celia got back to her unpacking, a smile hovering on her lips. Her life was turning out differently from Ruby's, but children had never been part of her own plan. Reminding herself of this helped keep the smile on her face.

Things were going to be fine.

After she'd emptied the two bags, Celia pulled a cardboard box out of the back of her closet. Opening it, she pulled out the stacks of photographs she'd stored there, pictures Danny had given her through the years. She transferred the stack into her blue trunk, setting them on top of Danny's old camera, locked the trunk up, and tossed her key back in her jewelry box.

She'd ask George and Gerry to take the trunk up to the attic for her after dinner, vowing to lock the memories and secrets away for good.

It was time to get on with her life.

CHAPTER TWENTY-EIGHT
GIFT OF TURNING A CORNER

"It's great to have you back, Celia," Preston said, smiling at her from his seat at the head of the small conference table. "I appreciate what you did this summer to get things back on track at Whispering Pines, and I thought today would be the perfect time for the three of us to discuss our plans for the office for the rest of the year."

"Gee, Dad, no 'and a big thank you to Tripp' for keeping things running in the office here while Celia was off playing at a lake resort all summer long?"

Celia inhaled, shocked at Tripp's audacity. How dare he address his father with such disrespect? She'd done her best to steer clear of Tripp since she'd arrived at 7:30 that morning. Looking at him now from across the table, the changes in him surprised her. His eyes were dull, and gray streaks fanned out from his temples. Even his hand, holding a pen poised over a pad of paper, had a slight tremor to it.

His son's biting sarcasm surprised Preston, too. "Tripp, I'm not sure what your problem is, but I will not allow you to speak to me like that."

Tripp squirmed at the reprimand, then sat straighter in his chair and folded his arms in such a way that his missing hand was less obvious—something Celia had seen him do countless times over the years. "I apologize. That was a poor attempt at humor. We're all glad to have Celia back and also relieved she didn't suffer any injuries in the storm that hit the resort at the end of the season. We'd have hated to have her end up in the hospital, or worse."

Tripp met her pensive gaze. His expression held a bland boredom. If he knew she *had* spent part of September in the hospital, he gave no sign. But she also wouldn't put it past him to hold on to salacious information he might have stumbled upon until he could put it to better use later. For some reason, Tripp's animosity toward her was growing. She may need ammunition in the future, too.

She turned her attention back to Preston. He updated her on progress for three large downtown projects and another one they were considering for development out by the highway.

"Rumor has it they're flagging federal money for infrastructure development, and I don't want to miss out on that opportunity."

"What about the subdivision we started work on last winter?" she asked. "Did those permits get granted so bid letting could begin?"

Tripp picked up his pen again, scratching on the paper. "You mean your little pet project to build a bunch of identical houses out in the sticks?"

Celia felt her blood pressure rise, a sensation she'd carefully avoided over the past five or six months. "I wouldn't call one of your father's missions to provide affordable housing for families on low to middle income a *pet project*. There's a shortage of affordable housing. Lots of would-be homeowners are veterans. I'd think you'd be in favor of helping your fellow servicemen."

If she hadn't been looking right at the man, she would have missed the way his eyes narrowed at her words. "I've given enough to my country," he said, his voice even and controlled. "Let someone else build little cookie-cutter huts so they can raise their two-point-five kids and live out the rest of their lives in obscurity. We are in business to make money. These large commercial projects do that."

It galled Celia that Tripp was right about the money part, despite the rest of his disrespectful observation.

"It's important to maintain a balance between profitability and social responsibility," Preston interjected. "It doesn't have to be one or the other here. We have the resources to support both."

Tripp mumbled something under his breath, but when Preston challenged him to speak up, the younger man stood and left the room, returning a moment later with a cup of coffee and his secretary, who followed close behind carrying two additional cups. She placed these before Celia and Preston and exited the room, closing the door behind her.

I'm surprised he didn't make the woman juggle all three at once, Celia thought.

It had taken Tripp five years before he stopped asking Celia to get him coffee. Coffee wasn't in her job description, and she'd never complied. That conflict was an example of the tension in their working relationship.

The meeting moved on, exploring scheduling options to allow staff time to work on both Tripp's and Celia's assigned projects. Celia assumed they were close to wrapping up when she heard a light knock on the closed conference door. Tripp's secretary, Annemarie, was back, letting Preston know his ten o'clock appointment had arrived.

"Show him in, please."

Preston rose, with Tripp and Celia following suit. Celia moved to leave the room, but Preston reached over and touched her arm. "No. We have one more item to discuss."

Celia nodded, curious about a mysterious visitor joining their meeting.

Her curiosity morphed into delight when Warren Arbuckle walked through the door.

"Celia, I trust you know Mr. Arbuckle?" Preston said, motioning for the man to take the open chair at the other end of the table opposite him.

"I certainly do," Celia acknowledged, both surprised and confused to see Helen's husband join them. "Warren married my dear friend, Helen."

"Indeed he did, and you also know I've been close family friends with Helen's parents since before any of you were born," Preston said, motioning around the table. "How's the family, Warren? Are the girls doing well?"

Warren raised one shoulder and smiled. "Perhaps it's *my* wellbeing you should inquire about, Mr. Whitby, given I'm now outnumbered five to one in my own home."

Preston, Celia, and Tripp all gave the obligatory chuckle at Warren's comment. Helen and Warren had welcomed a fourth daughter to their family while Celia was away at Whispering Pines for the summer. Celia had seen little of Helen in recent years. She still appreciated their long-lasting friendship, but their different lifestyles meant their paths seldom crossed these days.

For Warren's sake, she hoped the little girls didn't all share Helen's forceful personality. Celia couldn't imagine trying to raise *four* girls. Her friend never did pursue her dream of becoming a Parisian fashion designer, but if she still enjoyed the latest trends and clothed her daughters in a similar manner, Helen might be the number-one customer of some lucky designer.

Celia waited for the small talk between the three men to run its course, still curious about Warren. She didn't have to wait long before Preston turned to her.

"Celia, Warren is working for us now. He and Helen are moving to Chicago soon, where I'll be teaching him the ropes."

She blinked. "I'm sorry, did you say he works *here* now?"

Last she'd heard, Warren was running his father's business. Something to do with electrical components. While visiting, Ruby *had* insinuated Warren wasn't making quite enough money to keep Helen in the lifestyle to which she'd become accustomed.

"Yes. Warren will eventually oversee some of our commercial work in Chicago."

"And Helen agreed to this?" Celia asked, causing Tripp to snort. She suspected men rarely discussed whether their wives were in favor of a work-related relocation, so it didn't surprise her that Tripp found her question ridiculous. But this was *Helen* they were talking about.

"She did," Warren shared, offering Celia a warm smile. "It will be a chance for her to expose the girls to more *culture* than she'd find around here. That's a direct quote."

"We purchased Warren's family business this past summer," Preston explained.

This nugget gave Celia pause. Something of that size wouldn't be a small transaction, even for Preston. "I wasn't aware you were working on a deal of that size."

"Never assume you are privy to all the decisions that take place around here," Tripp said.

Something you never fail to remind me of, Celia thought, but she kept her thoughts to herself.

And just like that, the peace she'd found in the quiet of Whispering Pines slipped away, and Celia once again wondered if working for Preston, which she enjoyed, was worth it when Tripp was part of the equation.

Doing her best to ignore Tripp, she turned her attention back to the other two men. "I've been out of the office for a bit," she explained to Warren. Extending her hand, she gave him a hearty handshake. "Welcome to our little work family, Warren. It'll be a pleasure to have you as part of the team."

SPRING 1957

CHAPTER TWENTY-NINE
GIFT OF WINE WITH FRIENDS

*B*y the following spring, Celia needed a break. She jumped at the chance to head back to Whispering Pines, even if it was only for a few days. Preston couldn't get away, but he needed her to check on the progress his construction team had made under Nash's watchful eye. The original goal was to be back in business by Memorial Day. Now the project was behind schedule by at least three weeks. Celia needed to figure out why. A delay of that magnitude was unacceptable given the fast-approaching summer season.

Since returning home from Whispering Pines the previous fall, Celia had buried herself in her work, and Preston had clearly noticed. He praised her on the progress she'd made with the housing development, and he'd surprised her with a sizable bonus. For the first time, she could afford to buy herself a brand-new vehicle.

Celia ran an appreciative hand on the steering wheel as she drove herself to the resort, thinking back to the previous evening. She'd picked up a very pregnant Ruby in her new Cadillac, and the two of them enjoyed a nice dinner. Ruby appreciated the outing and went on and on about Celia's ability to buy herself a new car. Ruby herself shared a ten-year-old station wagon with her husband.

When Celia pulled into the gravel parking lot at Whispering Pines, her mind jumped back to the first time she'd arrived here. She'd come with Leo, Helen, and Ruby in Leo's brand-new Buick. Back then, she'd never have guessed she would someday arrive at the resort in her own new car—one she'd earned.

She'd dressed in jeans and work boots for this trip, a nice change of pace from her skirts and suit jackets. Regardless of what her workday at the office would bring, she always wore a feminine version of her male counterparts' attire. Her lack of wardrobe variety would bore the fashion-conscious Helen. She suspected her old friend would be enjoying the variety of shopping Chicago was sure to offer, although she hadn't talked to her since their move.

A knot of men stood at the west end of the parking lot. As Celia approached, Nash separated himself from the group.

"Mrs. Celia, it's nice to see you again," the older man greeted her.

"Nash, please drop the *Missus* part. And it's good to see you, too. Sounds like things are running behind out here?"

Nash nodded, and when a younger man walked over to join them, the caretaker made introductions. Celia recognized the man's name as the general contractor working on the rebuild. She'd done her research before arriving. Celia leveled a purposeful look at him.

"Why don't you update me on things around here then, Mr. Grady, and together we'll figure out a way to get back on track. None of us can afford a three-week delay."

A slow grin stole over the man's features. Celia braced herself, expecting the man to say something meant to placate her. She'd heard it often enough. But when he spoke with a noticeable southern drawl, he was agreeable. "Can't argue with that, ma'am. Why don't I show you where we're running into a few snags, and maybe we can figure out a solution?"

* * *

It turned out to be a productive day. Together they'd determined some relatively straightforward solutions to the handful of things causing delays. Bill, as the general contractor insisted she call him, was easy-going. Tomorrow she'd call Preston and secure his approval for the things she'd proposed. She didn't expect he'd have any concerns.

After a light supper alone, in what she considered her half of the duplex, Celia took a walk. The construction workers had left for the day, staying offsite somewhere, and she could hear Nash knocking around in the other half of the duplex.

Early perennials bloomed around the foundation of the lodge. Celia felt a pinch in her heart. She remembered watching Danny plant those bulbs. He'd promised they'd bloom for years to come, and sure enough, here they were.

So much had happened between them since those early days.

She wandered, her steps taking her into the woods. She'd spent the day going over the main resort grounds, and with at least two more hours of daylight, she felt drawn toward the tranquility of the woods. She doubted Nash would approve of her adventurous detour, but she'd be careful. Getting lost in the woods was not something she had any intention of doing. She'd even stuffed a roll of bright orange string in her pocket that she'd found on the floor in one of the three brand-new cabins. Before leaving the duplex, she'd cut foot-long sections of the bright string, and now she carefully marked her trail as she walked. Unless those ghost boys she'd heard of when she'd first come to Whispering Pines followed along behind her and pulled the strings off the trees, she wouldn't get lost.

A bird squawked loudly above her. Glancing up, she saw a flash of red. She stopped and stood still, hoping to get a better look at the colorful bird. Another loud squawk helped her find it, a red cardinal, sitting high above her and looking down.

Was this Beverly coming back to visit Whispering Pines with her?

Refusing to let her imagination get the best of her, Celia made to step away. Her foot kicked something hidden in the grass below. The clink of it sounded like glass rolling against rocks. Bending down, she felt around in the tangle of grass; her fingers found the smooth surface of a bottle.

Pulling it loose, she examined her find. A wine bottle, its label faded. She wondered for a moment who would leave a wine bottle out here, but then a vision flashed. The memory of four young women, enjoying a picnic on a hot summer day, passing a bottle of wine around as they shared dreams of their future.

This was their bottle. She was sure of it.

She could hardly believe she'd stumbled upon it, fourteen years later. The bottle would go home with her, and she could only imagine her friends' reactions were she to show it to them.

Another irritated call from a bird rang out high above. She couldn't see it now, but it sounded like the red cardinal. Did the bird want to accompany her down memory lane?

She'd wiped dirt from the bottle's label, so she brushed her soiled hand against the denim of her jeans. Checking her watch, she guessed she'd have just enough time for one specific trip down memory lane before darkness fell.

She walked on, not entirely sure she was going in the right direction. Hopefully her sense of direction was accurate enough that she wouldn't have to backtrack the whole way, using her path of bright orange strings to find the path back to the resort. As the light faded, she picked up her pace, confident now that she was heading in the right direction.

As she entered a clearing, she pulled up short. There was something familiar about the ring of trees, but the fresh scrapes in the dirt were new. She'd found it. This was where the old, rundown cabin had stood. The cabin where Danny and Mrs. Bell stayed before the duplex. The cabin where she'd first been with Danny.

It was gone, damaged beyond repair by the storm that followed the birth of their child. Remnants of the old foundation were all that remained. The footprint of the old cabin looked smaller now that they had removed the structure.

She wondered what happened to the family of raccoons that used to prowl here. She held the old wine bottle up to offer one last salute to the place's memory, and then she gauged how long it would be before the sun dipped below the horizon. She wasn't worried, but she would have to hurry.

Her heart knew the way back.

* * *

Things were on track with the rebuild by the end of Celia's brief stay.

"I have to hand it to you," Nash said, grinning down at her as she pulled a weed from the flowerbed on the side of the lodge. "You lit a fire under Bill Grady. Didn't matter what I said, I couldn't get him to move any faster. But he listened to you."

Celia tossed the offending weed. "Maybe it was my bubbly personality," she joked.

"That must be it. You leaving in the morning, then?"

"I am," she confirmed, although she'd have preferred to stay. It was always hard for her to leave Whispering Pines, and she didn't have any plans to return this summer. Preston had his staff lined up, and cabins rented. Some long-term customers were excited about the new cabins.

"Well, I'll say my goodbyes now, then. I'm heading out early in the morning for a day of fishing," Nash said, tipping his hat to her.

"I'm glad to hear it. You've worked hard getting this place back into shape. Enjoy yourself. Maybe I'll be lucky enough to come out next summer, spend more time here."

"That would be good," he said, then he strode purposefully out of sight, off to do yet another of his endless chores around the resort.

"Celia!"

Spinning, Celia was surprised to see Bill Grady jogging in her direction.

"Hey, Bill. What's up?"

"I'm glad I caught you. I was afraid I might have missed you. Now that you've finished your work out here, can I interest you in dinner?"

"Dinner?" she asked, surprised by his question.

He smiled his slow smile—the one she'd grown to like over the last few days. "Yes. Dinner. Maybe a little wine. You eat, don't you?"

"Well, sure. I was just going to eat a few leftovers out of my fridge. I leave in the morning."

Bill shook his head. "Please don't say no. You were a big help this week. I'd like to thank you."

"So . . . this would be a work meeting, then?" she asked, catching up with his meaning.

She really was rusty when it came to men. She hadn't been on a date since the infamous Christmas party where she'd left her dinner in the bushes. Maybe now was finally the time.

"Not exactly."

"Why, Mr. Grady, are you asking me out on a date?" Celia knew she was flirting, and she was enjoying it. She'd vowed to get back to her life, and that couldn't mean just work. Besides, Bill was handsome and fun to be around. He was also four years younger than she was—thirty to her thirty-four—but she didn't care. It was just dinner.

"You don't make this easy for a guy, do you?" Bill said, his ever-present grin refreshing. "What do you say?"

"I say . . . yes. I'd love to go out on a date with you. Pick me up at seven. I'm staying in the duplex, in the side with the cracked window you had your boy replace yesterday. And don't be late."

"I wouldn't dream of it," Bill said with a wink. "I'll make reservations over at Grand View Lodge. I hear they serve a great steak. Too bad it's not the weekend. I'd love to take you to one of their infamous dances."

As Celia watched him turn away, a cool gust of wind sent snippets of freshly cut grass skipping across the path in front of her. She inhaled the fresh scent of spring and looked forward to her evening out with an interesting new man. Perhaps a trip back to the lodge where she first met Danny was the perfect way to kick off a new chapter.

SUMMER 1960

CHAPTER THIRTY
GIFT OF SELF-SUFFICIENCY

*C*elia walked under the stone-and-iron archway marking the entrance to her favorite park. She'd needed to escape the office. A craftsman had woven the name O'Brien into the iron scrollwork comprising the top of the archway. Years earlier, when she and Beverly played in this park as little girls, their mother told them they'd named the park after a friend of their father. The O'Brien family was one of the founding families of the town. Her father, Charles Middleton, was also a member of one of those families. There had been family money back before he died and the stock market crashed.

Normally, Celia drove through the park, occasionally stopping to sit on the picnic bench that still bore her initials, but today the narrow road was under repair. She didn't mind walking. It felt good to stretch her legs. She should have left her jacket in the car. The hot summer sun was high. The brown paper sack containing her lunch crinkled against her leg as she walked.

As she passed beneath the arch, she caught the unmistakable buzzing of bees meandering between the bright blooms that formed a ring around each side of the entry. Bright orange chrysanthemums were just starting to open alongside purple asters. Day lilies offered bright yellow blooms against deep green foliage. The heavy heads of peonies drooped low, nearly spent, pink petals littering the dark soil below. Another summer was well underway.

She'd argued yet again with Tripp throughout the morning about the best use of their resources. He wanted all hands on the hotel project out along the highway. She hated to have their next dozen houses, so close to completion, sit idle during this stretch of perfect summer weather. Families were ready and waiting to move in. But Tripp's project was a big one for the company. He'd been more adamant than ever that his project take precedence, and she wondered why. He acted more focused—professional, even—and it had her suspicious. She liked it better when he busied himself with two-martini customer lunches and rounds of golf. It kept him out of her hair. When he was in the office and doing actual work, they frequently butted heads.

Her frustrations at work were growing. She still loved her job, but Tripp represented a legitimate roadblock. She used to think Preston tolerated the man because he was his only son, and not because she thought Preston hoped Tripp had legitimate business skills. But she'd changed her mind over the past few years. Tripp was talented and she worked in a family business. Preston would want to retire someday. When the older man put Tripp in charge of everything, what would be her fate?

No one was working on the park road as she strolled back to her favorite picnic bench. She sat on the tabletop facing the river, exactly as she'd so often done through the years. She loved this spot; sitting on the lower bench didn't provide the same view of the lazy waterway.

She pulled out a tuna salad sandwich wrapped in a paper napkin. It was still cold from the break-room fridge. As she nibbled along the crust, she considered what Tripp being in charge would mean for her career.

Tripp couldn't run the company from here. Wouldn't he have to move back to Chicago? Preston visited here regularly, but their largest customers were still in the Chicago area.

Maybe she'd finally be given the opportunity to run the local office. What would it be like to be in charge? To have the title that should rightly go along with all the work she was already doing keeping staff working, the doors open, and the lights on. Tripp never bothered himself with the more mundane, practical tasks. She knew those things were almost as important in keeping the company growing as glad-handing with potential customers.

Would Preston ever be brave enough to put her in charge? It would be an unprecedented move to name her as the local leader. She wasn't sure even Preston would take that chance, though she'd been working harder than ever, just in case.

As she caught the scent of pine on the breeze, she realized how much she'd missed Whispering Pines. It had been three years since her last visit: the spring following the tornado. She wondered what ever happened to Bill Grady, the general contractor. She'd enjoyed her date with him that evening, and although their paths hadn't crossed since, she had started dating again after that.

Not that she made dating a priority. Work kept her busy. But it gave her a break from constantly having to tamp down her femininity. In the office, she'd had to adopt a tough demeanor. If she didn't, some men automatically assumed they could take the upper hand. She seldom let them think that for long. The rare evenings when she'd put on a pretty dress and let a handsome man open the door for her provided a much-needed break from all the posturing and walls she'd had to erect. Perhaps she should return the call she'd received from another of Ruby's single male friends.

Ruby still hoped that Celia would marry someday. But Celia didn't need Ruby to find her a man. She was content with her life. That being said, she could humor Ruby and enjoy a night out with an interesting guy. She'd call him when she got back to the office. If she returned early from lunch, before everyone else, she could have a moment of privacy to arrange her date. Preston's open-door policy didn't allow for much of that when the office was hopping with people.

Crumpling her empty lunch bag, Celia stood from the bench, feeling the familiar twinge of pain in her toes and the balls of her feet.

Walking through the park in her pumps was less than ideal, but she didn't keep a spare pair of tennis shoes in her trunk. Maybe she should. Or maybe she should ditch the heels altogether. She was sick of her feet hurting.

Despite her aching feet, she grinned as she walked, entertained by the thought of everyone's expression in the office if she took to dressing exactly like the men, with pants every day instead of skirts, and flat, comfortable loafers.

Yeah, like that would be acceptable, she mused.

* * *

Pulling into the office parking lot, it surprised her to see Tripp's sleek black convertible parked in its premier spot—one he'd claimed for his own when the office first opened. While Tripp was often the first one in the office in the early morning, he was notorious for long lunches.

How am I going to arrange my date with him hovering?

Celia grabbed her handbag off the passenger seat and pulled out her pack of cigarettes, knocking one loose. She placed the slender filter between her lips and pulled the lighter out of her car's dashboard, lighting the tip and inhaling deeply. She allowed the smoke to calm her nerves.

It was a shame the sight of his car could so easily negate the peaceful feeling she'd captured in the park.

Jamming the small, circular lighter back into place, she turned off her car and got out. She unlocked the office door and tossed her lunch bag into the tall trash bin just inside the door. They always locked the office when they closed down over the noon hour.

Celia made her way back toward her own office, frustrated to see no one had bothered to turn the lights off as she so often requested. They shouldn't waste electricity when no one was around.

She noticed Tripp's closed office door—an unusual sight. Maybe he was tipping back a bottle, something even he wouldn't care to be too obvious about at work. The closed door was good news. Maybe he hadn't heard her return and she could still make that phone call.

Other staff would start returning in twenty minutes. Celia sat behind her desk, not bothering to turn her own office light back on. She took one last drag on her cigarette and snuffed it out in her ashtray. While nearly everyone she worked with smoked, she tried to avoid puffing away at her desk. She found it unprofessional.

Stowing her ashtray out of sight, she again opened her purse. She rummaged through it, sure she'd stashed the slip of paper with the name and number a secretary had jotted down for her when Ruby's friend had called the office looking for her. She took out her wallet and set it on her desktop, giving herself a better view into the other contents of her purse.

At the sound of Tripp's door opening and closing she looked up, startled to see Annemarie make her way back toward her desk. His secretary didn't notice Celia. She was too intent on adjusting her clothing and patting her hair. A few seconds later, Tripp came out, tucking in his shirt and adjusting his tie.

Celia froze. If Tripp noticed her, things would get ugly. But he didn't. He walked past Annemarie's desk, patted her bottom, then continued on toward the men's room. Annemarie bent down, stood back up holding her purse, then walked toward the door.

Nice of you to leave her with fifteen minutes to eat lunch, Celia thought, disgusted at what she'd walked in on. While she'd had little doubt Tripp engaged in extra-marital affairs, she'd never witnessed any. She felt a twinge of sympathy for his wife, Sofia, despite the woman's unfriendly demeanor. Celia couldn't imagine being legally bound to a cheater.

Filing this latest tidbit away for future use if need be, Celia flipped on her office light. Tripp would think she'd just come back from lunch when he returned from the men's room.

Turning her attention back to the contents of her purse, she finally found the man's name and number. With any luck, she'd catch him before his work began for the afternoon.

She was no longer concerned with the possibility of Tripp hearing her make plans for a date over the phone. *She* was single. No one could fault her for having a social life.

* * *

Celia spent her afternoon working on the complicated scheduling of their construction teams for the upcoming weeks. Then she transitioned to work their accountant had provided her related to Tripp's hotel project. Despite her lack of enthusiasm over the project, she needed to stay on top of the cost projections—Tripp would never bother himself with something so mundane.

She didn't notice the passing of time. A knock on her doorjamb had her jumping in her seat.

"I'm sorry!" The woman standing there laughed. "I didn't mean to scare you. I just wanted to let you know you're the last one here. I'm heading home. Will you be long? Would you like me to turn off the lights out here?"

"Don't apologize, Fiona," Celia said, leaning back in her chair and raising her arms above her head to stretch out the muscles that had tightened over the past few hours. "I can't believe it's already five."

The woman checked her watch. "Five-thirty, actually. Why don't you go home, too?"

Celia sighed. She knew the younger woman meant well. But it was a Tuesday evening and her mother wouldn't be home. No one was waiting at home for her.

"Soon," she replied, the noncommittal response not lost on her office friend, who frowned but waved good night. "And yes, please turn out the lights on your way out!"

As the fluorescent lights outside of her office flicked off, Celia glanced outside. Strong daylight still burned, although the shadows were lengthening on the concrete outside of her office windows. She'd leave the curtains open for now. If she was still here later, once darkness fell, she'd pull them closed.

Her bladder complained. As she went through the motions so she could get back to work, she let her mind wander, wondering how late her mother would be tonight. Tuesdays were her volunteer nights at the local hospital. Maggie would spend her evening reading books to lonely, sick children. It was something she'd done once her boys no longer needed her constant presence. Celia supposed it was her mother's way of giving back. When Beverly had been young, strangers had stepped in to help Celia's overwrought, widowed mother, too. She wondered if Maggie had missed her calling. Maybe her nursing skills had been born out of necessity, but she always had a knack.

Celia was glad Maggie had discovered the joy of volunteering. She supposed it gave the woman a sense of purpose and kept her mind occupied. They all worried about Gerry, off facing the horrors of war in the jungles of Vietnam. Celia both admired his sense of duty to serve and hated that her gentle brother was fighting somewhere out there.

She'd even wondered if Gerry would ever run into Danny. She hadn't heard from Danny since that fateful Thanksgiving night, but she knew he'd covered the war in Vietnam because she'd found pictures alongside news reports on the war. Seeing his name in the credits for an article still made her heart leap.

George was away at university, studying to become a teacher or college professor. Given his impish nature when he was younger, he already knew the tricks his students would try to pull under his tutelage.

She might as well spend her evening at the office. She'd been meaning to study the information Preston had passed on to her when she'd mentioned wanting to learn more about investing. She'd take some of the money she was earning and build a safety net for herself. While she loved her mother dearly, she hated the fact the woman struggled to be self-sufficient. Celia vowed to never find herself in a similar situation. If she ever lost this job, she wanted to have assets she could fall back on while seeking other employment. And she knew there would come a day when she didn't want to work so hard. Everyone had to retire eventually. Not that she'd face that for at least another twenty-five years.

Preston understood this desire for independence. He'd even put her in touch with his broker, and a personal referral from Preston Whitby carried weight. Celia was amassing a small portfolio of stocks and bonds, but she needed to be careful. She couldn't afford to take too big of risks. At least not yet.

She returned from the bathroom and sat at her desk, refocusing. No one was waiting for her at home, and she had work to do. No one was going to pay her way in this world. She refused to be like Tripp's wife, beholden to a man who showed her so little respect.

SUMMER 1963

CHAPTER THIRTY-ONE
GIFT OF HONESTY

"*I* still don't understand why you won't let me host a party for you here at the house," Maggie complained. Celia watched her mother rub at her left thigh; the damaged leg throbbed when the humidity was high. The habit was so engrained she doubted Maggie even knew she still did it.

"Mother, I appreciate that, but it isn't necessary. I'm turning forty, not four. I don't need cake and streamers."

Maggie practically dropped the plate of toast next to the newspaper spread out in front of Celia on the dining room table. The china plate rattled against the tabletop and tapped her daughter's mug of coffee, causing liquid to slosh out and soak into the newsprint.

Celia sighed. Maggie was displeased about something, and she doubted it was Celia's aversion to making birthday plans. "All right, Mother. Out with it. You haven't held a birthday party for me in twenty years. Something else is bothering you."

Maggie limped out of the room, shaking her head. "I've *wanted* to throw you parties."

Knowing her mother wouldn't share what was truly bothering her until she was ready, Celia returned to the morning paper and reread the first paragraph of the top story. The high summer temperatures and humidity that caused her mother's leg to ache were also providing a heated background for growing civil unrest, particularly in the southern states. Tensions continued to rise as blacks tired of the inequalities they faced. Rioting and marches were becoming more common.

Where would it all end? Could it all culminate in another civil war?

Celia massaged her temple against the telltale signs of a tension headache.

Maggie returned with a jar of her homemade chokecherry jam.

"Thank you," Celia said, dipping her knife into her favorite spread and lathering a thick layer across a piece of toast. She took a bite and groaned. "*This* is the best birthday present ever."

Maggie finally laughed and pulled out a chair. "You were never one of those kids who asked for a pony for her birthday."

"I never needed a pony," Celia agreed, between bites.

Maggie helped herself to a triangular piece of toast off Celia's plate. "You got in late last night. Don't tell me you were at the office the whole time."

"Why, Mother, are you keeping tabs on your forty-year-old daughter?" Celia grinned, picking up the knife to prepare a second piece of toast.

Even though the two women lived in the same house, they'd agreed years earlier that both were free to come and go as they pleased, without checking in. It was the only way it could work.

"Not intentionally," Maggie assured her, wrapping her fingers around what had to be a cold cup of tea by now. "I just didn't have time to pass on a phone message I took for you."

"Was it one of the girls? We're meeting for dinner this weekend."

Maggie stopped fussing with her cup and sat back, crossing her arms over her stomach. "No. It was a man."

Celia smiled and wriggled her eyebrows at her mother. "Oh, goodie. Did he sound handsome?"

"He sounded . . . *hesitant*."

This piqued her interest. "What do you mean?"

"Celia, honey . . . it was Danny Bell."

Danny?

The knife clattered against her plate, the last of her toast forgotten. She fingered the charm bracelet she'd gotten into the habit of wearing again a year ago. Time and distance had helped her heal to the point where the tiny charms made her smile. She had thought she'd made it through the heartache, but now that treacherous organ threatened to beat out of her chest.

"Danny Bell, huh? Did he say what he wanted?" she asked, attempting and—based on the look of sympathy her mother shot her —failing to sound nonchalant.

"He didn't say." Maggie shrugged. "He said you can reach him at the phone number he gave me. Celia, I've never been sure what happened between you two, but he breezes into town every few years, and once he's gone, you struggle to find your footing again. Maybe you shouldn't return his call this time. You seem content."

Danny rarely bothers to call first, Celia thought, the headache that threatened a minute earlier blossoming. *He just shows up.* And contrary to her mother's recollection, it had been more than a few years since she'd last heard from him. It had been over seven. She was painfully aware of the time span because her child, *their* child, would celebrate his or her seventh birthday at the end of the summer.

The fact she'd never been able to throw a birthday party for her own child soured her on the notion of such celebrations.

The grandfather clock chimed in the living room, marking the time as 7:30 a.m. Celia pushed her forgotten breakfast aside and folded up her newspaper. She stood and tucked it under her arm. She'd read it later. "Did you take his number?"

Maggie, unable to mask her disapproval, gave a brief nod. "It's on the notepad next to the phone in the kitchen."

Picking up her dishes, Celia went back to the kitchen and dropped them into the sink, her mind too preoccupied to toss the remaining toast in the trashcan. With the newspaper still stuck under her arm, Celia tore the top sheet of notepaper off the pad. The combination of seven digits, hastily recorded in her mother's handwriting, was a local phone number.

Danny was back, and she wasn't exactly sure what she was going to do about it.

* * *

Who was she kidding?

This was *Danny*! She couldn't ignore him. Despite her mother's warning, and the lecture from Ruby she could already hear if she knew Danny was back, Celia returned his phone call.

The sound of his voice had flooded her with a gamut of emotions.

When he'd left her the last time, she hadn't known if she'd ever see him again. Eventually, she had accepted that their time together had come and gone.

Promising herself she'd do a better job of protecting her heart this time, she agreed to meet him for coffee on Saturday morning. He'd suggested a dinner to celebrate her fortieth birthday, but she'd promised herself a different outcome from this meeting. Dinner could too easily set them on the same path they'd traveled before.

Her hand shook as she shifted her car into Park near the bakery they'd set as their meeting place. Easing back against the seat, Celia took a deep breath, willing herself to calm down.

Why am I so nervous?

She could have used a whole pack of cigarettes.

Get ahold of yourself, she thought, using her rearview mirror to check her makeup and hair. She'd primped for an hour after her mother left for her Saturday morning volunteer shift at the children's wing. Normally, Celia was out the door in twenty minutes for a date. But this was different. This wasn't a date. And he wasn't just any man.

Her mother was right. Regardless of how special Danny was to her —and she knew she'd never be able to change that fact—she always had to piece her heart back together after he left.

And he would *always* leave.

She needed to break the cycle, which meant (or so she told herself) she'd needed to look good for this last meeting. It would be her armor.

She touched up her lipstick before getting out of her Cadillac. If she didn't stop stalling, she'd be late. She was never late.

The bakery was bustling with patrons, just as she'd hoped. Glancing around, she recognized him immediately, even though his back was to the door. She'd recognize the set of his broad shoulders, the tilt of his head, anywhere. She took a fortifying breath, approached his table, and touched his shoulder.

Danny jumped in surprise, pushing back from the table to stand and greet her. He reached out as if to wrap her in a hug, but she held out her hands instead, and he took them. They stood like that for a beat as Celia searched his face. His skin was darker than she remembered, more weathered. There was a recent scar, running from the corner of his left eye up into his hairline. There was another, smaller cut that caused the right corner of his mouth to pucker. The years had left their mark, but they didn't dim the warmth of his smile—a smile that still reached his eyes.

"Celia," he said as he, too, scanned her face, not trying to hide his delight at seeing her.

Celia wondered if the two older women seated at the next table could hear the pounding of her heart.

Careful . . .

Pulling her hands out of his, she stood there, unsure how to proceed. This had been a mistake. She shouldn't have agreed to this. Her life had been fine without him back in it.

Hurrying around her, Danny pulled out the chair opposite his and motioned for her to sit.

"Do you still take your coffee black? And let me guess—you'll take a maple Long John, no filling."

And there it was. The years of separation fell away and her old friend was back, knowing her likes and dislikes. Not because they'd spent an inordinate amount of time together over the years, but because he paid attention.

She nodded, not trusting her voice, and he headed to the front display case. Ruby's old warnings echoed through her mind.

Stay away from him.

He disrupts your life.

Don't let him be the reason you end up alone.

But Ruby was wrong. Danny wasn't the reason her life was turning out this way. He was just one of the many choices she'd made throughout the last twenty years. And she wasn't alone. She had family, coworkers she considered friends, and she dated regularly.

"It's so good to see you, Celia." Danny set a cup of black coffee and a small plate containing the sugary doughnut in front of her. He sat back down, still smiling at her. "Thank you for agreeing to see me. It's been a long time."

"It'll be eight years this coming Thanksgiving."

He was taken aback by the preciseness of her reply, his eyes flicking away. "That long?"

She nearly reached across to touch his hand, her reaction to offer assurance still automatic. But she stopped herself, instead picking up the cup he'd brought her. She took a drink, grimacing as the scalding liquid burned her tongue.

"Careful. I should have warned you. It's hot," he said, smiling at something so obvious.

And once again, just like that, she felt more at ease in his presence. She didn't have to make this so hard. This was Danny.

"It surprised me you called. If I'm being totally honest, my mother wasn't too happy about it," Celia shared, and she could feel a smile hovering at his apparent unease.

"I sensed that," he acknowledged with a brief nod. "I wasn't even sure she'd remember who I was when I gave her my name."

"Oh, she remembers you."

He squirmed then, ever so slightly, as if he understood the true depth of the meaning behind her words.

"Danny, why *did* you call? Why, after all this time, are you here?" Celia asked. "Didn't we say our goodbyes eight years ago? Both of us wanted such different things out of life. But we've never been good at keeping things platonic, and anything more feels too hard."

Celia caught the curious glances of the two women next to them. She pinned them with a look that had them standing to gather their empty cups and trash. They'd barely reached the door before two teenage boys slid into their spots, locked in a heated debate about baseball.

Danny glanced at the boys, then winked at her. "Remember when we were young like that?"

"Barely," she conceded. "Danny, I'm serious. What brings you back to town?"

Tearing open a packet of sugar, he dumped it into his own coffee, giving the liquid a quick stir with his finger. "Damn, still hot," he muttered. At the look on Celia's face, he shrugged. "Sorry. Too many years in the field making due. I'm a little rusty in the manners department."

She waited. He stalled.

Finally, he reached across the small round table with both hands. Hesitantly, she laid her hands in his. When he closed his fingers around hers, she could feel the roughness of his skin. She noticed he'd lost the tip of his left pinky finger and her heart tripped.

What had this man been through?

His hands squeezed tighter. "I lost someone a while back. I guess I'm having trouble coming to terms with it, and I needed a friend."

His eyes held her gaze as tightly as his hands held hers. She couldn't look away.

"Someone?" she prodded when he got lost inside himself.

Her question brought his attention back. His eyes focused again. "Yeah. His name was Roberts. We'd worked together for years. He was like a brother to me. And then . . . he was gone."

It was Celia's turn to squeeze his fingers. She could see a deep well of pain in his eyes. "I'm so sorry."

He brought their clasped hands up and softly kissed one of her knuckles, then released them and sat back, brushing his thick sandy hair back from his forehead. It was a habit she'd witnessed countless times through the years, but his action revealed yet another scar that ran close to his hairline.

"We worked together. He reported the stories, I captured them in pictures. We were over in 'Nam," he said, and at the mention of Vietnam, Danny leaned his head back and stared at the ceiling. "I'll spare you the graphic details. We witnessed things too horrible to share."

Celia nodded. "My brother Gerry did an eighteen-month tour over there. He didn't say much about his experiences when he got back, but I can see he's a changed man."

Danny shook his head, his eyes sad. "Damn. I remember Gerry as an innocent young kid. I'm sorry he had to go through that."

"He made it back in one piece, and he got married last year. I know there are nightmares, but I pray he'll be all right."

"Give him time," Danny counseled. "Anyone that gets out of there alive has scars."

"Is that what happened to you?" Celia asked, motioning toward her friend's partial finger. Her heart ached at the idea he'd been in grave danger, though she'd always known it came with his job.

"We were chasing down a story," he said, his eyes again taking on that faraway look. "Our driver was a local. It was just the three of us in the Jeep, and it would be too generous to call the trail we were flying down an actual road. I still remember the way the palms slapped against us. The vehicle was open, no top."

Celia could picture it in her mind, could practically feel the jostling, the heat, the pulse of adrenalin. Had they come under enemy fire? The idea horrified her. An image of Danny, sitting calmly on the end of the dock with her at Whispering Pines that second summer, flitted through her brain. He'd wanted to see the world. To capture it with his lens. He couldn't have yet known the horrors he'd face in his quest.

"Next thing you know, I'm flying. We must have hit something. A rock, maybe? It was like time slowed to a crawl. I'd been in the back, and I can still remember how it felt, my body flinging up into the air, almost like I was on a Ferris wheel but without the cart. The Jeep rolled, end over end, in front of me. I didn't know if Roberts and the driver were still inside. Then everything went black."

Celia waited, giving him time to find his way back to her from the nightmare he was reliving in his mind. When he again caught her eye, she nodded for him to go on.

"After that, I just remember snippets. I'd ended up inside the tree line. Oddly, I remember lying on my back, staring up at a bright blue sky through the treetops. Everything was still for a second . . . peaceful, you know? But then the damn hum of insects picked back up, and I hurt *everywhere*. I remember calling out for Roberts, but there was nothing . . . nothing other than the blinding pain and the bugs. I blacked out again.

"When I came to the next time, I was inside a hut. This little old lady was cleaning my face. She didn't speak English, so we struggled to communicate. But she patched me up as best she could. Eventually, I was strong enough to make my way back to civilization."

He paused and sipped his coffee.

"I'll spare you any more of the details. There were times I didn't *want* to make it out of there alive. I think I knew, deep down, that Roberts was dead."

Given how Danny had started the conversation, Celia already knew his premonition was accurate. How odd it must feel for him now, sitting in a bakery smelling of fresh bread in the middle of the United States. He drew a deep breath and took another fortifying drink of coffee to chase away the nightmares born in a faraway jungle.

"Forgive me, Celia. I know my dropping in on you like this was probably confusing. But I needed a friend."

"At least you called first," Celia said, smiling to add some levity to their conversation.

It worked. He laughed. "I didn't think it would be fair of me to just show up on your doorstep again. But I wasn't entirely sure you'd still be at that number. Were you married by now, maybe even a mother to a family of kids?"

She knew he couldn't possibly know how those words would hurt her. She'd never told him about the baby. It was her turn to look away. He noticed her response.

"Wait. *Are* you married, Celia? Because if you are, I'm happy for you. I hope I didn't anger your husband, calling you like this."

She shook her head. "No, Danny. I'm not married. In fact, other than a few gray hairs and wrinkles, I'm the same person I was the last time you saw me."

But the minute the words left her mouth, she knew they weren't true. She was nothing at all like that thirty-two-year-old, idealistic woman she'd been when he'd given her the charm bracelet. He noticed it on her wrist then, reaching across the table to touch a finger to the golden pine tree.

"Are you still working for Whitby? If you are, I bet you practically run things by now."

She laughed, hating the touch of bitterness she felt. "I am. Still working for him, that is. Preston has been good to me. I *could* run things, if he'd let me. But he still has some preconceived notions about women in the workforce. Besides, he has his precious son to contend with, too."

Danny drew his hand back with a grimace. "Tripp Whitby? That man was always such an ass. Born with a silver spoon in his mouth."

"That about sums it up," Celia conceded, appreciating the fact her old friend also saw her nemesis for what he was. "He's still a woman-izer, a drinker, and riding on his daddy's coattails."

"Why have you stayed, then?"

Danny's question gave her pause. Why *had* she stayed?

She shrugged. "I guess because I like my work. And I'm good at it. Preston pays me well, despite his hesitancy to give me a title that matches the level of work I do. I appreciate his generosity regardless. He's even taught me a lot about investing. After being nearly destitute as a little girl, I vowed I'd never endure another time in life when my cupboards were bare."

A young woman approached with a pot of hot coffee, interrupting Celia. "Can you use a refill?"

Nodding appreciatively, Celia raised her coffee cup to accept the warm-up. Danny did the same.

When they were alone again, he turned his attention back to Celia, reaching across the small space and capturing Celia's hand once more. "I'm leaving tomorrow. Would you do me the honor of letting me buy you dinner tonight?"

Despite her resolve to keep their meeting on neutral ground, a quick hello between old friends, Celia felt her pulse jump at the touch of his fingers.

What is it about this man?

"I appreciate the invite, Danny, but I can't. I have dinner plans with Ruby, Helen, and Eleanor."

He patted her hand and sat back, nodding. "Let me guess. Fortieth birthday party celebration?"

"You could say that. But we aren't just celebrating my birthday. All of us turn forty this year, so we thought we'd do one joint evening out. Helen and Eleanor are both living in Chicago now, but they're driving in together. Good thing both my brothers are out of the house. Everyone's staying at my house afterward."

"That sounds like fun!" He suddenly bent over and rustled around in a bag at his feet. She hadn't noticed it earlier. He removed a small package covered in festive wrapping and topped with a red bow. He slid it across the table to her. "Happy Birthday."

Celia reached out to caress the red silk bow, touched. "I can't believe you remembered it's my birthday."

He grinned. "I could pretend I have the memory of an elephant, but your mother mentioned you might not have time to call me back because you had birthday plans this weekend."

Celia laughed at his admission. "That sounds like Mother. She worries you'll break my heart again."

His smile fell away, as if shocked at her words. "I broke your heart? Celia . . . I thought this was what you wanted. To stay here. I thought I was the only one who was miserable when I left the last time."

She felt her resolution slip ever so slightly. "Danny, you've always been special to me. Besides, Mother exaggerates sometimes."

Her flippant comment, meant to let him off the hook, instead caused him to flinch. Scooping up the present to change the subject, she flipped the package over, trying to figure out what lay hidden beneath the giftwrap. "Why, Danny, did you buy me a book?"

Grinning, he angled his head toward her hands. "Open it and see."

Carefully removing the bow and setting it aside, she tore off the paper, surprised to find a copy of *To Kill a Mockingbird*. "Oh, wow! I read a review of this in the newspaper not too long ago. Have you read it?"

"No, but I met Harper Lee at a publicity event a couple years ago." He grinned. "She really hates those types of events."

Setting the book down, Celia ran a finger over the cover. "Thank you, Danny. That was thoughtful of you. I can't wait to read this. It's a timely topic, to be sure. Have you covered any of the recent rioting down South?"

"No, but I wouldn't mind meeting Dr. King. He seems like a fascinating man."

"He does," Celia agreed, although she couldn't imagine ever meeting a man like King. Outside of work, her circle was much too small for those types of opportunities.

The bell over the bakery door jingled again, and a large group of teenagers filed in. The small eatery had become even busier while they'd talked. People were waiting for tables to open.

Danny noticed, too. "I've probably kept you long enough," he said, rising to his feet. "It's been wonderful to see you after all this time, Celia. Really."

Celia picked her purse up off the floor and her gift from Danny, taking a second to stow the bow safely inside her purse. As they stepped away, an employee swooped in and cleared their table for other patrons. Feeling as if they'd overstayed their welcome, Celia followed Danny out to the sidewalk.

It was a beautiful summer day, the sky a cloudless, crystalline blue that reminded her of the lake.

"What will you do for the rest of the day, then?" she asked, turning to face him.

He squinted against the bright sunlight. "Honestly, I have no idea. Maybe I'll check out early and head out. Seeing you was really the only reason I came."

She checked her watch. "It's awfully nice outside. How would a walk in the park sound?"

"The park where I vandalized the picnic table?" he asked, laughing.

The fact he'd even remembered that detail from so long ago warmed her heart. "Yes. We could check if your artwork is still there." She'd never admit to him she often enjoyed her sack lunch on *their* bench.

"Do you want to ride over with me, or should we meet there?"

Remembering her promise to herself, she took two steps back from him, toward her own car. "Why don't we meet there?"

Without waiting for a response, she turned on her heel and made her way to her Cadillac. As she climbed behind the wheel and glanced toward the bakery, it surprised her to see Danny still standing, exactly where she'd left him, watching her. Trusting he'd follow, she backed away from the curb and headed for the park, keeping her eyes on the road.

Driving under the iron archway, she eased down the road, toward the back of the park, the river, and their bench. The parking lot nearby was half full—not surprising on such a beautiful summer day.

She waited for Danny, watching as a young mother helped a toddler crawl onto a swing. Celia didn't need to hear the woman to know she was telling him to hold on tight, showing him where to place his chubby little hands. She felt the all-too-familiar pain in her chest at the endearing sight.

She jumped at the soft tapping on her window.

"And I thought all my years near battlefields left *me* jumpy," Danny teased when Celia opened her door.

"Something stung my leg," she lied, and she could see he wasn't buying a word of it.

"Should we walk or sit?" he asked, eyeing their bench, nestled between the road and the river.

"Let's check and see if your carving is still there," Celia suggested, knowing that it was but needing a diversion. She headed over with Danny close behind.

"Damn," he whispered, immediately spying their initials. "This was twelve years ago already. And you said it's been what, eight, since I last saw you? You know, I just realized something, Cee. You have been one of the few constants in my life. Thank you."

The sound of children's laughter floated over to them. That sound, the sound of what she'd given up, had become *her* constant in life. For the first time, she considered telling Danny about the child. Their child. The one she'd given up.

Did he deserve to know he had a child out there, somewhere in this world?

Danny had a questioning look on his face. "Everything all right, Celia?"

"I'm sorry. What did you say?"

He shrugged. "It doesn't matter."

"Danny, I'm truly sorry about what happened to your friend. To Roberts. If I didn't say that earlier, I apologize. I can't imagine losing someone like that, so violently. Did he have a family back home?"

"I appreciate that, Celia. And yes, he had a wife and a young son. When I felt sorry for myself over the accident, and missing Roberts, I thought of them. I stopped to visit them before coming here."

Celia had some experience in picking up the pieces and trying to go on after losing first her father, her sister, and then her stepfather. It was brutal, but they'd gotten through it. Eventually.

"Are they doing all right? His family?" she asked. "How long has it been since the accident?"

"About a year. And yeah, they are coping. A man stopped by just as I was leaving. So maybe Roberts's wife is moving on. I'm jealous."

Celia turned to Danny, surprised. "Of his wife possibly dating again?"

Danny laughed. "No, nothing like that. She's like a sister to me. I'm jealous of the fact they shared a son. Even though Roberts died, a piece of him lives on, you know? That's something I'll never have, and some days I regret it. It could easily have been me who died that day."

Celia let his words sink in. Neither spoke for a few heartbeats. The laughter between the young mother and toddler behind them continued, and in that moment, Celia trusted her gut.

"A piece of you lives on, too," she blurted out.

He nodded. "You mean in my photos? I know. But it isn't the same."

"No, I don't mean just in your photos."

Danny turned from the flowing river in front of them to face Celia. "What the hell do you mean?"

She took a fortifying breath and forced her eyes up from their initials in the tabletop to meet his, their intensity burning into hers like nothing she'd ever felt before. Rubbing her face with both hands, she scrambled with how best to tell him, now that she'd opened Pandora's box. When she dropped her hands, he grabbed her wrist.

"Celia, you don't get to make a comment like that and then clam up."

She tugged her wrist free and wrapped her arms around her knees, grasping her hands in front of her and training her eyes on the flowing water. Maybe it would be easier to tell him without his eyes burrowing into her soul.

"After you visited me that Thanksgiving, and we said goodbye for what felt like the last time, I felt out of sorts. I thought it was my heart, missing you. Turned out it was much more than that. When I got physically ill at our holiday Christmas party, I realized what was really happening."

Danny, having followed her lead, was gazing out over the water, too. "You were pregnant."

"I was pregnant," she confirmed.

She let her words float away, as if caught on the current in front of them.

"And?" he eventually prodded.

"And I couldn't raise a baby on my own, could I? Doing that wasn't in my life plan any more than it was in yours." She hated the defensiveness that crept into her tone, but she didn't feel inclined to sugarcoat things. She'd suffered, alone, for eight years.

Danny didn't look at her, but he reached over and pulled her clasped hands apart, wrapping her stiff fingers in both of his hands, comforting. Tears flowed, soundlessly, down her cheeks. She relaxed against him and allowed herself to cry.

"I'm so sorry you had to go through that alone, Celia. If I'd have known . . ." he started, but his words trailed off. Taking a deep breath, he tried again. "If I'd have known, I'd have been here for you. We could have decided what to do together."

She tilted her head slightly, burying her face in his shirt. "I know. But I worried if I reached out to you, we wouldn't make the best decision. We were both pretty clear in what we wanted—and what *didn't* fit with our dreams. A baby, as wonderful as it might have been, wasn't the path either of us envisioned. I did the only thing I could think of. I gave it up."

He wrapped an arm around her shoulders. Her tears dried up, and she straightened. Glancing down at his shirt, she couldn't stop the smile that teased at the corners of her mouth. "I'm sorry, I think you have more makeup on your shirt now than I have on my eyes. I must look a wreck."

Shifting slightly, he pulled a hanky out of his back pocket and handed it to her.

"Seriously?" she laughed, taking the white cloth out of his hands and dabbing at what had to be a mess underneath her eyes. Danny carried a hanky now?

"My eye waters more than it used to. Had some long-term damage," he explained, pointing at the scar running up from his eye. "Comes in handy once in a while."

They fell silent again, each lost in their own thoughts.

"Was it a boy or a girl?"

She understood his need for answers, though it hurt to talk about it. She turned her attention back to the water again, twisting his now-stained hanky between her fingers. "I don't know. Preston agreed to help me place the baby and keep the pregnancy a secret from everyone else at work. I didn't even tell my family, although I've always thought Mother suspected."

"Which might explain her animosity toward me," he interjected.

Nodding, she continued. "For the last few months before the baby came, I went to Whispering Pines. As far as the staff and guests there knew, I was a young widow, working in the office for Preston. As luck would have it, I delivered just after Labor Day. By the time I returned from the hospital, everyone had left except the caretaker. He minded his own business, didn't ask questions. I never knew if that was on Preston's orders, or if he just respected my privacy. He didn't ask why I returned to the resort empty-handed."

"Who took the baby?" His words were soft-spoken, full of heartache.

Celia shook her head. "Preston arranged everything. We agreed it would be better if I didn't know any of the details. Danny, I trusted him. And I needed someone's help."

He nodded, silent. Celia gave him time to process everything.

A child hollered behind them, causing both of them to glance over their shoulders. The young boy, the one from the swing set, was throwing a tantrum. His frazzled mother carried the squirming boy back to their vehicle. Neither was having fun anymore.

Danny and Celia grinned at each other. Despite the pain Celia had endured over giving up their child during the last eight years, and Danny's fresh pain, both suspected it had still been the right decision for them.

"We could have made great parents," Danny finally said, turning his full attention back to Celia. "But I understand why you did what you did. I'm sorry I wasn't there to help you through it."

"I appreciate that. I always knew you'd probably come if I called. And after, I never really considered reaching out to tell you. What purpose would that serve? But when you showed up today, out of the blue like this, and then your comment about a piece of you living on . . . I didn't think it was fair of me to keep this from you."

Pushing up off the bench, Danny stood, his back to the river now. He held out a hand to Celia and helped her down. He pulled her into a hug, and this time she allowed it. When his arms wrapped around her, it felt like coming home. Because that was what he'd always be for her, even when they were thousands of miles apart. She knew they would be apart again soon enough. He kissed her forehead gently and then released her.

"Thank you, Celia. Thank you for seeing the pregnancy through, and for telling me now. Even though I'll never meet our child, just knowing he or she is out there, somewhere, gives me a sense of continuity that's always been lacking in my life. Let's walk. We've been sitting too long."

They meandered through the park, moving haphazardly across the green expanse. At one point, Celia sat on a swing and Danny pushed her. They talked about their lives, their work, other relationships. Celia admitted to dating but never getting too serious with anyone. "If I'd have ever built a life with someone, it would have been you."

He'd grabbed hold of the chains on both sides of her swing as she spoke, jolting the forward motion to a stop. He walked in front of the swing then and kissed the tip of her nose. "We make quite the pair, don't we, Celia? Why do you suppose we're both such oddballs compared to everyone else?"

Grinning up at him, she kept a tight grip on the chains so she wouldn't be tempted to start something she knew she'd later regret. "Maybe that's what you get when two painfully independent souls become best friends. We don't fit any molds. But that's okay."

He laughed, and pushed her again, jumping out of the way when the swing swung back. Celia pumped her own legs, pushing her swing higher and higher, and a newfound sense of freedom flooded through her. There were no more secrets.

EARLY SUMMER 1966

CHAPTER THIRTY-TWO
GIFT OF PROMISES

Celia's heels clicked across the polished floor of the corridor as the still-familiar smells she'd grown up with enveloped her. Being inside a hospital always took her back to her earliest years —sitting beside Beverly, keeping her younger sister busy while doctors and nurses poked and prodded her. This hospital was new to Celia, but they all smelled the same.

The drive to Chicago was a blur, instigated by Eleanor's harried phone call. Her friend's father, and Celia's mentor, had suffered a massive heart attack. The doctors feared Preston had limited time left. They'd already brought in the man's three grown children, but Preston had asked for Celia, too. Could she come right away?

There was never a question. Preston was like a father to her. Her world would look so different if he hadn't taken her under his wing all those years ago at Whispering Pines.

She'd been pulled back to a hospital once again, first by her sister's weak heart when they were young, and now by Preston's damaged one. She'd always known the heart was the weakest link.

Maybe that was why she'd held so tightly to her own.

She spotted a man leaning against a wall down the hallway, bright light casting him into silhouette. Celia couldn't make out his features, but she knew it was Tripp, running his hand through his hair, his handless arm hanging at his side.

"How is he?" she asked as she rushed to him.

Tripp pushed away from the wall. If the haggard expression on his face was any indication, she might be too late. "It's bad, Celia. He won't pull through this time."

Celia had battled to accept this potential outcome throughout her drive. Eleanor's warnings to come quickly still haunted her. Preston had suffered a mild heart attack a year earlier, but had refused to change his ways. Now she could hear the murmur of Eleanor's voice coming from the room behind Tripp.

"Can I go in?"

Tripp sighed. "Yeah. You better. He's been asking for you."

Despite the animosity she felt toward Tripp, the pain in his voice tore at her defenses, as the threat of death so often does. She gave his arm a reassuring squeeze as she walked around him to enter the room.

She pulled up short. Eleanor was bent over Preston, gently kissing his cheek, while Iris sat weeping in a nearby chair.

"Am I too late?" Celia whispered, a new wave of fear gripping her at Preston's ashen complexion and closed eyes.

"Hell no, you're not too late," came the reply, drawing anxious laughs from all three women despite the gravity of the situation.

Celia walked over to Preston's bedside, opposite Eleanor, and took her mentor's hand in her own. "I should have known you'd be too stubborn to leave without saying goodbye."

"Who says I'm going anywhere?" Preston shot back, but Celia could see how much effort it took him to open his eyes. "Eleanor. Iris. Leave us for a minute, would you? Go find some lunch or something. I need time with Celia."

Eleanor patted her father's shoulder before motioning to Iris to follow her. "It's good to see you, Celia. Thank you for coming." Eleanor hugged her briefly, a sad smile accentuating the crinkles around her tired eyes as she walked out.

The look Iris gave Celia wasn't nearly as welcoming, but Celia couldn't say why. She barely knew Eleanor and Tripp's youngest sister. After so long in England, she'd had no interest in the business and kept to herself.

Preston's eyes drifted shut again as his daughters left, but he squeezed Celia's hand once they were alone and motioned for her to take a seat in the chair Iris had vacated. "Pull it close."

"I told you to quit smoking those damn cigars, Preston," Celia joked, trying to lighten the heavy mood as she did as he asked. "Didn't I tell you they were going to kill you?"

"You did, dear, but something is going to kill each of us. Whether we live a life of pure virtue or constant debauchery, there isn't a one of us getting out of here alive." His eyes were a watery blue as he met her gaze. She could see pain there, and perhaps regret.

"I know, Preston, but I still would have liked to have kept you around for a few more years. Things won't be the same without you."

He tried to take a deep breath, but the effort made him cough. When she went to stand, concerned, he waved her back into the chair. "Celia, we need to talk."

"I'd like that," Celia conceded, sinking into the chair once more. "I hope you know how much I appreciate all the opportunities you've given me through the years. I never quite understood why you did it, but I always appreciated it."

He nodded, his watery eyes looking beyond her now, at something outside the window—or maybe even into another time, when he wasn't lying broken in a hospital bed awaiting death. "Did I ever tell you I knew your father?"

Celia nodded. "You met Clarence when he and Mother came to pick us up at Whispering Pines that summer."

He gave a small shake of his head. "Not your stepfather. Your father. Charles. We went to university together. In fact, I worked for him for a short time."

Celia wasn't sure what to think. Was he confused, given the state of his health? She remembered the first time she'd introduced her mother to Preston. She'd been surprised when they already knew each other, but she had never pursued the history. "I don't understand."

"I was there that day. When the machine malfunctioned and cut his arm clean away. There was so much blood . . ."

Celia stared at Preston in horror. She'd known a work accident killed her father, but had never wanted to know the specifics. "That's *awful!*"

Preston must have heard the pain in her words. He pulled his eyes back to her. "I'm sorry. It was all so long ago . . . I shouldn't have shared so much. But you need to understand. Your father knew he wasn't getting out of there alive. He made me promise to watch out for his girls. You and Beverly, and your mother, were the last thing he was thinking about as I watched the life ebb out of his eyes."

"But I don't understand. Why didn't you tell me this before?"

Preston took his time with his reply. "I went to see your mother after the accident. I tried to give her money. But she didn't know me and wasn't looking for a handout. She thanked me, but sent me on my way. I could keep tabs on you through Helen and her family. When you came to Whispering Pines with them that first summer, I thought maybe it was my chance to do right by your father. He'd helped me when I was in a low spot in my life, and I felt like I owed him."

Finally, things made sense. Celia had never figured out why Preston practically treated her like another daughter. She'd worked hard for him through the years, but she had always felt as though there were some other, deeper connection.

"I'm sorry I wasn't able to do more for Beverly. The only thing your mother ever allowed me to do was help with some of her hospital bills. But it wasn't enough."

This shocked Celia further still, but for different reasons. She took a moment to compose herself before replying. "You did more than that. When you let Beverly spend that summer with me at Whispering Pines, she blossomed."

Preston's eyes closed, and he was quiet for so long she thought he'd drifted off. His chest still rose and fell, so she didn't panic.

Eventually, he spoke again. "I'm glad for that. I think that summer helped Tripp, too. He was different after that, at least for a while. I think he loved your sister. But then, when Beverly died, it was like the light switched off. I always knew Tripp felt betrayed by his mother, the way she'd left all of us like she did. Your sister gave him hope again. When she died, I lost a part of him, too."

"I never realized," Celia whispered.

Preston chuckled. "Why do you think he feels such animosity toward you? If he'd had his way, he'd have married your sister, gotten her the best care money could buy. Instead she felt safer going back home with you. Maybe he'd have been able to convince her to marry him eventually, but they ran out of time."

"I didn't know," Celia admitted, feeling foolish for being so blind. She'd witnessed Beverly sneaking off to meet up with Tripp that summer, but she'd chalked it up to a girlish crush. She hadn't realized Tripp reciprocated Beverly's feelings so strongly. Maybe her sister had experienced romantic love before she died after all.

"I'm not telling you this to make you feel bad. Life never works out exactly the way any of us expect. I wanted to tell you what an amazing man your father was, though. I thought it might help you understand why things have unfolded the way they have over the years. I'm afraid this is probably the end of the road for me. Hopefully, I've done enough to return your father's kindness."

Celia leaned forward and placed both her hands on Preston's arm, doing her best to ignore the tubes snaking out of him. "Preston, you've helped me do more with my career than I ever could have hoped."

He patted her hands with his own. "Please. I hope you'll stay on after I'm gone. I know it won't be the same, but Tripp will need you. Even though he can be an ass sometimes, deep down he knows he needs you, too."

"Sometimes?" Celia teased, but she sensed he needed a commitment. "Preston, I'm not going anywhere."

The old man sighed. "That's a relief. I know you are a woman of your word. You've kept up on that investment strategy we talked about, right? Will you be all right financially? I'd never want you or that stubborn mother of yours to want for anything ever again."

"Yes, Preston," Celia said, laughing softly. "You taught me so much. My portfolio is in decent shape. And I'll keep at it."

"Good. See that you do. I've also made arrangements in my will to convey two of my rentals to you. You need to own more real estate. There is security there."

Celia inhaled, surprised at the man's generosity. "That's too much."

"Nonsense," he said, cutting her off. "If it weren't for Tripp and my girls, I'd leave you my company, too, but you know I can't do that. I did warn Tripp to treat you fairly, and he agreed, for what it's worth."

Celia could hear Preston's family talking outside of his door. "I think the girls are back."

"They can wait," he said. "I have a couple more things I need to talk to you about."

Knowing Preston wouldn't change his mind, she turned her full attention back to him. She didn't want to keep him from his family if his time was near. "All right, go on," she encouraged the ailing man.

"First, I want you to know I placed your baby into a family where I knew she'd be well cared for and loved."

Celia inhaled sharply. *A girl.* She'd given birth to a girl.

"It was an honor that you trusted me to handle that situation for you," Preston went on, apparently not noticing his own slip of the tongue. "I didn't want to go to my grave without offering you that reassurance. If you want me to tell you what happened with your baby, now is your chance. You need only ask, but you better make it quick."

Celia's mind raced back to that day in the park with Danny, three years earlier, when they'd both worked to come to terms with the choices Celia made about their baby. Since then, she'd finally found true healing.

"I appreciate your offer, Preston. That was the most generous thing, on top of so many other wonderful things, that you ever did for me. But, no, I think it's best to leave that mystery in our past. The child would be nine now, almost ten. If you feel she is in good hands, I trust you. I've moved on."

He nodded, again patting her hand.

"Should I bring Tripp and your daughters back in? Or call a nurse? Your breathing is more labored, Preston."

"In a minute," he said, taking another deep breath without the accompanying coughing fit this time. "There's one more thing. Whispering Pines will transfer to Tripp. Neither Eleanor nor Iris can take care of it. You know better than most how much work it takes to keep the resort running. Hopefully Tripp will do right by it, but I'm not as confident in this as I am with transferring the business to him. Will you promise me to do all you can to keep Whispering Pines safe, no matter what?"

Celia could see the concern in Preston's fading eyes. Hadn't she promised him the same thing, that long-ago summer when he had to go to England where his estranged wife was dying? She considered how best to respond to what felt like this special man's last request. Tripp would do whatever he wanted with the resort, which made her blood run cold, and she wasn't sure what she could do about it.

Preston grabbed blindly for her hand, his eyes still on hers. "Celia. Promise me. Whispering Pines is a special place. Promise me you'll do anything it takes to keep it safe."

Despite her reservations, she took a deep breath and nodded.

"I'll do whatever it takes, Preston."

CHAPTER THIRTY-THREE
GIFT OF LOYAL FRIENDS

*E*verything changed after Preston died.

Tripp started spending more and more time in Chicago, which was fine with Celia. She appreciated having more autonomy with the man no longer constantly looking over her shoulder. She'd even hoped he'd eventually make her position official, seeing as how she was running the field office now.

She should have known better.

Early one Friday morning, two months after they'd buried Preston, Tripp strode purposefully into the office and called an impromptu staff meeting. His appearance was a surprise. Celia had heard through the office grapevine that he was leaving the country for an extended vacation with his wife, but she wasn't sure when. Tripp came into a sizable inheritance following Preston's death, but Celia had learned enough through the years to know his wife, Sophia, came from *old* money. She controlled the purse strings. When Sophia wanted something, she got it.

As Celia grabbed a seat at the conference table, leaving some lower-level employees to crowd around the outside of the room, she was in for more surprises. The door opened again and Warren

Arbuckle strode in, his appearance as unexpected as it had been years ago when Preston first brought him on board.

He nodded greetings to most everyone. Seeing there wasn't a chair for Warren, Tripp turned to Celia. Before he could open his mouth, Celia eyed Annemarie. She'd claimed the chair right next to the one Tripp always used. "Annemarie, I hear the phones ringing out there. Please go make sure it's nothing important. When you come back, bring another chair for yourself, would you?"

The woman rolled her eyes but did as Celia asked. No one would openly disobey Celia.

"Have a seat, Warren," she offered, motioning to the now vacant one. Having deftly avoided the potential embarrassment of Tripp ordering Celia to give up her chair, she crossed her legs, feeling anxious. She was flustered, but she'd never let it show. "Tripp, the floor is yours. What brings you here on a Friday?"

The look Tripp gave her conveyed his lack of appreciation over her invitation. She'd quickly figured out Tripp had no intention of honoring his father's wishes and treating Celia with respect. Things were growing more challenging at work, even with Tripp working more often from Chicago. She worried they were heading for the edge of a cliff, and she wasn't likely to be the one still standing at the top when the dust cleared. She was even considering looking for a position at a different company.

"I'm sorry for the short notice, folks," Tripp began, crossing his arms in front of his chest and tucking his stump out of sight. "I wanted to bring Warren by today to make some introductions. Celia, I know you've met Warren before, but some others haven't."

Now what is he up to? Celia wondered. *Warren married one of my oldest friends. Obviously I've met him before.*

A pit formed in her stomach. This could only mean one thing.

Tripp confirmed it. "I'm placing Mr. Arbuckle in charge of this office, effective immediately. This is home for him. Warren and his wife, Helen, and their four daughters are eager to move back. Chicago isn't for everyone. From here on out, Warren will set the tone for what happens here. We will instigate other changes, but not immediately. I want to give Warren time to become accustomed to how things are run here. This office has a history of strong production for the company, especially in prior years, although things have tailed off a bit in recent months."

Celia could feel her cheeks burn with embarrassment. Tripp's barely veiled jabs at her performance were impossible to miss. It didn't matter that his comments were a straight-out lie.

Tripp was putting Warren in charge of *her* office. If he was moving Helen and the girls back to town, this wasn't a short-term assignment. They would be back for good. She'd never be put in charge. She liked Warren, and of course this could mean a reconnection with Helen, but it also meant the end of her career aspirations. If she stayed.

Other employees around the room shifted uncomfortably.

"I'm surprised to hear you say things have slowed, Mr. Whitby," Flynn, an older man seated next to Celia, chimed in. Flynn had worked here since it opened, and Celia knew she'd earned his respect over the years. "Things have felt busier than ever. We're having trouble keeping up."

Celia could have hugged the man for his support. Tripp normally treated Flynn with respect, given he was closer to his father's age.

"That may be true," Tripp hedged, but Celia knew from the set of his shoulders he wasn't about to concede anything. "But most of our current projects are with our existing customers. Those are relationships I've nurtured for years."

Celia worried if he didn't stop talking, she'd fly out of her chair in either a fit of frustration or burst out laughing in Tripp's face. He wouldn't take kindly to either type of outburst. But even before Preston's second heart attack, Tripp's influence with their customers had been dwindling. Before moving to Chicago, he'd gotten into the habit of shorter days and longer weekends.

The door to the conference room opened again, and a disgruntled Annemarie attempted to drag a chair through the doorway, banging it into the doorjamb. Tripp held up a hand. "That won't be necessary, Annemarie. We're done here. I'll be taking Warren around town today, introducing him to our top customers. While he knows many of them socially, we'll be introducing him in his new capacity. So, back to work everyone. Now's your chance to impress the new boss."

Celia noticed the satisfied look Annemarie tossed her way. She'd missed Tripp's announcement, but clearly the woman knew what was happening. Celia wondered if Tripp was continuing his affair with his secretary when he was in town. It was all so inappropriate, so cliché. Did Tripp's wife have any idea?

It dawned on Celia that perhaps she was the only one who had discovered Tripp's office romance. Well, not exactly *romance*. Maybe she should do a little digging, find out if it was still going on. If Tripp ever had any dirt on Celia, she knew he'd use it. Given how things were falling apart now that Preston was gone, she may need more of her own ammunition.

* * *

Three weeks later, Celia accepted an invitation to visit Helen's new home. She navigated her way through a path of moving boxes, stacked three high, until she found Helen in the kitchen, delving into the contents of a box.

"Thank goodness," Helen said, her lack of a formal greeting evidence of their long-standing, even though recently neglected, friendship. She held up an exquisite Christmas ornament made of mercury glass and fashioned into a nutcracker. "Warren gives me one of these each year on our anniversary. The movers were so careless, I feared they might have broken these."

The sight of holiday decorations on a hot summer day felt as out of place as Celia did in Helen's new home. But she needed to hear what Helen had to say about their move, and she'd try to keep an open mind.

Helen carefully rewrapped the ornament and showed Celia to the sunroom that overlooked her friend's new backyard, shortly followed by the hiss of a kettle filled the air. Helen excused herself to fetch the tea.

Celia gazed through floor-to-ceiling windows, watching Helen's two youngest daughters frolic in an underground swimming pool. The two older girls reclined on large, colorful towels on a concrete patio that skirted the brilliant blue water. Celia had never visited a home with a private pool, and it seemed a silly luxury in a part of the country with limited summer weather. Not that Warren had ever worried about practicalities when it came to keeping his wife and four girls happy.

"Thank you for coming over for tea," Helen said as she returned with a tray. Celia turned her attention back to her old friend. "I have so much to do here. I couldn't get away. But I thought we needed to talk."

Celia sighed, leaning forward to remove a cup from Helen's tray. The bone china cup rattled against the saucer. "Helen, why didn't you warn me you were moving back? Tripp blindsided me in the office, announcing he was putting your husband in charge."

"That's why I needed to talk to you. To apologize. And to explain. It all came together so quickly. The girls were *not* happy about leaving Chicago. We had to get our house ready to sell, I needed to find this one . . ." Helen's voice trailed off.

"Helen, you knew I hoped Tripp would name me as the official leader at our local office once he moved to Chicago. I told you as much when we spoke at Preston's funeral."

Helen turned her head toward her girls. "It's not that simple, Celia."

How many times have I heard that before? Celia wondered. As one of Helen's oldest friends, she was familiar with her tendency to justify anything that helped her get what *she* wanted. And Celia knew Helen had never adjusted to Chicago, had wanted to move back here almost since day one.

"All right. Explain it to me, then."

Helen turned back to face her. "I suspect you already know this, but Tripp has never really liked you. He tolerated you because it was what Preston wanted."

Celia nodded. It hurt to hear the words, but Helen wasn't telling her anything she didn't already know. "Go on," she said, hoping her face didn't betray the fact that despite her dislike for Tripp, it still stung.

"A week after Preston's funeral, Tripp and Sophia invited us out for dinner. By the time they cleared the dessert dishes, the conversation was all business. I grew bored and excused myself to visit the ladies' room. I was touching up my lipstick when Sophia came in. Apparently she'd had enough shop talk, too. We visited for a bit, away from our husbands. She talked about a vacation she was planning for Tripp to take her to Venice."

Helen paused, sipping her tea, appearing uncomfortable. Celia waited. She knew Tripp was scheduled to leave the country on vacation the very next day.

Finally, Helen began again. "What she said next shocked me. She complained about her husband's philandering ways and planned to give Tripp an ultimatum while in Italy. He must quit seeing other women, or she'll divorce him."

"Other women?" Celia asked. "She knows there are other women in his life? I can't believe she told you that."

Helen narrowed her eyes at Celia. "There was plenty of wine with dinner. What part of this surprises you? The cheating? Or the fact his wife knows?"

"The cheating isn't a surprise. I saw him in, shall we say, a *compromising* position with his secretary, but he has no idea I know. It's the fact his *wife* suspects it and hasn't kicked him out that surprises me."

Helen burst out laughing, a sound Celia hadn't heard for years. "You did not! When, and *where*, did you see him? Not in the office?!"

This was the Helen she enjoyed, not the snobbish woman Helen had become. Her friend had always felt entitled, but with age came a boring level of reserve, too.

"It's good to hear you laugh."

Helen raised her cup of tea to Celia. "It's good to be back here. I hope to find more reasons to laugh. Now, where was I?"

"The ultimatum Sophia plans to give Tripp."

"Right. Celia, you need to understand. In some circles, love doesn't drive marriage. I sense that's the case for Tripp and Sophia. I doubt either stays entirely committed to their wedding vows, but that's not to say Sophia would tolerate any obvious indiscretions."

It was oddly satisfying though unsurprising to hear Tripp's home life was in trouble. "Helen, none of this surprises me, but why are you telling me this? What does it have to do with you moving back here and Warren stealing my dream job?"

If Celia's blunt comment put Helen off, she gave no sign. "Celia, how do you think other women view you?" Helen asked, setting her cup down, her expression turning serious.

The question surprised Celia. "Well, I suspect most women view me as a bit of an oddity. My career is my life. I've never married. I date a little, but I mostly work. I'm forty-three years old and share a home with my mother. I doubt other women think about me much at all, in fact. And if they do, maybe it's as an aging spinster."

Helen leaned back against the flowered sofa cushions and pressed the palms of her hands against her eyes with a groan.

Celia wasn't sure exactly how to interpret the theatrics.

Dropping her hands and leaning forward, elbows on her knees, Helen locked eyes with her. "Sometimes your naïveté simply shocks me."

"What the hell is that supposed to mean?" Celia asked, her defenses rising at Helen's tone.

"Women see you as a *threat*."

"A threat?"

"Look at you. Independent. Smart. Attractive. Money of your own. Dating handsome men, but never seriously enough to be under their thumb. A career woman. Things most of us only dream of."

Celia collapsed against the sofa back, shocked at Helen's words. She fought to process it all.

Finally, she said the only thing she could think of. "That can't possibly be true."

"Oh, Celia. Trust me, I've never spoken truer words."

Celia was both insulted and flattered.

Helen continued. "And because Sophia is a woman, and you work closely with her husband, she may harbor a touch of respect for you, but she also fears you. Imagine my surprise when she casually informed me, while applying a demure pink lipstick, that she'd already instructed her husband to get rid of you, now that her father-in-law isn't around to protect you."

Warren taking over the office had blindsided her, but Celia felt completely floored by Helen's news. "Tripp's going to *fire* me?"

Helen nodded. "Probably, if left to his own devices. But we all know what would happen if we allowed men to run the world."

Celia recognized the look shining from Helen's eyes. Her friend perfected it before she'd turned ten. Helen was a master manipulator. "What did you do?"

"Well, I *didn't* let on that you and I have been dear friends since we were in diapers. I assured her we wives need to be careful who we allow our husbands to associate with, and I left it at that."

"Gee, thanks. *That* was helpful," Celia quipped.

But Helen shook her head. "Let me finish. If I was going to figure out a way to protect you, I needed to be careful. And that brief discussion in the ladies' room wasn't my only surprise of the evening. When we got back to the table, Tripp was telling Warren about some real estate developers showing an interest in Whispering Pines."

Celia gulped, her blood running cold with her tea. A part of her had always worried she'd struggle to keep her position once Preston was no longer around, but Helen's mention of Whispering Pines pushed her anxiety to a whole new level.

"Oh my God, he can't do that! He can't sell Whispering Pines!"

Helen nodded. "I agree. Don't forget I was the one who first brought you to Whispering Pines. I love that place, too. Which is why I had to do something."

"What exactly did you do?"

Helen motioned around them. "Well, the first step was to protect *you*. I know how important your work is to you. You are talented. Dedicated. While most women might be jealous of you, I can see what you're really doing. You're paving the way for other women. I might not be living my career dreams, but when young women look at you, they see things are possible. People respect you at work. Warren has told me that."

Distraught, Celia fingered her charm bracelet, feeling for the golden pine. "Helen, I don't understand. How is this your first step in protecting me?"

"Driving home from dinner that night, I told Warren what Sophia said about getting rid of you. He hated to hear that, although he admitted Tripp would probably do it to keep his wife happy. I told Warren that kicking you out of the company was unacceptable, as was Tripp's plan to sell Whispering Pines. He let me know Tripp had hinted that he was considering asking him to move back here. Warren was uncomfortable with the idea—he knew you'd earned the spot— but when I told him about Sophia's directive, we realized the only way to keep you safe was for Warren to come here. When Tripp did offer Warren the job, he told Tripp the only way he would do it was if he could keep you on."

A beach ball slammed into the sunroom window, causing Helen to jump.

"I'm not getting fired, then?" Celia asked, barely registering the girls' antics in the pool. "I was afraid Warren's arrival meant the end of my career."

"On the contrary, dear. My husband's arrival *saved* your career."

While Celia hated that things had come to this, that the value she provided to the company wasn't enough on its own merit, she wasn't as naïve as Helen thought. Relationships made the world go around.

"Thank you, Helen. I owe you."

Helen grinned. "What are friends for? Besides, I'll find a way for you to pay me back some day. Now all we have to do is figure out how to save Whispering Pines."

Helen was right. Celia had made a promise to Preston to protect the resort.

No matter what.

"Helen . . . let me ask you this. What do you think Tripp values more? A marriage to a rich wife who keeps him living in the lifestyle to which he's accustomed, or unloading a piece of property on a lakeshore he cares little about?"

Helen grinned. "What are you considering, my friend?"

Celia sat tall on the wicker sofa, feeling that surge of confidence she often got when she knew she was on the cusp of closing a big deal. "I may have money of my own, but not enough to buy Whispering Pines outright. Besides, Tripp probably wouldn't sell it to me anyhow, just to spite me. Did it sound like he was in a rush to make a deal with the developers?"

"No. Their timeline would be to close next spring."

"Well, if you'll excuse me, I have work to do," Celia said, standing. "Tripp and his wife are leaving on that vacation tomorrow. If he doesn't walk the straight and narrow when he gets home, she might finally get rid of him. I'm going to devise a plan to make sure he *doesn't* give up on his philandering ways too quickly."

"Why, Celia, I like the way you think," Helen declared, getting to her feet. "Let me know how I can help."

Celia walked around the low wicker table and hugged Helen. "I'm sorry I was mad at you for moving back. I assumed you were the reason I'll never run this office. Now I can see that not only would you have done no such thing, but you helped me keep my job! My aspirations might have been too high for this company, but that doesn't mean I can't somehow get my hands on Whispering Pines. The Whitby Company may own my head, but Whispering Pines has owned my heart for more than twenty years."

"I know that look, Celia," Helen laughed, picking up their empty tea cups. "I pity any man that crosses you."

CHAPTER THIRTY-FOUR
GIFT OF LOOSE TONGUES

*L*aying a trap for Tripp would be easy. Celia had help, and the man himself possessed a bevy of self-destructive tendencies. The Monday afternoon following her meeting with Helen, Warren called Celia into his new corner office.

"Annemarie, hold my calls, please," he'd instructed his new secretary while standing in his doorway. "Celia will be walking me through the customer rolodex. I suspect we'll go past five, so leave the file cabinets unlocked in case I need to reference any of the master customer files. I'll lock them up before I leave and return your keys in the morning."

Celia heard the jingling of keys.

"Tomorrow, I'd like you to run down to the locksmith and have an extra set of keys made for all the cabinets," Warren continued. "I'll need access on nights, possibly weekends, too, and I can't be beholden to your nine-to-five schedule."

Celia exited her own office, carrying a stack of file folders. She enjoyed the stricken look on Annemarie's face as she passed.

"Certainly, Mr. Arbuckle . . . but Tripp—I mean, Mr. Whitby— never needed access after-hours. Are you sure that's necessary?"

"Are you questioning me, Annemarie?" Warren asked, straightening to his considerable height.

"No, sir. I'll leave my keys right here on the corner of my desk. And tomorrow I'll get a new set made for you. I've been meaning to catch up on my filing, too. If you think you'll be accessing the records on your own, versus me retrieving things for you, I'll straighten things up back there. I know where everything is, but my current system might be hard for you to decipher."

"I'm sure I'll manage," Warren assured the flustered woman, then waved Celia into his office, shutting the door firmly behind him.

"I think you threw her off," Celia pointed out as she took a chair at the small table in the corner of Warren's new office. "Tripp could barely sharpen his own pencil around here."

"You noticed that, too?" Warren said, taking the chair opposite Celia. "I wonder if she's hiding something in those filing cabinets. She seemed practically distraught over my request for an extra set of keys."

Celia grinned as she opened the top folder on her pile and raised a pen, preparing for a productive first meeting with her new boss. "That or she's behind in her filing and you've got her scrambling. Were you thinking you'd like to start with our highest revenue customers today? Or alphabetical? I'll be able to give you a summary of our relationship with each of them, regardless."

Warren waved a hand dismissively at her poised pen. "That can wait. I understand you spoke to my wife on Saturday."

Surprised, Celia nodded, setting her pen down. "I did. It was quite *enlightening*."

She'd always liked Helen's husband, but didn't know him well. She waited for him to say more, not wanting to misstep.

"First of all, I know exactly why I find myself in this corner office, even though you earned it. While you and I have done little work together, Preston always spoke highly of you. I've worked with Tripp long enough to know the extent of the role he plays in this company. Suffice it to say his influence, at least historically, has never been as impactful as he'd like everyone to believe. He does a decent job with customers, but working isn't always his top priority."

As Warren spoke, Celia liked him more and more.

"But we need to be careful. I held Preston in high regard. When my family's business was floundering, he stepped in and offered me a solution that allowed me to keep a modicum of pride and financial stability. You of all people can appreciate how important that is to my Helen."

Smiling, Celia assured him she appreciated that fact.

"I want you to know that we're on the same side here," Warren said, one arm resting on the table, his body angling toward her. She sensed his sincerity. "Moving back here and buying that monstrosity of a home for Helen and the girls is costing me a pretty penny. While I don't agree with some of Tripp's business methods, I need this job. We need to be careful," he repeated.

"I agree. I need this job, too," Celia assured him. "But Tripp is out to get me."

Warren sighed. "I think you've always threatened him."

"Well, maybe if he'd apply himself at work he wouldn't feel threatened. Customers do like him most of the time. Few see how he acts outside of their social interactions."

"Right. Tripp's biggest problem is he's upset his wife. And that makes it your problem, too. He'll do anything she asks."

"That's what Helen said."

"I think we need to shift Sophia's suspicion away from you," Warren said. "Will that be difficult?"

"I've had nothing but a business relationship with Tripp," Celia said, shocked that Warren might think otherwise.

He laughed at her expression. "You misunderstand my question. I've never thought there was anything inappropriate between you."

Celia took a deep breath, relieved. It had horrified her for a moment, thinking maybe people assumed Tripp's animosity might stem from an old romantic relationship between the two of them. "Sorry. Then are you asking whether I've come up with a masterful plan to bring about the ruin of Mr. Tripp Whitby since I left your wife on Saturday morning?" Celia was unable to keep the grin off her face despite the seriousness of their conversation. "Tripp isn't exactly pure of spirit. It shouldn't take much."

"Do you think he's done anything illegal?"

Celia considered this. "I don't think Tripp is stupid enough to try that. At least, it isn't something I've thought about. I could give two of the larger projects he's overseen in the past year a bit of extra scrutiny if you'd like, just to be sure."

"Yes. Do that," Warren said.

Celia liked his no-nonsense approach.

"Now, about the other topic you mentioned to Helen. She said you witnessed Tripp in a 'compromising' position in the office?"

She could see he was losing his battle to remain straight-faced.

"Technically the door to this office was closed, but they weren't quiet, and both were doing plenty of clothing adjustments when they came out."

"In the middle of the day?" Warren asked, disturbed.

"Over the noon hour. We close, as you know, and Tripp insisted everyone go out to eat. He thought it helped the local economy and opened up opportunities for the company."

"But you think it might have been so he could carry on an affair with his secretary?"

She laughed. "No. Tripp loves to network. He never understood that the staff can't afford to go out to lunch every day. Heck, I often bring a sandwich to the park to eat."

"We'll stop making everyone leave for an hour midday immediately. Folks can use the break room here if they like."

"People will appreciate having more options," Celia replied. "And anyway, I honestly have no idea if what I witnessed between Tripp and Annemarie was a one-time thing or ongoing."

"I need you to find out if it's ongoing. It's totally inappropriate, on many levels, and it needs to stop. But . . ."

Celia waited as his voice trailed off. She could see he was trying to decide whether to say more.

"But Tripp is volatile enough that we might both be wise to have something to hold over him."

"Why, Mr. Arbuckle, are you suggesting we blackmail the new owner of the company that employs us?"

He shrugged. "Tease if you must, but Tripp wouldn't hesitate to use something on either of us if it benefited him."

"True," Celia agreed. "I'll see what more I can find out about Annemarie. And maybe she's not the only one. Tripp has always been a ladies' man. There was a time when he set his sights on my sister. She was young and inexperienced."

"And before that, he defiled my wife."

Celia froze, shocked at Warren's comment. "Yes . . . that was a long time ago. You know about that?"

"Helen told me everything. Believe me, it's been difficult to pretend I don't know around him. Tripp might not even remember it. But I know Helen does. It scared her, no matter how cavalier she tried to be about the incident."

Apparently Warren had his own reasons to dislike Tripp.

"What is our endgame, then?" Celia asked.

"We make sure Tripp can't get rid of either of us."

"Agreed," Celia said, holding a hand out to Warren.

They shook hands, cementing their agreement.

"Say, Warren, what would you think about also helping me figure out a way to save Whispering Pines?"

"You know, I wondered if you were going to bring that up. Helen said that was the piece of the puzzle that upset you the most—even more than the risk to your job."

"You've been to Whispering Pines, Warren. You liked it, didn't you?"

He nodded. "What's not to like? And I know it was a special place to Preston."

Celia lowered her voice. "Preston asked me to keep Whispering Pines safe, *no matter what*." She'd never shared that with anyone before, but she felt Warren would understand.

"If our dear Preston gave you the green light to protect Whispering Pines by whatever it takes, then by all means, I'll help."

"We both have a lot to lose," Celia warned. It would be hard for her to start over somewhere else if they failed, yes, but Warren had a large family to support.

Warren grinned darkly. "We won't lose, Celia. Tripp isn't smart enough for that."

* * *

Once everyone else went home for the day, Warren and Celia came out of the corner office and got to work in the filing room. They weren't sure what they were looking for, but that didn't stop them from digging. Warren phoned Helen to let her know he wouldn't be home until late.

They methodically combed through the filing cabinets. Despite Annemarie's claim to the contrary, she'd kept organized, up-to-date files. However, they found nothing damaging or useful.

"What's that?" Warren asked, pointing to an old wooden file cabinet in a far corner.

"I don't know," Celia admitted. "I assume it's not used anymore. All the filing cabinets used to look like that when Preston first opened this office. He was frugal and brought them in from Chicago. The drawers stuck and the tracks would break. He replaced them all maybe five years ago."

Warren strode over and tried to pull open the top drawer. Locked. He pushed against the side of the cabinet, testing its weight. "It's not empty."

"Here, let me see if any keys on this ring work," Celia suggested.

She tried each of the keys, but none worked to unlock the old wooden cabinet.

"Could anyone other than Annemarie have a key?" Warren asked.

"I doubt it, unless it's Tripp himself. Why don't I go check her desk, see if she keeps any spare keys in there?"

They left the filing room. The sun had set while they worked. Celia flipped lights on as they went. Once at Annemarie's desk, she tugged on the center drawer.

"That's strange. It's locked. Who locks a pencil drawer?"

"Someone with something to hide," Warren pointed out. "Try the keys in your hand."

This time, one key unlocked all four drawers in Annemarie's desk. Celia rifled through the papers inside the larger drawers, and Warren rummaged through the pencil drawer. These drawers weren't nearly as neat as the ones in the filing cabinets.

Holding up a solitary key on a ring with a yellowed tag, Warren smiled. "Look familiar?"

Squinting at it, Celia nodded. "Yes! We used to use those tags to track the key inventory. That might open the old cabinet."

"Should I go try it?"

"Yeah." Celia nodded. "I'm almost done. I want to make sure there isn't anything interesting in here."

Celia felt a twinge of guilt as she thumbed through copies of old performance reports, grocery lists, and scribbled phone messages. While the files in the back were company assets, this felt more personal. Celia hated going through someone's personal things.

No matter what. Preston's last words echoed through her head. Tripp held the figurative keys to Whispering Pines, but Celia had promised to protect the resort. Nothing else mattered. She wasn't battling against someone with a conscience. She needed to set hers to the side, too.

Why would Annemarie keep old copies of phone messages?

One name kept showing up: Mr. De Luca. No first name.

The bottom drawer contained supplies. Not willing to give up, she piled the contents on Annemarie's desktop. Underneath everything was a pile of folded, lined notebook paper, bound with a rubber band. No one would go to so much trouble to hide meaningless office correspondence. Slipping the band off, Celia unfolded the top note.

"What an idiot," she said, her words echoing in the empty office area.

"Who's an idiot?" Warren asked, heading back toward her, a large file folder in one hand.

"I'll give you one guess."

"That answers that question. I found something, too," he said, holding the folder higher.

"I take it the key got you into the cabinet?"

"It did. And I found a file labeled *Whispering Pines*."

A pair of headlights swept through the interior. Someone had pulled into the parking lot in the back.

"Is someone here?" Warren asked.

"Shit!" Celia hissed, checking her watch. "I bet it's the cleaning crew. We switched to a weekly schedule."

"And they come in on Monday nights?" Warren asked, his eyes incredulous.

"It was the cheapest option!" Celia whispered, quickly replacing the supplies in Annemarie's drawer. "Go, get back in your office. I'll be in there in a second. I work late all the time. They won't be surprised to see me here, but they know this is Annemarie's desk, not mine. They leave their weekly invoice on her desk. I need to clean this up quick."

Nodding, Warren did as he was told, and by the time she heard the scrape of the cleaning team's key in the outer lock, she sat across the table from him.

"Let's see what's in there," Celia suggested, still feeling short of breath over the rush of possible discovery.

"What about them?" he asked, motioning toward the outer office area.

"We're working late on something. As long as they don't catch us digging through someone's desk, they won't think twice about us."

Flipping back the top of the folder he'd found in the older cabinet, Warren began reading through the contents. The folder was at least three inches thick.

Celia sighed. "Can I see some of that? We'll be here all night if I have to watch you read every single page."

"Sorry," Warren said, finding a divider and handing the bottom stack of documents over to Celia.

At one point, a man with a noisy vacuum waved at them and pulled Warren's door shut.

They kept reading.

"Oh my," Celia whispered. "I forgot about this."

Looking up, Warren rubbed a hand over one eye. The noises outside his office had quieted. The cleaning crew must have finished and left while they'd been lost in the contents of the folder. "What? Did you find something?"

"I think so. Helen said Tripp has been talking with some real estate developers, right?"

"Right?"

"How excited do you think developers would be to build on land purported to be sacred to the Chippewa? Over an Indian burial site?"

"I suspect that would probably be bad for business, if not outright illegal. Are you saying that's the case at Whispering Pines?"

Celia stood and walked over to Warren's side of the table. She laid the map she'd found over the pile of papers in front of him, pointing out what she'd been able to glean with a quick review. "Eleanor mentioned something about this way back when we first visited Whispering Pines."

"Damn," Warren said, leaning back in his chair and looking up at Celia. "If that's accurate, developing that land might prove problematic. You might have found the magic ticket to keep Whispering Pines safe."

The unexpected jangle of the telephone on Warren's desk caused them both to jump.

"I bet that's Helen, wondering if you got abducted," Celia said, glancing at her watch. She had to move her charm bracelet off the watch face to see the time. Out of habit, she fingered the golden pine tree.

Pushing up out of his chair, Warren crossed over to pick up the receiver. Celia could tell from his side of the conversation that it was

Helen, and something was up. "All right. I'll be home in ten minutes," Warren said, hanging up the phone.

"Duty calls?" Celia asked.

"Yes. Virginia must have eaten something that didn't agree with her. She's been vomiting for two hours. Trust me when I say Helen does not do well with stomach issues."

"I bet. Virginia's your youngest, right? How old is she now?"

Warren paused, as if he needed to do the math. She supposed that was normal when you had four daughters. "Ten. Well, almost. She'll be ten this fall."

"At least she's not three," Celia laughed. "A ten-year-old should at least be able to make it to the bathroom in time."

"Yes," Warren sighed. "But Helen is still squeamish. I'm sorry, but I have to head home."

"It's late. I should go, too. We did well tonight. We'll keep working on all of this, but I feel better than I did when you were scolding Annemarie about her keys."

"I wasn't scolding her," he insisted.

"Oh yes, you were. I think that was your 'father' voice we heard. You almost had *me* wanting to hand my keys over," Celia joked.

Warren grinned as he shrugged into his suit jacket and pulled his own set of car keys from his pocket.

Celia piled the papers back into the Whispering Pines folder. "Do you mind if I take this home with me?"

"Not at all. And I locked everything back up in the filing room. Come on, I'll walk you out. I don't like you in that dark parking lot alone. Leave her keys on her desk."

After quickly straightening the contents of Annemarie's drawers, not wanting to raise suspicions, she set the woman's keys on the corner of the desk and followed Warren out.

Celia felt optimistic about what they'd found. She hoped nothing would derail their progress.

* * *

"I'm surprised you joined us tonight," Annemarie said, eyeing Celia with a skeptical look over the top of her gin and tonic. "We've been meeting for drinks nearly every Friday afternoon after work for as long I've been here, and you've never come. Why this sudden change of heart?"

"Jeez, Annemarie, lighten up," Brenda, one of their accountants, scolded. "Look, Celia, we're all sorry that Tripp brought Warren in instead of promoting you when he moved to Chicago. I can understand why a drink might sound good."

Celia laughed. "What can I say? It's been tough. Tripp disappointed me, as usual. But us girls have to stick together. To answer your question, Annemarie, I never joined you because I didn't think I should."

"What do you mean?" Fiona, the fourth woman at the table, asked.

"Look. All of you have worked here long enough to know we all get treated a little differently than the men."

Brenda and Fiona raised their glasses in agreement.

"I see the payroll records and I know for a fact the men make twice what we do, and usually for less work," Brenda chimed in.

Celia gaped at her in alarm. Brenda shouldn't be sharing that kind of confidential information over drinks. But if what Brenda said was true, Celia couldn't ignore what she'd revealed. She knew pay inequities were the norm, but that didn't make it right.

"I don't know," Annemarie countered, swirling the liquid in her quickly emptying glass. "Men aren't so bad."

And it's women like you who keep us locked in the old stereotypes, Celia thought, but she held her tongue. She'd joined the three women tonight to pump Annemarie for information, but she needed to be careful.

The conversation shifted, flitting from topic to topic. There were plenty of work complaints, even though Celia expected her presence on this Friday night reduced the sheer number. Annemarie was single, but the other two were working wives. Some struggles they faced, such as reliable childcare, and balancing home and work, were eye opening for Celia. Here she'd been thinking she had it so difficult, working in a field dominated by men. But Brenda and Fiona were straddling two worlds.

The women with husbands waiting at home both made an early evening of it, saying their goodbyes after finishing their second drinks. Celia hoped she'd have time to speak with Annemarie alone before she took off, too.

She had to think fast when the secretary reached for her purse.

"Leaving already?" Celia asked, hoping her disappointment sounded sincere. "I was hoping to ask you what you think about working for Warren now. You're always so in-tune with what Tripp needs. He told me numerous times how valuable you are to the company."

"He did?" Annemarie asked, surprised. "He said that?"

"He did," Celia assured her, waving down the server. "One more round? I'll buy. And then I'll give you a ride home. I switched to Coke. More than one drink gives me a headache."

"Why the hell not," Annemarie conceded, raising her empty glass to the server and jingling the ice cubes.

"I'm trying to get a feel for how Warren operates," Celia improvised, testing how best to get Annemarie to confide in her. Helen's words surfaced in her brain about how other women felt around Celia. Plus, it wasn't like she was friends with this tipsy secretary. "Do you have any pointers yet?"

"You're asking *me* for pointers?" Annemarie asked, incredulous.

"Sure. Come on, Annemarie. It's obvious now that Tripp will never put me in charge. But I need this job. I want to impress Warren. Since you were so good with Tripp, I thought you might have some advice for me."

The server set two fresh glasses down, and Annemarie treated herself to another sip before replying. "I suppose you're right. I've always been able to connect with upper management."

Celia nearly choked on her drink as her mind conjured up an inappropriate image.

"I suppose it's because I'm willing to go beyond my normal job duties," Annemarie continued.

Is she going to go there?

"I mean, nothing inappropriate or anything," she quickly added. "Please don't take that the wrong way. I just meant things like buying gifts for Tripp's wife, or taking special care with certain phone messages I take for him. I do exactly as he asks, even if it's not in my job description. He appreciates my flexibility."

I bet.

The gin and tonics were hitting Annemarie. Her speech was slurring.

Celia felt another pang of guilt.

No matter what, she reminded herself.

"What kind of phone messages?" Celia prodded, hoping the woman was too drunk to suspect her question.

"Oh, you know, like when Mr. De Luca calls."

Bingo!

"De Luca? I don't recognize that name. He isn't a customer, is he?"

Annemarie laughed, then wobbled on her stool. A man passing by with a drink in his hand paused and took a step in her direction.

"Scram, loser," Celia hissed.

The man shifted his gaze to her in surprise, his eyes cloudy. He raised a hand and turned away, avoiding potential trouble.

"He was cute," Annemarie pouted.

"He was wearing a wedding ring," Celia countered.

Annemarie shrugged, unbothered. "Whatever. Now what were we talking about?" she asked, struggling to focus on Celia's face.

"Mr. De Luca."

"Ah. Yes. I think he's Tripp's bookie."

"Bookie?"

"Sure. You know Tripp likes to gamble, right? I'm sure it's harmless. Just a little fun. Life can be pretty boring around here."

"It sure can," Celia assured her.

It surprised her to hear Tripp gambled enough to have a bookie.

"Now that Tripp isn't in our office nearly as much, I save the messages for him. Tripp said to always tell him when Mr. De Luca calls, but to keep it between us. Tripp must be a *fantastic* customer."

"Why do you say that?"

"Because Mr. De Luca has been calling *a lot* lately. When I told him that Tripp was out of the country, he made me promise to have Tripp call him the minute he gets back. Hmm . . . you know what?"

"What?" Celia asked, uncomfortable with how easy it was to manipulate this girl. Her attitude toward the younger woman was shifting from contempt to pity.

"Maybe Tripp is in *trouble* with Mr. De Luca! He didn't sound too happy the last few times he called, even though he's always polite to me."

Maybe Tripp was in some trouble. A persistent bookie was never a good sign. She shifted the conversation, confident Annemarie had told her all she knew about this De Luca character.

No matter what.

"This is probably none of my business . . . but is Tripp generous with the gifts he gives his wife?"

Annemarie snorted, seeming to enjoy this girl-talk. "Is he ever! And it's gotten worse since Mr. Preston died."

"How so?"

"I really don't think I should say. I think I've already said too much," Annemarie declared, pushing her half-empty glass away.

"Interesting," Celia continued, pretending not to notice Annemarie's hesitation. "Maybe the rumors are true, then."

Annemarie straightened on her stool. "Rumors? What rumors?"

Celia shrugged and parroted Annemarie's words. "I've probably said too much, too."

"Come on, Celia, what have you heard?"

Celia hesitated, but then went all in. "I heard their marriage might be in trouble."

"Really?" Annemarie whispered, excited at the possibility. "I can't say I'm surprised. His wife really is quite heavy-handed. She tries to run his life, but he's too smart to let her. I figured it wouldn't last."

Hoped, more like, Celia thought.

"I even heard Tripp has a wandering eye. Can you believe it?" Celia asked, swinging for a home run.

"Oh, I can believe it," Annemarie said, grinning like the cat that swallowed the canary.

"Oh my, would you look at the time," Celia declared, as if she'd only just realized how long they'd been sitting there. "I have a date. I better get you home."

Nodding, Annemarie gathered up her purse, wobbling as she climbed off her barstool. Her eyes were clear, despite the three strong drinks. To Celia, Annemarie looked like a woman with a new focus.

She had little doubt Annemarie would be ready for Tripp when he returned to the States.

If Celia was lucky, Tripp would return to several surprises.

CHAPTER THIRTY-FIVE
GIFT OF A WELL-CRAFTED PLAN

*C*elia met Warren and Helen in the office on Saturday morning. Gloria, their oldest, was watching their two youngest at home. Helen never forgave Tripp for how he'd treated her when they were teenagers, and she wanted to help.

"The goal isn't to ruin his marriage then?" Helen asked, glancing between her husband and old friend. Celia heard a hint of disappointment in her voice.

"No. Sophia can help keep him out of our hair. We just want Tripp to believe I have the dirt to make that happen, should I decide to share it with his wife."

Warren sat back with a shake of his head. "I don't like this. I don't want you to shoulder all this on your own, Celia. Tripp might be dangerous. He has a temper, and desperate men can do desperate things."

Celia considered this. "That's why I need to be careful. If I play my cards right, I'll not only make Tripp see he needs my help, but offer him the solution that could save him."

"Tripp may be a reckless bully, but he isn't stupid," Helen cautioned. "To be honest, there has always been something about him that scared me a little."

"You can never let him know that, Helen. Bullies thrive on fear." Celia refused to admit she'd experienced that fear, too. But, after twenty years, she was tired of treading carefully around Tripp.

"All right, now that we've debated the lack of virtue in the junior Mr. Whitby," Warren said, "where do we go from here?"

"Now we set the trap."

"And how, dear Celia, do you propose we do that?" Helen asked.

Celia described her conversations with Annemarie and the other two women from the office the evening before. "And Warren, we need to discuss the fact that we are paying the women around here fifty cents on the dollar compared to men for the same work."

Warren fidgeted. "That can't be true. We pay you fairly, Celia."

Celia shook her head. "I'm not talking about me. I fought for every penny of that. You wouldn't believe the heated conversations I had around my pay increases through the years with Preston, God rest his soul. He was always resistant, though he'd eventually give in. Most women won't fight like that, and as a result they get treated unfairly. It isn't right."

Helen tapped the tabletop with her index figure. "Yes, be sure to take care of that, Warren. Celia raises an important point about pay."

Warren grimaced at the topic of pay inequities. Celia suspected it was easy to ignore the unfairness of it all when he wasn't on the hot seat in front of both his strong-willed wife and his most important employee.

"But let's set that aside for another day," Celia added. "We need to focus on Tripp."

Warren nodded. "Back to Tripp. What's our first step?"

"I couldn't sleep a wink last night. Eventually I gave up, went downstairs, and jotted down my ideas." Celia pulled both a notepad and the thick file on Whispering Pines from her briefcase. She started spreading the information out on the large conference table between them.

Helen and Warren leaned forward, curious.

"My primary mission here is to protect Whispering Pines."

Warren held up a finger. "And our jobs."

"Well, yes. I helped build this place. I'm not going anywhere. I need to stockpile some dirt to make sure Tripp can't get rid of me. Of us."

"Blackmail, then," Helen said, a wide smile stealing over her face.

"Why, dear Helen, you make it sound so nefarious!" Celia teased. "I'm shocked."

"Oh, stop!" Helen laughed. "We all know our dear friend Tripp protects what is his at any cost. We're following his lead."

"Ladies," Warren interjected. "How about we stop all this Tripp bashing and get down to the brass tacks?"

"Spoilsport," Helen said, sitting back with a pout.

"Right," Celia agreed. She referenced the list she'd penciled out during the quietest, darkest part of the night, when only the ticking of the grandfather clock was witness to her brainstorming. "Ultimately, I think the only way to save Whispering Pines—and to save it forever— is to find a way for me to buy it from Tripp."

This brought Helen forward in her chair again. "Wait. Seriously? You can afford that, Celia? I'm impressed."

"Don't be," Celia said, feeling a blush creep up her neck. "Preston helped me grow an investment portfolio over the years, but I don't have nearly enough set aside that I can afford to buy a lake resort."

"I don't understand, then."

Nodding, Celia tapped her notepad. "Let me explain, and then I'll need help from the two of you to find any holes in my plan. The trick will be to get Tripp to sell it to me for less than it's worth."

"Tripp would never go for that."

"Helen," Celia sighed. "Please. Hear me out."

Warren reached over and patted Helen's arm, as if to shush her. She shrugged his arm away, though her heart didn't seem to be in it.

"As I was saying, I'll need to get Tripp to agree to a lower price. How? By making him desperate. If he truly owes his bookie a chunk of money like I suspect he must, that could be our best leverage. I don't think the guy would call so often unless the debt was big."

"How could we possibly find out what he owes?" Warren challenged.

"Good question. Hold that thought," Celia replied. "Tripp already has an interested buyer in the resort. That's another problem. I'd never be able to pay more than a serious real estate investor. We need to kill that deal."

Helen nodded. "How do you propose we do that?"

"What if we find a way to let the developers know about the purported Indian burial ground on the property? Congress is considering legislation right now around protecting historical and archaeological sites. Real estate developers are up in arms over it. We make it look like Tripp thinks they should fast-track their purchase to avoid legal red tape, before any new laws are on the books. We let the developers think they are dealing with an unethical landowner directly. We sprinkle in little warnings about keeping this quiet to prevent negative press. We make it all sound risky enough that they walk away from the deal. There are plenty of mom-and-pop resorts lining the lakes of Minnesota, and many of them would probably be happy to sell for a pretty penny. Why would they want the headaches Whispering Pines could bring because of the Indian burial ground?"

Warren sat quietly, mulling over Celia's proposal. He nodded. "This might work. Celia, put together a letter to them capturing those exact thoughts."

Celia made a few notes. "I'll get that done this afternoon. But do I make it look like it's coming from Tripp directly? If we're putting something out in writing, I'm not sure we should sign his name. I don't want to tiptoe into any illegal activity. I can bend my ethics on this one for the sake of saving the resort, but none of us can land in jail over this."

Warren nodded again, more slowly. "No, don't sign his name. Use our letterhead but omit any signature altogether," he suggested. "It's unusual, but I think it might accomplish what we're after. With any luck, they'll wash their hands of the whole deal."

Helen stood. "Excuse me. While I find all of this highly intriguing, I need coffee. I'll go start a pot."

After her sleepless night, Celia could use a cup, too. "Thanks, Helen."

Warren spared his wife a quick smile, then turned his attention back to Celia. "I think your idea should take care of the developers. Now, as far as this bookie guy goes, I want to handle him."

Celia was relieved to hear him say that, as she'd struggled with that point. She had no experience working with men like that, nor was she inclined to want to gain some now. "How?"

"I'll tell Annemarie that the next time a Mr. De Luca calls, she's to put him through to me."

"Won't she question how you know about him?"

"Annemarie isn't as likely to question authority as you are, Celia."

Celia laughed at his pointed look.

"Besides, I can tell her Tripp suggested I talk to him. I'll pretend I'm interested in placing a few wagers, too. I doubt she'd suspect anything."

"That might work to put you in touch with the guy, but then what?" Celia glanced toward where Helen had run off. "Your wife would kill you if you started working with a bookie."

It was Warren's turn to laugh. "No. I'll take a different approach with De Luca. I'll meet him offsite. Explain that they hired me to come in and clean up a few messes. Push him for what it would take to make him disappear. I'm sure he's just a middleman. If he knows Tripp has left town for Chicago, paying him off will make him go away. He'll be getting pressure to collect."

Celia shivered. Getting involved with the underbelly of society made her blood run cold. "Thank you, Warren. Promise me you'll be careful."

"I'll be careful," he agreed, and he seemed sincere. "I'm just offering to help the guy solve a problem. I won't go in with guns blazing or anything stupid like that."

Helen strolled back in. "The coffee will be ready soon. What did I miss?"

"I'm going to get in touch with Tripp's bookie," Warren said, taking charge of this part of the conversation.

Celia expected Helen to balk at the idea, but she nodded in agreement. "Give him hell, dear."

"All right, then. Let's see," Celia said, referencing her list. "We do away with a potential buyer for Whispering Pines. We find out how deep Tripp is in with his gambling problems. With any luck, the number will be big enough that Tripp doesn't have many options, but not so big that selling Whispering Pines to me at a bargain can't make the problem go away."

"Sophia has plenty of money of her own. How do we make sure Tripp doesn't weasel the cash out of her to pay off his bookie?" Helen asked.

Celia smiled at Helen's question. "I think that might be the easiest part. You said Sophia is tired of Tripp's womanizing. She's probably giving him her ultimatum right now as they float down a canal in Venice."

Helen and Warren grinned at the picture Celia wove with her words.

"I've already set the bait with Annemarie. I suggest you bring him here for a meeting when he gets back to the States, Warren. That shouldn't be hard. After weeks away with his wife, he'll be ready for a work trip. Once he's here, we make it easy for Annemarie to corner him. Believe me, I could see the determination in her eyes when I mentioned Tripp's marriage might be in trouble. Annemarie is ready to swoop in. She thinks now's her time. We just make sure one of us catches him in the act, and we have our dirt."

Warren stood and stretched. He wandered over to the large window behind his desk and peered outside. "Remind me to never get on your nasty side, Celia. You are downright sinister when you set your sights on something."

The two women exchanged a knowing look. They were ready to bring Tripp down. He'd stolen Helen's innocence without a backward glance and he'd bullied Celia for years, stifling her career in the process.

"Tripp should have known better than to mess with us," Helen said. "And the funny thing is, he isn't even going to see it coming."

Celia nodded. "I hope you're right, Helen. This is too important. We can't mess it up. The thought of big bulldozers razing the cabins and trees at Whispering Pines makes me physically ill."

Warren turned back to face them. "That still leaves the dilemma of how you can afford to purchase Whispering Pines from Tripp, even at a discount. Even if he is desperate to get the bookie off his back and save his marriage, where will you come up with the cash for the purchase?"

Celia flipped the top sheet back on her notes, running a finger down the list she'd made. "Preston was generous. He'd been encouraging me to dip my toes into the real estate business. He left me a fourplex in his will. There's no mortgage now. I'll mortgage that property, but be careful to make sure the rent I'm pulling in from the units covers the monthly payment. I'll also mortgage my house."

Helen groaned at this. "Celia, you can't risk your home! What will your mother say?"

"I'll deal with Mother. Besides, don't you have a mortgage on *your* home?" Celia countered.

Helen looked to Warren, who nodded.

"I do also have an investment portfolio," Celia added. "Preston got me started on that years ago. I don't want to deplete it, but I can use some of it."

Helen reached across the table and grabbed Celia's hand. "Cee, I know how hard you've worked to build financial security. Be careful."

Celia squeezed her friend's hand, then pulled hers back. "I'm being careful."

"Maybe we could chip in," Helen suggested.

Celia couldn't help but smile when Helen avoided looking at her husband. At least Warren didn't flinch at the notion.

"I appreciate that. Really, I do. And I appreciate all the two of you are doing to help me. I know I couldn't accomplish this alone. Hell, maybe even as a team this will all crash and burn. But I made a promise to Preston to protect Whispering Pines, no matter what. I'm forty-three years old. I'll have at least twenty more years of working to replenish my coffers. I'm never going to raise children of my own, may not even marry. But maybe Whispering Pines could be my legacy. None of us like the thought of leaving nothing behind for our time here on Earth. You two have your four beautiful daughters. I know how crazy it sounds, for a single woman like me to want to own a small lake resort in the middle of Minnesota . . . but I do."

"Well then," Warren said, taking his seat again. "Let's make it happen. Helen, dear, why don't you get us that coffee. The three of us have work to do."

CHAPTER THIRTY-SIX
GIFT OF AUDACITY

$\mathcal{T}$he real estate development company walked away, exactly as they'd hoped. Celia sent the registered letter off to them on Monday and Warren intercepted their response from the daily mail delivery the following week. The company regretted to inform all parties involved that due to the recently discovered potential legal complications, they were pursuing other options.

Warren called Celia into his office first thing Wednesday morning and shut his door firmly behind her.

"You know, Preston had an open-door policy way back when," Celia joked, taking a seat at Warren's corner table.

He smirked, then shared the good news about the developers, but insisted he be the one to break it to Tripp. "I'll tell him the envelope landed on my desk—just as everything does now that he placed me in charge. This will be my chance to express my disappointment over his intent to sell Whispering Pines, a place so important to his dead father. I will offer as few details as possible. Maybe a dose of shame will have him cooling his heels on finding another buyer right away."

"That's probably for the best," Celia conceded. "As far as Tripp knows, you're relatively neutral on the whole Whispering Pines subject. If he thought *I* knew about the investment firm, he'd be suspicious. *Whew.* First step: success! Now, have you heard from De Luca yet?"

"Yes. I'm meeting him for a drink tonight. It should be interesting."

This part of their plan still scared Celia. "Promise me you'll be careful."

He nodded. "If I tell you something, swear you'll never tell Helen."

"I swear," Celia agreed, curious.

"I've had to deal with people like De Luca before," Warren admitted.

This surprised her. "Really? You don't strike me as the gambling type."

"Believe me, I'm not. But my father . . . he had a problem. It almost sunk our company."

Celia remembered Preston talking to her about Warren's family company being in financial trouble, which led to the senior Whitby bringing Warren into the fold.

"I've negotiated with bookies and loan sharks before. I'm not going into the meeting blind. Don't worry."

Celia appreciated it, but she knew she would worry regardless. "Do you already know this De Luca character, then?"

"No . . . not him personally. People don't last in that business for long. The deal with my father was years ago. But I feel like I know what makes them tick."

"Fine. Meet the guy. And please know how much I appreciate you doing this. But be careful. Be sure Helen knows exactly where you're meeting him and when you'll be home."

He grinned. "Why, so you can send the cops out to search the river for my dead body when I don't make it back?"

"Don't even joke about that!" Celia said, horrified. "Promise you'll call me when you get home. To let me know that you're all right and what you find out? I can't take another sleepless night."

"I'll call you. I promise. Besides, I can't wind up dead over this, because then Helen will kill you for dragging me into this mess, and I'd hate for that to happen. *You're* a decent human."

Celia appreciated his attempt to set her mind at ease. "Tripp will fly back into Chicago on Sunday. Is everything set then for him to drive over on Tuesday?"

"It is," Warren confirmed. "I've spoken with his secretary in Chicago and she's made all the arrangements. She didn't think he'd have a problem with leaving town so soon after his vacation."

Celia snorted. "That woman used to support Preston. She's privy to all Tripp's tricks."

"Have you done any more to encourage Annemarie to make a play while he's here?"

"Believe me," Celia assured him. "She's ready."

A knock on his closed door interrupted them. Annemarie let Warren know his nine o'clock appointment was there.

Celia rose from her chair. "Good luck tonight."

"Quit worrying, Celia. It's all coming together. Get to work on your end, lining up the money. We've set the bait, now we just have to reel him in."

* * *

Try as she might, Celia couldn't hear the conversation taking place behind Warren's closed door on Tuesday morning, even though their offices shared a wall, and it was killing her. Warren was sharing the disappointing news with Tripp that his potential buyer for Whispering Pines had walked away from their discussions. Try as she might, she couldn't imagine how Tripp would take the news. Would he be mad? Surprised the other party walked away? Uptight, trying to hide concern about his unpaid gambling debts?

From her desk, Celia could see Annemarie glancing toward Warren's closed door, too. She seemed as curious about the discussion going on behind that door as Celia.

While she waited for the two men to come out of the corner office, Celia flipped through the paperwork for the two new mortgages she'd applied for on her home and the fourplex. She needed to sign them, but she was still trying to come to terms with the treatment she'd endured during the application process.

Initially, her inquiry into potential loans against her properties was met with resistance, despite her long tenure at the Whitby Company. Her employer was a major customer of the bank, but lending personnel didn't like that Celia was a single woman, applying on her own. It had taken a heated conversation with the bank manager—not to mention the threat that she'd take her concerns about their treatment of her to Mr. Tripp Whitby, potentially putting the bank's whole relationship with one of their larger customers at risk—before they'd considered it.

Celia would never have involved Tripp, but the bank didn't need to know that.

The bank ended up approving both mortgages, without a cosigner, but the experience left a bad taste in Celia's mouth. Between pay inequities and limited access to credit, it was no wonder women faced an uphill battle in the business world.

She tapped her pen on her desktop as she tried to listen through the walls. She had yet to broach the subject with Tripp about buying Whispering Pines, and she recognized it was still a long shot, but she needed to be ready to act. Preston had instilled in her the need to always be prepared, and to have faith in her plans. It was a skillset that made her good at her job. She hoped it would serve her well now, too. If it all fell apart, she'd turn around and repay the mortgages immediately, and just be out the cost of interest and fees. It was a risk she was willing to take.

She signed both applications.

The number Warren had pried out of the bookie the week before had been big enough to make her pause. Her financial arrangements could still cover it, but just barely, and Tripp would come out of the sale of the resort with nothing more than a bookie off his back and a resort out of his hair.

As long as he didn't screw things up with his rich, spurned spouse, it just might be enough.

* * *

The last thing they had to do was throw Annemarie and Tripp together and hope they were both foolish enough to play into their plans. Warren had arranged for an early dinner in the office, fully catered, so Tripp, Celia, and Warren could hash out their bidding strategy on a new, large-scale commercial development on the edge of town. It was the type of thing Tripp loved to sink his teeth into. Warren also asked Annemarie to work late, promising her double pay for her overtime, implying they'd need her help to take notes. Since Tripp was leaving for home the following day, they needed to be efficient—and who better than Annemarie to help them do that? Tripp had eagerly agreed.

And Warren thinks I'm *diabolical.*

Tripp acted surly throughout the day, at one point yelling something about the terrible coffee. She hadn't had a chance to talk to Warren privately about how Tripp took the news of the developers walking away, but based on Tripp's mood, he wasn't happy.

Midafternoon, she noticed Tripp talking to Annemarie in hushed tones. Holding up a paper she'd been reading at her desk so she could discretely watch the two of them, she noticed Annemarie smiling flirtatiously up at Tripp. She couldn't hear what they were saying, and she tried not to stare, but Tripp's laughter sounded promising. Their office hussy was going to make this easy.

Twenty minutes later, the four gathered in the larger of the two conference rooms. Tripp offered to help Annemarie go out to the parking lot to pick up the food from the caterers. Celia suspected the caterers would have preferred coming in to set up the food themselves, but she welcomed a minute of private time with Warren. Everyone else had left for the day.

"Are we set?" she asked, glancing back over her shoulder.

"Oh, we're set, all right. As we'd hoped, he's plenty upset about the developers. When I pressed him on it, he made some backhanded comment about needing cash for a side project he was working on, but then he clammed up. He was definitely anxious about the lost opportunity."

Celia grinned. "With any luck, I can present him with a better alternative tonight. What time is Helen calling?"

"Seven. Virginia is going to fall off her bike shortly before that."

"You two are awful!" Celia laughed. "I'm never going to believe Helen's cries for help again."

Warren shrugged. "Four daughters give us plenty of real excuses, believe me."

The outer door opened and Celia could hear Annemarie and Tripp returning.

"Showtime," Celia whispered, winking at Warren.

* * *

The phone in Warren's office rang precisely at seven.

Celia glanced up from the charts they'd been referencing. "Annemarie, do you want to run and get that?" she asked.

"Fine," the woman said, setting her pen down.

Celia had noticed Annemarie checking her watch during the past hour, probably wondering when this meeting would wrap up so she could be alone with Tripp. She needn't have worried. They had that all worked out for her already.

"No, stay put," Warren said, standing. "It's probably Helen, given the hour. I'll be right back."

Celia watched him hurry out of the office.

"When Helen says jump, Warren always asks 'How high?' " Tripp said, causing Annemarie to laugh. Celia found the comment disrespectful—even if this particular instance was a trick—but she said nothing.

Warren hurried back into the conference room, running a hand through his hair as he walked, a look of concern on his features. "I'm sorry, but I need to get home right away. One of the girls fell off her bike. Helen is afraid she might need stitches. Can we pick this up again in the morning? Tripp, can you give us an extra hour or two tomorrow before you head out?"

Tripp, married but childless, sighed, his frustration over the interruption clear. (Annemarie, on the other hand, was having a hard time hiding her glee.) "Fine. But I need to be on the road by ten. There's a charity event at the Gala I need to attend with Sophia tomorrow night."

"I understand," Warren said, nodding and quickly gathering up the mess of papers in front of where he'd been sitting. "Again, I'm so sorry about this. I'd planned to get everything figured out tonight. I appreciate your understanding."

He rushed out. Celia needed to fashion him a pretend Oscar statue for his part in their little charade. He might have missed his calling.

Once Warren breezed out, Celia knew it was time for her to play her assigned role. She sighed and checked her watch. "What do you think, Tripp? Do you want to call it a day? I know you value *Warren's* input on this deal, so if you want to hold off on any further discussion until tomorrow morning, I'd be happy to oblige."

Celia was careful to keep just the right amount of snark in her tone, so she sounded like she often did when Tripp irritated her.

"You know, Celia, your attitude is exactly why Tripp is turning to Warren these days instead of you," Annmarie chimed in.

Normally, the secretary's complete disregard for organizational hierarchy would have infuriated Celia. This time it played right into her hand.

"Annemarie . . ." Tripp said, his warning clear.

Standing in a huff, Celia followed Warren's lead and gathered her papers and keys. She made sure the keys made a noise as she let them dangle from her fingers. "Never mind, Tripp. Cut her some slack. It's been a long day for all of us. I'm heading home. Do you want to start early tomorrow?"

Tripp sat back in his chair, looking haggard. The long day had taken a toll on him. Little did he know, they weren't done with him yet.

"Eight is fine. Goodnight, Celia."

She nodded first to Tripp, then Annemarie, and fled the conference room. She dumped the papers in her desk drawer, ignored her purse on the floor under her desk, and made her way outside, flipping the main lights off as she went. They wouldn't think anything of her turning out the lights, given her habit of harping on folks about wasting electricity. Since the conference room had no windows, it was as if she were leaving Tripp and Annemarie in a private little cocoon.

Hopefully, after his long day, Annemarie would jump at the chance to make Tripp feel better.

Celia climbed into her car and drove around downtown for ten minutes. Her right leg wouldn't stop shaking, making it difficult to maintain a steady speed. If this didn't work—if she couldn't get Tripp to sell her Whispering Pines—she'd be devastated. Her commitment to the resort went beyond her deathbed promise to Preston. Ever since she'd verbalized her dream to Helen of making the resort her legacy, it was all she could think about.

She was risking her home, her job, nearly everything on this.

At the appointed time, Celia drove back to the office, turning off her headlights as she rounded the corner and parking on the street. She eased her car door closed soundlessly and approached the building on the grass. She was suddenly thankful for the light cast on the backdoor by the safety lighting Preston had insisted on—he'd known people like Celia often worked late.

She was as quiet as possible with her key. With luck, Tripp and Annemarie were already distracting each other and they wouldn't hear her return. Leaving the lights off, she made her way through the darkened interior, delighted to see they'd closed the conference door after she'd left. She stopped at her office and picked up her purse, then strode purposefully back toward the conference room. With barely a knock, she swung the door open, light flooding out into the dark common area.

"Sorry, I just wanted to let you know I forgot my purse," Celia said. "I didn't want you to think . . ."

Her voice trailed off at the scene in front of her. She was thankful she hadn't waited any longer to come back. As it was, Annemarie sat on Tripp's lap, facing him, her legs straddling him. The only nudity was the secretary's bare breast, held aloft in the palm of Tripp's hand.

There could be no disputing what she'd walked in on.

Annemarie struggled to extricate her legs, but the way she'd woven them through the chair to sit on Tripp's lap made it difficult. Tripp swore while Annemarie fought to get untangled. The prudent thing would be for Celia to close the door and pretend she'd seen nothing.

She was tired of always acting prudently.

Instead, she stood there, watching the scene play out in front of her, arms crossed over her chest, her toe tapping impatiently.

"Celia, what the hell are you doing here? We thought you left!" Tripp barked, still trying to push Annemarie off his lap.

"Obviously. Do you two need a little help there?" she asked, keeping her tone even—business-like, even. She had the upper hand now, and she intended to use it.

"Shut up, you bitch!" Annemarie screamed, finally getting her legs out from the knot she'd found herself in. "You did this on purpose!"

Fighting to keep her expression neutral, Celia shook her head. "I have no idea what you're talking about. I suggest you go on home now, Annemarie. You've done enough damage here tonight. We'll deal with you in the morning."

Huffing with rage—and embarrassment—Annemarie did as she was told. She gathered her things, threw them on her desk, and left the office building in record time.

Celia kept a close eye on Tripp as she walked back into the conference room and took her chair again. He just sat there, eying her warily, clearly unsure how this would play out. Despite their careful planning, Celia was terrified. She tried not to let her clasped hands shake as she rested them on the table. Tripp had a mean streak. Was she in physical danger? Tripp could be a bully.

But before the bullying came the placating. "Look, Celia . . . I can explain," Tripp said, slipping behind the mask he used to charm customers. It usually worked, but it wouldn't tonight. Not with her.

Doesn't he know I can see right through that?

"Explain what? Your little dalliance with her? Believe me, I've known about that for some time."

His face blanched. "What?"

"Tripp, your womanizing isn't exactly news. But I suspect it would upset your wife greatly if I made a phone call and passed the news to her. She may not like me, but Preston trusted me, and she knows that. She'd believe me."

"You wouldn't," he hissed.

"I could, and I might. But as long as I feel my position here at the company is secure, I'll keep your little escapades to myself. As far as I know, no one else is on to you, although you should be more careful. Women like Annemarie don't give up easily, and clearly she has her sights set on you."

Celia could almost see the wheels turning in Tripp's brain. She suspected he'd send Annemarie packing first thing in the morning. Celia wouldn't let herself pity the woman.

Tripp stood. "Fine. You keep doing your job—working for *Warren*," he emphasized, "and you can stay. But if one word gets out about this, you are finished."

Celia nodded. "I understand. I only wonder which one of us would suffer more if word of this gets out."

Tripp crossed his arms, staring down at her. She no longer worried about her job. She had him where she wanted him in that regard.

"Look, Celia. It's been a hell of a day. Go home. Let's forget any of this ever happened."

"I'll set it aside for now, but trust me, I'll never forget. Do you understand?" she said, keeping her voice low and serious. She needed to keep the upper hand for what would come next.

He nodded his head once, then turned for the door.

"Stop. Sit down, Tripp. There is something else I've been wanting to discuss with you."

She could see his shoulders tense, and she half expected him to walk out the door. But he turned to face her yet again, his face starting to blotch in frustration.

"What now? I'm exhausted."

Celia held her hand out in a flourish toward his chair—the one she'd just caught him in with Annemarie.

He collapsed into it. "Make it fast. I'm getting a headache."

A crude comment skipped through Celia's brain, but she let it go.

"I have a proposition for you."

"For *me*?" Tripp said, his face registering surprise. All frustration fled and the hint of a smile teased the corner of his mouth. "I've always suspected you've wondered what we'd be like together."

Celia could have screamed. The man was incorrigible.

"Not that kind of proposition, you pig."

He shrugged. "Hey, you said it. Not me."

"Listen closely, Tripp. Coveting another woman's husband isn't Annemarie's only vice. She has a loose tongue."

Tripp narrowed his eyes. "Explain."

"She mentioned the name De Luca in conversation one day."

A moment's pause. "She did not," he insisted, but his cheeks flushed at her words.

"Look, Tripp, I don't give a damn what kind of trouble you might be in—with either your wife *or* your loan shark."

"He isn't a loan shark!"

Celia waved his words away. "Whatever. Semantics isn't important. The fact De Luca has been eager to talk with you since you left tells me you might have some gambling debts to take care of."

"How do you even know who he is?"

Celia held Tripp's eye, arms crossed, but offered nothing more.

"Fine. Get to the point."

"I think you need money. I think maybe your inheritance from Preston isn't liquid enough for you to pay this De Luca fellow off. You wouldn't dare go to your wife for money to pay off gambling debts you can't afford. That would require admitting to secrets, and then where might that lead? On top of that, you'd never be stupid enough to steal from the company."

He moved to protest, but she held up a hand.

"You need cash," she repeated, "and I have cash. You have something I want, as well. I think we should make a deal."

He pulled his chair closer to the table, rested his arms on the surface, and pointed at her with his stump—something she'd never seen him do. "You want Whispering Pines, don't you?"

She blinked. She supposed she shouldn't be surprised at how

quickly he caught on.

"I do."

Those two simple words reverberated around the windowless room.

He lowered his arm and laughed, the sound harsh against her ears. "You can't afford it."

She unfolded her arms and put them on her hips. "Try me."

"I've had people approach me with a hefty offer."

She feigned surprise at this. "Really? Did you accept their offer already? Am I too late?"

He fidgeted, tucking his stump under his armpit again as he leaned back in the chair. "Not yet. It didn't work out. But there will be others that want it."

"Tripp, Preston taught us both years ago that something is worth exactly how much another party will pay for it, and not a cent more."

"Name your price, then," he spat out.

She pretended to consider this, although she and Warren had already worked up what they thought he'd bite on. After some feigned deliberation, she tossed that figure out to him.

He rolled his eyes. "You aren't even close."

But she was in the ballpark, and she sensed the interest he was trying to hide. This was her chance. She could feel it.

No matter what.

"Fine," she said, getting to her feet. "Take it or leave it. I just hope your wife doesn't catch wind of this De Luca guy."

She was halfway to the outer door before he stopped her.

"Celia. Wait."

She couldn't hold back the smile as she turned back to face Tripp, silhouetted in the lights of the conference room, still sitting in the chair that had ruined him. She'd ventured into murky waters to take what she wanted. She wasn't proud of her methods, but in that moment, she knew she'd won.

Whispering Pines would be hers. It would be safe. She'd keep her promise to Preston.

No matter what, Preston. No matter what.

EPILOGUE
MONDAY, OCTOBER 3, 1966

$\mathcal{C}$elia turned onto the drive that would once again take her to Whispering Pines.

She wished the big old sign that used to mark the turn still stood tall to greet her, but the tornado had damaged it beyond repair a decade earlier. She wanted to hang a new sign. Maybe she'd use the same welcoming message and bright red letters as the previous one:

WHISPERING PINES
A Family Destination
Serving Minnesota Since 1926

As she pulled into the resort's gravel parking lot, she rolled down her window, not caring about the dust as it floated in. She sat for a moment, examining the lodge and noticing, for the first time, the paint peeling around the windows and door. The lodge was brand new when she'd first visited the resort in 1942. Preston had it built when he took over. Twenty-four years of harsh summer heat and brutal Minnesota winters were taking a toll. She climbed out of her car and leaned back against the cool metal. The sun was bright but had lost most of its warmth. A gentle breeze teased her nose with the ever-present scent of pine.

It felt amazing to be back.

And for the first time, Whispering Pines was all hers.

Challenging negotiations with Tripp meant she ended up paying more than she'd hoped, but she could cover the difference. Once the sale was final, she'd phoned Eleanor to share the news. She could hear the relief in her old friend's voice. It delighted the woman to learn the old resort would now be safe in Celia's hands. She'd worried her brother might do something rash with her father's beloved Whispering Pines. She agreed that there was no better new owner than Celia.

Pushing away from her car, Celia glanced at the door to the lodge, knowing she'd likely find Nash inside. It had come as a relief to learn Tripp had kept him on after Preston passed away. But first, she wanted to reacquaint herself with the old place before getting down to business.

The beach was quiet; the sand was littered with golden leaves. Her old dock, the one she'd sat on so often through the years, waited for her. She remembered fishing off the end with Leo, and, later, spending hours there with Danny. She even recalled the day angry waves pummeled the dock as the violent storm rolled in, shortly after she'd given birth to their daughter. She promised herself she would head out there again later to contemplate what she'd gotten herself into.

Following the walking path through the resort, she smiled at the three newer cabins, built after the tornado demolished the white ones that used to sit closer to the water. Already ten years old now but still in excellent condition.

She glanced toward the trees, but knew the shack where Danny spent that summer was gone. Meandering on, she came upon the large log-sided cabin where she'd first stayed with Helen and her family. The cabin could benefit from a bigger screened-in porch; the current one was too small, and on summer evenings in Minnesota the bugs were horrendous.

Next came the smallest cabin, the one she'd done so much living in. She'd shared it with Ruby, then with dear Beverly, and finally with her own baby, before the child's birth. So much had changed through the years, yet the cabin still looked the same. The only exception was the paint, which also showed signs of age, peeling and curling in places.

Purchasing Whispering Pines wouldn't be the last hit to her finances, but she'd make it work.

No matter what.

Moving on, her wandering eventually took her to the duplex, tucked back in the trees. She would stay in her half while she was on site. Nash, ever loyal, still lived in the other half of the duplex. She hoped to do some of her work from here the following summer. Warren would most certainly allow her to find a balance.

Celia's mind skipped back to the night Danny first showed her the new foundation of the place. They never could have guessed how their lives would play out in the years ahead.

Sinking down on the steps leading up to the duplex, Celia rested her arms on her bent knees. Her memory hadn't failed her. The peacefulness of Whispering Pines surrounded her, seeped into her, and chased away the exhaustion she'd felt after all of her work to wrestle this place away from Tripp.

A mosquito nipped at her ankle. She slapped it away.

Then she saw them. Initials, carved into a backside corner of the wooden step.

C.M. + D.B. '51

Her eyes welled with tears. These matched the initials Danny carved into their picnic bench back home. He must have carved these when he stayed here at the duplex for Eleanor's wedding. It was when they'd first reunited, after years apart.

A tear spilled from Celia's cheek, plopping onto their initials and turning the wood dark.

Celia heard footsteps and raised a hand in greeting to Nash. He smiled back, and right then and there she knew the older man would help her keep Whispering Pines, the place that was so much a part of her soul, going.

She'd already experienced some of her very best and very worst days here.

She looked forward to what the future would bring.

"*I* wish someone would have dated these when they hung them up on the wall," Jess said before taking another sip of her beer. The heat made the bottle sweat, and she had to keep wiping off the glass so it wouldn't drip moisture on the pictures they were trying to organize. "Some have dates, but some don't, and there seem to be some big time gaps."

Renee slipped her glasses off and rubbed her eyes. "Getting these into chronological order might be tougher than we thought."

"They dated the one with the girls standing by the old Ford as 1943. This photograph of an outdoor wedding"—Jess squinted at the back of another frame—"is . . . hmm . . . they used a pencil. It's hard to read, but I think it says June 16th, 1951. I wonder who the lucky couple was?" She glanced over at her sister. "Guess you weren't the first couple to get married out here."

Renee smiled, thinking back to that sunny afternoon two years earlier when she'd married Matt in their outdoor ceremony. She held her hand out and Jess handed her the framed photograph. The colors in the picture were fading, but the expressions on the young couple's faces were still clear. "They look happy. It would be fun to know their story."

Jess snorted. "Since that was taken sixty-eight years ago, I think we'd have to make up the story. I doubt anyone who was in attendance is still around."

"Don't be so negative, Jess. It looks like a young crowd. College kids, maybe. Maybe the happy couple was related to whoever owned Whispering Pines back then."

"Have you ever considered hosting weddings out here? It could be another stream of revenue for you. I'm honestly surprised we hadn't thought of it before."

Renee shuddered at the suggestion. Owning Whispering Pines had opened up a whole new career for her, and she loved it. Hosting guests in the summer and retreats for women in the off months was incredibly rewarding. But wedding planning was a whole different level of stress and organization. "No, thank you. Holding my own wedding out here was enough. And it was fun to fix up the Gray Cabin for you and Seth to use on your honeymoon. But I'm afraid turning this place into a destination wedding would be torture."

Laughing, Jess got up and took their empty bottles over to the recycle bin. "You're probably right. Forget I even suggested it."

"Oh, I've already forgotten," Renee assured her. She picked up the steak knife they'd been using to remove photographs from their frames and carefully sliced through the backing on the wedding photo.

"Don't forget to transfer the date to the wedding picture itself."

Renee sighed. "Jess, we've been at this for two hours. I know the drill."

Peeling the backing off, Renee was surprised to find another stack of photographs, similar to the one Jess found behind the picture from 1943. "What do you suppose the deal is? Here's another one with more than one picture stacked inside the frame."

"Don't know." Jess shrugged. "I used to do that with school pictures of my kids I kept on my desk in the office. Every year I'd layer the new one on top, inside the frame. It was always fun to flip through them and see how the kids were changing."

Nodding, Renee fanned through the five photographs. Unlike the stack Jess found, these were all in color instead of black and white. They weren't as crisp as the older pictures. "Maybe it was just a way to keep them all together, without giving each one its own frame?"

"Any good ones?" Jess asked, returning with bottles of water instead of beer and handing one to Renee.

Renee grinned. "Yes! These are great. They seem to all be from about the same time, too. Maybe they're all related to the wedding. Look, I think this is Celia! Doesn't she look happy?"

Jess took the photograph from Renee's outstretched hand. "Is she dancing? Why am I not surprised? Celia knew how to have a good time."

"I bet it was the wedding dance. And here's another bonfire, down on the beach. Maybe they were guests from the wedding, too." Renee studied the faces, but features were difficult to distinguish in the firelight.

She shrieked when she flipped to the next photograph in the stack. "You won't believe this one, Jess! Check out the cute little paper bell, hanging above the door on this cabin. That has to be the Gray Cabin! Looks like you weren't the first couple to honeymoon in there."

"There have probably been a few weddings—and plenty of honey-mooners—out here through all the decades this resort has been in business," Jess said, looking over Renee's shoulder.

Next in the stack was another picture of a cabin. Renee didn't recognize this one. The setting was different, the cabin in rough shape. Woods surrounded it instead of the open areas around the other cabins at the resort. "Maybe this is at a different resort? Or in the mountains somewhere?"

Jess reached over Renee's shoulder and took the photograph. "Renee, what if this is the cabin that used to stand where your new house is now?"

Renee snatched it back, studying it more closely. Nothing about it looked familiar. "I don't know . . . the trees are different."

Pulling out her chair again, Jess sat back down next to Renee. "But these pictures are probably all almost seventy years old, right? Trees fall down, or they grow up. We've never been able to figure out what was back there in the woods, just that old foundation you and Matt found. I think it's possible."

Renee shrugged. "I guess you could be right. It doesn't look like the mystery cabin in that book we found about Minnesota resorts. You know, the book that included Whispering Pines? I'll show Matt. He'll get a kick out of it, either way."

"What else is there?"

Renee took one last look at the mystery cabin and flipped to the final picture. This one wasn't in focus. She searched again for her reading glasses, pawing through the mess of photographs and emptied frames. "I don't know if I can handle finding any more surprise photos. I'm getting a headache."

Jess pointed to Renee's head. "Maybe if you'd leave them on your face, instead of the top of your head, you wouldn't strain your eyes trying to focus."

Grimacing, Renee slid the glasses back down into place. She took another look at the picture. "It's a guy and a girl by the water. Standing out on a dock, maybe. Whoever took it didn't focus on their faces."

"I suppose cameras weren't as easy to use in the fifties compared to our phones today," Jess pointed out.

Renee turned the photograph over. "Oh wow, this one has names . . . and the girl is *Celia*! I can't believe I didn't recognize her."

"Who's the guy?"

"It says 'Celia and Danny,' then below it someone listed what looks like initials. 'CM + DB '51.'"

"What?" Jess asked, again snatching the picture out of her sister's hands.

"Jeez, Jess, what? Does that mean something to you?"

Jess took Renee's readers again and studied the scrawled note on the back of the picture. "I've seen these initials before."

Renee smirked. "Yeah, right."

"No, Renee, I'm serious. Someone carved these same initials into the back corner on a step at the duplex. I think it might even have the '51, too, but I can't remember for sure. Haven't you ever noticed them before? They're old, but you can still read it."

A brief knock on the back door interrupted them and their father walked in. "Hello, ladies!"

"Hi, Dad," Renee and Jess said simultaneously.

"Nathan called. Said he and Robbie might have blown up that old boat motor. Thought I'd stop by and see if I could help. They around?" George noticed the mess they'd made on the long, collapsible table. "Looks like you've opened up a can of worms yourself here," he said, crossing the kitchen to take a closer look. "Those from the wall back there?"

"Yep," Renee confirmed. "Hey, Dad, have you ever heard of somebody named Danny? A friend or maybe boyfriend of Celia's, way back when?"

George took the picture Renee held up to him, looking first at the couple on the front. He grinned at the image of his older sister. "I don't remember seeing this picture before. It's so fuzzy, I'm surprised she kept it. Danny, you say?"

"Yeah, turn it over," Jess said, pointing to the words on the back.

"Hmm . . . no, it doesn't ring a bell. Might have been an old boyfriend. She had a few. She was almost twenty years older than me, so I didn't know the men she dated."

"Were there lots of them?" Renee asked.

"Lots?"

"Lots of boyfriends, I mean."

George shrugged. "I wouldn't say *lots*. You girls know Celia never married, but she did date through the years. She used to say she missed out on someone special once, and that no one else ever quite measured up. But she'd never say his name." He handed the photograph back. "Where are the boys? I should go see if I can be of help."

"They're outside somewhere. Probably down by the water, tinkering with the boat or swimming to cool off. Just holler for them."

With a wave, he headed for the door, grabbing water out of the fridge on his way out. "You girls need a fan in here. It's hot."

Renee smiled at her dad's back. After the screen door slammed shut behind him, she picked up the picture of her aunt again. "Men. They have no sense of romance. I'd love to know who this guy was. Maybe he was *the one* that Celia let get away."

"Hey, maybe we uncovered that little mystery we were hoping to find about Celia after all! Or at least a 'mystery man.' Like Nathan said, these pictures give us a glimpse into the stories behind the history of Whispering Pines," Jess said, rubbing her hands together. "I'm glad we're finally doing something with all of these."

Renee grinned at her sister. "We should do some digging. At least look into this Danny guy."

"We should, but where would we start?"

Renee pulled her phone out of her pocket. "How hard would it be for Matt to figure out who got married out here at Whispering Pines on the sixteenth of June in 1951? There must be records."

Jess laughed. "Sure pays to be married to the sheriff. That's probably a good place to start. Who was this Danny guy, and was he the one Celia let get away?"

As Renee waited for Matt to pick up, she tilted her phone away from her mouth. "I still think the bigger mystery is how Celia ever came to own Whispering Pines in the first place. She bought it in the mid-sixties. Back then, women were fighting for rights that we take for granted today."

When Matt didn't pick up, Renee left a message. Tossing her phone down, she sighed. "I wish we'd have asked Celia more questions when she was still alive."

Jess nodded, picking up the photo they both thought epitomized summer at the lake. She couldn't help but smile at the laughing faces of the four young women as they splashed through shallow water, hand in hand. "I guess all we can do now is try to use these pictures to piece together the puzzle."

"You never had much patience for puzzles," Renee said with a laugh.

"True," Jess agreed. "But this is one time I'd like to see the whole picture."

Reenergized to finish what they'd started, Jess and Renee got back to work, organizing the snippets of time from a bygone era. Pieces of their dear aunt's life would undoubtedly remain a mystery, but there was no denying that Celia's long-ago challenges and victories were still shaping their own lives, much like the ripple effect of a stone tossed into the waters off their dock at Whispering Pines.

Thank you!

Dear Reader,

I would like to thank you for taking the time to read **Celia's Gifts**. I am so grateful you selected it and I hope you enjoyed this fifth book in my Celia's Gifts series.

If you don't mind taking a few more minutes with this book, I'd appreciate it if you would leave a review. Reviews are extremely helpful and much appreciated.

Next up in the series is **Celia's Legacy** (Book 6). Celia's life was simply too big to fit into one book!

For links to all my books and to sign up for my newsletter so I can keep you posted on new releases, please visit my website at

www.kimberlydiedeauthor.com.

Wishing you my very best,
Kimberly

AN INVITATION

If you enjoyed any of the books in my Celia's Gifts series, please visit my website to join my mailing list for periodic updates on new releases and my other writing projects.

www.kimberlydiedeauthor.com

When you join my mailing list, be sure to watch your email for a FREE copy of my novella:

First Summers at Whispering Pines 1980

ACKNOWLEDGMENTS

When I first sketched out my Celia's Gifts series, I planned to write four books: one for each of Celia's three nieces and one nephew. The series kicked off shortly after Celia's death. But somewhere along the line, I fell in love with the idea to travel back in time to get to know the real Celia, not just the woman her family thought they knew.

Eventually, I didn't feel like I even had a choice. Celia's story needed to be told. The writing of the first four books, along with the related holiday novel, served as a powerful reminder to me of just how much of a person's story dies when they draw their last breath.

My new plan was to tell Celia's story in one book. I was going to wrap up some of the many mysteries, both large and small, related to Celia that surfaced in earlier books. I even had a robust outline!

But I lost myself in the magic of Whispering Pines in the 1940s through the 1960s. It will take two books to tell Celia's whole story. Maybe it felt so good to escape to another time because I wrote this within the confines of 2020. I hope I stayed true to the different decades in this fictional account. I did my best.

One of the powerful themes that emerged was the blessing of life-long friendships. Celia held tight to her childhood friends throughout her entire life. My own "Aunt Mary", my inspiration behind Celia's character, also had a close-knit circle of friends.

I like to include a quote at the beginning of each book, and decided I wanted this one to be about friends. But I wasn't finding one that felt right. I decided to check a dictionary's definition of "friend." My dad gave me a massive, vintage Webster's dictionary a few years back. I pulled that one out. The tome (over 1400 pages) is dated 1899. Here is a partial look at the old definition:

FRIEND *1. One who is attached to another by affection; one who entertains for another sentiments of esteem, respect, and affection, which lead him to desire his company, and to seek to promote his happiness and prosperity.*

Aside from the glaring singular use of him/his (kind of like the blatant discrimination Celia would have faced), and the expected formality given the age of the dictionary, I liked the definition. Friendships are never perfect, because we are human, but this was the type of relationship Celia had with her friends.

I'm blessed to have friends like Celia and Aunt Mary. These fabulous women are integral parts of my best memories from high school and college. Miles separate us now, but our bond runs bone deep. Thank you Deneen Axtman, Darlene Lauridsen, Jodi Anfinrud, and Lynn Lambrecht for your love. Even when a year or two passes between our time together, we pick right back up again. This is genuine friendship. Thank you for your encouragement and inspiration. Fiction is life reimagined. You've given me plenty of building blocks!

I wouldn't be able to put these books together without the unending support of my family and the talented contributions by both my editor and cover designer. Thank you again.

We should all be lifelong learners. I have found an incredibly supportive community of other authors within the online world. If you've ever wanted to write a book, know that the support is there for you, too. Don't die with your story or words still inside you. Take a chance. You'll be glad you did.

New friends are amazing blessings, too, and I've found so many of you when you've taken a chance and read my books. Thank you. I wouldn't be doing any of this without you.

ABOUT THE AUTHOR

Kimberly Diede writes contemporary novels that weave together family, hope, and romance. She writes family sagas, suspense, and women's fiction that you'll find hard to put down. She truly believes we are never too old for second chances at love and at life.

Kimberly enjoys spending the short months of her Midwest summers on the lakeshores of Minnesota and North Dakota. Nothing is better than time with her family at their cabin. Her love of tradition and all things vintage comes through in her stories.

Be sure to follow Kimberly on social media to catch glimpses of the junk she drags home to repurpose and to get updates on her latest books.

f facebook.com/KimberlyDiedeAuthor
instagram.com/kimberlydiedeauthor
pinterest.com/kdiedeauthor

Made in the USA
Coppell, TX
06 September 2021